D0549458

Since her explosion onto the publishing scene more than ten years ago, Suzanne Brockmann has written more than forty books, and is now widely recognised as one of the leading voices in women's suspense writing. Her work has earned her repeated appearances on the *USA Today* and *New York Times* bestseller lists, as well as numerous awards. Suzanne Brockmannn lives in Florida with her husband, author Ed Gaffney.

The Unsung Hero
The Defiant Hero
Over the Edge
Out of Control
Dark of Night
Hot Pursuit

Suzanne
BROCKMANN

Out of Control

headline

First published in 2002 by Ballantine Books,
an imprint of the Random House Publishing Group,
a division of Random House, Inc., New York.
This edition published in arrangement with Ballantine Books.

First published in Great Britain in 2012 by
HEADLINE PUBLISHING GROUP

1

Cataloguing in Publication Data is available from the British Library

ISBN 978 0 7553 7117 4

Typeset in Palatino by Avon DataSet Ltd,
Bidford-on-Avon, Warwickshire

Printed and bound in Great Britain by Clays Ltd, St Ives plc

Headline's policy is to use papers that are natural, renewable and
recyclable products and made from wood grown in sustainable forests.
The logging and manufacturing processes are expected to conform to the
environmental regulations of the country of origin.

HEADLINE PUBLISHING GROUP
An Hachette UK Company
338 Euston Road
London NW1 3BH

www.headline.co.uk
www.hachette.co.uk

For the brave men and women who fought
for freedom during the Second World War.
My most sincere and humble thanks.

Acknowledgments

A gazillion thanks (again!) to Mike Freeman for advice, information, hours of reading drafts and emails, and solid friendship.

Special thanks to fellow writers Pat White and Liana Dalton. Thanks for listening and for being there.

Thanks as always to Deede Bergeron, Lee Brockmann and Patricia McMahon – my personal support staff and early draft readers.

My deepest thanks to Shauna Summers, my editor and teammate at Ballantine, and to my wonderful agents, Steve Axelrod and Damaris Rowland. Without all of you, this book would not have been possible!

And thanks, of course, as always, to Ed.

Any mistakes I've made or liberties I've taken are completely my own.

Prologue

At about 0530 that very morning, Ken 'WildCard' Karmody became a terrorist.

It wasn't a career move he would normally have made, especially on such short notice, with no time to prepare properly. But seeing how it was a direct order, he had no choice but to embrace it completely.

'You believe you'll be rescued in a matter of a few short hours, don't you, Mr Bond?' he asked his hostage – an SAS enlisted named Gordon MacKenzie who was sitting, tied up, on the sagging floor of the hut they'd finally chosen as Tango HQ. 'But such an easy escape – no, it is not to be.'

'Ah, Christ.' Gordie rolled his eyes along with his *r*s, sounding as if he were doing an excellent imitation of Scotty from *Star Trek*, except, hot damn, Jim, the Scottish accent was for real. 'Here we go, on the move again, is that what you're trying to tell me?'

Kenny slipped neatly from Evil Overlord to Yoda. 'Try not,' he told Gordie solemnly as he untied the rope that held the Scot's feet. 'Do. Or do not.' He grinned. 'And in this case, my friend, what I need you to *do* for me is strip.'

Gordon sighed. With his dark hair cut close to his scalp, his dark brown eyes and his lean build, he looked more like George Clooney than the rather portly chief engineer

1

of the Starship Enterprise. 'Kenneth. Be reasonable, lad. It's a training op. You're only supposed to *pretend* to be the bad guys. Don't you know if you let my boys catch you and liberate me, you'll be home in your girlfriend's bed before 2230?'

His girlfriend's bed.

The rest of the SEALs who were playing the part of Ken's merry band of nasties got very quiet. Too quiet.

What, did they honestly think those three words – *his* and *girlfriend's* and *bed* – would set him off? He could feel their uncertainty bouncing around the rough-hewn walls of the shack.

Yup. No doubt about it.

Jenkins and Gilligan and Silverman and even Jay Lopez, whose first name was short for Jesus, were all expecting him to go postal.

Ken laughed. He supposed it served him right. Once upon a time, he *would* have lost it at the merest reminder of Adele.

But, come on. That was then, this was now. Hadn't they noticed how fricking serene, how absolutely Buddha-like he'd been lately?

Imperturbable. Oh, yeah. That was him, all the way. In fact, his picture had gone up next to that word in the dictionary.

He unfastened Gordie's hands. 'Kinda crowded in my girlfriend's bed these days, considering she got married to some rich dickhead last weekend.'

Gordie winced. 'Shite. We're in for a night of it then, are we, boys? Up til dawn's early light?' He glanced at Jenk, at Lopez, at Gilligan, at Silverman, sending them each a silent individual apology for having said the wrong thing. As if

Ken were some kind of special-needs child who had to be handled with extra care – instead of the imperturbable son of a bitch he'd worked hard to become.

He let the flash of annoyance roll off him as he shook his head. 'Naw, it won't take until dawn. We'll take 'em out long before midnight.'

The Scot laughed aloud. '*You'll* take *them* out? Is that what I heard ye say?'

'You bet your pointy ass. Now strip,' Ken ordered.

'No focking way.' Gordie was still chuckling to himself. 'A fully outfitted SAS team – they're youngsters, true, and fresh out of . . . No, I won't bet any body parts, but I *will* wager a crisp hundred-dollar bill that if there's any taking out to be done, my boys will be the ones doing it.'

Ken knew what MacKenzie was thinking. The men from SEAL Team Sixteen were playing the part of the tangos – terrorists – as the six-man SAS team from England trained, practicing the rescue of a hostage. That hostage being, of course, the one and only Gordie MacKenzie, so freaking full of himself it was a wonder he wasn't bobbing against the ceiling like a helium balloon.

MacKenzie was thinking about the fact that his SAS *boys* were dressed for a rescue mission. They had the gear and the MRE's – Meals Ready to Eat – in case they got hungry. They had the firepower.

So to speak.

The automatic weapons both teams were using didn't shoot real bullets. They were part of a kickass computer program that worked like a state-of-the-art, high-tech paintball game. Except instead of covering the other players with bright-colored paint, a direct hit was registered, via satellite, in the mainframe computer. A hit severe enough

3

to 'kill' disabled an individual player's ability to use any of the weapons – even one stolen from the enemy.

The weapons Ken and his SEALs had been given – only two to split between the five of them – didn't work quite as well as the seven pseudo-machine guns and sidearms that the SAS team had in their possession. Nah, unless tangos were bank-rolled by a wealthy patron, they often couldn't afford anything but cheap-as-shit, rusty, or obsolete weapons. And the computer program, in an attempt to make the T's weapons seem as rusty, obsolete, and cheap-as-shit as possible, would occasionally and randomly cause them to jam.

That program was a neat little piece of training software. Ken knew it inside and out.

He ought to, he'd helped design it.

Its one major flaw was that it could be uncomfortable to train with in hot weather – something they didn't have to worry about on a freeze-yer-balls-off winter day like today. It required all the players in the training op to wear specially designed, long-sleeved uniforms, the fabric laced with a sensor grid.

So, in actuality, the computer didn't register the fact that a *player* died. It registered the fact that the player's *uniform* died.

'You know, it's tempting,' Ken told Gordie, 'but I'm not a thief. I'm not going to steal your money by taking that bet.'

'Ach, but I have no problem stealing *yours*. Humor me, lad.'

'If you insist. But don't say I didn't warn you. Now, take off your *focking* clothes, MacKenzie, or we'll take 'em off for you.'

Gordie stared at him. 'You're serious.'

'Yes, I am.'

'You're going to cheat, aren't you, you bastard—'

Ken nodded to Gilligan, Jenk and Silverman, who wrestled the Scotsman to the ground. He hummed happily to himself as he untied his own boots and kicked them off to get his legs free from his pants. This was going to be fun. 'Hey, Lopez, you got scissors in your medical kit?'

'Absolutely, Chief.'

Jenk tossed him Gordie's pants and Ken stepped into them. Yeah, the two men had the same height and build. Gordie's uniform shirt quickly followed, and he slipped that on, too. 'You know how to cut hair?' he asked Lopez.

The SEAL team's hospital corpsman looked at him, looked at Gordie who was now being dressed in Ken's uniform like a giant, uncooperative Barbie doll, and smiled. 'How hard could it be?'

'Let's go with something nice and short today,' Ken sat down on a partially charred log someone had dragged inside, either to sit on or in an attempt to burn the place down. 'I'd like the look that all the SAS *boys* are sporting these days. I think it would look *smashing* on me.' He caught a glimpse of his reflection in the hut's only remaining window.

With the exception of his hair – which grew much too quickly and tended to stand straight up when he ran his hands through it – in a certain light, especially when he tipped his head a certain way, Ken looked a little bit like George Clooney, too.

'Captain,' he murmured to himself in a perfect imitation of Scotty, honed from years of watching way too much Star Trek – a lonely, dorky, smart-ass loser of a kid who longed for a father more like Mr Spock, ruled by logic

5

instead of the kind of raw emotion that could make a man put his fist through walls. 'The warp engines cannae take anymore . . .'

It was the waiting that was the hardest part.

Ken had been born without the patience gene. His biggest challenge in becoming a SEAL had been in learning to wait, learning to lie silently in ambush, constantly alert as the seconds became minutes became hours became days.

Gilligan, Lopez, and Silverman were out there now, dug into the dirt, communing with the bugs that were still alive under the blanket of brown leaves and fallen pine needles.

Somehow it was easier to wait in an ambush position. But Ken was here, waiting for a signal, sitting on his butt in this stupid hut.

Ach, laddie, but he was nae Kenneth Karmody any longer. No, he was handsome Gordon MacKenzie now and, aye, he had the short hair and overinflated ego to prove it.

The sun was low in the sky and the shadows nice and long when Gilligan – Dan Gillman – finally gave forth with one of his freakishly authentic turkey calls. Apparently, Gillman entered turkey-calling contests and county fairs and won first prize all the time. Ken wasn't sure exactly what he won – a trophy of a turkey or a trophy of a grown man standing on a stage and acting like a turkey.

But the signal was his heads up. The SAS boys had finally moved into position outside the hut. What the hell had taken them so long to find this place?

Ken ignored Gordie's reproachful eyes as he tested the ropes that bound the man and checked the bandanna he'd stuffed in his mouth as a gag. 'Won't be long now.'

Gordie made a string of muted noises that might've been him trying to say, *You dumb focker, when I get free, I'm going to kick your bluddy arse.*

'I'm sure you'll try, me wee laddie,' Ken murmured back to him as he jammed his own favorite winter hat – the one with the ear flaps that completely covered his hair – onto Gordie's head.

He glanced at Jenk, who also appeared to be tied and gagged, at least at first glance. In case any of the naughty SAS *boys* peeped in through the windows.

'Ready?'

Jenk nodded. With his cheeks rosy from the chill in the air, and his eyes bright with excitement, he looked more like a kid who'd just put a frog in his teacher's drawer than a deadly Navy SEAL. But that was part of his particular charm.

Ken squeezed the trigger of the pseudo-automatic. Two short bursts, aimed at the floor.

'Get down,' he shouted in Gordie's accent. 'Get on the focking floor! Yer dead – so dunna ye move!'

He counted out the seconds it would have taken him to bind and gag two men, and then, crawling on his stomach, pulling his weapon behind him, he pushed at the door, propping it so that it would stay open. With great drama, aware that all eyes were on him, he dragged himself down the steps and into the dirt, leaves, and fallen pine needles outside of the hut.

He was Gordie, he was Gordie, he was Gordie. Keep the accent up, keep his face down in the shadows.

'If you're out there, boys, I sure enough now could use some help,' he called in a low voice. Gordie's voice. Allie, allie in free, boy-Os. 'I had a bit of a fall and my ankle's focked up good. I think it's broken for real.'

Ah, shite, that last bit sounded far more like John Lennon than Gordie MacKenzie. Still, maybe Gordie sounded like John Lennon when he was in serious pain, because – jackpot! – here they came.

Four of 'em, silently slipping out of the brush and shadows like ghosts, coming to his aid. That meant two were hanging back.

And there it was again. Gilligan's wild turkey. Which meant his teammates had pinpointed the locations of the other two SAS boys who were cautious enough to stay hidden.

Once these four got close enough to see his face in the twilight, the game would move to the next phase. The chaos phase. His favorite. Ken clenched his teeth so he wouldn't smile.

'I've got two kills in the cabin,' Ken reported à la Gordie, 'which means there's only three of 'em out there, with one weapon between 'em. Because I've got their other right here.'

He pulled it up into a firing position, and damn, Gordie was at least half right. His boys were pretty good, considering the fact they never should have left the cover of the brush in the first place.

Either they had great intuition or twenty-forty vision, because he didn't get a single shot off.

They fired, he was hit, and then he *couldn't* get a shot off. The sensors in the uniform screwed with the computer in the automatic weapon, rendering it useless.

To him.

Although he was dead, his aim was still good, and he neatly tossed the weapon back through the open doorway of the hut.

Then Jenkins was there, popping out like a nightmare jack-in-the-box, weapon blazing. And just like that, the game was over for those four wee brave SAS laddies.

It was over for the two in the bush, as well.

And the sun hadn't even fully set.

Ken went into the hut to cut Gordie free. 'You lose.'

'You son of a whore,' Gordie accused as soon as the gag was out of his mouth.

'Actually, my mother's quite nice. Kind of conservative. You'd like her. She attends church—'

'Is everything a focking joke to you?'

Kenny considered the question carefully. 'No. In fact, I took this training op very seriously – enough to completely kick your ass in record time. Six SAS boys *and* the hostage dead – killed by friendly fire no less. The computer will make a special little note of that.'

'They didn't kill me, they killed *you*.'

'Details, details. As in your *boys* missed an important one – such as the fact that I was wearing your uniform. If they really were the elite force that they're supposed to be, they should have been paying attention. *I* would have made a point to know everything there was to know about the computer program that was running this show.'

'Sure,' Gordie grumbled, 'and since you're some kind of focking computer genius, you would've gone in and rewritten the program so that your opposition's weapons wouldn't fire. That's called cheating, Karmody.'

'Not according to my definition, it's not,' Ken said, still able to sound serene in the face of Gordie's anger because he was right. 'It's called *being prepared*.'

'What about throwing your weapon to Jenkins that way? I saw you, you know. When you're dead you're supposed

9

to play dead. That was cheating for sure. I'll bet you do it because you know you wouldn't win in a fair fight.'

Ken's cool slipped a notch. 'Yeah, gee, sorry, MacKenzie, you're abso-fucking-lutely right. Of course we all know real terrorists *never* cheat. And we also all know that there's never been a case of a tango – even one who's been shot in the head – managing to squeeze off a few more rounds and killing his attackers after he's as good as dead.'

A year or so ago, this was where Kenny would've followed up on Gordie's insult by challenging him to a fight right then and there. Bare fists and no rules – let's see who walks away and who crawls. Come on, dickhead. Hit me. Just hit me . . .

But a year or so ago, he hadn't yet made chief. With the higher rank came the responsibility to not be an asshole – particularly not in front of his men.

'I'm going to see that the results of this op are challenged,' Gordie blustered. 'Your CO is going to hear about this from me.'

'From me, too,' Ken countered, managing to smile because he knew that Gordie was baiting him and he knew that by staying cool he was completely pissing off the other man. 'My team did one fine job today. I'm going to make sure Lieutenant Commander Paoletti knows all about it.'

Gordie made himself large. 'My boys were supposed to learn something here today.'

Ken nodded. 'Yeah,' he said as he stepped around MacKenzie. 'Let's hope they did.'

One

Several Months Later

Savannah von Hopf's life spiraled even further out of control when she opened her cell phone and discovered that the batteries were completely dead.

She stared at the phone in disbelief, unwilling at first to accept any explanation other than that she'd suddenly and horrifically been plunged into an alternate reality. She'd charged her phone last night in her hotel room – same as she charged her phone every single night of her life. She wouldn't have forgotten something as important as that, and she hadn't. She'd plugged it into the outlet in the bathroom and . . .

And then turned out the light to go to sleep. Without the light switch in the *on* position, the outlet hadn't worked and the phone hadn't charged.

Of course.

She wasn't in an alternate reality. She was merely an idiot.

So now here she was, sans phone, in a rental car with a flat tire, in an unfamiliar part of San Diego.

Okay. Cross using her cell phone to call the car rental company for roadside assistance off the list that had the heading 'What To Do Now'. Savannah kept the motor on and the air conditioner running while she tried to think. What were her other options?

Knock on doors and ask to use a phone?

She peered out the windows of her car. The houses in this neighborhood was extremely small, and many of them had a grayness to them – as if the people living inside had had to choose to spend their money on something more vital, like repairing the roof, rather than on a fresh coat of paint.

The yards were all neatly kept, but still, this entire part of town had a desperate feel to it, a hopelessness.

The thought of having to get out of her car made Savannah a little uneasy – let alone the idea of getting out of her car and knocking on some stranger's door.

And wasn't that just great? If she were too chicken to get out of her car in some middle-class neighborhood in San Diego, how on earth was she going to get off the plane in Jakarta?

Of course, that was why she was here in the first place. Because she *didn't* want to get off that plane in Jakarta – at least not without a hand to hold.

Specifically, Kenny Karmody's hand.

She'd gotten what she'd come into this neighborhood for before the thumping front tire had forced her to pull to the side of the road.

She'd driven past Kenny's house and made certain there was no circumstantial evidence in his yard that would signal he was married with kids. No swing set, no big wheels, no Barbie hanging by her hair from a tree. No minivan parked in the drive.

Adele had told Savannah that, to the best of her

knowledge, Ken was still single. But she'd had experience back in college with 'the best of Adele's knowledge', and she'd wanted to see where Kenny was living before she called him.

And asked him to travel halfway around the globe with her, as a favor.

God, how was she going to ask a favor like that? Of a man she hadn't seen in over six years? A man with whom she'd had only one brief conversation, who probably wouldn't even remember her?

Savannah could see Ken's house in her rearview mirror – it was one of the better kept ones on the street. Miniature, sure, but not quite as drab.

She wasn't going to have the opportunity to ask the man anything if she didn't get back to the hotel and call him.

And say what?

Adele had been adamant that Savannah not mention her when she spoke to Kenny. According to Adele, he still wasn't over their breakup.

'Don't even tell him you met him while you were at Yale,' she'd said. 'He hates Yale – hates all Ivy League schools and everyone who went to one.'

So what was Savannah supposed to do? Lie?

'Tell him you met him at that technical college he went to in San Diego,' Adele had suggested.

No, the last thing she was going to do was lie. She was going to call him and say she got his name from a friend of a friend – which was a variation of the truth since Marla had stayed friendly with Adele after college, and Savannah still met Marla for lunch in the city every few months.

She was going to tell Ken that she needed some advice, and would he meet her for dinner at the Hotel Del

Coronado? Her treat. Her plan was to get him to show with the promise of a gourmet meal, and then, once face to face, tell him about Alex and the money and the trip to Jakarta. And – somehow – get up the nerve to ask him to come along.

Without making it sound as if she were propositioning him.

Although, truth be told, the idea of spending a day or two in the exotic port of Jakarta with a man she'd had the hots for since she'd first laid eyes on him, left her considering the possibilities.

Considering? Try fantasizing.

Savannah turned off her rental car's motor, and stepped out into the five-billion-degree heat. Didn't it figure? San Diego had perfect weather nine hundred and ninety-nine days out of every thousand.

Today, however, there was a heat wave that could put her mother's beloved Atlanta to shame.

Her hair wilted instantly as she bent to look at her front right tire.

Pancake city.

If Savannah had been even just a little less practical, she might have sat down and cried. Instead, she just sat down. Right there on the curb. Crying wouldn't get her out of there.

Driving on that tire wouldn't get her out of there, either.

And walking to that service station she'd passed two or three miles back also wasn't going to do the trick. Her high-heeled pumps matched her beige linen skirt and jacket with such perfection, her mother would have swooned with pride. However, her shoes didn't do such a terrific job matching her feet. After a half a mile, she would be in such excruciating pain, she'd have to crawl the rest of the way on her hands and knees.

So that left the final option. Changing the tire.

Savannah opened the trunk and there it was, under the rug. The spare tire. And the metal thingy that would prop the car up so the bad tire could be removed and the new one attached.

She'd driven past someone who was using one of those things once. A jack. That's what it was called.

How hard could it be?

'Please.' Joaquin's mother knew only a few words of English, but the anguish in her eyes said it all. *Save my son.*

Molly Anderson's first-aid training made her the closest thing to a doctor on this remote mountain in this remote corner of Parwati Island in this remote part of Indonesia. But she wasn't a doctor, and she had no clue as to what was causing the little boy to struggle so just to breathe.

She couldn't radio the hospital for advice. The camp's radio had been stolen three weeks ago for the third time in a row. Short of guarding it 24/7, Father Bob had decided not to replace it.

'Please,' the little boy's mother whispered again.

The trip down the mountain to the port of Parwati – the island's sole metropolis, population a whopping 3,500 – would take five days via treacherous mule trail.

As the parrot flew, it was only a few hundred miles.

A relatively short trip via airplane.

'Gather the things you need,' Molly said in the local dialect. 'You may be at the hospital for some time. I'm going to go find Jones. You know Mr Jones, right? Meet me up at his airstrip.'

There was only one airplane in the neighborhood, and it belonged to an American expatriate who went by the name *Jones*. Just Jones. And Molly was willing to bet that that wasn't the name he'd been given at birth.

Jones was a loner. A quiet man who kept to himself.

He'd shown up about six months ago, looked her up and down in a manner Molly was sure was meant to be insulting, then hired twelve men from the village to help him clear the old WWII-era airstrip that had been cut into the valley a short distance up river.

He'd worked the men hard – and paid them fairly, too, Molly had noted.

The next time she'd seen him, he'd been buzzing overhead in his battered red Cessna.

She suspected he was a smuggler. She knew he was a black marketeer. She'd heard he'd be willing to carry anything in that dilapidated old plane of his – even a gravely ill child – if the price was right.

And today the price would be right, because Jones owed Molly a big favor.

She slowed her pace as she approached his camp, uncertain as to her reception. Although she'd never been up here, the man was a hot topic of conversation in the village among both the locals and the missionaries. Depending on who was asked, he was a dangerous thief, a killer, a lost soul, a good employer, a card shark.

He'd appropriated one of the deserted sagging Quonset huts as his living quarters. More often than not, his plane – which was held together by chewing gum, rubber bands, and prayer – lay in pieces on the runway.

Today, thank goodness, it looked ready to fly.

He was out on the field, shirt off, machete in hand,

working hard to keep the jungle from reswallowing the airstrip. Molly watched him work, aware that with a runway this size he had to spend literally hours each day cutting back the brush.

She knew he'd seen her. A man like that had eyes in the back of his head. Still, he kept doggedly working, the muscles in his back and arm straining with each wide swing of his razor-sharp knife.

As she got closer, she could see the latticework of faded scars on his back, scars that meant he'd been lashed, beaten within an inch of his life. Even knowing they were there, even faded as they were, she was still taken aback by the sight. She knew they weren't his only scars. He had others on the lower half of his body as well.

'Mr Jones. Mr *Jones.*' It wasn't until she said it again, until she was within ten yards of him, that he stopped working and turned, wiping sweat from his brow with his forearm.

The men in the village often worked without their shirts, but they always made a point to cover themselves respectfully when she came around. Jones just looked at her, his dark hair slick with sweat, his usual four-day growth of beard darkening his chin, his tanned muscles gleaming.

Lord, he was . . . masculine. And she was staring, which was pretty dumb since she'd seen him without a shirt quite a few times before. In her bed, even. With some tropical form of the flu that had knocked him off his feet – quite literally.

She'd held him and wiped his face with a cool cloth after he'd been violently sick. During the three days that the bug had gripped him the hardest, she'd wiped him clean in some other places, too.

17

She'd dozed beside him, on a cot, for three nights until his fever broke. She'd stayed on that uncomfortable cot for another night, as he slept a full twenty-four hours, regaining his strength.

And then he'd left. Without a word, without a note of thanks, without giving her a chance to ask him about those scars. She'd come back to her tent, and he was gone.

She'd sent Manuel up to Jones's camp, to make sure he was all right, but both Jones and his Cessna were gone.

A week later, she came back to her tent to find a package on her bed. Two new sets of sheets and towels to replace the ones he'd soiled. And books. Ten of the most recent bestsellers, both fiction and nonfiction. Obviously, he'd taken a look at the overflowing bookshelves in her tent and noted her love for reading.

It seemed kind of odd that a man who was that perceptive – who would know to buy her books rather than something more traditional like chocolate as a thank you gift – hadn't noted that her interest in him wasn't merely that of nurse for her patient.

She'd sent him a note, thanking him for the books and inviting him to the village's traditional Sunday evening barbecue.

He hadn't shown.

She'd sent him a second note, inviting him to come calling whenever he found the time.

A month had passed and he'd never found the time.

As he looked at her now, his eyes were so completely devoid of emotion, Molly felt a surge of satisfaction. He was working so hard to hide what he was feeling – therefore he must be feeling something. It was probably embarrassment, but she preferred to think it was deep remorse for not having responded to her invitations.

However, there was neither time nor reason for small talk or embarrassment on either of their parts.

'I'm here to call in the favor you owe me,' she told him. 'I need a ride into Parwati for a sick child, the boy's mother, and myself.'

Jones didn't bat an eye at the idea that he owed her a favor, even though she herself believed nothing of the sort. She hadn't helped him when he was sick because she'd expected to get something in return. Her world didn't work that way, but his did, and she used that now to little Joaquin's advantage.

'I can take you tomorrow,' he said.

Molly shook her head. 'This child needs to get to the hospital now.'

'Now.' He took a drink from the water bottle he wore clipped to his belt, his eyes never leaving her, as if she were some kind of poisonous snake that might attack if he dropped his guard.

So she attacked. 'I don't think he's going to be alive tomorrow. You know I wouldn't even be here if this weren't life and death.'

The muscle jumped in the side of his jaw as he glanced at his watch. He swore softly. 'I can only take you one way. I've got a . . . job that starts tonight, and I won't be back near Parwati for a couple of weeks.'

Molly nodded, nearly giddy with relief. He could take them. 'That's fine.'

'It's hardly *fine*. It means you'll have to take the mule trail back up the mountain.'

She smiled at his pitiful attempt to discourage her. 'Oh,

19

well, then . . . in that case, forget it. I'll just let the little boy die.'

He didn't laugh at her joke. 'That's not what I meant. I meant, I'll take the kid and his mother – you don't have to come along.'

'They need someone to go with them to the hospital. To translate for them.' Joaquin's mother would need a hand to hold. 'I'm going.'

He shrugged as he headed toward the Quonset hut. 'Suit yourself. But I need you back here ready to leave in twenty minutes.'

'I'm here and Joaquin and his mother are already on their way.'

He laughed humorlessly. 'Pretty sure of yourself, weren't you?'

No, but she *was* pretty darn sure of Jones. When a man like him booted his lunch on a woman's only pair of running shoes, it was a pretty sure thing that he'd be desperate to make it up to her. 'Just hopeful,' she told him.

'After this,' he said, 'we're even.'

'Hey.' Ken knocked on the front window of the car. 'You know, it's not a real smart move to have the car running while it's up on a . . .'

He realized he was looking down at a young woman who'd hiked her skirt all the way up to the tops of her thighs. She had the AC on full blast and her blouse unbuttoned so much that he could see the lace of her bra. It was red. Holy God.

'Uh, up on a jack,' he finished.

Dear *Penthouse*, I never thought I'd write a letter like this, but . . .

'Oh, my God,' she gasped, and wrestled her skirt back down with one hand while she buttoned her blouse with the other. When she was covered again, she pushed the button and the window slid down with a whir. 'I'm sorry. Excuse me. I was just so warm. I was trying to cool down and—'

'Relax – I didn't see a thing,' he lied. 'Why don't you turn off the car and I'll give you a hand with that tire?'

She looked at him. Looked at him again over the tops of her sunglasses. She had wispy blond hair that curled around her face. Her eyes were an almost electric shade of blue and loaded with complete horror. 'Oh no!'

'What, are you trying to earn your Girl Scout flat tire badge or something? You need to do this yourself or you won't win enough points?'

'No,' she said. 'No, I'm . . . No.'

As far as a *Penthouse* encounter went, the promising start had petered out. She was either apologizing or looking at him as if he were an ax murderer.

Whoever she was, she had grease on her nose. She had grease on her cheeks, on her neck, on her chest, on her arms and her hands. She had grease all over her designer clothing, too.

Beneath all that grease, she was unbelievably pretty. Delicate looking. With that hair and those eyes, that angelic face, she looked like a fairy princess – a very grubby fairy princess.

As Ken watched, she took a Kleenex and used it to keep herself from getting the key dirty as she turned off the car.

She didn't bother to be so careful as she reached down to

21

slip her shoes back onto her feet. He could see her discarded pantyhose next to her on the seat and the day got even hotter.

He opened the door for her to keep her from having to use a Kleenex to do it. She first slipped her million-dollar pair of legs out of the car and then followed with the rest of her body, careful to keep her skirt from riding up again, much to his disappointment.

Ken tried not to think about the way her skirt hugged her hips, tried to forget he'd seen that pair of pantyhose she'd left back in the car, tried to ignore the burning question of the day – did she have anything on at all, underneath that skirt?

She was even shorter than he'd guessed, and had to tilt her head up to look at him, which was cool, since he was not extremely tall himself.

'Please,' she said in a husky, low voice that belonged to a stripper named Chesty Paree, not some sweet, Disney-big-eyed pixie. 'I'd love it if you could help.'

He'd gotten out of his truck with the intention of helping – whether she was a little old lady or a three-hundred-pound corporate CEO named Bob. But this was just too good to be true. She was pretty, she was red hot, and she wasn't wearing a wedding band on her left ring finger.

He could feel the testosterone flooding his system. Big Strong He-Man to the rescue. Why, sure, lil' lady, I'll save you. You just sit back and get ready to screw me blind in appreciation.

Oh, please Heavenly Father, don't let him say something stupid or hopelessly rude that implied he was unable to think about anything but sex. Even though it was true –

98 per cent of the time he was completely unable to think about anything but sex.

But despite his errant thoughts, he was simply going to change her tire and then wave as she drove away. And then he was going to go home, unload his melting ice cream from his grocery bags, go for a swim in his pool, have an early dinner and veg out in front of the TV, watch some of the shows he'd videotaped this past week. The closest he was going to come to having sex tonight would be lusting after Buffy or Seven-of-Nine.

And in a month or two, he'd finally stop thinking about this woman, this nice, well-to-do, intelligent, and completely undeserving-of-any-lewd-thoughts woman, and her underwear. Or lack thereof.

Please Jesus, as long as he was asking for divine favors, don't let her be a mind reader, okay?

'But I don't think anything short of explosives is going to do the trick,' she was telling him in that voice. 'I managed to get one of the bolt thingies off, but it took twenty minutes. The others I worked on for close to an hour, but they didn't even budge. What I'm really ready to do is blow this stupid rental car to hell.'

Ken laughed, wishing he could see her eyes again. But they were hidden behind her sunglasses. 'My neighbors might not like that very much.'

'What neighbors?' she asked. 'I've been out here for hours and not a soul drove past.'

'It's a dead end.' And on a Friday night, everyone but the most pathetic losers went straight from work to the local bars. She was lucky he was such a dweeb, and that for him, a hot Friday night meant watching TV, alone. 'What are you doing down here, anyway?' he asked her.

She stared at him as if he'd suddenly started talking to her in one of the funky languages that his pal Johnny Nilsson spoke so fluently.

'Did you get lost?' He simplified the question.

She cleared her throat and gave him the strangest little wavery smile. 'I was . . . just driving around. I'm in town for only a few days and . . .' She cleared her throat again.

Man, she was a terrible liar. Apparently she was too polite simply to tell him that he'd crossed the line and asked her a question that was none of his goddamned business.

He crouched down next to the tire. 'These lug nuts *are* tight.' He had to put some muscle into it to get them to move.

She sighed as he got the second one off. 'God, I'm such a wimp.'

'I've got slightly more body weight to throw into it.'

'Couldn't you sweat just maybe a *little*?'

Ken laughed. 'Believe me, babe, I started sweating as soon as I walked over here.' Oh, crap, that sounded as if he'd meant . . . He glanced up at her, and found her looking at him over the top of her sunglasses again. *Blue* eyes. 'I mean, as soon as I got out of my truck,' he tried to clarify. 'Hot day, you know?'

Yeah, right. Ah, he was smooth as shit.

But she nodded as she hid behind her sunglasses again. 'I thought it wasn't supposed to get this hot in San Diego.'

'This is unusual. This heat should break by tomorrow.' Yes, they *were* talking about the weather. He'd definitely freaked her out. Freaked himself out as well. 'I'm looking forward to getting home and jumping into my pool.'

'You have a pool?'

The third and fourth lug nuts dropped into his hand. 'Yeah, it's the reason I rented this house – it's just down the street. The house is nothing special, but the pool's huge. I can actually swim laps.'

'That's what I need right now,' she told him. 'A swimming pool. You can swim laps, but I'd like one of those floating chairs with a place to put a drink. And a frozen piña colada, please. A *large* one.'

Man, he was stupid. She must've been incredibly thirsty – out here God knows how long, in this kind of heat . . . 'I've got some pop and some beer in the truck. Help yourself.'

'Are you sure?' She held herself back, but he knew from the way she was standing that she wanted to run to his truck and rip the door open. She was incredibly thirsty, but terminally polite.

'Grab me a Coke while you're at it, will you?'

Ken glanced up to see her actually use the tail of her blouse to keep from getting grease on the door of his truck. That gave him a glimpse of her pale stomach and another flash of that red bra, Jesus save him.

The final lug nut came free, and Ken took off the tire. What the hell – what did he have to lose? Go big or stay home, alone, watching TV, for the rest of his life. 'You know, if you want, you could—'

Come back to my place and go for a swim. He didn't get a chance to ask because, as she handed him the can of pop, at the exact time he spoke, she also said, 'Your ice cream's melting. Did your wife—'

They both laughed at the conversational head-on collision.

'Sorry,' she said. 'Go ahead.'

'No, you go.'

She shook her head, her cheeks tinged pink, as if she weren't going to say anything. But then she took a deep breath. 'I just . . . You've got a lot of groceries in your truck. I was thinking how nice that must be, you know, for your wife? Do you . . . Do you pick up groceries for her all the time?'

Hel-lo. That was a full-fledged, deep-sea fishing expedition if he'd ever heard one. I don't have a wife. Want to come for a swim in my pool? Naked? With your legs around my waist?

Ken clenched his teeth, locking in all the things he shouldn't say, all the things that would reveal just how pathetically inexperienced he was at this kind of social and sexual game.

It was at times like this that he really, truly missed Adele – not because he still loved her. No, he was finally done with that. What he missed was belonging to her. They hadn't been married, but they might as well have been. On again and off again, but mostly on again, from senior year in high school until just over a year ago – he wasn't counting months any longer – they'd been a couple. He, at least, had been faithful for all those years – almost ten of them. The relationship had been long distance and way, *way* less than perfect, but he still missed the relief that came with not having to play this will-she-won't-she, if-I-say-this-then-maybe-she-will game with every beautiful stranger whose tire he changed.

He took a long drink of the cold pop before he answered her. 'I'm not married.'

It came out matter-of-fact. Casual. No big deal – certainly not as if inside he was running around and crashing full speed into walls in his blind hope that this good-looking woman, whose name he didn't even know, would sleep with him tonight. She was interested. She was *definitely* interested.

'Oh,' she said, equally casually. And then, obviously casting her fishing rod again, she asked, 'You have a lot of vegetables in your bags . . . Do you live alone? I mean, stereotypical bachelors live on tacos and pizza, but I suppose that's just the stereotype . . .'

'You caught me on a good day,' he told her. Wanna go have sex? No, no, no shit-for-brains. Ask her her name. Tell her yours. He cleared his throat. 'I'm Ken Karmody, by the way. And yes, I live alone. Completely. Alone.'

Oh, Jesus. Not *quite* as casual as before.

She took off her sunglasses. X-Men's Cyclops, with his laserbeam gaze, had nothing on this chick. Those eyes were incredible. Forget about her underwear, forget about sex, all he wanted to do was stare into her eyes for the rest of his life.

'You are so fucking pretty.' The words were out of his mouth before he could stop himself. 'Whoa,' he said. 'Excuse me. Wow, I'm sorry. I spend most of my time with a bunch of guys who—' A siren sounded, a few blocks over. 'Great. Here comes the language police, to lock me up.'

She was laughing, thank God. 'I'm Savannah.'

'Savannah. That's um . . . very pretty. It suits you. You got a last name, or are you like *Cher*? One name says it all.'

It was a lame joke, but she laughed again, and he teetered, on the verge of falling desperately in love. Just like that.

Ken knew he was prone to losing his heart to the girl behind the cash register at McDonald's before he even got his super-sized fries, but this was even more ridiculous

27

than usual. Savannah had said she was in town for only a few days. If there was going to be something between them, it was going to end almost before it began. And as far as getting a strenuous workout, his heart was not the primary organ he wanted to exercise here.

'Savannah von Hopf,' she told him. She held out her hand, but pulled it back, wrinkling her nose at the grease that was on her fingers.

Ken held out his own hand, showing her there was no way she could get him dirtier than he already was. 'Savannah von Hopf – that's a mouthful.'

She smiled again as she put her hand in his. He tried to keep breathing, tried to keep his heart from stopping at the warmth of the contact.

But her fingers were long and slender, her palms soft. He held onto her longer than he should have, turning her palm up and running his thumb across it. 'So you dig ditches for a living, huh?'

'No. I'm . . . an appellate attorney.' Her eyes were wide and she'd stopped smiling, but she didn't pull her hand away, so he didn't let her go.

So what do you say we jump in my truck, drive up to Vegas and get married?

His brain was definitely shorting at her touch. He knew there was something he should ask her that lay somewhere between 'Wanna go have sex?' and 'Wanna get married?' but his mind was completely blank.

'I'm from New York,' Savannah told him, and the reality of a three-thousand-mile commute from his house to hers crashed onto him like an anvil from the sky.

'The city, or . . . ?' As if it actually made a speck of difference to him.

'I live about forty minutes north of New York City,' she told him.

'I live in San Diego.'

'Yeah, I know.' She smiled weakly, turning to gesture down the street toward his house. 'You said.'

What the hell did that smile mean? He turned back to her car. Where was the goddamn spare? He should put it on her car, push her inside, and make her drive away. Letting himself fall for this woman would be idiotic. 'How long did you say you're here for?'

'I'm not sure exactly,' she said. 'Just a few days.' She cleared her throat. 'I'd like to repay you in some way for . . . I mean, not repay but, rather, *thank* you for helping me like this and . . .'

Unbelievable. 'The spare's flat.'

She stopped trying to get up her nerve to ask him whatever it was she was going to ask him, and came to look at the tire. 'It *is*?'

'Look at it.' It was completely soft.

'It's not supposed to be that way?' She was serious.

'Nope.' He tossed the spare back into the trunk, quickly put the old tire back on the rim, fastening the lug nuts loosely. 'You got the rental information in the glove box? There's probably a number to call for assistance.'

She nodded. 'I feel so stupid. If I had known . . . Instead I got all dirty, and *you* got all dirty, and I . . . I completely wasted your time.'

Ken cranked the jack and lowered the car to the ground. 'No sweat. Grease washes off.' He put the jack in with the spare, closed the trunk.

'I'm so sorry.' She was actually upset about this.

'So you're automotively challenged – so what? You want

to see real trouble? Ask me to practice law.'

Jackpot. He'd coaxed a smile out of her. 'Are you always so nice?' she asked.

'Nah, like I said, you caught me on a good day.'

And there they were, standing next to her flat tire, smiling at each other like a pair of fools.

Ken cleared his throat. 'So, um, where are you staying?'

'At the Hotel Del Coronado.'

The Del. Holy God. She either had money or worked for a company that did. 'Okay, look. If you can give me five minutes to put my groceries in the house, I'll give you a lift back there. Or—' Or you could come over to my place, call the rental car company, have 'em tow the vehicle while you stay and have a swim in the pool, stay all night, stay for a week, stay forever . . .

'Will you have dinner with me?' Savannah asked.

That was it. *That* was the question that he should have asked her.

He had to clear his throat so the words could come out. 'I'd love to.'

She actually looked relieved – as if there was a snowball's chance in hell he'd turn her down. 'There's a restaurant at the hotel that's supposed to be wonderful—'

'At the *Del*?' She wanted to have dinner with him at the freaking Del? That place was pure gourmet – five stars on a scale of one to four. 'Uh, Savannah, you know, we're not exactly dressed for the Del.'

'Well, of course I'd have to change—'

Oh, man, he didn't want to go to the Del and sit there all starched and uncomfortable. And while he was all for her taking off the clothes she was wearing, he didn't want her putting on anything else.

'Honey, you're going to have to do more than change. You have to hose yourself down. You've got grease, like, behind your ears.' Ken looked at his watch. It was already almost 1830. 'And it's a Friday night.'

She looked so disappointed, he felt himself cave. Maybe going to the Del wouldn't be a bad thing. He could put on his dress uniform – some women really dug that. 'If your heart's set on it, I could try calling for a reservation,' he told her. 'But I'd bet big money the place is booked solid from 1900 on.'

'I should have made a reservation this morning.'

Ken had to laugh. 'Yeah, if only you checked your crystal ball, you would have known you were going to meet Prince Charming this afternoon.'

She gave him the oddest look, and he kicked himself for being an ass. He'd meant it as a joke, but it came out sounding as if he was serious. Him, a prince? Yeah, right.

'What do you say we hit the Del tomorrow for lunch, instead?' he suggested quickly, before she could run away, screaming in horror. 'You know, the restaurant outside on the deck?' That would be a little easier on his wallet, too.

'Oh.' She looked worried. 'Are you busy tonight?'

'No, it's just . . .' Ken tried to explain. 'Friday night, it's a pain in the ba— backside to get a table for dinner just about anywhere. I'm not a fan of crowds, so I thought . . .' Oh, Christ, just *say* it, loser. 'I thought, if it was okay with you, we could maybe have dinner at my place. I've got a steak I could put on the grill, and some salad, and I thought we could go for a swim, you know, I could lend you one of my bathing suits, and—'

'That sounds great.' She was smiling at him.

31

'Great,' he echoed. 'Yes, it does sound very great. Extremely great.' God, he sounded like an idiot, but Savannah just kept on smiling back at him as if she liked idiots. As if she liked *him*.

Holy shit, she was going to go home with him.

He looked into her eyes, lit up the way they were from her smile and he knew.

Forget about writing to *Penthouse*.

This one was going to be a story for their grandkids.

TWO

'Tell him I'm not here, Laronda.' Alyssa Locke turned, heading back toward her office, and came within inches of slamming into Max Bhagat, the head of the FBI's most elite counterterrorist team.

Max Bhagat, her boss.

'Funny,' Max said, 'you don't look like you're not here. Who exactly are you hiding from, Locke?' He leaned over the receptionist's desk to get a look at the rows of monitors showing the downstairs lobby. He pointed to Dwayne, who was standing there looking like Mr Perfect in his Dockers, his shirt sleeves rolled boyishly up to his elbows. 'This guy? What's wrong with him?'

He wasn't Sam Starrett.

'He's arrogant, egotistical and insincere, he thinks he's God's gift to women, and he doesn't understand that no means no.' On the other hand, when she put it that way, Dwayne sounded an awful lot like Sam. 'Dwayne's a school teacher, but he can't seem to learn that I'm not interested in dating,' Alyssa explained. 'I've told him, many times, that I'm focusing on my career right now.'

'Which thrills me to no end,' Max shot back at her. 'But I'm a little concerned when one of my top agents runs and hides from a teacher. What's going to happen

SUZANNE BROCKMANN

when you come face to face with an AK-47-toting terrorist?'

'I shoot him,' Alyssa said flatly. 'I didn't think that that was the correct response in dealing with Dwayne, sir, and since talking to him hasn't seemed to work, I was going with plan B. Become invisible in the hopes that he'll get tired of chasing someone who's never there.'

Laronda was watching and listening with unabashed interest. It was no secret that the receptionist had a crush on Max. He may not have been extremely tall – not as tall as Sam, anyway – but he had the dark and handsome part down pat, with deep brown eyes to die for. A lot of people in the bureau had crushes on Max. Including Alyssa's own partner, Jules.

'Please tell him I'm not here,' Alyssa told Laronda again.

'Hold on,' Max ordered. He turned to Alyssa. 'You really want to lose old Dwayne once and for all? Because I can help you get rid of him.'

Oh, God. 'No, thank you, sir. I'd prefer to do this myself—'

'By going back into your office for another thirty minutes until you're sure he's gone? Look at you. You were ready to go home, weren't you?'

There was no denying it – she was standing there holding her briefcase. 'Yes, but I have plenty of work to—'

'Laronda, tell our pal Dwayne that you're not sure, but you think Special Agent Locke may have just headed down to the lobby,' Max said as he took Alyssa's arm and pulled her toward the elevators.

'Max.'

He pushed the call button, but there was already an elevator right there, waiting. The doors slid open, and he pulled her inside.

'Max.'

He smiled at her, a picture of innocence. 'Yes?'

'Don't you dare do what I think you're going to do.'

'Well, I have no intention of shooting poor Dwayne if that's what you mean.'

The bell rang, the doors slid open, and Max slipped his arm around Alyssa's shoulders as they went out into the main lobby.

Alyssa knew it looked as if he were holding her casually, but his grip was like a vise. She couldn't get free without creating a giant scene. And it was possible, even with a scene, that she *still* wouldn't have been able to get free. She kicked him in the ankle, hard, but to his credit he didn't even flinch.

'I just bought an entire case of Alligrini Amorone, 1996,' Max was saying loudly enough for everyone in the lobby – in both this building and the next – to hear. Both Dwayne and Lenny, the security guard, were watching them from the other side of the room. 'It's supposed to be magnificent and I'm thinking it'll taste twice as good if we have a glass or two in the hot tub.' He laughed and lowered his voice to a perfectly projected stage whisper. 'Of course, Bud Light tastes amazing in the hot tub with you.'

And then he kissed her.

His mouth was warm, his lips were soft, and he tasted like coffee and cinnamon. As far as kisses went, it wasn't awful, the way kissing Dwayne had been. It was actually nice. Sweet.

Safe.

And when he stopped kissing her, she saw that, just like magic, Dwayne had finally vanished.

But oh my God! She'd just kissed her team leader – her boss – in the lobby of the Washington, DC FBI Headquarters.

She pulled away from Max, punching him hard in the arm, and this time he let her go. 'Don't you ever do that again.'

'I'm sorry. I really didn't mean for it to be more than just a quick—'

'I can take care of my own problems myself,' she told him hotly. Lenny was still watching them. 'That wasn't real,' she told the guard.

Max followed her out of the building and into the steamy early evening heat. 'You have to admit it did the trick. So long, Dwayne.'

'Yeah,' she said. 'Perfect. Now Dwayne thinks I was lying when I told him I didn't want to date him, that I didn't want to date *any*one. Thank you very much.'

'Some guys have such big egos, they'd never believe a woman would prefer to be alone instead of with them. Some guys just never give up. Unless you *wanted* him following you around—'

'Don't be a dickhead.' Alyssa stopped walking and turned to face him, giving him her widest eyes and most innocent face. 'Oh, excuse me. Did I just call you a dickhead? I probably shouldn't do that, considering you're my boss. But wait. You *kissed* me. In front of Lenny. Talk about inappropriate and *actionable* behavior, Mr Bhagat.'

Max laughed. 'You know, I really like you, Locke.'

Alyssa felt her glare falter.

'No,' he said, quickly. 'I don't mean like that. Although to be honest, that kiss was a little more than I bargained for. It was a little too nice, you know – considering we're both in love with other people?'

Alyssa turned away. The evening was so humid, the sidewalk was actually damp. 'I don't know what you're talking a—'

'I know about you and Sam Starrett.'

She went for a major bluff, turning back to face him dead on, eye to eye. 'I don't know what you think you know, because there's nothing going on between me and Lieutenant Starrett. He's married now. He's got a daughter.'

Little Haley. Sam had sent Jules, her partner, a picture of Sam and his wife, Mary Lou, holding a scrawny little, red-faced, yowling newborn. Alyssa had taken only very slight satisfaction from the fact that the baby was ugly, that Mary Lou had gained about seventy extra pounds from her pregnancy, and that Sam looked weary.

'I didn't say there was something going on between you,' Max said gently. 'I said, you're in love with him.'

'Well, I'm not,' she lied. 'I spent some time with him last year, yes. But that ended.'

When he found out he'd knocked up his old girlfriend. When he went back to California to *do the right thing*. Damn him for being so honorable. Damn *her* for loving him for the fact that he was so honorable.

Max nodded. 'Okay. But you should know that I make a point to know what's going on with the members of my team, and I happen to believe that you're in love with not just a married man, but a married Navy SEAL. That's got to suck.'

'As long as you believe I'm a good agent, capable of getting my job done, I don't care what else you believe,' Alyssa told him. 'If we're done here, sir, I'm going home.'

Max shifted so that he was standing directly in front of her, blocking her way to the parking garage. 'What? And miss secret-sharing time? It's my turn. Don't you want to hear that I'm hung up on this girl – and I'm not being politically incorrect by calling her that. She's really

SUZANNE BROCKMANN

a girl – she's almost half my age; she's not even out of college. And if that weren't bad enough, she's a former hostage from that hijacked plane we helped take down last year in Kazbekistan.'

Alyssa remembered the plane, remembered the girl. 'Gina.'

He nodded. 'Gina Vitagliano.'

Alyssa was completely surprised, both about the relationship and the fact that Max was telling her about it. 'You've been . . . seeing her?'

Max correctly read her hesitation, her use of the words 'seeing her' to imply a sexual relationship. His smile was rueful. 'I've met her for coffee, even dinner, gone to visit her at her parents' house – that was weirder than hell. Her father's my age – but no, I haven't been seeing her. Not the way you mean. She was . . . assaulted on the plane.'

It was his turn to speak euphemistically. Gina had, in fact, been violently gang-raped by the hijackers as part of a power play. And Max had listened via the microphones the SEALs in the counterterrorist team had planted on the aircraft, unable to do a goddamned thing to stop her from being attacked.

'Do you really love this girl?' Alyssa asked him now. 'Or do you just feel guilty because she was raped on your watch?'

That was one hell of a harsh question to answer, but he didn't turn away. 'Honestly? I don't know. The shrinks all say that her feelings for me aren't real. It's all transference, and that she's still fixated on the fact that I was her lifeline throughout her ordeal. They say that I'm doing her more harm than good by seeing her. So I stay far away from her, and what does she do? She calls me on the phone.

'I try not to be home at any regular times, but somehow she always knows when to call. And I end up talking to her, two, three hours a night, a couple times a week. This past week, I've stopped answering my phone, and I'm going crazy, missing her.'

Alyssa knew all about what that was like. 'I'm sorry.'

He cleared his throat, forced a smile. 'Yeah, well, I didn't mean to get all pathetic and maudlin. I just wanted you to know you're not the only one in this unit who has a secret.'

She nodded. His was one hell of a secret, too. Continued involvement with a former hostage. Despite the fact that he was careful to avoid sexual contact, there had to be rules against that. If the wrong people found out . . . 'Your secret is safe with me, sir.'

'As yours is with me.' He started walking with her. 'So since my life really sucks, and your life really sucks, you want to go get some dinner?'

She looked at him sharply. 'No. And I also don't want to have sex with you, thanks, despite the fact that we're both so dreadfully lonely. Isn't that the line that comes next?'

He laughed. 'Honest to God, I'm really just hungry. And if you're hungry, too—'

'Max, what is this really about?' It was Alyssa's turn to stand in front of him, to keep from going anywhere. 'You know damn well if I have dinner with you, someone's going to see us, and word's going to get out. The assumption's going to be that if we're eating together, we're sleeping together.' And there it was. She'd answered her own question. Max didn't move a muscle, his expression didn't change, but Alyssa knew. 'You want the word to get out, don't you? Because you think that somehow it'll get back to Gina. You want her to stop calling you.'

'Yes. In fact, it would help me enormously if you could come to New York with me in a few weeks, so we could "accidentally" run into her . . . Then she'll make some discreet calls, find out that yes, indeed, I *have* been seeing you . . .'

'What about me?' Alyssa asked. 'Didn't it occur to you that the entire bureau will think I'm getting ahead in my career only because I'm getting with the boss?'

'I didn't think you cared what other people thought. I know you're very private with your personal life, but as far as conventional behavior . . . I mean, come on, your partner – whom you chose over any other partner, and you had your pick – is gay.'

Alyssa gasped. 'Oh, my God, he is? Jules? Really?'

'Think about what happens when word gets out that we've been spotted together, wiseass. Spec Ops is a very tightknit community.'

She knew what he was saying. It wouldn't take long for SEAL Team Sixteen – Sam's team – to hear that Max and Alyssa had hooked up.

'You don't want Starrett to think that you're out here pining away for him, do you?' Max asked.

She couldn't answer that.

'Okay,' Max said. 'No pressure. Just . . . think about it, all right? I mean, you have dinner all the time with Jules, right?'

'Jules is gay.'

'Yeah, well, you're just as safe with me. I'm a pedophile.'

Alyssa had to laugh at that. 'Max, I know for a fact Gina's over twenty-one.'

'Yeah, well, back when I was thirty, she was only twelve. Hey, before I forget . . .' Max dug into his briefcase and pulled out a book. He tossed it to her. 'I want you to read this.'

Double Agent: From Brooklyn to Berlin

It was an autobiography of a woman named Ingerose Rainer von Hopf. Alyssa quickly skimmed the front cover flap. Apparently Ingerose – or Rose as she was called by her friends – was a German American who was recruited by the Nazis to provide information on American aircraft manufacturers in the early days of World War II. Apparently, they targeted a large number of first-generation German Americans, especially those who, like Rose, worked for companies like Grumman. Pretending to be eager to help the Fatherland, she signed up to be a Nazi spy during a trip to Berlin. But upon her return to New York, before she even stopped at home to kiss her mother and father hello, she went to the FBI. At age eighteen, she became America's first female double agent.

'Hey, I just heard an interview she did for NPR,' Alyssa said. 'She sounded amazing.'

'She's even more amazing in person.'

'You've met her?'

Max nodded. 'You're going to have a chance to meet her, too. Rose doesn't know it yet, but Alex von Hopf, one of her sons – she's got twins – just went missing in Indonesia.'

'Oh, no.'

'Once she gets the news, I'd give her twenty-four hours before she charters a flight to Jakarta, straps on an automatic weapon, and marches into the jungle to look for him.'

'You're kidding, right?' Alyssa looked at the photo of the woman on the back of the book. It was from the 1940s, showing a girl in her early twenties with the devil in her smile. There was an inset of an elderly woman with the same smile. 'She's got to be, what? Seventy-five years old?'

'Eighty,' Max said. 'And no, I'm not kidding. Don't get into a fight with Rose von Hopf. Eighty or not, she'll kick your ass.'

He pointed the opposite way down the sidewalk. 'I'm parked this way. Unless you changed your mind about—'

'I haven't.'

'Then see you later, Locke.'

'Good night, sir.'

'Hey,' he called back to her. 'You might want to start packing. The team's going to Indonesia. Maybe not tomorrow, but definitely by the end of the week.'

Savannah came out of the bathroom wearing one of Ken's bathing suits and a T-shirt, feeling a little shell-shocked.

This was surreal. She was here in Ken Karmody's house, wearing Ken Karmody's clothes, about to sit down across from Ken Karmody himself and eat his food for dinner.

She hadn't planned to meet him this way. Now how was she going to tell him about Alex, and ask him to go to Jakarta with her without having to confess she'd been in his neighborhood because she wanted to see where he lived?

No matter how she worded it in her head, it came out sounding as if she were just short of stalking him.

There had been several little windows of opportunity when he'd first approached her, the first when she'd looked up and realized it was, in fact, Kenny Karmody standing there outside her car. Another had opened after he'd asked her why she was in his neighborhood, but she'd frozen, again unable to tell him why she was there without sounding like some complete and total freak.

The inside of Ken's house verified the fact that he did, indeed, live by himself. There was a package of clean socks and underwear from a laundry service in the living room, in a prime position on the coffee table. The art on his walls tended to be mostly movie posters from science fiction and action films. His home entertainment system was enormous and state of the art. And in the kitchen, he was clearly on the once-a-week plan in terms of loading his dishwasher.

The bathroom bore all the telltale signs of a recent visit from a cleaning service. While in there, Savannah scrubbed the grease from her hands and face – how had she gotten so much on her forehead and nose? – succeeding in washing off most of her makeup as well.

Still, as she emerged, Kenny gave her a smile that was lit with appreciation. *You are so fucking pretty.* She actually believed it when she looked into his eyes. Even dressed the way she was.

He'd already put away the groceries, cleaned up the dirty dishes, and had filled a bowl with salad.

'Can I help?' she asked.

'Nope.' He put a glass of wine in her hand, and carrying the raw steak and the salad, led the way through a set of sliders into the backyard.

Not that there was any kind of real yard back there. It was totally in-ground swimming pool, surrounded by a wooden fence, with a small deck right by the sliding doors for a table and the gas grill.

The water looked incredibly inviting, cool and clean and blue.

Ken put the steak on the grill then took the wineglass out of her hand. One firm push to the small of her back, and with a splash, she was in the water.

It felt as amazing as it looked, so she just stayed there, suspended, beneath the surface, surrounded by the delightfully cool silence.

But then there was a flood of bubbles, and Ken grabbed her, hauling her up and out into the air.

'Holy shit,' he gasped, grabbing onto the side of the pool with one hand, still holding tightly to her with the other. 'I didn't even think to ask if you knew how to swim.'

'I do.' She was pressed up against him, practically nose to nose, his muscular thigh between her legs, his arm around her waist, his hand up underneath her T-shirt, against the bareness of her back. 'I was just floating.'

'No, you weren't. Floating means you're up at the surface. You were at the goddamn bottom of the pool.' He wiped the water out of his eyes. 'Christ, you scared me.'

She could feel his heart pounding. Hers was going fast, too. She was holding onto his arm and shoulder and he was impossibly solid. He didn't release her, and she . . . well, she wasn't about to pull back. She'd dreamed about feeling his arms around her too many times not to want to savor the real thing. 'I'm sorry.'

'No,' he said. 'I'm the one who should be apologizing. I pushed you. I just thought . . . You're so polite. I didn't think you'd go in while I was cooking – not without a little help.'

He was right, she wouldn't have. 'I like lying on the bottom and looking up at the sun through the water,' she tried to explain. There was water on his eyelashes. Up this close, she could see every hypnotizing drop, every long, dark lash. He had beautiful lashes, beautiful eyes, a beautiful mouth . . .

'I should take you diving. You ever go diving?' He was

wearing his hair short these days, and his face wasn't as thin as it had been back in college. He'd filled out all over, in fact.

'I went on a cruise once, and there was a class, but . . .' He was staring at her mouth, and she knew. He was going to kiss her. Finally. After years of wishing and dreaming.

But he didn't move. And rather than just hang there like an idiot, she kept talking. 'I'm not very brave. Once I heard the stories about people's lungs exploding . . .'

Oh, terrific. Way to get the man to kiss her. Talk about exploding lungs.

He smiled, and sure enough, the moment was gone. The mood had been broken.

'That's only if you're an idiot,' he said, 'and you don't follow some really simple rules.'

'I'm good at following rules, but I'm not very brave,' Savannah admitted. He loosened his hold on her, and she knew she'd blown it. She'd brutally murdered that romantic moment. She *was* an idiot. She deserved to have her lungs explode.

But there was one lock of his wet hair that was dripping onto his nose, and without thinking, she reached up and pushed it back, and suddenly there she was, with her fingers in Kenny Karmody's hair.

And just like that, the moment she thought she'd lost was resuscitated. Instead of letting her go, Ken's arm tightened around her. And with a flash of heat, the way he was holding her didn't feel even remotely as if he were rescuing her anymore.

Even the water felt hot.

His eyes were so dark brown they were almost black. 'Savannah, I have to . . .'

He kissed her. He kissed her! His mouth was so sweet, his lips so gentle. It was a perfect first kiss – tender and respectful, practically reverent – like something out of a Disney movie with a G rating, featuring a nun.

She was the one who bumped it up to the next level. She was the one who practically inhaled him. She wrapped her arms around his neck and opened her mouth and . . .

And Ken was completely up for the challenge.

Adele had always said Kenny was a terrific kisser. She'd said that unlike some men, Ken didn't use kissing merely as a stepping stone to sex. She'd said he'd liked to kiss purely for the pleasure of kissing.

Savannah finally understood what Adele had meant.

And then she stopped thinking about Adele altogether.

At least until Ken gently pushed himself away from her and swam all the way down to the other end of the pool.

'You're dangerous.' He climbed out and dripped his way over to the grill. 'This is filet mignon, you know, and for a minute there, I was completely prepared to let it burn into a blackened cinder.'

'But you didn't.' Savannah climbed out of the pool, too, unsure whether she should be charmed by the fact that he hadn't assumed that one kiss gave him a green flag to take off her clothes, or insulted that she'd been pushed aside in favor of saving a piece of meat.

'It occurred to me that I should attempt to follow through on my offer to feed you dinner and hello, Jennifer Lopez, I knew there was a reason I should've given you a black T-shirt instead of a white one.'

Savannah looked down. Her shirt had gone transparent and, plastered against her body, it left absolutely nothing to the imagination. Not that she had all that much to imagine.

She tried to pull the fabric away from her skin, but that didn't really help. She folded her arms across her chest, but then she realized that after that one brief glance, Ken was carefully keeping his back to her.

'Third drawer in the dresser in my bedroom. That's the T-shirt drawer,' he told her. 'Help yourself.'

She went into the house, dripping onto his carpeting. It was easy to find his bedroom – only one of the two rooms at the end of the hall had a bed.

The other was filled with computers.

She stuck her head into that second room. Ken must've had four different home computers and a full array of scanners, cameras, zip drives, and high-tech things she couldn't even identify.

The king of all computer geeks, Adele had called him, claiming that when it came to computers, Kenny was a genius.

'He's like Albert Einstein,' she'd said. 'No, make that Albert Einstein with ADD. I swear, if Kenny would just learn to sit still, he'd be filthy rich. Instead, he's too busy playing soldier.'

There was only one thing Ken loved more than his computers, Adele had lamented. And that was being a SEAL. She'd come third in his life. Could she really be blamed for going out with other guys during their months of separation?

Yes. As a lowly college freshman to Adele's exalted senior status, Savannah had kept her opinion to herself, but even back then she'd thought Adele was a fool for cheating on Ken. And now, after having kissed him, she *knew* Adele had been a fool.

47

She went into his bedroom, a dim, cool, quiet room where the curtains were still shut. His bed was unmade, and he had packages of clean clothing out on every available surface.

The T-shirts weren't in the third drawer – that was empty. Instead, they were in a pile on top of the dresser, right next to his SEAL pin.

Half of the clothing in his room had various types of camouflage prints. Two different naval dress uniforms hung in the open closet under a thin sheet of dry cleaners' plastic. It was painfully obvious just from being in there that Ken was a Navy SEAL.

Savannah took one of the camouflage T-shirts and went into the bathroom to change. So now what was she going to do? He might think it really strange if she came out of his bedroom and didn't say anything about his uniforms. He hadn't mentioned to her that he was in the Navy. He hadn't said that much about himself at all.

Nor had she. Ever vigilant to keep away from the topic of where she went to college, she'd already changed the subject more than once. She didn't want to lie to him, but really, she already had. She'd been lying by omission ever since she rolled down the window of her car, recognized his face, and didn't admit that they'd already met.

A million years and a different lifetime ago, for both of them.

Catching a glimpse of herself in the mirror, Savannah attempted to make her hair look a little less as if she were a wet rodent. What would Rose, her grandmother, do? She took a deep breath, and went back outside.

'So . . . you're a SEAL.'

'So . . . I am.' Ken glanced up at her, his expression suddenly shuttered. 'Is that a problem for you?'

48

This was it. Her big chance to try to explain about Alex and Jakarta. 'Actually, no. It's not. In fact, I was looking—'

'You know what?' he interrupted. 'If you're a SEAL groupie, I don't want to know about it.'

'Excuse me . . . ?'

'A groupie. A woman who fucks SEALs just because they're SEALs.'

She recoiled from the harshness of his language, but he either didn't notice or didn't care as he carried the steak to the glass-topped table.

'I'm having a really good time believing that you're here, Savannah,' he said, 'because you felt the same jolt that I did when I looked into your eyes. Because we connected. If that's not true, I'd just as soon not know.'

'I'm *not* a SEAL groupie,' she said. How could he think that?

Except she had come to California to look him up because he was a SEAL. Now probably wasn't the best time to tell him that. Except, she realized with a sinking heart, there was *never* going to be a best time to tell him.

'If you are,' he said quietly, 'I'm not going to kick you out. I'm not that stupid. I'm going to take whatever you want to give me. I'm just . . . I'm looking for something more than a one-night stand, that's all.'

'I'm not a SEAL groupie,' she said again. 'Oh, my God.'

'Let's just talk about something else, okay? You want more wine or something else to drink with dinner?'

'No,' Savannah said. 'Let's not talk about something else. Let's talk about this. Because I *didn't* come here to have sex with you. And if you think otherwise, maybe I should just leave right now, because I have absolutely *no* intention of having sex with you.'

Well, *that* was a lie. 'Tonight,' she added. Which kind of ruined the effect of her impassioned, indignant, outraged speech.

But then it was okay, because he smiled. Ken Karmody had a smile like sunshine after a week of rain. 'Really?' he asked. 'Does that mean you'll have sex with me tomorrow?'

Somehow she'd said the right thing. Somehow she'd convinced him she wasn't – oh my God – a groupie. He believed her, and now he was teasing her, but she answered as if he were serious.

'I don't know,' she told him. 'We hardly know each other. Tomorrow still seems kind of soon. Doesn't it?'

'Maybe not if we, you know, stay up all night talking.'

If that was a line, it worked. The thought of this man – who was upset by the idea of a one-night stand, who, oh my God, was looking for something *more* – being intrigued enough by her to want to spend the whole night talking made her knees a little weak.

'I apologize for my, um, profanity,' he said. 'I tend to, uh, jump to conclusions sometimes. I have a history of being a worst-case scenario thinker and . . . A couple of months ago . . . No, it's been longer than that now, but anyway, to make a long story short, Janine, the last woman I dated, was pretty much a groupie. And I really don't want to do that again.'

Savannah didn't know what to say. And when he pulled out the chair for her, she sat down.

God help her, she had to tell him the truth.

And she would.

Right after dinner.

New York City. January 23, 1943.

I walked into the party at my boss's penthouse apartment expecting just another decadent attempt to ignore the fact that, as Americans, we'd been in the war for over a year now, and things weren't going quite the way we'd hoped.

Our allies in Great Britain were still getting the spit kicked out of them every night from bombing raids by the German Luftwaffe. Our own boys in the Pacific were fighting and dying in their attempts to regain one small island after another from the Japanese.

But in New York, we laughed and danced and drank champagne.

I was twenty-two, and thought I was quite the experienced and cynical woman of the world. I'd graduated from college. I'd traveled to Europe. I'd had my heart broken. I'd worked for nearly four years now as a double agent, code name *Gretl*.

Most of the other young women I knew complained about the inconveniences of the war – the lack of silk for stockings, the shortage of men and chocolate, and the fact that the blackout was disrupting the glitter of the city at night. What was the point of turning off the lights? We were far from Europe, far from danger.

I sometimes had to bite my tongue to keep from telling them that the war was closer than they thought – that I was fighting it every day from my office at Grumman, where as part of my cover I actually worked a full ten hours a day as Jonathan Fielding's secretary while I also maintained my Nazi contacts and fed false information to the Third Reich. All the while, I constantly prayed that today wouldn't be the day that my Nazi 'friends' discovered my allegiance was not to *der Vaterland* but rather to the land of the free and the home of the brave – not to mention my beloved Brooklyn Dodgers.

Yes, because I was 'Gretl', I knew far more than the average twenty-two-year-old woman in New York City. I knew that German U-boats moved silently and unseen just outside of New York Harbor. I knew they often came close to shore just off Long Island to allow Nazi spies and saboteurs to disembark.

I had been told by my Nazi contacts that if I found myself facing 'discovery' by the Americans, I should head to South America. There was apparently a Nazi stronghold in Brazil, the idea of which gave me nightmares of squads of German soldiers – similar to the ones I'd seen in Berlin in 1939 – goose-stepping their way through Mexico, up into Texas and beyond.

No, we were *not* far from danger. Yet on the evening of January 23, I put on my best gown – a low-cut dark blue number. The color set off my fair hair and eyes, and the daring neckline set off my other attributes.

In this war, my pretty face and female figure were my weapons and my gown was my uniform. I marched forth that night, heading into the thick of it – Nazi hunting.

I'd heard rumors that a high-powered Nazi agent, code name Charlemagne, was due to arrive in New York at any moment. I was planning to hit the Supper Club and the Bubble Room – and all the other popular nightspots – to scan for new faces, after stopping briefly at Jonathan's party.

I remember the disdain with which the maid took my winter wrap and my hat at the door to the Fieldings' apartment. She glanced pointedly down the hallway, as if looking for my missing escort, who, of course, didn't exist. In 1943, if a woman went out only when she had an escort, chances were she wouldn't go out at all.

And, considering that I was supposed to be Jonathan Fielding's mistress as well as his secretary, the scandal of my appearance at his party far outweighed the scandal of my lack of escort.

Evelyn Fielding, Jon's wife, greeted me with the warmth of a glacier. She was so good at hating me, I nearly always laughed aloud when we came face to face in public.

She knew darn well that I wasn't her husband's mistress, that I was a double agent working for the FBI. Jon had told her the truth from the start.

At first, I'd been terribly upset by this. It was bad enough that Jon had to know who I really was, but his wife . . . ? My very life – and the lives of my dear mother's brothers and sisters back in their tiny village outside of Freudenstadt – depended on total secrecy.

But then I met Evelyn and she became the older sister I'd never had. I knew instantly why Jon trusted her so completely, why he adored her. And once a week, when Jon would take me – his 'mistress' – for a daytime rendezvous at the Grand Hotel, Evelyn would meet us there, and we'd all have a cozy luncheon *à trois*.

She was always so worried for me, always bringing cookies and homemade soup. She was sure that I wasn't taking the time to eat properly, and Lord knows she was right.

'I'm afraid I can't stay long,' I told her now as I took a glass of champagne from a passing tray.

'What a pity,' she drawled, so beautifully disingenuous, I couldn't help but laugh.

Fortunately, anyone watching would think I was laughing at her out of spite, or maybe nervousness at such close contact with my lover's wife.

'Careful.' She leaned close to whisper with a near perfect sneer that made her look as if she were quietly threatening to boil my panties if I didn't leave immediately. 'Euro-God at nine o'clock. He's got you in his radar, Rose. You're in trouble now.'

She was always saying things like 'at nine o'clock' and 'radar'.

53

Even though I'd told her again and again that the life of a double agent in New York City wasn't all that exciting, she didn't believe me. One of these days I vowed I'd show her the paperwork – the endless encryption of messages with ridiculous codes, the endless searching through classified ads in the *New York Times* for messages that contained phrases such as 'Grandmother's favorite dog missing' or 'Attic room to let' – and let her see first-hand what I spent most of my time doing – waiting for contact. Aside from the threat of being found out, it could be pretty dull.

Except, of course, when I was out Nazi hunting.

'Don't count on it,' I told Evelyn, not bothering to lower my voice, since my retort worked equally well both for her true comment and any potential threat to boil my underwear or slit my throat. I turned to see exactly what her idea of a 'Euro-God' was this week.

And nearly dropped my champagne flute.

It was Heinrich von Hopf. Right here in Manhattan.

Needless to say, he wasn't wearing his SS uniform.

Rose stopped reading, silently counted to five, then said, 'May I take a short break?'

The microphone from the engineering booth clicked on and Delvin's voice came through her headphones. 'Absolutely, Miz H. Can we get you some coffee?'

Rose stretched as she stood up from the desk. Old bones, old muscles, old aches and pains. There was actually one twinge in her hip that she'd had longer than the engineer, Delvin Parker, had been alive. *Way* longer than his assistant, a baby-faced, fresh-mouthed, smart-assed boy named Akeem, who swore he was twenty-five but didn't look a day over sixteen.

'Actually, one of the reasons I could use a break is because I've already had a little too much coffee.' She set the headphones down next to the computer screen and headed for the door.

Akeem beat her there, coming from the other side. He pushed open both sets of soundproof doors that isolated the recording studio from the mixing booth and propped them open. 'This shit you're reading – this Nazi spy story – is it all true?'

She had to laugh. 'Here's a hot tip, child.' She knew it made him squirm when she called him that. 'When you're speaking to an author, you might think of a more flattering word to use to describe her book.'

He followed her into the hallway. 'I didn't say it was *bad* shit. Matter of fact, it's *good* shit. Usually I fall asleep.'

'Ah,' Rose said dryly. 'Quite an endorsement.'

'Yeah, it is. Did it really happen like this, or did you jack up the action to make the *Times* list?'

She stopped outside of the ladies' room door. 'What do you think?'

He looked into her eyes for several long moments. She liked that about him. Too often today young people didn't take the time to look at the person to whom they were speaking. And forget about young people, the entire world tended to ignore the elderly altogether. But not Akeem.

He grinned. 'I think you're a crazy woman now. I think you probably were worse when you were twenty-two. I think you dialed it *down*, instead. I think you left out all those games of strip poker, and all those times you streaked through Times Square – so as not to embarrass your uppercrust family.'

She laughed.

'I'm right, aren't I? Okay, don't admit it. But answer me this – you ever meet Hitler when you were in Berlin?'

'Why don't you read the book and find out?'

'I did read the book. I read it the night after your first recording session. Like I said, it's good shit. But I figure if you ever met Hitler, he woulda hit on you. You know, *Ach du liebe, vat a hot goil. Vant to join me for some Nazi nookie?*'

'Yes, that was the first thing I noticed about Adolf Hitler,' Rose said. 'That he had a heavy Jewish accent, just like a Catskills comedian.' She shook her head. 'No, dear, I never met him. I tried my best to keep from being noticed by the *Obergruppenfuehreren* – the upper level Nazi leaders. And if you've read the book, you know that I was not alone in Berlin.'

'Yeah, that occurred to me.'

'Rose. There you are. How are you?'

She turned to see a man at the end of the hall, in a perfectly tailored, very dapper dark suit. He was better dressed than most FBI agents, but she'd been with the bureau long enough to know one when she saw one.

But good heavens, was it . . . ?

'George Faulkner,' he identified himself as he moved closer.

It *was*. Anson Faulkner's boy, George. Except he wasn't a boy anymore. Lord, how the years – decades – flew by.

She could tell from his face that this wasn't a social call.

'Oh, yeah,' Akeem said. 'I'm supposed to tell you, Rosie – suit here wants a word with you if you've got a sec.'

Rose's heart was already pounding and her damned eighty-year-old knees felt weak. A visit, not a phone call. That wasn't good. She forced herself to stand tall, to face whatever was coming with her head held high. 'Who's dead?'

'No one's dead, ma'am.' George pointed to the ladies' room door. 'Were you on your way in or out? Because this can certainly wait a few minutes.'

No one was dead. Thank God. Still . . . 'Have you come to tell me I've won the lottery?' Rose asked.

George, like his father, was an exceptionally handsome, almost pretty man. They both had the kind of face in which lines of stress and strain – both mental and physical – stood out. And somehow, in a way that was entirely unfair to women everywhere, those lines only made them better looking. If he were a woman, he would look haggard and hideous. But George managed to look attractively exhausted. 'I wish. But, no.'

She turned to dismiss Akeem. 'Please excuse us.'

'Oh,' he said, backing toward the studio door. 'Right. Except . . . Are you sure? You know this guy, right?'

'Yes. I need to speak to him privately,' Rose told the young man. 'Now, please.'

George waited until the door closed. 'This may be nothing—'

'Alex or Karl?' This had to be about one of her sons. Her daughters were too smart to get into any kind of real trouble.

'Alexander. He went to Jakarta on a business trip,' George told her.

'He travels to Jakarta all the time.'

'This time, he failed to appear for a scheduled conference call with his office in Malaysia. Bob Heath, his personal assistant back in Kuala Lumpur, called the US Consulate in Indonesia after – over the following two days – he failed to reach Alex at his hotel. Because of who Alex is—'

'My son.'

'Yes. Because of that, the State Department was given the heads up for a possible abduction.'

Oh, Alex . . . 'He's diabetic, you know. He needs insulin shots every day.'

George got out a small leather-bound pad and made a note. 'I didn't know.'

Still, it had been only two days. 'He might've met someone,' Rose said. 'Gone off on a spontaneous holiday without letting anyone know. It wouldn't be the first time.' Or the last.

'Absolutely,' George said.

'But you don't think so. Why else would you be here?'

'I'm here,' he told her, 'because I love you. Because of all the times you went out on a limb for Dad. Because someone made a decision not to notify you about this, and I believe – with your service record – you have the right to know.'

Rose knew that George was going to get into serious trouble for telling her this.

'It may be nothing. They might've already found Alex,' he continued.

'Or they might not have. Who's heading the investigation?' she asked.

'I don't know. Our local guys in Jakarta will find out if Alex is missing or if he's *missing*. If it *is* an abduction . . .'

'Max Bhagat will get it.' Rose was certain. 'Do you know him?'

George exhaled a burst of air that might've been a laugh. 'I assume you mean, do I know *of* him? Yes. It's kind of hard to miss him. The man has his own page on the Urban Legend website, right next to Superman's. But I've never met him. I mean, other than in my dreams.'

'If Alex *is* missing, you'll be assigned to Max's unit,' Rose decided.

George laughed. 'I appreciate the thought, ma'am, but . . .'

She looked at him sharply. 'You don't think I can do it?'

He shifted his weight, clearly uncomfortable. 'I'm not sure I *want* you to—'

'You don't think I'm doing this for you, do you?' Rose asked him. 'I'm doing this for *me*. If Alex is missing, I want to know exactly what's going on. I want you in the thick of it.'

'When my boss finds out that *you* found out about all this from me . . .' George shook his head. 'Let's just say that I'm not going to get a promotion. Certainly not a transfer into the top counterterrorist team in the country.'

'I found out about this from Bob Heath,' Rose informed him. 'Alex's assistant. Go home, George, because after I call Bob, I'm going to call you for the details. It would be nice if you had some new ones to tell me. Oh, and start packing. You'll be going to Jakarta via Washington.'

George sighed. 'Rose.' He was trying hard to be diplomatic. 'It's just that, well, I happen to know that Bhagat handpicks his team.'

'He'll be told to handpick you.'

He laughed in exasperation.

'You don't think I can do it,' she said. She took her cell phone from her purse. 'Just watch me.'

A week ago, Savannah had gone out to dinner for the third and final time with Vladamir Modovsky, an actual Romanian count, a man accessorized with a title and a real crumbling castle.

He also had a mortgage that was coming due, but that wasn't to be spoken of – certainly not in public, definitely not with Vlad-of-the-big-white-teeth. And in private, in phone conversations with her mother, the subject was either ignored or heavily glossed over. There was no doubt about it – old Vlad was Priscilla's latest favorite candidate for the role of Savannah's husband-to-be.

Savannah had been out with him three different times – which was three times too many in her opinion – enough for her to feel as if she'd given him a fair shot.

Each time, they'd been followed by paparazzi. Most of the photographers were from eastern European newspapers. Only one of the photos had shown up in an American rag, and in the back pages, thank God.

Vlad had actually enjoyed the attention. He played to it, throwing kisses to the photographers.

Savannah had gritted her teeth and gone home after that last dinner – Vlad's third and final strike – and left a message on her mother's answering machine, telling her that under no condition – not even as a favor to the president of the United States – would Savannah go out with him again.

Of course, her mother was out of town and unlikely to receive the message for another week and a half.

'Are your parents still alive?' she asked Ken, over a second glass of wine. Unlike big-toothed Vlad, he didn't have a clue that he was dining with the daughter of one of the richest men in America. He had absolutely no idea that, as an only child, she stood to inherit an enormous fortune, that she already had more money in her personal bank accounts than most people earned in a lifetime.

His interest in her was genuine.

Well, okay, sure. Ken's interest in her was based on sex. He wanted to sleep with her. She knew that. Still, even if that was his sole motive in gazing into her eyes as if he'd be content to sit there talking all night, it was refreshing.

The light from the candle he'd lit when the sun had gone down flickered over the planes of his face, making his dark eyes even darker. Mysterious. 'My dad died of a massive stroke about four years ago,' he told her quietly.

Oh, God. 'I'm sorry.'

'Yeah, well . . . thanks, I guess. He was. . .' He shook his head, flashed his smile. 'My mother's still alive. Still lives in New Haven.'

New Haven. Home of Yale University, her alma mater.

'What's her name?'

'Mary. Dad was John. How's that for keeping it simple?'

'Mine are Priscilla and Karl.' She rested her chin in her hand as she looked at him across the table. 'Do you ever think of your mom by her first name?'

He laughed. 'No. Not really.'

'I do. My mother can be . . . kind of like a human steamroller. It helps me remember this is my life and that I don't have to live it on her terms if I think of her as Priscilla.'

'Hmmm,' he said. 'I've had a little experience in trying to live life on someone else's terms. I had this girlfriend who—' He stopped short, taking a long slug of his beer.

'Who what?' she asked, fascinated, knowing he was talking about Adele. He had to be.

He looked at her dead on, the flame from the candlelight reflecting in his eyes, making them seem twice as warm. 'Nah, I don't want to talk about her. She doesn't matter anymore. She doesn't have anything to do with me, and she certainly doesn't have anything to do with you.'

Oh, God. Savannah leaned forward. 'What's the one thing you've done that you regret the most?'

This was how she was going to do it, how she was going to tell him the truth. She would get him to bare his soul and then she'd bare her own. It had come to her a few minutes ago. It was something Rose would have done, something right out of the story of her grandmother's life.

'Jeez, it's kind of hard to narrow 'em all down to just one.' Ken leaned forward, too. 'Right now I'm really regretting that when I said we should talk all night, I forgot that I've got to be on base for training at 0430.'

Savannah tried not to be distracted by the fact that he'd reached across the table and taken her hand, that he was playing with her fingers, that he was looking at her as if, were the table not between them, he would kiss her again. 'I'm talking about . . .' She had to clear her throat. 'About serious regrets.'

'I don't think I've ever been more serious in my life.' But then he smiled. 'You know, you still have this big streak of grease on your neck.'

She froze. Oh, God. 'I do?'

'Yeah. Right under your left ear.'

Savannah pulled her hand free. 'You let me sit here all through dinner with . . . ?' She pushed back her chair, ready to run for the bathroom and the soap, but he stood, too.

'Hey, Van,' he said, catching her. 'Whoa. I didn't tell you so you'd run away. I just . . .'

At close proximity, she could see that he was probably as nervous as she was. That he wanted to kiss her as much as she wanted to kiss him.

'You're so beautiful, it scares me a little,' he said softly, 'because I don't really get what you're doing here with someone like me. All during dinner, I was having these real freak-out moments, you know? But then you turn your head to the right and there's that grease under your left ear, and I think, well, okay. This is all right. I think, she's here because she's not afraid to get her hands dirty, because she's not afraid to get up to her neck in things, because she's willing to take chances, to go for it, to get real.'

Savannah gazed up at him, unable to respond.

People usually saw her quietness as timidity, her politeness as conservativeness. But when Kenny looked at her, he actually saw someone strong.

And instead of running for the bathroom, she kissed him.

It was quite possible that she was never going to wash her neck again.

Three

Slow down. Slow. Down.

But, great holy God, when Savannah slipped her hands up underneath his T-shirt, when she kissed him just as eagerly as he was kissing her, slowing it down was the last thing Ken wanted to do.

No, the sensation of her cool fingers against the heat of his bare back was not one that would normally evoke feelings of caution and deliberation.

She was pressed full against him, and sweet mother, the idea of taking a step back from *that* . . . Well, he'd have to be a saint or a madman, and he was neither.

'Savannah,' he managed to say. 'I don't want to wait until tomorrow.'

She stood on her toes for another soul-shattering kiss. He took it as a good sign. But her real answer came when she slipped one of her hands out from under his T-shirt, and down beneath the elastic waistband of his swim trunks to cup his buttocks. Talk about mind-blowing surprises. This woman knew what she wanted and, thank you, *thank* you, Jesus, it sure as hell seemed as if she wanted him.

'I don't want to wait either, Kenny,' she breathed, looking up at him with those incredible eyes.

Kenny. It was what Adele used to call him, and for two-

64

tenths of a second, it threw him. But this woman was not Adele. In fact, she was the opposite of Adele. She was small in stature, slight in build, while Adele had been tall and stacked. Savannah was sweet and polite and honest.

They were as different as two women could be.

Except, of course, for the fact that, like Adele, Savannah lived on the freaking other side of the country. If he let himself fall for her too hard, he'd either wind up broke or frustrated as all hell.

Or both.

Ken tried to stay cool as he swept Savannah into his arms and carried her into the house, into his bedroom.

But she laughed as he kicked the door closed, as he dumped her onto his bed, and he knew he was screwed. This wasn't going to be a one-night or even three-night thing. He was going to New York. A lot. And it was going to be okay. Somehow, some way, this time, he'd make it work.

Savannah was too freaking amazing for him not to try.

She pulled him down with her and he found himself exactly where he wanted to be – between her legs. All they had to do was lose the few pieces of clothing they had on between them, and find a condom.

Bedside table, top drawer. He kept a stash there in the eternal hope that Sarah Michelle Gellar would come to San Diego for a party, meet him and follow him home.

He pulled off his shirt – Savannah helped.

He pulled off her shirt – she helped with that, too.

God, he loved everything about women, but he especially loved breasts. Savannah was not voluptuous in any sense of the word, but she was so perfectly feminine, he briefly considered weeping with joy at the sight of her, lying there, bare-breasted in his bed. But that would've taken way too much time.

Instead he kissed her, caressed her, licked her, touched her. She smelled like his soap, like the chlorine from his pool, like his clean laundry on top of her fancy perfume. She smelled like he'd already, at least partially, claimed her as his own.

God, what a turn-on.

The sounds of pleasure she was making were inspiring, too. When he lifted his head to look at her, her eyes were half closed, the expression on her face an image he'd take with him to his grave.

She didn't say a word. She just pulled him down and kissed him, pressing herself up, rocking against him, leaving him with absolutely no doubt as to what she wanted.

What he wanted, too.

He kept kissing her as he pushed at his swim trunks, as he reached for the drawer where he kept his stash of prophylactics. Somehow they both managed to get naked amidst a tangle of arms and legs, her skin heart-stoppingly smooth against his. Somehow he covered himself in spite of the fact that he couldn't stop touching and kissing her, that she couldn't stop touching him. His world became a blur of her bare skin beneath his hands, her soft hands exploring him, her mouth and his, the wet rasp of tongues, kissing, tasting, licking . . .

'Please,' she was saying. 'Please . . .'

The sound she made as he entered her was enough to bring him dangerously close to losing it. But then he realized she was coming. She was shaking apart, completely unraveling beneath him. Just like that. Just from his being inside of her.

It was too much of a turn-on, and, combined with the too many months since he'd last had sex, it pushed him over the edge.

Four more thrusts and he was done, too, in a blinding rush of pleasure.

'Oh, my God,' she gasped, clinging tightly to him. 'Oh, my God.'

Good thing she didn't seem to want him off her, because he wasn't sure he could move. He just lay there with his face buried in one of his pillows, completely trashed by the mind-blowing intensity.

Jesus, that had been fast.

It would've been completely embarrassing if she hadn't been even quicker on the trigger than he'd been.

He lifted his head, suddenly filled with trepidation. 'That *was* you coming, wasn't it?'

She opened her eyes and smiled. It was all the answer he needed.

God, she had beautiful eyes, a beautiful body. He rolled off of her, propping himself up on one elbow, head on his hand, so he could just look at her.

'Did you have a dog growing up?' she asked, reaching up to trace his lips with one finger.

What?

She laughed at the look he knew was on his face. 'I figured even though we jumped the gun, this is the part where we should talk all night. At least until you have to go.' She hesitated, suddenly uncertain. 'Is that all right?'

His heart grew in his chest, just like the Grinch's, only his had already started out a little too big for his own comfort. Man oh man, he was in trouble when she gave him that big blue-eyed look.

'How about after my morning training session, I put in for a few days leave, and we talk all day tomorrow?' he asked. 'How about right now I kiss you for about a half an hour, and then we do what we just did all over again, only this time in slow motion?'

He kissed her, and she welcomed him with an answering kiss that was slow, deep, and hot. It sent a bolt of desire clear through him. Forget a half hour. Try ten minutes.

He kissed her again, and forgot all about time.

Molly Anderson had never flown in a Cessna quite like this one before.

It occurred to her that she should probably be afraid for her life, considering she was all these thousands of feet up in the sky in a plane that spent more time in pieces on the ground than in the air.

But then Joaquin's mother became frantic, crying out over the roar of the engines. Her son had stopped breathing.

To Molly's complete surprise, Jones answered the woman in the local dialect. 'Check his air passage, clear any foreign obstruction, and start mouth to mouth—'

He turned to Molly, his eyes hidden behind sunglasses. 'I'm not sure she knows how to do that.'

'I do.' Molly climbed into the back.

Oh, dear God, the little boy truly was in trouble. His lips were blue and his face was mottled and swollen. In fact, his fingers were swollen, too.

'Check to make sure he's really not breathing,' Jones ordered crisply. 'Check for cyanosis.'

'What?'

'Is he turning blue?'

'You're a doctor,' she realized.

'Come on, Molly. Answer the goddamn question. Is he turning blue?'

'Yes.'

'Check for an obstruction,' he ordered.

She opened Joaquin's mouth and . . .

'Nothing I can see,' she reported. 'But his throat looks swollen.'

'It's probably anaphylactic,' Jones said. '*Shit*.'

'What?'

'Allergic reaction. Christ, I thought you were a nurse.'

'I'm not. But if you tell me what to do . . .'

'He needs you to give him a tracheotomy.'

Oh, dear God. Molly had watched enough episodes of *M*A*S*H* as a kid to know that that involved cutting a hole in Joaquin's throat and inserting a tube through which he'd be able to breathe. 'I can't do that.'

'Know how to fly a plane?'

Yeah, right. 'No.'

'Get your ass up here, because you're going to learn.'

She scrambled to the front, telling Joaquin's mother that Jones was going to help, Jones was a doctor.

'I'm not a doctor,' he said, pulling her onto his lap. He was as hard as he looked, all muscle and bone and grit, not an ounce of softness anywhere.

'Hold this steady,' he added, putting her hands onto the oddly shaped steering wheel as he slid out from beneath her. He tapped a dial. 'This is your altitude.' He tapped another. 'This represents the horizon. This thing here is our wings. Keep everything steady. Try not to crash.'

Some lesson.

Of course, there was no time for Jones to be more precise. Joaquin was running out of time.

Molly held the controls of the plane with white knuckles, listening to the murmur of Jones's voice as he spoke to Joaquin's mother. The woman's voice rose in panic as Jones took out his knife, but Jones kept on talking to her, his voice low and reassuring. Joaquin was going to be okay. Jones was going to make it possible for him to breathe, and then they were going to get him to the hospital. Trust him. She had to trust him. He knew she trusted Molly. And Molly, she trusted Jones.

It seemed like forever, but Molly saw from the clock in the dashboard – did planes have dashboards? – that it was only a few minutes before Jones was back.

'Thank God for Bic pens.' He was trying so hard to be blasé, she knew he was feeling anything but. 'He's breathing again, but I need to push this crate faster. Outa my seat.'

This time she slid out from beneath him. 'Can you radio ahead to have an ambulance waiting?'

'I could if I had a radio that worked.'

Joaquin's mother was cradling the boy in her arms, murmuring a steady stream of prayers.

'Go sit with her,' Jones ordered. 'She needs another dose of God. Takes a lot of faith to let a stranger stick a knife in your kid's throat. She probably needs some of hers restored.'

'Her faith is fine,' Molly said. 'She trusts in God.'

Jones laughed, glancing up at her, his eyes filled with disgust. 'Yeah, God really took care of that little boy.'

Molly smiled. 'He certainly did.'

He snorted. 'And on the eighth day, God created Jones, his pocket knife and a Bic pen, right?'

'Mr Jones, I do not doubt for one second that you are one of God's more magnificent masterpieces.'

'Jesus H. Christ, give me a break.'

'Or should I call you Dr Jones?'

'Only if you want me to wind up dead in some Parwati back alley,' he said flatly. 'Please take your seat and prepare our other passengers for landing.'

Savannah stirred as Ken searched his dark bedroom for his clean T-shirts.

His T-shirt drawer was empty, and as he discovered the pile on top of his dresser, he also managed to knock about fifteen dollars in coins onto the floor.

Amazingly, it wasn't that that seemed to wake her, but rather his whispered epithet.

'Kenny?' She was barely awake, barely able to lift her head.

'Shh,' he said. 'I'm sorry, Van. Go back to sleep.'

'Are you leaving?'

'Yeah, I gotta go. It's nearly 0400.' He made the mistake of moving close enough to the bed to see her in the dimness. She was only half covered by the sheet, and when she stretched, he actually found himself considering facing Unauthorized Absence charges. How bad could it really be to go before a Captain's Mast?

Bad enough that he'd kiss goodbye his chances of getting leave for the next week – and *that* he absolutely didn't want to do.

Still, he couldn't resist sitting on the edge of the bed and kissing her. And that was his second mistake. She pulled him down on top of her, kissing him back that way that she always kissed him – as if she couldn't get enough of him. As if he were some kind of freaking sex god who made her world spin.

It was wild, because she was barely even awake.

71

Savannah breathed his name, and he was doomed. He was going to walk around with a serious woodie for the rest of the morning.

And that was going to look swell in a wet suit. If there was a God, the water would be nice and cold. And it would stay good and dark outside until he was submerged.

'I don't suppose I can talk you into staying right here, just like this, until about 1100,' he murmured. He had about ten minutes before he had to walk out the door but he couldn't stop kissing her.

'Don't go,' she said. 'Please, Kenny. I need to . . . I have to ask you to go to Indonesia with me tomorrow.'

Ooo-kay. *What* was she dreaming about? Ken had to laugh. And in the manner of the not-completely-awake, her question was of vital importance to her.

'I didn't get a chance to ask you—'

'Shh,' he told her, between kisses. 'Don't worry about a thing. Go back to sleep – I'll be home before you know it.' And if she woke up, he'd already written a note and left it on the kitchen table, on top of her purse.

'But—'

He kissed her. 'I'm going to get leave,' he told her. 'I'll take a couple of weeks – I'm long overdue.' In fact, Senior Chief Wolchonok had all but ordered him to take some vacation time, and to take it soon. 'Then we can go to the moon if you want, okay?'

'I don't want to go anywhere,' she mumbled, 'but I have to.'

'Don't worry,' he said again, kissing her face, her throat, lower. 'We'll figure it all out later, all right?'

'Please,' she said, arching against him. 'Don't go without . . . I want . . .'

At first consideration, pulling back the sheet that covered her didn't seem to be a move worthy of a man with his enormous IQ, a man who knew there'd be hell to pay if he were late. But then again, his enormous IQ was not what she wanted right this second.

She pushed down his shorts, and – proof that not all of the oxygen-carrying blood in his system was being diverted to his lower extremities, that at least a small amount was still going to his brain – he grabbed for a condom. Number three for the night.

He had three minutes before he had to be in his truck and heading for the base.

But he wasn't the only one in a hurry here. He'd barely managed to cover himself before she pressed her hips up and pushed him deep inside her, surrounding him with her slick heat.

And she did it again. Just like the first two times they'd made love. Just as he'd hoped she would.

She exploded.

She was so freaking hot for him, she just went off as soon as he was inside of her. He knew that if he had even just a little more time, he could make her come once, maybe even twice more – outrageously long, lingering orgasms that left her gasping and giddy and weak with laughter and pleasure – before he lost his own somewhat tenuous control.

And that was just after only one night. After just a few short hours of exploring one another. They hadn't even gotten past the missionary position. Imagine what he could do to her with his mouth.

It was the thought of going down on her that made him explode in a heated rush.

He got himself cleaned up and dressed and kissed her

goodbye, leaving her sleepy and satisfied – at least temporarily. It seemed so ridiculously rushed, but he was out of time. He kissed her again, then ran for his truck, just a few minutes behind schedule.

There was no real traffic at this time of the morning, so he leaned on the accelerator, quickly making up the lost time.

He was going to spend the morning diving – which he loved to do. And then he was going to arrange for leave and meet Savannah, either at his house or her hotel. He would kiss her hello, then peel off her clothes and . . .

Ken drove through the empty streets, grinning like a fool.

He was, without a doubt, the luckiest son of a bitch on the face of the planet.

Berlin. Early summer, 1939.

The loss of some amount of innocence is always a necessary step in the journey each girl takes to become a woman.

My path was one in which I lost more at age eighteen than most women lose in a lifetime.

I went to Berlin that May, at the end of my first year of college, a proud – and remarkably innocent – recipient of what I thought was the Brooklyn German American Club's All-Around Merit Scholar Award. It turned out to be something else entirely.

But as I, the daughter of a carpenter from Bremerhaven and a cook from a small town in the German Black Forest, boarded the ship that would carry me across the Atlantic Ocean, the pride on my parents' faces went with me.

As did my memories of having seen Benny Goodman and his band, live and in person, just a few weeks before I left New York.

I may have been the recipient of an award that lauded both my ability to read and write in German and my studies of German literature and history, but I was an American girl, through and through. I loved music and I loved to dance and I loved Hollywood movies – especially the ones with Jimmy Stewart. I loved Coney Island in the summer and Fifth Avenue at Christmastime. And oh, I passionately loved my Brooklyn Dodgers.

I was not just an American, I was a New Yorker – loyal to my borough of the city, down to my very toenails.

My trip was fun – at first.

Days one through three had been filled with visits to my mother's brothers and sisters in their tiny Black Forest village. *Vati* – my father – had been an *einziges Kind* – an only child. He'd come to New York with his father, also a carpenter, after his mother had died when he was quite young. *Mutti*, my mother, had come as a teenager, to work in the kitchen of the great house in which her aunt was a cook.

She met my father at the Brooklyn German American Club, and the two fell deeply in love. They had me almost immediately. But then my father contracted the mumps, which ensured that I, too, would remain an *einziges Kind*.

I still often thank those mumps for the opportunities I was able to enjoy as a result of my lack of siblings. Not having a son, my father took me to baseball games with him. He taught me how to frame a wall, how to fix the broken plumbing, how to pour concrete, how to install a lock, how to plant a vegetable garden on our apartment building rooftop. And he and *Mutti* saved their pennies and nickels to send me to college.

So here I was in Berlin, after winning this wonderful opportunity to see the land of my parents' birth, the home of Goethe and Bach. I'd met my mother's younger brothers and sisters – my *Tante* Marlise was just a few years older than I – in the fairy-tale village in which *Mutti* had grown up. I met my cousins – more cousins than I'd ever dreamed of – little sweet-faced blond-haired children who stared with wide eyes at my American clothing and shoes.

And then I was brought to Berlin to have an official congratulatory lunch with the spokesman from the prestigious university, a balding, bespectacled little man named Herr Schmidt.

We spoke at length – or rather, he spoke and I listened, about the glory of the German Fatherland, about the magnificence of the Nazi Regime, of their glorious Reich that was destined to last a thousand years. Was I not impressed with this beautiful country?

I was.

Was I not impressed with Der Fuehrer, Herr Hitler?

Well . . . I diplomatically replied that it seemed as if he'd done much to bring Germany out of the Depression. His Autobahn was certainly going to be quite an achievement. I refrained from mentioning that his Gestapo frightened me, that his policy of ruling through fervor and fear was against everything I believed in as a staunch American, and what I'd heard about Kristallnacht and his attacks on Germany's Jewish citizens shocked me.

Did I not feel the stirrings of great German pride when I looked on the glory of all that was Deutschland?

Of course I agreed – because it seemed rude not to, like shrugging off a proud grandmother's photos of her latest grandchild without oohing and ahhing over the dazed and drooling infant.

He talked about duty and honor and pride, and all the time I nodded and smiled and tried to keep him from looking down my blouse.

But then the other shoe dropped.

'You work for Grumman, the American aircraft manufacturer in New York, *ja*?' Herr Schmidt asked.

I explained that yes, during my first year of college, I got a part-time position as a filing clerk, as an assistant to the secretary of the vice president. It was what we referred to at school as a charity job. The VP was an alumnus, and although he didn't really need a filing clerk, he enjoyed being a benefactor to the students at his alma mater. I did a little filing, but I mostly studied as I sat behind the receptionist's desk during her lunch hour, answering the phone when it occasionally rang.

And it didn't ring that often. We were not the manufacturing division, or even general management. We were R and D – research and development. Which of course, meant we dealt with information that the Nazis were most eager for.

Herr Schmidt offered to pay me quite handsomely to keep him abreast – yes, my pun is intended – of new developments at Grumman. And a lightning bolt of realization charged through me, ripping at my innocence. This man wanted me to be a spy for Nazi Germany.

I played dumb, giving him my best Katherine Mulvaney smile. Kat was one of the girls in my college dorm. She was a physics major, a sheer genius in fact, but she'd learned early on that the boys didn't appreciate that. So she'd developed a smile that suggested she moved her lips when reading. And sure enough, she had a date every Saturday night.

'Oh, but Mr Fielding – he's my boss. I'm afraid he doesn't let that information go public,' I told Herr Schmidt with that smile. I even batted my eyelashes a little bit.

Unfortunately, Schmidt knew I was smarter than that. 'Such industrial secrets should be shared – for the betterment of all mankind. Think of how much easier it would have been had you not had to travel by ship from New York. If Germany had access to this information, we could help make air travel affordable.' He leaned closer and upped the ante. 'A girl with your scholastic record would be eligible for a scholarship to the university here in Berlin. After you finish your studies in New York, you would be welcome to further your education here.'

Yes, I was a very smart girl. And I suspected that the Nazis weren't after mere industrial secrets. They wanted to know what kinds of military planes the Americans were developing.

I later found out that people like me –young, first-generation Americans born to German immigrants – people who belonged to German American clubs, or studied German language and literature in school – were frequently targeted by the Nazis, particularly if they worked, as I did, at places such as Grumman.

This trip to Berlin was an attempt to woo me to their cause.

Somehow I managed to smile. 'I'll certainly consider such a generous offer.' I was lying through my teeth, but all I wanted was to get out of there. To end this luncheon and—

'Did you hear what happened?' Jules came into her office without knocking.

'Go away.' Alyssa didn't even look up from the book. 'I know it doesn't look like it, but I'm working.'

. . . *all I wanted was to get out of there, Rose had written. To end this luncheon and breathe some air that didn't stink of wrong-doing. Of treason.*

Jules came and started reading over her shoulder, which always bugged her, and she closed the book. 'Do you mind?'

Of course, her closing the book was exactly what her partner wanted. He hopped up on the edge of her desk, letting his feet dangle. 'So this new guy, George, he shows up this morning. Like, here I am, reporting for duty. And Laronda figures, okay, this is nothing new. Max has left her out of the loop again. She's got no information on any George joining any aspect of the team, but she buzzes Max, tells him George is here. And *he* goes, George *who*?'

Jules laughed. 'I'm standing there, collecting my phone messages, pretending I've got a reason to be there, and George, he's right next to me, he kind of closes his eyes and says *shit* about four times, under his breath. Have I mentioned that he's really good looking?'

'No,' Alyssa said.

'Very Armani ad. Dark blond hair, starting to thin, but gracefully. *Nice* suit. Italian shoes. Not a thread out of place – it was like he was trying to out-Max Max, except I don't think it was an act. He's like a taller, thinner, blonder Max.'

Jules was enjoying himself so much, she almost kept her mouth shut. But she had work to do. 'Is there a punchline to all this?'

'I'm not sure I'd call it a punchline, but it definitely gets even more weird,' Jules said. 'You're going to love it. Mysteries abound. But before we go there, aren't you dying to ask me if George is gay?'

'Actually,' Alyssa said, 'his sexual orientation doesn't particularly—'

'He's not.'

'You didn't *ask* him . . . ?'

'Yeah, I've definitely learned that works really well,' Jules scoffed. 'To frighten the hell out of the straight guys who are going to work with me by letting them know at our very first meeting that I think they're hot?'

'Then . . . ?'

Jules slid down off her desk, did a slow spin like a fashion model on a runway. 'Look at me.'

And Alyssa had to laugh, because she knew exactly what he meant. Today he was wearing black jeans that hugged his perfect hips and drool-worthy, subcompact, tiny butt, and a black T-shirt that was molded to his perfect upper body. His hair was back to a more natural shade of dark brown, and cut extremely short the way it was, it accented his dark eyes and classic cheekbones.

On a scale of one to ten in cuteness, Jules was a four million. He could have gone on an audition for a boy band and been signed without even singing a note.

'I'm a Village People fan's dream come true,' Jules said, 'and our new boy George barely even glanced at me.' He hopped back onto her desk. 'I'd suggest you try for him – no wedding band I could see – except rumor has it you're off the market. Word is, you've snagged the boss.'

Oh, crap. Alyssa was already shaking her head. 'Not true and you know it.'

'Laronda said you kissed him. Why do I always miss things like this?'

'He kissed me,' she explained, 'to make Dwayne go away. It was pretend.'

'Yeah, right,' Jules said. 'Pretend.' He winked. 'Gotcha.'

'You are very close to getting your ass kicked out of here.'

'Okay.' He held up his hands in a gesture of surrender. 'I'm sorry.' He went serious on her. 'I just . . . well, if it could be true, you know, about you and Max, I think it would be a really good thing for you, sweetie. You know, to help you stop thinking about what's-his-name.'

Alyssa sighed. 'Now would be a really good time for that punchline.'

'Okay, so we have George standing in front of Laronda's desk, saying—'

'Shit,' Alyssa said. 'I got that. *And . . . ?*'

'And Max comes out of his office.' Jules grinned. 'And there they are, face to face. The designer suit twins. And Max just looks at George, you know, with that look. That "if you have interrupted me with anything less than information about an impending nuclear attack, you are about to learn the true meaning of pain" look. And I'm close enough to George to see that even though he's playing it cool, he's got this one bead of sweat right by his left ear. And he introduces himself to Max and says, "I guess I arrived in advance of the phone call."

'And Max just waits for him to explain. I would've run away, weeping. But George, he just kind of laughs, and says, "You're going to hate this, sir, but I've been assigned to your team."

'And Laronda's jaw is on the floor, she's just sitting there staring at George, and she turns to look at Max, probably wondering like me if he's going to pull his gun on this obvious imposter, because everyone, *every*one knows that people don't *get assigned* to Max's team.

'And the phone rings, and Laronda answers it, still watching Max, who's stone silent, just staring at George. And she puts whoever it is on hold, and says . . .' Jules laughed and imitated Laronda's husky voice. '"Excuse me, Mr Bhagat. The president. Of the United States. On line one, sir."

'And Max just slowly turns and goes back into his office, but before he closes the door behind him, he calls back to George, "How long have you known Rose?"

'And George says, "She's my godmother, sir."

'Max just nods and says, "Welcome to the team. I'll be with you in a minute." Sure enough, he's on the phone for maybe thirty seconds, and then he opens his office door and waves George inside. I look at Laronda, because who the hell is *Rose*? But she doesn't know either.'

Alyssa held up her copy of *Double Agent*, letting him see the cover. 'Rose,' she said. 'Mystery solved. Former agent. VIP.'

'No shit she's a VIP,' Jules said, taking the book from her hands and flipping through it. 'What's going on that no one has bothered to tell little ol' me?'

'Possible kidnapped son,' Alyssa said. 'Alexander von Hopf. Businessman traveling in Indonesia, gone AWOL from his hotel. Just to make it more complicated, he's a diabetic. Max gave me this book last night, told me to read it.'

'After the pretend kiss?' Jules waggled his eyebrows.

'Don't start.'

He looked at her bookmark. 'For an overachiever, you didn't get very far.'

'Tyra called with an emergency.' Alyssa's sister was a drama queen whose entire life was in italics followed by multiple exclamation points. 'A real one this time. Her father-in-law had a heart attack, and she needed to go to the hospital with Ben. I rushed over to baby-sit Lanora, and like a genius left the book on my kitchen table. Which was probably just as good, since Lanora kicked my ass and ran me ragged the whole time. On her way out the door, Tyra was like, "She had a really long nap this afternoon so don't worry about putting her to bed until she gets tired." And then it's midnight, and we're not just reading *Good Night, Moon* for the four thousandth time, we're acting it out. And I'm thinking, what do they feed this kid and where can I get some, and how long *was* that nap?'

'Hey,' Jules said, still leafing through the book, 'this girl became a double agent when she was only eighteen.'

'Did you hear a single word I said?' Alyssa asked.

'Good night, kittens. Good night, mittens,' Jules said, still buried in the book. 'I would've loved to have seen that. I bet you were a great mitten. You know, I should write *my* memoirs.'

She took the book out of his hands. 'The book has to come *after* you retire. Makes it hard to go undercover when your face is in every bookstore in the country.'

'Excellent point. Can I read it after you?'

'Yes. Shut the door on your way out.'

He actually did.

Alyssa opened the book.

After that hideous luncheon, I found myself walking, just walking rapidly through the city, for hours, until it was nearly dark. I was angry and frightened and disgusted that my hosts could think I would be so easily for sale.

I didn't know what to do.

I wanted desperately to go home, to throw myself into *Mutti*'s arms, but I had three more days before my ship even set sail for New York. And – God help me – there was another luncheon scheduled for tomorrow. For which I would plead illness, I vowed to myself. I'd stick my finger down my throat if I had to.

Finally, exhausted, and not sure I could find my way back to my hotel, I sat down on the steps of a bakery, the door locked up tight, the owners long since gone home.

The evening air was starting to get chilly, and I didn't have a sweater. I buried my face in my hands and allowed myself some childish tears of self-pity.

'Are you lost?'

The man standing in front of me on the sidewalk had spoken to me in English. I guess it was obvious to the entire world that I was an American. I quickly wiped my face, embarrassed that a stranger should see me cry.

'This isn't a particularly good part of town,' he continued. His English was remarkable. It was British accented, with just a trace of Germany in the percussiveness of his *ds*. *Goodt* instead of *good*.

He stood with his hands in his pockets – I realized later that this was intentional, that everything he did was intentional. He'd wanted to appear as nonthreatening as possible because sitting there the way I was, I surely looked utterly pathetic and completely vulnerable.

He was dressed in a baggy pair of trousers and a tweed jacket with patched elbows that made him look like the boys I went to college with. Except he was older than those boys – older than me – by at least ten years.

He had dark blond hair and hazel eyes and the kind of too-handsome face I'd seen adorning the Nazi propaganda posters that littered the country. A perfect straight Aryan nose. Strong, almost flat, Teutonic cheekbones. An elegantly shaped mouth and a proud chin.

'The first time I came to Berlin,' he told me, 'I got hopelessly lost, as well. My parents actually sent out a search party, looking for me.' He smiled. 'Of course, I was two years old at the time.'

He had a Prince Charming, fairy-tale smile that lit his face, his eyes, his very soul and made him even more handsome. I had to work very hard not to fall in love with him right there on the spot. Like most eighteen-year-old girls, I was in the habit of quickly falling in love with extraordinarily handsome men.

'I'm a little older than that, I'm afraid,' I told him. I glanced

84

up and down the street – there was no one else out there, just a long line of neatly closed shops and pristine cobblestone.

But I wasn't alarmed. A man like this one didn't have to attack unsuspecting girls in the storefront of a bakery. All he had to do was snap his fingers, and a literal harem of women would come running. Myself included if he kept smiling at me like that.

'This doesn't seem like such a terrible part of town,' I said, wishing I could take a moment and freshen up my lipstick.

'Most of these shops are Jewish owned,' he informed me. 'Their window panes are prone to breaking – especially after dark.'

'That's terrible,' I said without thinking, and then I realized that, like most German citizens, he was probably a Nazi. Nearly everyone I'd met on this trip was, and anti-Semitism seemed to be a major part of the Nazi party manifest. Still, I said it again, staring right into his perfect eyes, daring him to contradict me. 'That's *terrible*.'

'Yes, it is.' He smiled at me again, and neatly changed the subject. 'Where are you staying?'

I told him the name of my hotel as I stood up and brushed off my skirt.

'That's eight miles across town. You walked all that way in those shoes?'

'It didn't seem that far.' At the time. Now my feet were burning. And the rest of me was freezing. I hugged myself, and he took off his jacket.

'Please,' he said, draping it over my shoulders.

It was warm from his body heat and it smelled faintly of cigarette smoke, frying sausages, and sauerkraut. He must've just come from dinner at one of the local *Bierhalls*. I'd passed several on my journey, but hadn't dared enter alone. My stomach rumbled now. 'Thank you.'

'My pleasure, Fraülein.' His hazel eyes were like warm liquid. Men should not be allowed to have such beautiful eyes. 'Do you have any objections to getting a ride back across town?'

I didn't have the kind of money I'd need for a cab ride all the way back to my hotel. 'Only if I can catch a bus or street car.'

He made a face of dismay. 'Only . . . ?'

I was determined to use the small amount of spending money I'd brought to buy a present for my parents. Even if it meant walking another eight miles in the crisp night air in shoes that weren't made for hiking.

I pulled the young man's jacket together in the front, trying to get as warm as I could while I still could. 'Would you happen to know how late they run?'

'I'm afraid I don't. But if you want, I could ask my driver. He might know.'

'You have a—' I shut my mouth. He didn't look like the kind of man who would have not just a car but a driver. And yet . . .

'It makes it much easier to get around Berlin,' he said as if he could easily read my mind. 'I'm not a native, I'm actually from Wien— Vienna.' He held out his hand. 'Heinrich von Hopf. My American friends call me Hank.'

'I'm Ingerose Rainer,' I told him. 'My American friends call me Rose.' As for what my German friends called me . . . well, I didn't seem to have too many German friends. The Nazis who had paid my passage from New York to recruit me as a spy under the guise of a scholarship prize were not my friends.

'Rose,' he said, melting my knees with another of those smiles. He was still holding my hand, and I gathered my wits about me and gently tugged it free.

'You're one of the American students visiting the university. I read something about it in the paper. How wonderful to have a cultural exchange with our American friends. Are you enjoying your stay?'

'Do you want to hear the polite answer or the honest one?'

He laughed and his eyes sparkled. 'Oh, definitely both.'

I gave him Kat Mulvaney's smile. 'Oh, yes, sir. I'm having *such* a wonderful time.'

'Oh, my,' he said, 'You *are* a good liar, aren't you? And the honest one now . . . ?'

'Berlin is nothing like New York. I love the history – the buildings are so *old*, but I don't like not knowing my way around. And the papers don't have the baseball scores . . .'

'Horrors,' he murmured, pursing his lips to hide a smile.

'I'm homesick, speaking and listening to German constantly is much harder than reading it in a book, and the people I've met *aren't* very nice.' I amended that. 'Most of the people.'

My stomach growled again, and Hank laughed. He had a truly magical laugh. '*And* you're hungry and chilled,' he said. 'Shall we find you something to eat and perhaps a glass of May wine to restore you?'

I hesitated, thinking of the limited funds in my pocket. Back at the hotel, I could order room service and the charges would be covered by my hosts. My Nazi hosts. I would be putting myself further and further into their debt simply by eating.

God save me, I didn't want to go back there. I just wanted to go home. To my horror, I realized that my eyes had filled with tears. I fiercely blinked them back, turning slightly away from him, hoping he wouldn't see.

He was the kind of man who saw everything. But he chose to pretend not to notice.

'My car's right there.' He turned and gestured, and sure enough, a car engine started, its headlights switching on. 'It would be my honor and privilege to treat such an esteemed guest of the Reich both to dinner and a ride back to her hotel.'

Which was worse? Being indebted to a man I didn't know, or being indebted to Nazis who wanted me to spy for them? I wouldn't have gotten into his car if he were alone, but a man with a driver . . . Was the driver going to abduct me, too? It didn't seem likely. Still, I hesitated.

Hank put his hands into his pockets. 'Let me be your friend,' he said quietly. 'I think you could use one right now, yes?'

God, yes.

The car approached and I saw that it wasn't just a car, it was a Rolls-Royce. The driver – an older man dressed in a livery uniform – hopped out, and opened the back door, bowing.

Hank stepped forward. '*Danke schön, Dieter, aber*—'

'Your highness,' the man intoned loudly, and Hank winced.

If my jaw hadn't dropped at the sight of the Rolls, it hit the ground now. I managed to get my mouth closed, and turned to stare at this man whose American friends called him Hank. No doubt his German friends called him something else entirely. 'Something tells me you left out a few minor details from your introduction, your highness?'

'Don't be mad,' he said. 'I just . . . well, I know how un-impressed you Americans are about things like titles and . . . and . . .' He was actually stammering. 'And it's foolish, really. Absolutely foolish. I'm Austrian, Fraülein, and I had the good fortune to be born a prince in the house of . . . oh, it's too complicated. And it's ridiculous. After the War, Austria became a republic, and use of such titles was no longer allowed. But after the *Anschluss* – the annexation of Austria by Hitler and his Reich – our titles were restored, except we no longer have Austria to rule. Hitler and his Nazis rule now. So what good is a prince without a kingdom?'

His smile was tight and it occurred to me that he might be in need of a friend, too. Someone who wouldn't fawn over his wealth and – as he called it – his foolish title that, despite saying otherwise, he cared very much about.

My stomach rumbled again.

'Please come with me before you starve to death right here in the street. I know a lovely place not far from here . . .'

But I didn't want to go anywhere lovely with Prince Anyone and have to sit at a table covered with white linen while waiters and wine stewards danced nervously around, and looked down their noses at me for using the wrong fork. I was tired and cold and done with feeling under siege for the day.

'It's not very fancy,' he told me as if he could read my mind. 'Just a *Bierhall*. There's an open grill. Tables and benches. Music. No one will know you're American. Or that I'm too often called something other than Hank. I go there all the time. The food is wonderful.'

I held the sleeve of his jacket to my nose and breathed in the scent that was so like my mother's cooking.

'Please,' he said again.

'All right.' The smile he gave me was brilliant, and it got even broader as I smiled back at him and added, 'Hank.'

Four

Savannah von Hopf woke up all alone in Kenny Karmody's bed.

The house was silent the way houses often were when there was no one else around.

In the daylight, his bedroom looked less dim and mysterious and more like a laundry package holding station.

When she sat up, she encountered her reflection in the mirror that was on the closet door. She pulled up the sheet to cover herself, unable to face the sight of her nakedness. The fact that her hair was completely out of control was bad enough.

She flopped back onto Kenny's pillows. What had she done?

She'd slept with this man on the equivalent of a first date. Somehow that hadn't seemed like such a bad thing last night, when Ken was here, distracting her by being so intensely attractive. So darkly good-looking. So ripped with all those delicious muscles. So hot, so utterly, devastatingly sexy, so tempting.

She hadn't been able to help herself. She'd wanted him for so long. Yes, it had all happened so fast, but so what? It had happened fast for Romeo and Juliet, too.

Ah, but look where that got *them*.

Now that Ken was gone, doubt flooded her. What if the fact that she'd gone and jumped him last night really *wasn't* romantic? What if it was cheap? What if he now thought of her as easy?

The real irony here was she was the least easy person she knew – in more ways than one.

He hadn't left her a note. At least not as far as she could see, and she tried to convince herself that that didn't matter. Before he'd left, he'd told her that he'd try to get time off. And he'd told her he'd go with her to Indonesia. He'd seemed remarkably blasé about it, in fact.

Of course, she hadn't yet told him why she had to go. Or that she'd come to San Diego expressly to talk him into going with her.

Savannah got out of bed, pulling the sheet off and wrapping it around her. God, his house was quiet. She went to the bathroom, then headed into the kitchen, praying he had coffee.

There on the table, held down by her purse and far better than the best Columbian blend she'd ever tasted, was a note from Ken.

'Sorry I had to leave,' he'd written. He had scratchy, kind of spidery handwriting – as if he didn't spend too much time with a pen in his hand. 'I should be back by 1100. Feel free to stay, help yourself to whatever you find in the kitchen that's edible. Coffee's in the fridge.' Thank God. He'd also left a cell phone number. *'If you get up early, call me.'* That was underlined twice. 'With luck, I'll be in range.'

He'd signed it, 'Love, Ken.' And there was a P.S. 'I hope this doesn't sound too hokey, Savannah, but you're the best thing that ever happened to me, and I'm counting the minutes til I can see you again.'

She almost started to cry. Instead, she picked up the phone on his kitchen wall and dialed the number he'd left.

He answered before the second ring, his voice that of a stranger's – brisk, businesslike. 'Karmody.'

Suddenly shy, all she could manage was, 'Hi, it's, um, it's me.'

'Van.' His voice got a whole lot warmer. Thank God he knew who she was, that he remembered her, calling her by the nickname he'd used so often last night. 'I was just thinking about you. I spoke to the senior chief. There's going to be no problem at all with me getting two weeks leave.'

Her heart leapt. 'Two whole weeks? That's *great*, Kenny. Starting . . . ?'

'As soon after 1100 as I can do the paperwork. Things are really light right now, it's a good time to be away.'

Savannah closed her eyes. Thank God. They could catch a flight out tonight. 'That's wonderful.'

'You bet. Look, I gotta run. You gonna hang there at my place or . . . ?'

'No,' she told him. 'I'm going back to the hotel. I'm just going to call a cab.'

'Okay,' he said. 'Then I'll meet you there.'

'Ken?'

'I'm still here.'

'It wasn't too hokey,' she told him. 'What you wrote. It was lovely.'

'Yeah, well, it was either that or tell you just how badly I'm dying to go down on you.' He was laughing, but it was that laughter she'd come to recognize. He was being funny, yes, but he was also dead serious.

Savannah had to sit down. 'Well,' she said weakly. 'That's a . . . a lovely thought, too.'

He laughed again. 'You bet. Hey, I really gotta go. See you in a few, babe. Love ya.'

With a click, the connection was cut, and Savannah was left staring at the phone. Had he just said . . . ?

No. Love ya was definitely not I love you. He'd signed his note *love*, as well. It was his default farewell to the woman he was sleeping with. It didn't mean anything.

It certainly didn't mean half as much as the fact that he'd gotten two whole weeks off, that he was willing and ready to travel halfway around the world with her.

That he wanted to . . . Savannah laughed aloud, feeling herself blush even though she was completely alone. Lovely thought, indeed.

But it was going to have to wait.

You're the best thing that ever happened to me.

The next time she came face to face with Kenny, she was going to have to come clean with him. She would tell him everything, tell him she'd come here looking for him, shoot, she'd even tell him about getting his address from Adele.

They'd have a good laugh about how silly she'd been not to tell him the truth from the start, and then he'd take off her clothes and . . .

And later, they'd catch the evening flight to Jakarta, she'd deliver the money to Alex, and that would be that. She and Ken would have two whole weeks together. They could go to Hawaii. Or Australia. Or even back here to San Diego.

Love ya.

This was definitely going to work out.

*

93

Jones was at the bar in the Tiki Lounge, nursing a beer when Molly came in.

He didn't try to hide, but he didn't try to catch her attention either. He didn't even look directly at her in the cloudy mirror behind the bottles of hard liquor.

Maybe she was here because she was thirsty. Maybe if he ignored her, she'd order a rum and something with lots of ice, and take it out onto the veranda where the other tourist types sat and watched the sun set over the harbor.

And maybe Ed McMahon was going to come in next and announce that Jones had just won ten million dollars in the American Publishers Clearinghouse sweepstakes.

Why not? This was turning into a night of unexpected visits. Jayakatong Tohjaya – Jaya for short – had left just moments ago. Jaya was an Indonesian entrepreneur who'd recently joined forces with the rebel leader Badaruddin, a self-important military wannabe asshole who had his biggest camp of followers on the island just north of Parwati, and waged an ongoing war with not just the government but also the Zdanowicz brothers, gun and drug runner assholes who operated out of Jakarta.

Jaya was no fool, he hadn't joined Badaruddin's private army because he wanted the beret-wearing, camouflage uniform-clad self-awarded general to become Indonesia's dictator. No, he simply could make more money and have access to better modes of transportation while working as the general's right-hand man.

Jaya had come right over and sat his skinny butt down next to Jones. He'd heard – island gossip was faster than the digital internet – that Jones's plane was down, that a vital part of the engine had burned out during the afternoon's frantic rush to the hospital.

Jaya had even known – somehow – exactly what part Jones needed to fix the Cessna.

And he had a way to get his hands on that very part.

For an exorbitant finder's fee, Jaya would deliver that part to Jones sometime between tomorrow morning and early next week.

They'd struck a deal, and Jaya had skittered off into the night, on a quest to find insulin shots for a guest of the general's.

But now Molly appeared. She sat down, of course, on the stool Jaya had recently vacated, of course, and ordered a glass of tropical juice.

Jones took another slug of beer, still not looking at her. But he could see her too well. His peripheral vision had always been too damn good.

Molly Anderson. She'd recently tried to rebraid her thick reddish-brown hair, but she was the kind of woman who moved too quickly ever to achieve real tidiness. Bits and pieces of her hair had escaped, some curling wildly in the humidity, some clinging damply to her neck and face.

It was a face that wasn't even really that pretty. It was too broad, with a too generous mouth that would have been sensuous if she'd bothered to wear lipstick. Which, as far as he knew from his days of living in her tent, she never did.

Her eyes were pretty enough – a light, almost golden, brown. But they had laughter lines around them, showing her age. She had to be closing in on forty, fast, and she'd lived, if not hard, then certainly enthusiastically.

She was wearing the same drab green T-shirt and the cargo shorts that came down nearly to her knees that she'd had on during the flight to Parwati. Leather sandals on her feet.

Pink nail polish on her toes. It was such a contradiction to the lack of lipstick, it fascinated him. He refused to let himself so much as glance at her feet again.

'Joaquin's going to be okay,' Molly said. 'You were right, Mr Jones. It was an allergic reaction to black market penicillin. His mother gave it to him, thinking it would clear up an infection in his foot.'

He shrugged, still hoping rather futilely that she'd get a clue and leave him alone.

The bartender put a tall glass of juice in front of Molly, and she thanked him, then nearly drained the glass in one long chug.

With her head tipped back, she looked as if she were inviting vampires to dinner. All that pale skin, that long, elegant throat.

Jones was probably the only man in the place who wasn't staring at her. Terrific, now he had to worry about one of these lowlifes following her out of here.

No, he wasn't going to think about it. That was her problem. He'd made up his mind weeks ago not to think about her anymore.

But when she put the glass down, and drew a line in the frosty condensation on the outside with one of her long, elegant fingers, he had to force himself not to remember her hands, so cool against his heated forehead and face as he lay, feverish, in her bed.

'I heard about your plane,' she continued. Of course she had. Everyone on the island had heard about his plane. 'That you burned out the something or other and have to wait two weeks for the part to come in from Jakarta. I'm so sorry.'

Jones finally looked at her. Because of her, he'd missed his appointment, lost more money than he could believe, *and* pissed off some very dangerous men in the process. He was stuck in this shithole until tomorrow – and that was absolute best-case scenario. It could well take Jaya a full week to get that part.

And she was *sorry*.

The real stupid thing was, she *was* sorry. Most people didn't mean it when they said it, but Molly Anderson did.

How did she manage to be so goddamn beautiful all the time? Her eyes, her face – they just seemed to shine despite her lack of cosmetics, despite the fact that she wasn't conventionally pretty, despite the wrinkles and lines. Or maybe because of them. Jones couldn't figure it out.

'I know you've been seriously inconvenienced,' she was telling him, 'but if it weren't for you, Joaquin would have died. So finish your beer. I'm taking you to dinner.'

Oh, no. No way. He was absolutely not going to have dinner with Molly Anderson. 'No, thanks.'

'Mr Jones, I refuse to take no—'

'Look, we're even now.' His voice came out louder and edgier than he'd intended. He took another pull on his beer and when he spoke again, he managed to sound more matter of fact, more like his normal bored but deadly self. 'By flying you down here, I paid you back. I don't owe you anything else.'

Molly laughed and he had to look away. He pretended to be fascinated by the picture of the *Playboy* Playmate of July 1987 that was pinned up behind the bar. Faded and tattered around the edges, she hadn't aged quite so well as Molly.

'I want to treat you to dinner,' she told him. 'That means I'll pay. Honestly, I don't expect anything else from you.'

'You wanna bet?' He turned slightly on his stool to face

her. 'You don't want to take *me* to dinner. You want to go out with some watered-down, defanged version of me. And I'm telling you right now, I no longer have an obligation to act like some goddamn choirboy around you. We're even. You still want to have dinner with me? Fine. But you've been warned. You're going to be getting way more than you bargained for.'

He looked directly into her eyes, and let her see that he wanted her, that when he looked at her, when he thought of her, he thought of sex, pure and raw, primitive and pounding. Him hard inside of her, her face flushed with desire as she clung to him. No finesse, no promises, no emotions – just a good old-fashioned banging.

But he should've known she wouldn't scare easily.

She didn't look away, didn't blush, didn't rush out of the bar, scandalized.

No, she just stared right back at him, a slow smile spreading across her face.

'Well,' she said. 'You're mighty sure of yourself, aren't you, Mr Jones?'

He let himself look at her wide mouth, imagining just what she could do with lips like that.

And she laughed, rich and thick and throaty, genuinely amused.

'What do you really think is going to happen? That during the hour or so that we have dinner, I'm going to find you so irresistible that I'm going to beg you to come back to my room so I can have you for dessert?' She actually licked her lips, the witch.

And *he* was the one who started to sweat.

But then she leaned forward so that he had to look into her eyes, not at her mouth anymore. 'Get over yourself.

Even if you showered and shaved, it's not likely I'm going to succumb to your *vast* charms tonight – although I have to admit, your chances would be greatly improved. I do so prefer a man who doesn't stink.'

This was *not* the way this scenario was supposed to play out. She was supposed to run away. He was supposed to sit right here at this bar and have another five, six, seven beers until he was too drunk to care about the hard-on she'd just given him.

Molly slipped down off the bar stool. 'So cut the macho crap, get off your butt and come have dinner.'

Jones finished his beer and stood up. Let her see what she did to him. Maybe that would give her pause. 'You've been warned.'

'Yeah, yeah,' she said as she led the way out onto the street. She glanced at him, glanced down and smiled. Again, she was genuinely amused. 'I'm terrified.'

Love ya.

Ken had actually said, *Love ya*, right before he'd hung up the phone.

Maybe Savannah hadn't noticed.

But holy God, maybe she had.

Well, there wasn't much he could do about it now. The words had slipped out, shocking the hell out of him. Did he really love this woman? After knowing her for just a few hours? After only one night?

One freaking great night.

Savannah clearly felt something for him. She was so not the type to just randomly shack up with a stranger.

Wasn't she?

Jesus, he'd been hideously wrong about women before.

He headed for Lieutenant Commander Paoletti's office, paperwork for his two weeks of vacation in hand, both anticipating and dreading seeing Savannah again.

What if he'd royally screwed things up by using the L-word too soon? What if she thought he really meant it and decided he was an emotional imbecile for thinking he could fall in love that quickly?

What if he *was* an emotional imbecile . . . ?

Johnny Nilsson and Sam Starrett were in the hallway, no doubt exchanging diapering tips. The two officers were his best friends in the world, and they were both married, both relatively new fathers, and lately both as boring as hell.

These days, it seemed as if they were unable to talk about much besides the various types of bowel movements of their children.

It was mind numbing how long they could keep that conversation going.

Well, that wasn't what *he* wanted to talk about today.

'Hey,' Ken said in greeting, interrupting Johnny mid-sentence. 'What do you guys know about multiple orgasms?'

Both Johnny and Sam turned to look at him – Sam with the bleary eyes of the sleep deprived. He looked shell-shocked and confused – and as if he might've actually forgotten what an orgasm was.

'I'm wondering what it's like for the woman?' Ken got more specific. 'Is it like riding one big perfect twenty-minute wave? Or is it like catching an excellent string of three or four smaller but equally perfect waves?'

Johnny laughed. 'Surfing as an analogy for orgasm. I like that. Kowabunga.'

'Three or *four*?' Sam repeated, interest returning to his bloodshot eyes, as if he were waking up. He laughed. 'Ho,

WildCard, you're shagging a woman who comes three or four times inside of twenty *minutes*?'

Count on Starrett to bring it down to the crudest possible level.

'I didn't say that,' Ken countered stiffly. He hadn't brought this up to engage in a locker room discussion of last night's exploits.

'You didn't have to.' Sam laughed again. 'Holy shit. Who is she?'

Yeah, like he would tell. 'Look, asshole, I'm not *shagging* anyone.'

'Ah. Right. Forgive me. You're making beautiful, respectful love to the Orgasm Queen of the World. Congratulations, man. Is this normal for her, or is there something important that you've discovered about women, that you need to teach the rest of us mere mortals?'

'I think you really need to ask *her* about it,' Johnny advised, pretty much ignoring Sam. 'Women's orgasms are different from men's. With us, it's over when it's over, right? With a woman, if you do it right, you can keep it going for a nice long time.' He smiled the smile of a man who knew. 'But I don't think that necessarily qualifies as a multiple orgasm.'

John Nilsson had been married for nearly two years, and he and his wife, Meg, were so freaking happy, at times it seemed abnormal. Ken and Sam both tried their hardest to be sincerely glad for the guy, but it got a little hard to deal with at times – for Ken, because he was so relentlessly alone, and for Sam because he'd been roped into a loveless shotgun marriage when a former girlfriend, Mary Lou Morrison, showed up four months pregnant.

The situation was made worse by the fact that Sam was

crazy in love with someone else at the time. And probably still was.

And Ken was one of the very few who knew Sam was hung up on FBI agent Alyssa Locke. Despite the fact that they claimed to despise each other, Ken had come across Sam and Locke in a serious liplock right before Mary Lou had dropped her little bomb and detonated Sam's life.

'So who is she?' Sam asked again, persistent son of a bitch.

'I was speaking figuratively,' Ken lied.

'He's such a fucking liar,' Sam said to Johnny. He turned to Ken. 'Why the big secret? Jesus, you're not seeing Adele again, are you?'

'God, no!'

'Well, that's good. Even if she came every sixty seconds like a clock, you'd still be better off a hundred miles away from her.'

'I was just looking for information,' Ken said. 'I was with Adele for so long and . . .' He wasn't like Nilsson or Starrett. Before Johnny got married he'd been a real ladies' man. And Sam had never suffered from lack of female company either. But in his entire life, Ken had been with a grand total of four different women – including Savannah – and the first one had been back in high school, before Adele even, and didn't really count. 'I was just wondering if there were any rules that I don't know about.'

'Rules?' Johnny repeated. 'Like . . . ?'

'Don't do it in animal masks while swinging from a trapeze until the third week of the relationship,' Sam suggested. 'That's a rule I always followed religiously – along with the one about not having sex in her parents' kitchen in the middle of a black-tie party. Broke that one once – got into *real* trouble.'

Ken ignored him. 'Like, there's a rule – it's unspoken, but it's definitely a rule – make sure the woman comes first, right?'

'Oh, shit,' Sam said. 'Really? Maybe that's what I've been doing wrong all these years.'

Ken continued to ignore him. 'But what do you do if the woman comes right away? I'm talking *right* away. And then she comes again, and you know if you keep going she'll come a third time, except by then you're completely crazed because she is *so* freaking hot and . . .'

The expressions on both Johnny's and Sam's faces would have been funny as hell if this weren't so important to him.

'And I think I just got the answer to one of my questions,' Ken had to laugh anyway. 'I'm guessing that it's not one in every four women who can—'

'No,' Sam said emphatically. 'Try one in four hundred.'

'You're in uncharted territory. You're going to have to make up the rules as you go along, man,' Johnny told him.

'That is one very dangerous thing to tell an operator whose nickname is WildCard.' Senior Chief Wolchonok and Team Sixteen's commanding officer, Tom Paoletti, came out of Paoletti's office. 'Do I need to know what this is about?'

'No, Senior,' Johnny said. 'Karmody's got it handled.'

'You got something for me to sign, Chief?' the CO asked Ken.

'Aye, sir.' Ken handed him the papers, and Paoletti took out his pen, motioning for Ken to turn around and give him his back to use as a table.

'What's up?' Johnny asked.

'Two weeks leave, Lieutenant,' Ken said as Paoletti signed.

'Well, all right,' Sam said.

'He's finally taking a vacation.' The senior chief turned to Ken. 'Don't just stay home and watch TV. Go someplace good. That's an order, Chief.'

'No worries, Senior,' Sam drawled. He grinned at Ken. 'I happen to know Chief Karmody's going someplace *really* good.'

'How old are you?'

Molly smiled. Jones had been asking her questions like this ever since they'd sat down to dinner. Too blunt, too personal, too rude.

She'd answered them all.

She didn't have a favorite position when making love – she liked them all.

She didn't wear lipstick because she'd traded the last of her makeup – except for one bottle of nail polish that had fallen behind her bookshelf – to a neighboring village in return for beads to sew on a wedding dress for one of the young women who worked with her.

She was born in small-town Iowa and her mother lived there still.

She'd first had sex at age fifteen – much too young for most girls, but she'd never regretted it. The boy had been killed in a car accident several months later, and yes, she loved him still. A dead boyfriend was a hard act to follow, even now, all these years later.

'I'm forty-two,' she told him now. 'How old are you?'

'Thirty-three.'

He was much younger than she'd thought. 'Tough age.'

'No tougher than thirty-two was.'

'Really? You're not having a Jesus complex?' she asked.

He laughed. Despite his scruffy growth of beard, the lank hair hanging in his face, despite the scowling badman attitude and the fact that he needed a shower, his laughter transformed him. He had no doubt been a remarkably beautiful child.

'Yeah, right,' he scoffed. 'Me and Jesus – we're so much alike, people often get us confused.'

'Sometimes people – men in particular, for some reason – experience a sense of impending doom in their thirty-third year because that was when Jesus died. The thinking is, "I'm not even half the man He was, so why should I be allowed to live longer than He did?"'

'If that's the case, I should've been hit by lightning when I was seven.' Jones laughed again. 'No, I don't spend much time thinking about Jesus. It's not my thing.'

'Do you believe in God?'

'Nope.'

Molly nodded, took a sip of her coffee. He'd answered that awfully quickly. 'Why did you leave my tent without saying goodbye?' It was her turn to ask the blunt, personal questions.

He didn't hesitate with this one, either. 'Because I wanted to fuck you, and that didn't seem like a good way to repay you for your help.'

'I see.' Molly set her coffee down, glad that she hadn't been taking a sip when he'd said that. Years of working in unusual places and dealing with unexpected people and situations enabled her to sound as cool and matter of fact as he'd sounded, when in fact her heart was racing.

She knew it. Despite their age difference, this attraction she felt wasn't a one-way street. When he'd ogled her back

105

in the bar, that had just been for show – an attempt to frighten her away.

But what he'd just said now smacked of a raw honesty.

'I don't know. That might've been a perfect thank-you gift.' She managed to lift a casual eyebrow. 'Are you any good at it?'

He laughed at that. He'd been trying to shock her with his language, and she'd managed to turn it around on him. Score.

'Yes,' he told her. 'I am.'

'Well, I'll certainly keep that in mind the next time you get the flu.'

He shook his head, still laughing. 'You are so full of shit.'

She gazed at him across the table. 'Takes one to know one, Mr Jones.'

Out of all the things she'd asked and said, *this* made him most uncomfortable. 'Look, don't call me that, all right?'

'Well, if you told me your first name, I could—'

'It's Jones,' he said.

'Your name is Jones Jones?' Molly shook her head, enjoying his discomfort. 'Sorry, I don't believe it. If you want me to call you anything other than Mr Jones, you're going to have to give me a first name. And I have to be frank with you. I'm not going to have sex with someone I know only as Mr Jones. I mean, talk about awkward. "Mr Jones, kiss me there again . . ."' She laughed. 'I'm sorry, there's not a chance of that happening.'

His gaze was unwavering in the candlelight. 'So if I tell you my first name, then you and me—'

'Thank you so much for the box of books,' she interrupted him sweetly. 'I read them all in about three days. I wrote you a note—'

'I got it. Go back a sec, will you?'

She leaned forward. 'Actually, let's go back to the day you left my tent after being so sick. After vomiting on my running shoes. Doing diarrhea on my sheets and in my bed. After all that, you were finally starting to be pleasant to be around, and you just left.'

He pretended to be absorbed in peeling the label off his bottle of beer. She suspected that if the light were any better in here, she would see that he was blushing. There was no doubt about it. He absolutely *hated* his memories of her washing him clean, particularly now that he knew she wasn't a nurse.

He glanced up, but he couldn't hold her gaze. 'I sent you new sheets.'

'And they were very pretty, thank you very much. But that was unnecessary. Sheets can be washed. Didn't it occur to you that if you really wanted to fuck me, as you so eloquently put it, you'd have a better chance getting what you wanted by sticking around? By visiting in the evenings? By occasionally dropping the word *please* into your speech? By smiling at me, oh, every few days or so?'

He put down the bottle. 'So you're telling me that if I tell you my name, if I come to see you, if I say pretty please and *smile* . . .' He gave her a big fake grimace of a grin.

'And mean it,' she interjected.

'You'll have sex with me.'

'Don't forget the shower and shave.'

'Check,' he said. 'Shower and shave.'

'Very important.'

Jones laughed. 'You're completely conning me, aren't you? Jerking my chain.'

Molly shrugged. 'Maybe. You want to hear a fact?'

107

He was staring at her mouth again. 'Absolutely.'

'All those things . . . ?'

'Yeah?'

'If you *don't* do those things,' she told him, 'you definitely *won't* have a chance with me. I'm an old-fashioned girl. I like being courted before being fucked.' Molly pushed back her chair and stood up. 'It's time for me to go. I'm staying with some friends from the local church. They're picking me up, they're probably already outside, and I don't want to keep them waiting.'

'Stay with me tonight,' Jones said, still sitting back in his chair, but looking up at her as if he wanted to eat her alive. All sense of banter was dropped from his voice. It was thick, vibrant with desire. 'Please,' he whispered.

Somehow Molly managed to smile. 'My oh my,' she whispered back. 'The P-word puts in an appearance. Maybe the man can learn.'

If he had been anyone else, she would've kissed him. But Jones was far too magnetic, far too attractive. She didn't trust herself to get that close. Instead, she slowly backed away. Blew him a kiss from the distance.

'Good night, Mr Jones. Sleep well. And thank you, again, for saving Joaquin's life.'

Savannah looked so completely different when she opened the door of her hotel room that Ken froze.

He'd imagined her greeting him with a smile as she leaped into his arms. He'd pictured them shedding their clothes right in the entrance to her room, barely getting the door closed first. He'd imagined pulling her down to the floor and . . .

'Hi,' she said.

She was . . . beautiful. Perfect. Too perfect. Scary-looking perfect. Her short curls were tamed and obediently in place. She was wearing makeup that accentuated her incredible eyes, lipstick that outlined her lips. No way was he going to kiss her and risk marring all that perfection.

And her clothes . . .

She wore the kind of high heels that managed to be both sternly practical-looking and yet still impractical as hell. No way could you run in them – not without twisting an ankle.

Pantyhose glimmered on her legs, as if she'd shrink-wrapped them to protect herself from germs. Her light-colored business suit, a skirt and jacket over a similarly colored blouse, was crisp and neat and well tailored.

He'd washed up before leaving the base, but he'd need to scour himself before he risked touching her in a suit that color.

'Hi,' he said back to her like the dumbass chickenshit that he was. 'You look . . . uh . . . nice.'

There was definitely one freaking weird vibe here. Because the smile she gave him was some stranger's smile. A little too polite, a little nervous. 'It's nice to be back in my own clothes.'

Jesus, did she actually *like* wearing that shit? Ken clenched his teeth over the question. Obviously, she did.

'I'm not quite ready,' she informed him.

Ready for what? He'd come here with the belief that they were going to have immediate sex so anchored in the forefront of his brain, he had no clue what she was talking about.

'Oh,' he said lamely. 'That's okay.'

God *damn*, he should have just grabbed her and kissed her when she opened the door. So what if she was dressed like Barbara Bush. Beneath that suit was a warm, funny, intelligent woman who was capable of multiple orgasms. And once he got the clothes off her, messed up her hair and smudged her makeup, his more user-friendly version of Savannah would be back – hot and eager and ready to blow his mind.

He'd keep her naked for two weeks straight, then take her to the mall and buy her a pair of blue jeans and some T-shirts.

But he'd blown it. Instead of kissing her, he'd stood there, like an idiot. And now, here they were mired in Weirdville with all the exit routes to Normal-land completely blocked.

'Won't you come in?' she asked politely, as if he hadn't made her come five different times last night.

Screw this. Ken grabbed her and kissed her and – glory alleluia – she melted against him, hot and soft and eager. As long as he kept his eyes closed, this could've been an extension of last night.

Except for the part where she tried to pull away from him. God, but he didn't want to let her go.

'Don't,' she said. 'I'm sorry . . . Kenny, *stop*.'

He released her and she took more steps back from him than necessary. Jesus, what did she think, he was going to grab her again after she'd shouted *stop* at him like that?

He could take a hint. They weren't going to start up today from the place they'd left off last night. That sucked, and it also sucked that he didn't understand why. He had absolutely no clue. It didn't compute. What had happened between the time that she'd called him and now?

Then he saw her suitcases. Two large ones and one of those hard metallic briefcases with a combination lock, all packed and ready to go, right by the door. *Two* suitcases for someone who was in town for only a few days? This was making less and less sense.

'There's something I have to tell you,' Savannah said. Her face was pale, and her hands were fidgeting.

And he knew. She was going back to her husband. Or to the nunnery. Or to Mars. It didn't really matter which.

'You're leaving,' he said flatly.

God, he was such a gullible schmuck. She'd completely played him and now she was going back to wherever she'd come from.

She saw he was looking at her luggage. 'Oh,' she said. 'Well, yes, checkout's at noon. But there's a room downstairs where they'll hold my bags until it's time to go to the airport.'

He wanted to ask her if it had been something he'd done or said. Had he come on too strong? Was it that note he'd written or was it what he'd said on the phone? *Love ya.* God, he was a fool. She'd probably been laughing her ass off.

Instead he asked, 'Where you going?' Amazing how matter-of-fact he could sound while his heart was breaking. Amazing how much it could matter to him even when he'd already told himself that where she was going was moot.

She got very still, just looking at him. 'I told you last night,' she finally said. 'Indonesia.'

What? It was his turn to stare at her. This was too god-damn hard to figure out. His voice cracked. 'Jesus, you were *serious*?'

'You weren't?'

This was getting weirder and weirder. She didn't want him to kiss her, but she *did* want him to come with her to flipping *Indonesia*. He wanted to call a time-out, or maybe

111

start over. Just leave the room and come to the door again.

'I thought you were having some kind of funky dream,' he told her. 'So, no, I didn't think you were serious.'

'I was,' she said. 'I am. Kenny, I bought tickets. The flight leaves at 9:45 tonight.'

'You bought me an airline ticket to freaking Indonesia?' Last minute like this, that kind of fare had to cost a small fortune.

Savannah nodded. 'To Jakarta.'

This wasn't Weirdville, this was fricking Wonderland. Alice here was all grown up, but she was still chowing down on too much of that psychedelic mushroom.

Maybe it was the lack of sleep that was making this seem so wack. He'd had about three hours total last night, which normally would be fine. He could get by on even less sleep. But combined with the intensity of the sex and the exercise his pathetic, lonely, ever hopeful heart had gotten as well . . .

Ken sat down on the bed. 'Why in God's name would you want to go to Jakarta? Things aren't so swell over there right now. The American Consulate's office issued an additional travel warning for Indonesia three weeks ago. It's not considered a safe place to take a vacation, what with terrorism and religious disputes among the locals. Oh, and did I mention pirates? Don't plan to go anywhere by boat. Except the entire country is ocean and islands. You can't get around if you don't go by freaking boat.'

'I don't want to go to Jakarta,' Savannah said. 'I *have* to.'

'If you want to be relatively safe while you're there, it's a good idea to find one of the better-known drug runners or terrorist leaders and hang with him. He's got security and protection that rivals the US Secret Service. Of course, rival gangs will be gunning for him, so . . .'

112

'I thought I would be relatively safe by traveling with you. I knew since you were a SEAL . . .' She closed her eyes. '*Shit.*'

Ken stared at her. Imperturbable. She knew he was a SEAL. Since *when* did she know he was a SEAL? Something about her delivery shook him, but he was determined *not* to lose it.

'Okay,' he said, trying to make sense of this. 'Help me out here, Savannah, because there's obviously something I'm missing. Let's start at the top. Why do you *have* to go to Jakarta?'

'This wasn't the way I wanted to tell you about this.' She was obviously upset. 'Kenny, please don't—'

A loud knock on the door made her jump, but she quickly composed herself. Completely. It was kind of freaky to watch.

She opened the door to a bellhop with a luggage cart, and dealt with him smoothly, in total control, smiling as if absolutely nothing was wrong. The kid left with the two larger bags and a hefty tip, and she closed the door behind him.

'I'm sorry about that,' she said to Ken.

'Will you stop being so fucking polite and just answer my question?' Well, that wasn't quite as imperturbable as he'd intended. He took a breath. 'Why do you have to go to Jakarta?'

'My uncle's there. He's in some kind of trouble,' she told him. 'He called me a few days ago and told me that he needed two hundred and fifty thousand dollars in cash and he needed it by the end of the week.'

Ken looked at the metal briefcase.

'Yes,' she said. 'It's in there.'

113

No fucking way.

He laughed and stood up. He had to get out of here. 'Okay, Savannah. You completely win. Whatever you intended to do here, whatever mind game you're playing . . . you win. Hands down. This is just too freaking weird for me and—'

She hefted the briefcase up and onto the bed, quickly spun open the combination lock.

And holy Lord Almighty God Jesus, the case was filled with hundred-dollar bills. Twenty-five hundred of them, he would've been willing to bet.

'Where did you get this kind of money?' He couldn't manage more than a whisper as he sat back down.

'I had it in the bank.'

Of course.

'So, let me get this straight. Your uncle calls and says hi, how are ya, bring me a quarter of a million dollars, and you take the money out of the bank and jump on a plane? You have one freaking strange family.'

'Uncle Alex and I have a special relationship.'

Ken closed his eyes. 'I don't know if I want to hear this.'

'Oh, my God, Kenny, not like that! It's just that, well, he's gay, all right? When I was thirteen I found out somewhat . . . unexpectedly. Alex sat down with me and talked about it, about who he was, about what it meant to be gay in the world he lived in – in the world my parents and I live in. He was very honest with me. I'd always loved the way he treated me like an adult and this was no exception. So I kept his secret from the rest of the family – my father, my grandmother. Can you imagine – fifty-something years old and still in the closet? But that was his choice, and I respected it. So I call him when I'm in trouble and he calls me when he's in trouble. We trust each other. It's *that* kind of special relationship.'

'So where do I fit into this, Savannah?' He already thought he knew – *I knew you were a SEAL* – but Jesus, maybe she had some good explanation for that, too. 'We didn't meet by chance yesterday, did we?'

She closed and locked the briefcase, pushed it back and sat down heavily on the bed. Not a good sign.

'Who gave you my name and address?' he asked her.

She finally spoke, only briefly meeting his eyes. 'Adele.'

It was a knife hit to the heart. A searing hot flash of pain that made him want to double over and howl.

He'd wanted her to laugh in disbelief. To say 'Oh, my God, you're wrong. We *did* meet completely by chance. It was the biggest coincidence of my life. I needed to go to Jakarta, and then I met you, and . . .'

'This was what I wanted to tell you,' she said quietly. 'This is why I didn't want to kiss you when you got here. I knew if I let myself kiss you, we'd . . . well, we wouldn't talk, and I had to tell you the truth about everything, so we could, you know, laugh about it, and move on.'

Laugh about it? *Laugh* about it? 'Yeah,' Ken said numbly. 'It's really funny that you slept with me to get me to go to Indonesia with you.'

'No,' she said. 'That's not true. I didn't—'

'How do you know Adele?' What did it matter? Still, he needed to know.

'From college. She was on my floor of the dorm. We met, you and me, a couple of times when you came to visit. You probably don't remember me.'

He didn't. He'd been so wrapped up in Adele.

'You went to Yale, too,' he realized. Yes, this was his

worst freaking nightmare. Another rich bitch Ivy League liar. He should have known. His stomach churned. 'So what did Adele tell you? Besides where to find me, I mean. Did she tell you how to get me into bed? That speech you made last night was inspired, by the way. I bought it completely. Is that what she told you to do? Act sincere and innocent? What else did she tell you? How to make me unbelievably hot for you?' His voice was getting louder and louder, but God *damn*, he was furious. 'Was it her idea to make me wonder for a couple hours if you were even wearing underwear? Jesus, I should have known. Did she fucking tell you where I like to be touched, Savannah? Answer me, goddamn it.'

'No,' Savannah said. 'Kenny, I swear, it wasn't like that.'

He was furious and hurt. Jesus, this hurt. 'What did she fucking tell you?'

To her credit, she didn't cower, didn't burst into tears, didn't back down. 'She gave me your phone number and your address and told me you were still single. That's all. And I . . . I wanted to make sure. That's what I was doing when I got that flat tire. I was checking to see if there was any sign of a family at your house.'

'And if there was, what? You'd screw me back here instead?'

'Okay,' she said. 'Okay. You're mad at me, and I deserve this. I should have told you who I was and that I was there looking for you when you first came over to help with the tire. I apologize.'

'So do you do this all the time when you need help?' he asked her. Apology *not* accepted. He wasn't going to fall for her innocent crap again. At least not in *this* lifetime. 'Find

116

some guy who fits the bill and use sex to get him to do what you want?'

'No!' Her eyes were so blue. 'I was afraid to go to Jakarta on my own, and I remembered you, remembered that you were a SEAL. And ... well ...' She actually bit her lip. It was a nice touch. 'I always had a crush on you, Kenny.'

'Don't call me that.' Kenny was Adele's nickname for him. 'You can call me Ken or WildCard or Karmody or Fuckhead – I don't care. Just don't freaking call me *Kenny*.'

'I'm sorry. I'm *sorry*. You've got to believe me – the sex wasn't supposed to happen. My plan was to call you and tell you I got your number from a mutual friend—'

'Yeah, me and Adele, we're best friends these days. *Shit*.' God, he wanted to cry. But no way was he going to do that in front of her. He focused on staying angry. There'd be plenty of time to nurse his hurt later. He suddenly had two weeks free.

'My plan was to ask you to dinner,' Savannah was determined to explain. She didn't seem to get the fact that nothing she could say was going to fix this. 'At dinner I was going to tell you about my uncle and ask you to go with me to Jakarta. I think, I don't know, I think I was going to offer to pay you.'

'Well, you did pay me, didn't you? Oldest form of barter in the world. Except you got it backwards, babe. You weren't supposed to sleep with me until *after* I did you the favor. You gave away the prize too soon.'

'I didn't mean to sleep with you.'

'Oh, yeah, right. Last night – three times – that was a total accident. Whoopsie daisy. Or – I know – aliens were controlling your mind, right?'

117

'That came out wrong,' she said tightly. 'I *meant* to sleep with you. I wanted to sleep with you. I *loved* sleeping with you. But I didn't *plan* for it to happen.'

'I gotta get out of here.' He stood up. 'Look, I've got a friend, he's a SEAL, too – Cosmo. He's got a thing for lying Ivy League types like you. He'd probably be up for a trip to Indonesia in return for some sex. If you want, I'll put in a good word for you. Despite the bullshit, you were a very good lay.'

The blood completely drained from her face. 'How dare you?' she breathed.

'How dare *you*?' Ken asked. He managed not to slam the door behind him.

Imper-fucking-turbable as always.

Five

When Hank – Heinrich von Hopf – dropped me at my hotel that night, he asked if he could see me the next day. He wanted to take me on a driving tour of the countryside, to picnic near the local Schloss (castle).

I told him of my dreaded luncheon at the university.

'I have some influence,' he told me. 'I'll make a call, see if we can't get you free.'

Sure enough, within fifteen minutes of my return to my hotel room, I received a phone call from Herr Schmidt, informing me that plans had changed. I was to meet Prince Heinrich von Hopf in the lobby of the hotel at 9 A.M. Sharp.

The next day, the weather was glorious. Hank left his driver and Rolls at home. We headed into the country in a sports car, a picnic basket in the trunk.

The scenery was gorgeous, and my host was a perfect gentleman – charming and witty, respectful and gracious. If this had been any other place or time, I would have been sorely tempted to fall in love.

All day long, we talked of anything, everything. The coming threat of war, America's isolationist attitude, women's rights, the Brooklyn Dodgers, my job at Grumman, my studies at school. He wanted to know everything there was to know about me. In return, he told me all about his childhood in

Vienna, his memories of the Great War and its aftermath on his homeland.

The more we found out about each other, the more fascinated we both became. He liked my honesty. I liked his sense of loyalty to his country, his code of honor. And we both liked to make each other laugh.

'Tell me your plans for the future.' He was lying on the picnic blanket, his head propped on his hand.

I was leaning back on both elbows, just looking up at the patterns of the clouds in the sky. It was late afternoon. Almost time to go.

'Will you work at Grumman after you graduate?' he asked.

'I suppose I might . . .'

'Hmmm,' he said. 'You don't sound very excited.'

'I'm not.' I sat up. 'Do you know what I'd really love to do?'

'Tell me.'

'I'd like to travel the world and write travel guides for women.' I glanced at him. He wasn't laughing, so I went on. 'All of the guides that I found were written for men, or for women who were traveling with men. Before I left New York, I wanted to know where in Germany I could or couldn't go by myself – and where I'd be safe, as a woman, to go alone – but there was no information.'

'So you like to travel.'

'I like the adventure,' I admitted. 'Yes. Can you imagine me as this famous adventuress? I'd always dress in men's trousers and smoke cigars.'

'And wear a pith helmet,' he suggested.

'And carry a loaded pistol in my evening bag.'

'Have a boa constrictor for a pet.'

'I'll name him Hank,' I declared. 'After you.'

'I'm honored,' he said. 'But that could get confusing – having two Hanks about. Because I'll be in your entourage – one of the besotted men who follow you everywhere, desperately trying to be the one to refill your martini glass.'

'My canteen,' I corrected him. 'And while we're in the Sahara, I'll accept the refill and bestow a kiss of gratitude upon your lips.'

'After which I shall be positively dizzy with pleasure.' He was laughing, but his eyes were suddenly so intense, I felt the need to change the subject.

'What about you?' I asked. 'Your future. You know, I don't think you've ever told me what it is exactly that you do.'

'Do?' he asked. 'Princes don't *do*, my dear. I simply lie around looking princely. Occasionally, I go to the zoo. Or take beautiful American girls on picnics.'

'What did you do before the *Anschluss*?' I persisted. 'You told me that before Germany annexed Austria you weren't allowed to be a prince.'

'I wasn't allowed to be *addressed* as prince,' he told me. 'Not in public, anyway.'

'Seriously, Hank. What do you do with your time?'

'My family owns a number of vineyards,' he finally admitted. 'And I was involved in the Austrian government. I am still, but . . . It's a joke, Rose. We could debate an issue for weeks, but in the end, we do what Hitler tells us to do.'

'That must be difficult.'

He shrugged. Forced a smile. 'There are many things in life that are difficult. The *Anschluss* happened, and when such things happen, you do what must be done.' He paused and his next words shocked me. 'I think you should come over here and kiss me. That would make all my frustrations bearable.'

He wasn't teasing. He was completely serious.

He sat up. 'May I kiss you, Rose? I want to so very much.'

121

I didn't know what to do, what to say, so I said exactly what I was thinking. 'I'm going home day after tomorrow.'

'You better kiss me quick then – we're running out of time.'

'Hank, I don't . . . want to.' That was an outright lie. I was desperate to kiss him, too, but I knew if I did . . . 'I don't want to fall in love with you.'

If I did, then where would I be? In New York, in love with an Austrian prince who lived on the other side of the Atlantic Ocean. No, thank you very much.

'I think you already have,' he said with the kind of confidence that in any other man would have been lofty and egotistical. 'I think it's too late for both of us. May I see you tomorrow?'

I shook my head. My day was completely filled with a program on German literature. And there was a formal reception in the evening. 'I'm sorry.'

'Then may I see you tonight?'

'Hank.'

He was determined. I had no chance. 'I'm going to take that as a "Yes, Hank." We'll have dinner. I'm going to take you out to—'

'A place just like the one we went to last night,' I told him, determined to keep this at least partially in my control.

His eyebrows went up. 'A *Bierhall*?'

'Yes.'

Hank smiled. 'I wish I'd met you sooner – when you'd first arrived. We could have had a whole week of knackwurst and sauerkraut.'

That smile made me raise my defenses. 'I agreed to have dinner with you. I didn't agree to kiss you, so stop looking so satisfied.'

'Ah, but I never agreed not to try to get you to change your mind.'

'I won't,' I said.

But of course I did. I was eighteen and he was charming and handsome and very, very determined.

He found a *Bierhall* with a band, and we of course danced. And in the laughter and the music the uncertainty of the future seemed to slip away, leaving only the present. Only *now*. His arms felt too good around me. His eyes were so beautiful.

And when he whispered, 'May I kiss you, Rose?', I whispered back, 'Yes.'

We were in public, and I expected him to brush his lips across mine. Instead, he kissed me, *really* kissed me. I was shocked. We were on the dance floor, in front of the entire world. And yet I couldn't resist him. I wanted *more*.

I'd been kissed plenty of times before, but never like that.

'*Mein Gott*,' he murmured, pulling back to rest his forehead against mine. He was breathing hard, and I must confess I was, too.

I risked a glance around. It was the most remarkable thing. My life, my entire world had been turned upside down. But no one had even noticed. No one paid us the least little bit of attention.

'We have to go,' he told me. 'Now.'

'But . . .' It was barely even midnight. He'd said that the dancing and music would continue until the wee hours of the morning.

'I have to take you back to your hotel,' he said, as he practically dragged me through the crowd and out to the street where his car was parked.

He all but threw me into the car, and took off, tires squealing. He didn't say another word, he just stared straight ahead and drove – both hands on the steering wheel.

I didn't know what to think, what to say. But as I began to

recognize some of the landmarks near my hotel, I knew we were almost there, and I had to ask. 'Did I do something wrong?'

'Yes,' he said tightly. 'We both did. You were right. I shouldn't have kissed you. Because once wasn't enough. And since I don't trust myself enough not to kiss you again . . .'

And here we were. At the hotel. Hank took the car out of gear and finally turned to look at me. 'It feels like someone made you just for me,' he whispered. 'Everything about you is . . .' He took a deep breath. 'Rose, I know it's crazy, but . . . I'm so in love with you.'

I couldn't speak.

'May I write to you?' he asked.

I nodded.

'Maybe this isn't so bad,' he said. 'Who knows when I might come to New York. Right? And who knows? Maybe you'll come back to Germany some day soon.'

'I don't think so,' I managed to say. 'I mean, yes, who knows. But . . . Hank, the only reason I'm here now is because the German American League paid my way. I don't have the kind of money to—'

'Maybe if you continue to get good grades, they'll reward you with another trip to Berlin. Maybe you'll be given a scholarship to the university here.' The intensity of his gaze was unnerving.

I *could* get a scholarship. I'd already been promised as much. But first I'd have to become a spy for the Nazis. And I couldn't do that. Not even for a chance to be near Hank. Dear, sweet, wonderful Hank. Who *loved* me!

I was too much of an American, but when he kissed me again, I came the closest I ever have to thoughts of treason.

'If this world weren't so damned complicated,' he whispered, 'I wouldn't let you out of this car. We would drive away together. All the way to . . . to *Hong Kong*.'

I had to laugh. It was either that or cry. 'Hong Kong?'

'Yes.' He kissed me again, fiercely. 'We'd get married, explore the Far East and write his and her travel guides.'

'Married?' He'd told me that one of the more tedious things about being a prince was that his family expected him to marry a princess. Or at least a member of the Austrian royalty.

'You could be known for wearing trousers, and I'd be known for giving up my fortune and title to marry an American who wears trousers.'

'What if I said yes?' I asked. 'What would you do then?'

'I'd beg you to wait a few years,' he told me, kissing my hands, the tips of my fingers. 'I'd beg you to wait for me, to wait for a time when my country doesn't need me so desperately.'

He kissed me again, and all I could think was, I didn't want to wait.

I was completely inexperienced. I'd kissed my share of boys, and some of them had fumbled their way inside my blouse, but that was it. I knew that I was supposed to want to wait for marriage before giving up my virginity, but all I could think was that it could be years before I saw Hank again. That should have been a powerful incentive to keep my distance, but oh, how I loved him. And he'd said he loved me. Enough to *marry* me. And of course I'd believed him. I was only eighteen.

'You should go inside,' he finally whispered.

You should come with me. I was far too shy to speak those words, but I wanted to. I just sat there, instead, looking at him.

I'm certain he knew what I was thinking. He was holding his breath, as if waiting, praying for me to ask him up to my room. And yet, at the same time, I think he was fearful that I actually would.

But I couldn't do it. He finally got out of the car and opened my door for me.

125

'This isn't a goodbye,' he told me softly. 'I *will* see you again before you leave. Even if I have to be at the train platform at dawn to see you off two days from now.'

Yet, still I hesitated. 'Hank—'

Max Bhagat had the habit of knocking on a door while he opened it. It was pretty obnoxious, but since he was not only the boss but some kind of law enforcement genius, Alyssa didn't make him go back outside and knock again.

She did, however, refuse to give him her full attention – at least until she found out whether or not Rose was going to get it on with her Prince Charming.

Yet, still I hesitated. 'Hank—'

He waited.

'Good night,' I said and went inside.

Alone.

What a fool. Alyssa knew that that kind of love and passion didn't happen very often in life. Anyone lucky enough to experience it should take full advantage – before it was too late.

She marked her place and closed the book, setting it down on her desk.

Max was already talking to her. '. . . introduce you to George Faulkner. I'm going to team him up with you and Jules. The three of you are going to be in charge of making sure that Rose von Hopf is as happy as humanly possible over the next few days or weeks if necessary.'

He'd brought the new agent into her office. Jules had been right. George Faulkner could've stepped out of *GQ* magazine.

Alyssa came out from behind her desk to shake his hand. 'Nice suit.'

'Thanks. I'm looking forward to working with you.'

No kidding. Most agents would sacrifice a vital organ to work under Max Bhagat. Even though this assignment was only temporary, after it was over, George was going to put it at the top on his résumé.

'Have we verified that the son's actually been kidnapped?' Alyssa asked Max.

'Not yet.'

Poor George. If Alex von Hopf turned up red-faced and sheepish, having gone on some drugging or whoring binge, the extent of George's 'work' with Max's team would be going to give Rose the good news.

'I'm still hoping Alex will show up,' George told her. 'That this has all been a mistake. Alex is . . . something of a free spirit, so it really is possible.'

'And then you'll go back to . . . ?'

'Philadelphia,' he said, with a smile. 'Quite happily.'

He was either the best liar she'd ever met, or he really was being sincere. Both thoughts were equally disconcerting. He was either Satan or Pollyanna's big brother. She wasn't sure which was worse.

Her intercom beeped. 'Is Max in there?' Laronda's voice squawked over the speaker.

Alyssa pushed the button. 'Yes, he is.'

'It's the call you've been waiting for, sir.'

'Excuse me.' Max hurried back to his own office.

And there she was, alone with the new guy.

'Have you met Jules?' she asked.

'Uh, yes, I have.'

'Any questions?'

George thought about it. 'Just . . . do you and he drink coffee?'

'I meant about . . .' She shook her head. 'Never mind.'

'I know what you meant,' he said easily. 'But I can't think of a single question about that that's any of my business. However, since I'm a Starbucks addict, I like to stop and pick up a cup a coupla times a day. If you guys drink coffee, I could pick up something for you, too. I like mine black, half decaf and as large and hot as possible. In case you ever want to return the favor.' He headed toward the door with a smile. 'I'll let you get back to work.'

'We're going to get along just fine,' Alyssa told him as he started to close her door behind him.

He poked his head back in. 'So much that you're going to cry to see me go.'

'I don't cry.'

'How *do* you like your coffee?' he asked.

'Black and high octane, although when I have too much in the afternoon, I don't sleep at night.'

'What's your cutoff time? You want a cup right now?'

'Your job here isn't to get me coffee, George.'

'Right now my job is to make everyone around me as happy as possible,' he countered. 'I'll get you some.'

'George.'

He came back.

'When you cut the coffee with decaf – does that help you sleep any better at night?'

He thought about it. 'No.'

'Yeah, I didn't think so.'

Savannah picked up the phone and punched in Ken's number, her heart securely lodged in her throat. She'd always thought that expression was an exaggeration, but there her heart was. Neatly choking off her air supply.

She'd spent the past two hours figuring out exactly what she was going to say when he answered the phone. But he didn't answer. His machine picked up, and her mind went blank.

'Karmody,' came his recorded voice. 'Leave a message.'

The machine beeped, and it was her turn to talk.

'Kenny – I mean, Ken, it's me. Savannah. You know. The anti-Christ?' Oh, that was brilliant. Make it sound as if she were laughing at him – maybe he'd get even angrier.

She cleared her throat. 'I called to tell you how sorry I am, how completely wrong I was, not to be honest with you from the start. It was just . . . there you were, and there I was, and you were acting as if you liked me and . . . I was so afraid you might think I was stalking you or something. I didn't know what to say. And you know that expression, "Oh, what a tangled web we weave . . . ?" Well, it's true. It just kept getting worse and worse. And I was going to tell you, I really was, right after dinner, but then all of a sudden, we were . . . you were . . . and it was . . .'

She closed her eyes. 'It was so good, Ken. It felt so right.'

She had to work to keep her voice from shaking. She would *not* cry in front of him. Not even on the phone where he couldn't see. 'I just want you to know that I understand why you said the things you said. You were wrong, and you really hurt me, but I know I hurt you, too, so I understand, and I forgive you.

'Again, I am so, *so* sorry for not being completely upfront with you about why I came to San Diego. But I'm not sorry I slept with you. I'm not going to apologize for the best – the *very* best – night of my life.' Her voice wobbled. She tried, but she couldn't steady it. 'I'm going to call you in a few days. I'm going to come back from Jakarta via San Diego. Will you please try to forgive me? Because I really want to see you again.'

She forgave him.

She fricking forgave *him*.

Ken keyed the phone and message replayed. *Kenny* – He'd *told* her not to call him that. Of course she caught it right away. She corrected herself and called him *Ken*.

He knew he was torturing himself by listening to her message again, but he couldn't make himself hang up the phone.

It felt so right . . .

Yeah, it was remarkable just how great meaningless sex could feel. It was one of the biggest jokes in life, as a matter of fact.

I'm not going to apologize for the best – the very *best – night of my life.*

Good try, Savannah. Excellent job, especially with the wiggle in the voice, but it wasn't going to work. He wasn't going with her to Indonesia. She was going to have to do this completely on her own.

How hard could it be to deliver an attaché case of money to her uncle? It wasn't as if the guy was going to lead her into any serious danger. She'd probably hand off the money at his office, or in a hotel lobby.

And then she'd turn around and come back to the States. She'd leave another message on Ken's machine – she said she'd call when she returned. He wouldn't call her back – he wasn't that stupid – but at least he'd know she got home safely.

Ken hung up the phone and turned on the TV, flopping

down onto his sofa and putting his feet up on a package of clean laundry. Restlessly, he flipped through the cable channels, but absolutely nothing was on. He stopped on the Weather Channel. They were showing a travelers' report, a quick twenty-second overview of the weather in the South Pacific.

The weather patterns looked pretty normal for this time of year. No major tropical storms brewing.

The weather guy started in on the forecast for the Northeast, and Ken turned off the TV and headed for his computer. Five seconds, and he was on-line, scanning the US Consulate's website for the most recent updates and travel warnings for Americans heading to Indonesia.

Nothing had changed. Indonesia wasn't the safest place in the world for an American traveler these days, but it was a far flipping cry from Algeria or Kazbekistan.

In fact, he'd been to Indonesia several times over the past few years, and had had absolutely no trouble at all.

Of course, he wasn't a five-feet-four-inch blonde fairy princess lookalike. Jesus, Savannah couldn't be more vulnerable if she had the words *potential victim* tattooed on her forehead.

But God damn, he didn't want to go with her. He didn't want to spend all those hours on a plane with her; he didn't want to spend another second in her company, being reminded of what a total fool he was.

Absolutely no way was he going. No fricking way.

Ken pushed his chair back from his computer and rolled across the room to his laptop's workstation.

This computer held the prototype software for his programming masterpiece. He'd designed both the software and the hardware for a clandestine tracking system that utilized cell phone satellites that hung in orbit all around the world.

He'd had something of a techno-nerd fantasy this morning, as he was coming back to shore after the diving exercise. He'd imagined bringing Savannah here into his office, and showing her his tracking system. Explaining how it worked. Showing her the miniaturized signal devices – ball-bearing-sized transmitters, their edges roughened so they could be fastened to someone's clothing without that person knowing, kind of like a high-tech burr.

The software worked fast and sweet and was idiot proofed.

The entire system was hugely sexy in a very James Bond way.

At least Ken thought so.

And so did Tele-Kinetics, Corp. A month ago they'd offered him a seven-digit figure for the system – a flat buyout deal. If he signed, this puppy would belong completely to them. And he'd belong to them, too. The take-it-or-leave-it terms of the contract had him finishing up his current tour with SEAL Team Sixteen and going directly to TK's research and development lab for two years, at another quarter mil per year.

Not bad for a loser who'd once been told by a high school science teacher that the best he could hope for in life was a part-time job saying, *Do you want fries with that?*

Not that he was going to take TK's deal. In fact, he'd already turned them down once, but they kept calling. He'd told them flat out that he wasn't ready to quit the SEAL teams. There'd be plenty of time to work in a technolab after he was too old to be a spec warrior. Until that time, he was having too much fun jumping out of airplanes and blowing shit up.

Still, the fact that he'd built this thing, that he'd taken an idea and made it work – and that strangers wanted to pay him lots of money for it – made him proud.

But who knows what Savannah would have really thought. She probably would have made all the right noises when he showed it to her – oohed and aahed and stroked his ego.

Yeah, she would have stroked more than his ego. She would've sat on his lap right here in this chair and . . .

Shit.

He'd done the right thing by walking away. He knew that he had. What was the point in tormenting himself.

He activated his tracking software, took one of the transmitters from his drawer, got it up and running and slipped it into the pocket of his shirt.

That didn't mean he was going anywhere. It didn't mean anything. Shit, he didn't know if his system would even work in Indonesia. All that ocean . . .

Then again, maybe he should go somewhere. Maybe he should go to Hawaii, spend his two weeks doing some serious surfing.

He rolled back across to his internet computer, intending to check the times of the military flights heading south. Somehow he found himself checking the commercial airlines, looking to see which carrier had a 2145 flight that would eventually get to Jakarta.

He told himself that this way he'd know if something happened, like if Savannah's flight crashed. Yeah, that was definitely why he wanted that information.

No way was he going to do something really asinine, like go to the airport and get on a plane to Jakarta with a friend of Adele's.

No way. He wasn't that freaking stupid.

Ken went into his bedroom to look for his passport.

Molly found Jones easily enough at the Parwati airport.

He was running the checklist, getting ready to take off.

'I got your phone message at the church,' Molly said as a greeting. 'Thank you so much for taking the time to call.'

'The part came in,' he told her, 'and it actually fit. I figured if you could get here by the time I was ready to leave, I might as well take you back with me.'

As far as she could tell, he'd taken advantage of the shower at the hotel, but like her, he'd had to put his same dirty clothes back on. He hadn't managed to locate a razor, and he'd gotten a brand new layer of grease on himself while fixing the plane.

'The guy I spoke to in the terminal said you've been ready to go for about four hours.'

Busted. He didn't know what to say, so he glared at her. 'So what?'

'So thank you,' she said. 'For waiting for me.'

The glare became a glower. 'Just get in the plane.'

She climbed in, and he started taxiing to the runway before she even got the door closed and her seatbelt fastened.

He still hadn't gotten his radio fixed, and the tower – if you could call it that – signaled him with a flag when it was time for him to go.

Molly managed to hold her tongue until they were in the air. Until they were almost home. 'I really do appreciate this,' she finally said. 'You've given a full eight days of my life back to me.'

While she'd been prepared to return without complaining to the village with the mule train up the mountain, she was exceedingly grateful not to have to endure that camping nightmare. Not to mention the fact that the five-day trip wasn't scheduled to leave for another three days.

'How much?' Jones asked.

'How much what?'

'How much do you appreciate it?'

Molly laughed, rolling her eyes. 'Must we have this particular conversation?'

'See, I figure if you appreciate it enough, I might be willing to give you a ride into town just about whenever you want to go.'

She knew exactly what he was getting at, but she wanted to see just how low he would go.

'Are we talking one-way or round-trip flights?' she asked.

'One way.'

'Of course,' she said.

'It doesn't have to be you on the plane.' He was warming to the idea. 'Say some other kid gets sick. He and his mother need a ride to the hospital. I'm there.'

Molly nodded. 'All I have to do is . . . Four times, and they get there and back.'

'Guaranteed.'

She sighed dramatically. 'I don't know, Mr Jones. That's an awful lot of time I'd spend on my knees – *praying*. Because that's what you meant, didn't you? That I should show my appreciation by *praying* for you?'

He looked at her. 'What did you think I was talking about? Blow jobs? No way. A blow job'll only get you part of the way to town. I was talking full penetration sex. Me inside of you as far as I can possibly go. And then some.'

Molly laughed. 'Wow,' she said. 'Last night really scared the hell out of you, didn't it? *I* really scare you, too, don't I?

Well, guess what. It didn't work. I'm not going to be insulted by your outrageously crude proposition. I think . . . yes, I'm going to be flattered instead. So thank you very much for being so terrified of me, but we'll stick with my list of requirements before you get inside of me as far as you can possibly go – and then some.'

'Yeah, right,' he scoffed. 'Except that little list's going to keep growing and growing. I've got to start going to church, right? And before I know it, I'll be shuttling every kid with sniffles to the doctor in town with no end in sight. I'll have to help you train the villagers in animal husbandry – getting animals to get it on, that's lots of fun. And oh, yeah, after I do all that? When I'm all showered and shaved and saying please every other smiling word?

'That's when you sweetly let me know that church ladies like you believe that extramarital sex is a sin. I've got to marry you if I want you, right?' He laughed in disgust. 'Thanks but no thanks.'

Molly laughed, too. She just laughed and laughed. 'You're afraid you want me enough to marry me. Oh, my! Mr Jones, I'm flattered, but really. I'm not looking for a lifetime commitment.'

'You're crazy,' he said flatly. 'Because that's *not* what I just said.'

'It's not what you *think* you said,' she countered. 'But you did say it. You know, it really is your lucky day. I like you, despite your attempt to pretend to be the lowest scum-sucking, slime-eating, godforsaken worm on the face of the earth. And I have to confess, I find you physically attractive, too – despite the Han Solo outer crust. I'm dying to be friends with you. Intimate friends who have – as you so eloquently called it – full penetration sex as often as discreetly possible. No wedding ring, no promises, no stupid games with changing rules.

'I'm not any kind of saint, but yes, there are things I believe in, completely, with all my heart. I believe that the sin lies in not taking precautions to prevent an unwanted baby. Sin is in not using protection against AIDS. Sin is the dishonesty with which so many people – both men *and* women – get other people to sleep with them.'

They were approaching Jones's airfield, and she waited until he brought the little plane in before she continued. She wanted his full attention.

The landing was bumpy – no doubt on purpose. He was, after all, scared to death and trying to scare her, too.

But they taxied toward the Quonset hut that Jones called home, and he cut the engines. The silence was remarkable.

'If you want to be friends with me,' she told him quietly, 'I'll welcome your visits with a cup of tea and a smile. If you want to be intimate friends, and I think you want that as much as I do, we've got to be regular friends first. I need you to be completely honest about what you want and who you are. I'm not looking for you to share *all* your secrets with me – just a few. I know you don't really want to marry me. Believe me, neither one of us is looking for a lifetime commitment here.'

'I thought all women wanted to get married.' It was the most honest thing he'd said to her today.

'You thought wrong,' she informed him.

He was holding on to the funny-shaped steering wheel with both hands, as if he didn't trust himself to sit so close to her without touching her. Molly could relate.

She reached out, even though she knew she shouldn't, and brushed his hair back from his face. It was as soft to touch as she'd imagined. 'I suspect a woman would have to be a saint to spend the rest of her life with a man like you. And as I said, Mr Jones, I'm no saint. But an occasional night or two with you might be exactly what I need.'

He turned toward her, but she unlatched the door and slipped out of the plane.

'Have a nice day, Mr Jones.'

'Molly.'

She stopped walking but she didn't turn around.

'I can't do this,' he said tightly. 'I can't be your friend.'

It was something she'd already considered – that it was possible that Jones was simply too scared of this powerful pull between them. Lord knows it frightened the hell out of her.

He could very well just pack up and leave. There was a large chance that once she walked away, she was never going to see him again.

It took every ounce of faith Molly had not to turn around and beg him not to go. But she knew that that probably would scare him into running.

'Too late,' she called back to him as cheerfully as she could manage, then headed down the trail to the village without looking back.

Six

'You're wearing *that* for a flight to Jakarta?'

Ken. Savannah nearly dropped her attaché case as she spun to face him. It really was him. He was really here in the airport.

He must've heard the message she'd left on his machine. He must've forgiven her. It took every ounce of control she had not to burst into tears.

'Where's your luggage?' he asked. 'Because the first thing you've got to do is change out of *that* shit. Forget about the fact that you're going to be traveling for twenty-three hours straight and you're going to be as uncomfortable as hell. That skirt's too short, and you need to wear something that buttons all the way up to your neck.'

Savannah looked down at her pale yellow suit. The skirt was by no means too short. 'Why?' It was not really the question she wanted to ask him, but it was all that came out.

His mouth turned into an even more grim line in his angular face. 'Because I say so. If I'm coming with you, I'm going to make goddamn sure you don't get yourself kidnapped or killed. And that means you're going to do exactly what I say, without question, or I walk, is that clear?'

What was clear was that he hadn't forgiven her. Now the tears that threatened were from disappointment.

Yet somehow he'd decided to help her, to come along. That was something, wasn't it? It was a start.

'I've already checked my luggage,' she told him, careful not to cry – not for any reason.

He swore, obviously no longer bothering to watch his language around her. 'Okay. Then the first thing we do when we hit Jakarta is claim your bags – provided they make it there. Of course, there's a good chance they won't. But if luck's on our side, once we get there, you can change into something *more suitable* in the ladies' room.'

Savannah nodded, willing to play by his rules. 'All right. Although you're going to have to give me a bigger hint about what you mean by more suitable. Because I'm not exactly dressed like a stripper, so . . .'

He didn't even crack a smile. It was as if he'd had a sense-of-humor-ectomy between last night and right now.

'Chances are your uncle got himself into trouble with the locals, and the money is some kind of payoff. The majority of Indonesians are Muslim – I'd be willing to bet that's who we'll be dealing with when we get there. The more religious sects have tougher rules about what a woman can and cannot do – down to the clothes you wear. It's a good idea for you to go in covered – ankle to wrist. That way you can't offend anyone and make things worse for your uncle.'

Ankle to wrist? 'But isn't it really hot there?'

'Yeah,' he told her. 'This way I won't be the only one uncomfortable.'

She looked at him. He was wearing cargo pants – the kind with lots of pockets, and an untucked green and brown Hawaiian-style shirt, open over an olive drab tank undershirt, sandals on his feet. He was dressed for hot weather – loose, cool, comfortable clothes.

'Do you still have an airline ticket for me?' he asked. He was carrying a small duffle bag, and a day pack was over his shoulder.

'Yes.' Savannah forced herself to hold his gaze. 'I didn't cash it in because I was hoping you'd change your mind.'

'Well, shit, aren't I predictable?'

'Thank you so much for coming with me,' she told him.

'Yeah, well, I got the time off and I didn't have anything better to do.'

'I'm prepared to pay you for your time.' Savannah knew the instant the words were out of her mouth that it was the wrong thing to say.

'Oh, that'll make it all better,' he replied. 'Does that really work for you? To throw money at all your various problems?'

'No,' she said. 'I'm sorry—'

'Screw your money,' he told her. 'I don't want your money. No, I'm accepting your original offer. I'll take my payoff for this job in sex.'

It couldn't have stung more if he'd reached out and smacked her across the face.

'Then you might as well go home, because I'm not sleeping with you ever again.'

'Gee, last time you said something like that, you jumped me within two hours. Good thing I packed a lot of condoms.'

Savannah lost her temper. 'Why are you here?' she asked him. 'If it's to make me feel terrible, good job – you can go now. You obviously have no intention of forgiving me, you act like you hate me—'

'I don't,' he said. 'I don't *hate* you. Jesus.'

'I'm not going to sleep with you,' she said again.

'I know,' he said. 'I was just . . . I don't know. Trying to be an asshole, I guess.'

'Well, you can stop trying. You succeeded.'

Ken actually smiled. 'Yeah, I'm told that's something I'm particularly good at. Come on. I better get checked in.'

'I'll wait here,' she said.

'No.' Ken shook his head. 'Starting right now, you've got to get used to sticking close to me. Once we're in Jakarta – once we hit Hong Kong for that matter – you're not going to go anywhere without me making like your little shadow. You're not going into the ladies' room alone. I'm going to be inches from you, twenty-four-seven, and if we're in a crowd or a situation where I don't feel like I'm in complete control, I'm going to have to touch you. I'm going to have to hold your wrist or arm or hand or the waistband of your skirt, whatever – or if I need two hands free, you're going to have to hold onto me. Do you understand?'

She did. And she understood, too, what he'd meant when he'd spoken about not being the only one uncomfortable.

This was really going to suck.

Jones found himself standing stupidly outside of Molly's tent.

What the hell was he doing here?

He'd intended to pack up and leave despite the fact that his airfield – *his* by squatters' rights only – was a sweet little gem. It was the perfect base of operation, except for the fact that it was too damn close to the village where Molly Anderson and her friends were messing things up the way only true do-gooders could mess things up.

But instead of packing, he lay down for a couple of minutes and took a nap. He hadn't slept much last night, and a couple of minutes quickly turned into the entire afternoon.

When he awoke, he found he'd made up his mind. He didn't want to leave. He wasn't going to leave. But he *was* going to make damn sure he didn't run into Molly ever again. He'd stay far from the village, and if she came up to see him, he'd hear her coming and lose himself in the jungle.

How hard could that be?

Grimly happy with his decision, he thought about making himself dinner. But the next thing he knew, he was in the shower. Shaving.

And when he dressed, he not only put on clean clothes, he put on new clothes. A silk shirt in a deep shade of blue he'd picked up in Hong Kong. A pair of pants he'd been saving for a special occasion.

Like he was ever going to have a special occasion. What did he really think? That his mother was going to come visit him or something? She didn't even know he was still alive.

He even cleaned off his boots before he put them on.

It was then, with the rag in his hand, that he knew. He was completely fucked. He had been from the first moment he'd caught sight of Molly, right after he'd found the airfield.

He couldn't stay away from her. He'd tried, and failed.

Miserably.

He sifted through the boxes of supplies he'd brought back from the city until he found what he was looking for. Three books – a mystery, a romance, and some old lady's autobiography. All three were on the *New York Times* list as of two weeks ago, and they'd cost him a small fortune.

He knew without a doubt that Molly was going to like the romance best. So he'd save it for last. He took the nonfiction book, wrapped it in rice paper, and tied it with a piece of twine.

It looked nearly as ridiculous as he did.

Jones slipped his handgun into the back of his pants, and, pathetic gift in hand, he headed down the trail to the village, cursing himself every step of the way.

He didn't stop walking until he got to Molly's tent. And then he stood there, recognizing the total insanity of what he was about to do. Maybe Molly had been right about him having a – what did she call it? A Jesus complex. Maybe some part of him actually wanted to die this year.

She opened the flap and stepped outside before he could walk away.

'I thought I heard someone out here.' Her hair was down around her shoulders and she was wearing a sarong-style skirt that flowed around her as she moved. Her feet were bare, save for the pink nail polish. The smile she gave him was glowing. 'Good evening, Mr Jones. What a wonderful, *wonderful* surprise. Have you come for a cup of tea?'

He wanted tea about as much as he wanted to be struck by lightning, and she knew it. She knew what he really wanted, and she knew he was going to do whatever it took to get it. To get *her*. But that seemed to be okay with her. In fact, she seemed pretty damn happy about it.

'I'm so glad you're here,' she continued. As she touched the sleeve of his shirt, her fingers brushed his arm, and it was crazy the way his heart pounded. What was he, in high school again? 'You clean up nicely, don't you?'

'Don't be fooled,' he murmured. 'Rotting wood looks great with a fresh coat of paint.'

144

'Hmmm,' she said, her eyes dancing. 'That's very profound. And quite noble of you to try to warn me.'

Noble? Not a chance. 'Are you going to invite me in, or what?' Jones caught himself. 'Please, may I come in.'

'What the hell are *you* doing here?'

'Language!' Molly said.

'Sorry.'

Jones turned to see one of the missionaries – a tall, lanky, long-haired man with a beard, whose name was Bobby or Jimmy or something equally gee-whiz – stomping toward them, scowling. His scowl was aimed unerringly at Jones.

'Mr Jones is here for a cup of tea,' Molly announced. 'Have you two met? Mr Jones, this is Bill Bolten. Billy's with the mission.'

'Yeah,' Jones said. 'I noted his warm Christian greeting.'

Billy was carrying a bouquet of flowers and he gave them to Molly with a kiss. He would have planted it on her lips if she hadn't turned her head at the last minute.

'I'm glad you're back safely,' he told Molly, gazing meaningfully into her eyes.

Oh, come on. Billy couldn't have been more than twenty-five years old. Did he really think he had a chance with a mature woman like Molly?

Except she was smiling back at him, with real warmth in her eyes. She brought the flowers to her nose. 'Mmmm, thank you. These are lovely.'

Shit. He should have brought flowers instead of some stupid-ass book. Books weren't romantic. Books didn't say 'I want to do you,' quite the same way flowers did.

He was on his way to shifting, so that he could hide the book behind his back, but it was too late. She'd already seen it.

145

'Is that for me, too?' she asked him.

So he handed it over.

And great. She was opening it right in front of Jesus's angry little brother.

'It's a book,' she said, feeling it through the paper. 'Please let it be a book . . .' She took the paper off as if it were a precious resource as valuable as the gift inside. 'Yes!' She quickly scanned the back cover. 'This looks fabulous.' She hugged it to her chest as she gazed at him. 'Thank you so much.'

Jones wanted her to hold him the way she was holding that book. And if Billy hadn't been standing there, he would've reached for her and made an attempt to kiss her. But no way was he going to give the kid the satisfaction of seeing him bounce one off of her cheek the way he had done.

'Come in,' she said. 'Both of you. I'll put on a kettle.'

The dead last thing Jones wanted was to go into Molly's tent with Billy. But if he left, that meant Billy would be going inside alone.

So Jones went into the tent.

Billy followed on his heels, jockeying for position.

It was pretty big for a tent, with a wooden floor and flaps that could be raised to let the breeze in and lowered for privacy. Molly opened all the flaps as Billy sat down at the table one of the villagers had made for her.

There were only two chairs, so Jones headed for her bed. Before he sat, he took out his gun and set it on the crate she used as a bedside table, next to her lantern. That was where he'd kept it while he was sick.

'Oh, that's nice,' Billy said. 'Did you ask Molly if you could bring a gun in here?' He looked at Molly. 'Did you know he was armed?'

'Everyone here is armed,' she replied evenly as she filled a real tea kettle – with a whistle and everything – from a container of bottled water. 'You, me, Colin, Angie, and Father Bob are the only people on this entire mountain who don't carry a gun. You know that.'

Yeah, Billy. Don't be stupid. Except, oops, guess you can't help it. Being stupid comes naturally to guys like you.

Jones leaned back on Molly's bed, supporting himself with his elbows, enjoying Billy's obvious discomfort. He watched Molly light a can of Sterno and set the kettle above the flame while Billy watched him.

'I have Mr Jones to thank for flying me home this afternoon,' Molly told Billy. 'He didn't have to wait for me, but he did.'

'It wasn't that big a deal.' Jones gazed at Molly's ass with undisguised admiration as she moved to a cabinet to get out a tea strainer and a tin of tea. 'I used the time to take on a load of cargo.'

'Oh, yeah?' Hostility dripped from Billy's voice. 'What did you carry?'

Jones shrugged as he turned his attention back to the younger man. 'The usual. You know.'

'No, I don't know. What's the usual for you, Jones? Drugs?'

'Yeah, that's right,' Jones told him. 'I loaded the Cessna with heroin and cocaine and headed on home.'

'And you invite this man into your tent . . . ?' Billy sputtered.

'He's kidding,' Molly told him. 'Think about it, Bill. The drugs come down *off* the mountain, into the cities, where they can be distributed.'

'Guns are a different story,' Jones said helpfully. 'Guns go up into the mountains. Guns go up, drugs go down. D, drugs, down. That's how I remember it.'

Molly shot him a don't-be-mean look.

He smiled at her. This was actually kind of fun. He liked leaning back on her bed, fantasizing that instead of sitting across from Billy at that little table, she would join him here. She'd lie down beside him, so soft in his arms, her head against his shoulder, and . . .

'And how many guns were in the cargo hold of your plane this afternoon, Mr Jones?' she asked.

Jones pretended to think about it. 'None,' he admitted.

'Your usual cargo is, in fact . . . ?'

'Canned goods, fresh vegetables, and the ever popular toilet paper. I am, in fact, the Indonesian King of Toilet Paper. Although I think I'm onto something that's going to make me even more money. That book cost nearly as much as a four week supply of TP. I think I'm going to fly to Hawaii, buy a couple crates of books and finally make my fortune.'

'A flying bookstore.' Molly smiled at him. 'Be still my heart.'

'So you're saying you've never carried illegal drugs or guns in your plane?' Billy was a pit bull in his determination to prove to Molly that Jones was in league with Satan.

'No,' Jones said. 'I'm not saying that.'

'Then you *have* carried—'

Enough of this bullshit. 'It was nice meeting you, Billy,' Jones said. 'Too bad you have to go now.'

'Fuck you, scumbag. I'm not going anywhere.'

Them was fightin' words, but Jones didn't let himself move an inch. Every muscle in his body had tensed, but the key was in continuing to look – and sound – relaxed. 'Watch your mouth around the lady, junior,' he drawled. 'Do yourself a favor and say good night and go.'

'Not on your life—'

Jones did his own version of a fast draw, reaching for his handgun as he got to his feet all in one quick, smooth motion. He knew from the look in Billy's eyes that the kid had barely seen him move. One minute he was on the bed and the next, he had his gun pointed at the kid's head. 'How about on *your* life?' he asked softly.

'Okay,' Molly said, clapping her hands to get their attention. 'That's it. Both of you. *Out.*'

She stepped directly in front of the gun as she pointed at the door, and Jones pulled it up and put the safety back on.

'Why are you kicking *me* out?' Billy protested. 'I'm not the one who pulled the gun.'

Molly put her hands on her hips and blasted him. 'Maybe not, but you were rude beyond belief. This is my home. You don't come into *my home*, insult my friends, and use that kind of language – which, by the way will cause real problems for you in the seminary. I'm a dedicated pacifist, but I nearly pulled a gun on you myself for being such a jerk.' She turned to Jones. 'And you. Wipe that self-satisfied little smile off your face.'

'What?'

'I'm certainly not on your side, so stop looking as if you've won. How dare you bring this kind of violence into my home?' She was really mad.

'Hey, I wasn't really going to shoot him.'

'And on top of that, you're a hypocrite! "Watch your mouth around the lady . . ."? After what you said to me this afternoon, sewer-man? Give me a break!'

'Yeah, about that. I was hoping to get a chance to apol—'

'Get out of my tent,' she ordered again. 'Both of you. And don't come back until you're ready to stop acting like idiots. You know what? I'm going to make a big sign for the door. *No Idiots Allowed*.'

Jones found himself outside, staring at Billy as Molly closed all the flaps in her tent with no small amount of violence.

'Stay away from her,' Billy said tightly. 'You're not welcome here.'

He stomped off toward one of the other tents.

'God bless you and keep you, too, my son,' Jones called after him, and he could have sworn he heard a burst of hastily stifled laughter from inside Molly's tent.

And he knew what he had to do. He headed for the trail to his camp at a jog – fast enough to get there as quickly as possible, and slow enough to keep from raising a sweat and messing up his pretty clothes.

As the flight to Hong Kong achieved cruising altitude, Ken pretended to sleep.

Sitting next to Savannah was bad enough without having to endure her bouts of small talk that came in fits and starts. She was too polite to sit there without saying anything, but really, what was there for them to say?

The second time they discussed the three-hour layover in Hong Kong, Ken had had way more than enough.

He'd reclined his seat, closed his eyes, folded his arms across his chest, and concentrated on breathing.

But even then, Savannah managed to intrude. She was wearing perfume. The same kind she'd had on last night.

As a result, he was going to – forever – associate that particular scent with incredible sex.

He could hear her, too. Her breathing was ragged, and he knew without a doubt that she was on the verge of tears.

Great. That was all he needed. A crying woman – his personal kryptonite. He was completely unmanned and defenseless when women resorted to tears. Adele had learned that early on. No doubt she'd passed the info on to her protégée.

Ken forced himself to keep his eyes closed. Ignore her. Pretend she wasn't there.

But as the seconds turned into minutes, he realized that Savannah was trying – desperately – *not* to cry.

He opened his eyes and saw that she'd turned away from him. Her eyes were closed, too, and she was ignoring him as resolutely as he'd been ignoring her just a minute ago.

That was new. Adele had used tears mercilessly to get her way.

But he now got the sense that Savannah would rather die than cry in front of him. She was unbelievably tough. She fought it hard for a long time – nearly a half an hour – and won.

By the time she finally fell asleep, *he* was exhausted.

She was tough. Far tougher than she looked in that stupid yellow suit. Far tougher than she looked naked, too.

Ken spent too much time – far more than he would have liked – thinking about Savannah, naked. He forced himself to stop, to remember instead how completely she'd fooled him, how completely he'd misread her.

He watched her as she slept, this friend of Adele's, who had gotten him dreaming again of forever.

151

What a joke.

He watched her breathe, studied the way her eyelashes lay against her cheeks, the way her curls had escaped from whatever hair-care products she'd used to get that carefully coiffed look that had terrified him back in her hotel room. Her lipstick had faded too, and save for the suit, she looked like the woman who'd begged him not to leave this morning without loving her one more time.

Loving. Yeah right.

Sam Starrett had been closer to the truth. Shagging was the word he'd used. The word Ken should've used, right from the start.

What a joke, indeed.

As the plane headed west, toward Hong Kong and the Far East, Ken closed his eyes.

It was his turn to make goddamn sure he didn't cry.

It took him twenty-two minutes to come back.

Molly put down the book Jones had given her – she was already over forty pages in – as he knocked on her door again.

'Molly. It's me.'

She went to the door and spoke softly so that no one in the tents nearby would be able to hear. 'I know. I'm still mad at you. Go away.'

'I didn't get a chance to tell you what I came here to tell you this evening,' he said just as quietly, through the door.

'Let's see, that you're sorry, right?'

'That my name is Dave.'

She laughed. Then opened the door a crack. 'It is not. You are *so* not a Dave, you liar.'

He held something up for her to see – another wrapped package. Another *book*. Oh, the man was a devil!

'Can I come in?' he asked.

Molly looked from his eyes to the book and back. He was smiling his triumph, the beast. He knew she'd let him in. She opened the door wide enough to let him slip through. 'God, I'm easy.'

'I *am* sorry,' he said. 'About what I said to you this afternoon. In the plane.'

'But not about pulling a gun on Billy?'

'No,' he agreed. 'Not about that.'

He was still smiling at her. He'd shaved about ten years off with the stubble and grime, and with his smooth face and clean clothes, with that melting smile, he actually looked closer to Billy's age.

She had to give him credit. He was smart enough not to assume that he could leap on top of her simply because she'd let him in the door. But he did look around, and she saw him take in the fact that the flaps were all down. No one could see in.

It was comical – the way she could practically see the wheels turning in his head.

'I'm sorry it's so warm in here,' she told him pointedly. 'I need to keep the flaps down at night when I read. It's amazing how determined the bugs can be when it comes to finding little holes in the tent.'

'Moths to the flame,' he murmured. 'I can relate.'

Molly laughed. 'Which are you, Mr Jones? The moth or the flame?'

'Dave,' he said. 'I'm Dave, remember?'

'Dave. David Jones.' She snorted. 'Not very original.'

'I'm not trying to be original.'

He held out the package – the book – and she took it. 'Thank you.' He made certain that their hands touched, and she smiled at him so that he'd know *she* knew it was no accident.

She unwrapped it, careful not to tear the paper. But oh, wonder of wonders! 'The new Robert Parker!' She danced around the tent, jumped on the bed.

Jones laughed – real laughter – and she caught a glimpse in his eyes of how he'd been as a child. 'It's a good one, huh?'

'They're all good,' Molly told him from atop her bed. 'If it's got pages and a spine and I haven't read it before, it's fabulous. Even if it's a how-to guide for building an igloo. But *Parker* . . . For a new Parker, okay, yes, I'd have sex with you.'

'Well, all right,' Jones said. 'Let's get naked.'

She got down off the bed. 'I was kidding.'

'So was I.'

She narrowed her eyes at him. 'No, you weren't.'

'Okay, I wasn't,' he agreed.

He didn't reach for her. He didn't move closer. He just stood there, still by the door, smiling into her eyes.

'I love it when you smile,' she whispered. 'You should smile more often.'

'Make love to me. I'll smile the entire time, I promise.'

Neither one of them was smiling now. Now there was only heat between them.

Molly turned away and set the book down on her table, next to the other one, next to her tea cup. *Yes.* She wanted to say yes. But that would be crazy. Wouldn't it? 'I don't think we know each other well enough,' she said as much to convince herself as him. 'Not yet.'

'I came over here so that we could get to know each other better,' he said.

Molly laughed at that. 'You came over here hoping I'd take one look at you in that pretty blue shirt and find you irresistible. I'm afraid I'm going to have to disappoint you, Mr Jones. I have a rule about what goes on inside this tent. Nothing happens in here that can't happen out in the middle of the village plaza. Canvas walls are very thin and—'

'How about you come have tea up at my camp?'

'Well I'm not sure—'

'Tomorrow.'

'Tomorrow's Sunday,' she told him, relieved she had an excuse. 'We hold an evening barbecue in the village every Sunday night. It's not my turn to cook, but I still have to attend. Would you like to—'

'Yes.'

She laughed. 'How do you know what I'm going to ask?'

'I'll come to the barbecue,' he said. 'I'll go to hell with you, if you want. As long as ol' Billy keeps his distance.'

'You're not really jealous, are you?'

'No.' Jones met her eyes. 'Yes. A little.'

'Don't be. He's just . . . I don't know. A lonely little boy. Looking for a diversion, I guess. He's tired of being alone.' She smiled. 'Of course, I could probably say the same thing about you.'

'You'd be wrong.' Jones looked her in the eye, looked away, then forced himself to look back, to hold her gaze. 'I can handle being alone. In fact, I, uh, I'm more . . . comfortable alone. I'm used to it, you know?'

Molly nodded. He was telling her things he didn't normally tell anyone. And he wasn't finished.

'You were right,' he continued. 'What you said this afternoon, I mean.' He cleared his throat, gave up on the eye contact. 'You scare me to death.'

155

She slowly sat down on the bed. That was something she'd never expected him to admit. Not ever.

And still, he wasn't done.

'I don't really know what this is about,' he admitted. 'I mean, look at me. I'm ready to roll over if you give the command. But it's not just about sex. If it was just me being horny, I could . . . you know, I could go get laid. There are plenty of women both on the mountain and in town who'd . . . you know. Take care of me. That way.'

Molly knew that she shouldn't laugh. He was being so serious. So earnest. And she knew he didn't really mean for his words to sound so utterly egotistical. 'I'm sure there are,' she murmured. 'You're a very beautiful young man.'

Very beautiful and very young. Maybe too young. But she'd been honest about how old she was last night at dinner. He hadn't so much as blinked.

He smiled. 'Well, that's something I've never been called before.'

'So if it's not just about sex . . .' she prompted gently.

'I don't know what it's about,' he admitted. 'But whatever it is, it's powerful enough for me to risk my life by becoming friends with you.'

'Risk your life?' She didn't understand.

Jones, bless him, actually tried to explain. 'Lovers are no big deal. Walking away from a lover is easy, as long as you keep everything right on the surface.'

'As long as you keep it only about sex,' she clarified.

'Yeah. Which is why I said what I said this afternoon.'

'You mean, about your personal frequent-flyer program?'

'Yeah.' Dear Lord, was it possible that he was blushing? That he was actually ashamed of himself? 'I figured either you'd go for it, or you'd never want to see me again. Either way, I'd win.'

She had to laugh. 'If that's winning . . . What do you get when you lose?'

'Dead,' he said, looking over at her. 'You get dead.' He could see she didn't get it. 'Friends are a luxury,' he explained. 'A dangerous one. Having friends gets guys like me killed. Friends make you hang around too long when you need to get gone. Friends are a weakness – a way to get to you, to use as leverage. Friends get to know your secrets and they don't always think before talking, so those secrets don't stay secret for very long.

'But here I am. Ready to be your friend if you still want me.'

Molly didn't know what to say.

And still he wasn't done. 'You want to know the name that's on my birth certificate?' He lowered his voice. 'It's Grady Morant. If you tell anyone, if you forget and call me that in front of anyone, if you *whisper* it and someone overhears, I'm dead.'

'Oh, God, I don't want to know it then,' she breathed.

'Too late.' They were the same words she'd thrown back at him this afternoon. It *was* too late. For both of them. They were both in this now. Together.

His honesty awed her. Oh, she knew exactly why he was telling her all this. She knew he still had hopes that she'd break her rule and take him to bed, right here and now.

But the fact that he wanted her enough to talk to her like this . . .

It was possible he was making it all up. But it was also possible that he wasn't. She wanted to believe that he wasn't.

'I know you're curious about the scars on my back,' he said quietly. 'But that's something I can't . . . I can't talk about. Not now. Not ever.'

'That's okay,' she said. 'I won't ask you about them.'

'I wish . . . I wish I could, but . . .' He shook his head.

'It's okay,' she said again. 'Really.'

'I'm not a doctor,' he told her. 'I know you think I am, but I'm not and I never was. I did have training as a medic, but you can't tell that to anyone. If people knew that about me, about *Jones*, they might make the connection, figure out who I really am, and then I'd be dead. Do you get the pattern here?'

'Yes,' she said, blinking back the tears that had filled her eyes. 'Dave.'

He smiled, but it faded far too quickly. 'Knowing this about me . . . Maybe it would just be easier if . . .' He cleared his throat. 'You want me to go away and just never come back?'

If he was bullshitting her, he was doing a damn fine job.

'No, I don't,' she told him.

He started toward her, and she knew that he was going to kiss her now. She stood up. God forbid he sit down next to her on her bed, pull her back with him. She'd break every rule in her book.

'Tomorrow morning,' she said, talking fast so that she could get it all in before he reached her. It was too soon, she knew it was too soon, but that was just too bad. She didn't want to wait. 'After church? I was planning to take the mission boat up river. There's an elderly couple who live way up north, a couple hours ride. I was going to pack a picnic lunch, go check on them, and then spend the afternoon just drifting back down. Do you—'

'Yes,' he said.

'. . . want to come?'

He kissed her.

Feeling his arms around her was nothing like her fantasies. It was nine thousand times better. He was both hard and soft. Hard body, soft mouth, soft hair, soft touch. In about twelve hours, he was going to be with her, in the middle of nowhere, alone on a boat. She was going to let him in, going to give him everything he so desperately wanted, and take more from him than he'd probably dreamed he was capable of giving.

This was, no doubt, one of the shortest courtships in the history of the world. Unless, of course, she counted back to those days he'd spent in her tent. She would, she decided. Everything that was happening between them now *had* started then.

Jones kissed her longer, deeper, pulling her more tightly against him, molding her to him, reaching between them to cup the fullness of her breast.

They were breaking her rule, but it felt so good, she nearly didn't pull away.

Somehow she managed though, pushing him gently toward and then out the door.

'Tomorrow,' she reminded him softly.

He just laughed and she knew what he was thinking. Yeah, like he was going to forget.

My last full day in Germany started with a bang at 6:17 A.M., with a frantic phone call from my *Tante* Marlise.

She was the youngest sister of my mother, only three years older than I. Pretty and vivacious, when she was my age, Marlise had married a handsome young cobbler's apprentice named

SUZANNE BROCKMANN

Ernst Kramer. Poor in the pocket, their humble home was rich with love. When I'd met them earlier in the week, they'd already had two sweet-faced little children, with another quite happily on the way.

The Gestapo had come shortly after ten last night, Marlise told me through her tears. They'd banged on the Kramers' door, frightening the babies and waking the neighbors. They'd dragged Ernst from the house, thrown him into an automobile and taken him away.

Marlise had brought her children to her sister's house and walked the twelve miles into Freudenstadt, to find out where Ernst was being held and why he had been taken. He was a good man, an honest man, a hardworking man. He paid his taxes and he never spoke ill of the Nazi Party.

She told me she'd sat in a waiting room at the local Gestapo headquarters for hours. Finally, just before dawn, she was brought into a room and interviewed. Yes, instead of being able to ask the questions, the questions were asked – none too kindly – of her.

Was it not true that Ernst had attended a recent Communist rally in Munich?

No! Ernst had never been to Munich. Not ever. Neither he nor Marlise had ever traveled more than twenty miles from their village.

Would she know of a reason why his name would be on a list of dangerous Communist dissidents?

Marlise was stunned. *Her* Ernst?

The questions went on and on and on, until finally, the last one: Were she and her husband related to an Ingerose Rainer, an American student who was visiting Berlin this very week?

Marlise wasn't told where Ernst was being held, or if he were even still alive. But she'd hurried home to call me at the hotel, to find out if I knew why the Gestapo would have been asking about me in connection to Ernst.

And I *did* know. I knew right away. Ernst's arrest was arranged to put pressure on me to spy for the Nazis.

I knew with a certainty that was chilling, that were I to go to Herr Schmidt and agree to send him American military secrets from Grumman, Ernst would be returned to his family.

I also knew that were I to continue to refuse, my mother's other brothers and sisters would be arrested. And maybe even executed.

I was beside myself with anger and fear. I didn't know what to do, or even what to think.

I quickly threw on some clothes and, taking only a minute to study the route map of the streetcars, I headed for Hank's house.

House?

It was a palace. As I ran up the drive, I could see his Rolls out front, engine idling. His driver, Dieter, was holding the door open, standing sharply at attention as a man, dressed in the uniform of the Nazi SS, swastika on his armband, came out of Hank's ornate front door.

I stopped short, filled with terror. Had they come for Hank, as well? Was he also in danger because of his association with me?

I hurried closer, ready for what? I'm not sure. Maybe to try to wrestle the entire Nazi machine to the ground. All I knew was that I had never hated anything or anyone so completely before in my entire sheltered life.

'*Entschuldigen Sie mich!*' I called out imperiously. (Excuse me!)

The officer turned.

And my innocence died.

It was, of course, Hank wearing that uniform. Or rather, Prince Heinrich von Hopf. It was hard for me to think of him as

SUZANNE BROCKMANN

Hank while he wore that hideous crawling spider, the emblem of the Nazi Party, on his arm.

'Rose?' He was as shocked to see me as I was to see him. Or at least he was pretending to be shocked.

How much did he know?

All of it, no doubt.

I'd spent the day with him with Herr Schmidt's blessing, I realized with dread. The truth was hideously apparent – Hank was part of this attempt to recruit me as a spy. What better way to tie a romantic young girl to the country of her parents' birth than by providing her with a handsome man who claimed to adore her?

It all made so much sense now – an older, sophisticated man, an innocent girl. What could Hank possibly have seen in me to have been so attracted, unless it was my ability to provide the Nazis with this information they wanted?

I was devastated, but somehow I managed to keep my wits. I think I realized at that moment that Marlise and my mother's other siblings weren't the only ones in danger from these odious people. I wouldn't have put it past the Nazis to create some terrible 'accident' to befall me, should I refuse to cooperate.

'I didn't recognize you,' I told him, somehow knowing instinctively that I should stick as closely as possible to the truth. 'Is this the uniform you wear as you help govern Austria?'

'No,' he answered. 'I have additional duties that I perform for the Reich, and . . . Are you all right? What are you doing here?'

He looked so concerned, but it was all an act. It had to be an act.

'It's too terrible,' I said, erupting in noisy tears. They weren't hard to fake. In truth, they were all too real.

He took me into his car and ordered Dieter to drive.

He held me close, my head against his shoulder, his arms

162

around me tightly. I could feel his lying heart beating in his chest, and somehow, it gave me strength.

And I knew in that instant what I had to do. I had to agree to be their spy. But the moment I stepped off that boat in New York Harbor, I would go straight to the FBI.

I would be a spy for the Nazis, indeed. But I would only feed them information that my country wanted them to see and hear.

With my new resolve burning within me, I was able to stop my tears long enough to tell Heinrich about Marlise's phone call, about Ernst's arrest and the charges of communism. And with tears clinging to my eyelashes, I asked him, please, for his help.

'It must be a mistake,' I said. 'Ernst Kramer is no more a Communist than I am. Why, he even had a framed picture of Der Fuehrer in his living room.'

I was, as my granddaughters are prone to say, pinning the BS meter with that one.

But Hank didn't seem to notice. He barked out a street address in rapid-fire German to his driver. To me, he said, 'Perhaps I can help. Not directly, but . . . We have a mutual friend, Herr Schmidt, who has connections in the Gestapo. I am certain he'll be able to give you the assistance you require.'

Herr Schmidt was, of course, the horrible little man who'd asked me to spy for the Nazis. If I had any lingering doubts that Hank was somehow not involved, they were now crushed.

We arrived at a nondescript building near the university, and Hank led me out of the car. Up four flights in an elevator, down a hall. I remember it so clearly – the floor was hardwood and it gleamed from polish.

I was shown right into Herr Schmidt's office. Hank was asked to wait outside. At first, he refused, but I reassured him. I would be all right. I was, in fact, quite relieved that he wouldn't be there. I suspected that he would be able to see through the lies I was about to tell.

The door to Herr Schmidt's office closed, and I sat in front of his desk, telling him about Marlise and Ernst. 'It's all been a terrible mistake,' I said again. 'If you could help my family, if Ernst could be allowed to return home, I would be so grateful.'

And then, God help me, I said the words that were to change my life forever. 'I would be willing to show my gratitude and my loyalty to my parents' Fatherland by providing you with as much information from my employer as I can obtain after my return to New York.'

It was 8:30 in the morning.

Marlise called the hotel to tell me that Ernst was home by noon.

'I'm so glad they realized their mistake,' she told me as she wept. 'I'm so glad it's over.'

For me, the only thing that was over was my childish love affair with Heinrich von Hopf.

My career as a spy, however, with all its danger and intrigue and heart-hardening cynicism, had just begun.

Rose was ready to go on to the next section they were re-recording due to 'tape glitch', whatever that was, but Akeem's voice sounded in her headset.

'Sorry to stop you, girlfriend,' he said, 'but the MIB squad is here to see you.'

'Who?'

'Men in Black,' he clarified. 'Or in this case, men and very hot woman in black. It's your buddy George, and this time he brought some friends.'

Friends. Plural. That wasn't a good sign. Alex had been kidnapped. George was here to tell her that, and the other two agents were handlers, assigned to make sure Rose didn't pressure George into taking her out into the jungles of Indonesia to search for Alex herself.

Oh, Alex. Why do you insist on living in a part of the world where you're always in danger? Why don't you just look me in the eye and say—

The door opened and George Faulkner came into the studio. 'I'm sorry to have to interrupt—'

'Is he alive?' she asked.

'We have no reason to believe he's not.'

Rose nodded, glad she was still sitting down. 'Do we know yet who took him?' A man and a woman had followed George into the studio. Neither of them were so full of themselves that they had to be introduced before she was given the facts.

'No,' he said. 'We're still working on that.'

'What *do* we know?' she asked.

'He was taken from a restaurant in Jakarta called The Golden Flame on Monday night, apparently against his will. A number of people saw him dragged into a plain white delivery truck. He was shouting, but no one could make out the words – apparently there aren't too many English speakers in that part of the city,' George told her.

'Was he the only one taken?' she asked.

'Apparently, yes.'

'Who was he dining with?'

'According to the restaurant owner, his dinner companion hadn't yet arrived. He'd made a reservation for two.'

Rose nodded. 'His hotel room has been searched? As well as his apartment in Malaysia?'

'We're in the process of doing that,' George said. 'But as of right now, we haven't managed to find his appointment book or a scrap of paper saying "Dinner at eight on Monday with so and so, and by the way, I suspect so and so wants to kidnap me."'

'It's been my experience,' Rose said, 'that there's always some kind of paper trail. Anything else?'

George shook his head. 'That's all we've got so far.'

She turned to the female agent, a pretty young woman who was at least part African-American. 'Is there anything he's not telling me that I should know?'

'No, ma'am. His job is to be forthcoming with all information he receives.'

Rose looked from her to the other man, a shorter young fellow with nearly as pretty a face as the woman's. 'Well, then maybe I should be asking the two of you. Is there anything *you're* not telling *George* that I should know?'

The young woman laughed and became even more strikingly beautiful. 'No, ma'am. We're not going to play it that way. You're going to have access to all information at all times.' She held out her hand. 'I'm Alyssa Locke. I'm honored to meet you, Mrs von Hopf.'

Alyssa Locke had a good, firm, no-nonsense handshake.

'And this is Jules Cassidy,' George told her.

He shook her hand, too. 'Ma'am.'

'He'll be in need of insulin,' Rose told them. 'Alex will. He's diabetic. If he's been a prisoner since Monday . . .' It had already been too long. 'If they intend to keep him alive, they'll need to get their hands on insulin. We should watch for any thefts in pharmacies – it may be a lead in tracking him down.'

Alyssa stepped slightly away from them as she flipped open her cell phone. 'Get me Max Bhagat.'

'Max and the rest of the team are already en route to Jakarta via LA,' George told Rose as Alyssa relayed the information about the insulin directly to her boss. 'You're welcome, of course, to join us, but if you want to stay here in New York, there's no need to—'

'I'm packed,' Rose announced. 'Shall we take my car or yours to the airport?'

Seven

'This your first trip to Jakarta?' Ken said in Savannah's ear as he steered her through the crowd at the airport.

She nodded, obviously overwhelmed by the people, the noise, the energy, the complete non-Western-ness of it all. He had her by the elbow, and he just kept pulling her along.

'Keep the attaché case between us,' he ordered. 'I'll carry it if you want.'

She was clutching it with both arms. 'Just . . . stay close. Please.'

'I'm right here,' he said. 'I'm not going to let go of you.'

'Thank you.'

It was their lengthiest conversation since leaving California, and Ken knew from the sudden sheen of tears in Savannah's eyes that he wasn't doing her any big favors by being kind.

'How're your feet holding up in those stupid-ass shoes?' he asked. 'They weren't exactly designed for running through airports.'

'I'm fine.' She was a terrible liar. Her feet had to hurt like hell.

Ken was tired and hungry and jet-lagged and grubby from spending over twenty-four hours in the same clothes – she had to be feeling ten times worse because she wasn't used to it. But damn, she refused to complain.

'Do you think . . .' she asked haltingly, gazing at him with those eyes. 'Would it be okay if we, like, started over? I mean, here we are, halfway around the world, and you wouldn't *really* have come all this way if at least a part of you didn't want—'

'Miss Savannah von Hopf?'

The man who was blocking their path was large with a capital ARG. His suit was tailor-made and obviously expensive. Even Ken – who didn't give a damn about clothes – could tell it had cost big bucks.

The rest of the crowd managed to flow around the big man, but he and Savannah were temporarily trapped. The giant held up a sign that said *VON HOFP*. 'I am here to take you to your uncle,' he said in heavily accented English. He wasn't Indonesian. Ken guessed Russian.

'You spelled her name wrong,' he pointed out.

'How did you even know which flight I'd be on?' Savannah – who wanted to start over – wondered.

Good fricking question. One he should've thought of himself, if he hadn't been thinking with his dick, the part of him that was enthusiastic about the possibilities of 'starting over' with Savannah.

'Thanks, pal,' Ken told the best-dressed driver in the entire world – yeah, right, this guy was a chauffeur. And yeah, like hell they were going to go even two feet with him. 'But we'll get our own ride to the hotel. Why don't you go pick up *Mister* von Hopf and tell him we want to meet him there? I'm sure he'll understand our need to be cautious.'

Large looked at him. 'Who are you?'

'A friend of the family,' Ken said. 'Who the hell are *you*?'

'I want to go with him,' Savannah said.

What the . . . ? Ken turned to look at her. It was the weirdest freaking thing – she'd gone completely pale. 'Oh no you don't.'

'Yes,' she said. 'I do.'

This was just perfect. What happened to *Can we start over?* 'What did I tell you in San Diego?'

'I want to get this over with.' Savannah wouldn't look him in the eye.

'You do it *my* way,' Ken reminded her, 'or I'm outta here. I was serious about that.'

'Okay,' she said with the weirdest freaking smile he'd ever seen. 'That's okay. It's . . . it's great, actually. Great. And . . . and . . . if you hurry, you can probably even catch the next flight back to Hong Kong.'

She sounded as if she desperately wanted to get rid of him. She sounded . . .

Ken realized far too late that Large Guy wasn't alone. There was another man standing directly behind Savannah.

He was carrying a coat over his arm – a coat, in tropical Jakarta. It was a time-honored but none-too-original way to conceal a weapon – in this case, some kind of big-barreled Dirty Harry-sized handgun he was jabbing hard into Savannah's side.

'So goodbye,' Savannah told Ken. 'I definitely don't want to do this your way, so yes, you should *just go home.*'

Holy shit, she was trying to protect him from the bad men with the guns. She was trying to send him away so he wouldn't be hurt, while she went off to meet her unhappy fate.

If Coat Man had been holding one of the usual cheap shit popguns native to most third-world countries, Ken would have put himself between Savannah and the barrel while he disarmed the two sons of bitches.

But that elephant gun wouldn't just blow a hole in him if the guy's trigger finger accidentally slipped. The bullet would go right through Ken and it would make a big hole in Savannah, too. And neither of them would get back up, not ever again.

'Okay,' Ken said easily. 'Let's do it your way, babe. Let's go with this gentleman.'

Surely there'd be an opportunity between here and the parking lot to get that weapon into his hand and to regain control of the situation. Two guys, one weapon? Even if Large was carrying, these punks were amateurs. It'd still be a breeze.

Savannah, however, was determined to make it as difficult as possible. 'There's a man behind me, Kenny,' she said from between clenched teeth, 'and he's got a gun on me.'

No shit, Sherlock. 'Yes, I knew that, thanks. And now, unfortunately, *he* knows that *I* know it, too.'

'Go away,' she said.

'And don't call me Kenny,' he added.

'Please come with me,' Large said. '*Both* of you.'

Savannah turned to face the Russian, suddenly fierce. 'This has nothing to do with him.'

Him being Kenny. Jesus. This was why she wanted him to come along, wasn't it? To protect her? Did she really think, then, that he'd run at the first little sign of trouble?

Ken took her elbow and moved her forward. 'I can take these guys,' he breathed into her ear. 'Just . . . don't say anything else. Please.'

'But—'

He squeezed her elbow and she fell silent, thank God. All she needed to do was let slip the fact that he was a US Navy SEAL, and she'd be on her own. The SEALs had a reputation for kicking terrorist ass in this corner of the ocean. There would be no 'evil warlord' scenario, no tying him up, no taking him prisoner if the truth came out. No, guys like these were so scared of SEALs, he'd have a bullet in his head so fast, he wouldn't know what hit him.

Large led the way, and as they moved, Ken realized there were three additional guys, also carrying coats, moving through the crowd with them.

Shit. Five to one wasn't going to be quite so easy.

And the goatfuck factor went to an eleven on a scale of one to ten as Large led them not to the parking area, but rather to a fricking heliport, where a twin engine Puma was ready to fly.

Okay. Okay. Maybe this wasn't as bad as it looked. So what if they were flown to some desert isle and held for ransom. He did, after all, have one of his tracking devices in the pocket of his shirt.

As soon as he turned up missing, Johnny or Sam or Cosmo or *some*one who knew him would eventually go to his house and check his laptop and see that he was broadcasting a steady signal from Middle-of-Freaking-Nowhere, Indonesia – provided there was cell phone satellite access in the area. And if there wasn't, well, his pals could bring in some temporary sat towers and, presto, he'd be found. At which point, if he hadn't already managed to escape from whatever bush-league bamboo and vine hut he and Savannah were being held in, the SEALs would come and liberate them.

Of course, he was assuming these guys really were terrorists of some kind. It *was* possible that this helo would land on the lawn of some fancy estate, and Savannah's Uncle Alex would stroll out to meet them, piña coladas in both hands.

'This is the money, no? I will take it now,' Large announced, reaching for Savannah's briefcase.

'I don't think so.' Ken stepped between them, and all the coats came off. A pair of Uzis and one HK MP5 that he itched to get his hands on all came into view, leveled at him. But it was the Magnum .44 still aimed at Savannah that stopped him cold.

Large motioned for Savannah to hand over the case, and she surrendered it quickly.

'Okay,' Ken said. 'Here's how a kidnapping works. You get the money, you let the hostages go. Simple. Basic. Easy even for stupid shits like you to understand. You have the money now, so now you need to—'

Wham.

Large hit him. In the back of the head with the metal briefcase. Jesus, that rang his chimes. He didn't see it coming, didn't brace, and the force from the blow sent him down to the pavement, onto his hands and knees.

He realized, as he was down there staring at his four hands, that the fact that he *wasn't* braced was probably what kept it from being a knockout blow. As it was, it just hurt like fucking hell and – big pain in the ass – made him dizzy, too.

Savannah scrambled down to the pavement next to him, no doubt tearing the knees out of her fancy pantyhose.

'Oh, my God,' she said. '*Kenny* . . .'

'I'm okay,' he managed to say. 'Skull's pretty thick.' He

just needed another minute down here to get his eyes back into focus.

'Please,' she said, touching his face. Her hands were cool despite the sun's heat. 'Don't do anything else to make them angry.'

'Can't help it,' he said. 'It's that asshole thing again. It's in my genes.'

She actually laughed. But it turned into a shriek as Large hauled her back to her feet.

That got Ken very vertical very quickly, too. He shook off the last of the dizziness. 'Keep your fucking hands off her!'

And *that* got him the butt of the HK submachine gun right smack in the kidneys. That searing pain came with the bonus of knowing he was going to pee traces of blood for the next day or so. But the pain was nothing he couldn't handle.

He'd had the shit beaten out of him enough times in his life – thanks, Dad – to know that he could win a fight with just about anyone simply by staying on his feet longer. By ignoring the pain and pushing himself off the ground when another man would've stayed down.

But he wasn't fighting one man here. There were five of them. And if he got himself killed now, in the first few minutes of this funfest, Savannah would be left all alone.

She was looking as if she were ready to jump into the fray, to fight alongside of him. That wasn't good.

Besides, after tossing her into the helo, Large was keeping his fucking hands to himself. So Ken shut his mouth and climbed into the open sliding door after her.

'You okay?' he asked, pulling her down next to him on the corrugated metal floor. There weren't any seats. This was a cargo helo. In fact, it was filled with small crates. Large had wedged the briefcase in between one of the stacks and the farthest bulkhead from the open door.

She nodded, all big blue eyes. 'Are *you*?'

'I'll live.'

'Kenny, I'm so sorry I got you involved in—'

'Shh,' he said. 'Savannah, don't talk. Just zip it completely, okay?'

'But—'

He looked at her, and she cut herself off. But only for a second.

'If you get a chance to escape, please go,' she said as quickly as possible. 'Get yourself to safety. You can always come back for me.'

'Zip,' he said. 'It.'

'Promise me.'

'Fuck, no!' He couldn't believe her.

'But you'll be able to get away.' The woman would *not* shut up. 'You're a S—'

SEAL. He kissed her. She had been about to announce to a helo filled with terrorists that he was a SEAL. So he shut her up the only way he knew was guaranteed to work – by covering her mouth with his own.

He just kissed the shit out of her as the helo blades started turning, creating a wash of sound that you had to shout to be heard over. And then, as they lifted into the sky, he brought his mouth right up to her ear, so no one could read his lips. 'If they find out I'm . . . what I am, they'll kill me. Don't even let it slip that I'm in the Navy, do you understand? Or I'm dead.'

Savannah nodded. She was trembling. He would've liked to have thought it was the kiss that had put her into

175

such a state, but he suspected it was the result of the potential threat to his life.

He was the one shaken by that kiss.

Ken looked out the open door. As far as he could tell, they were heading northeast. They were already away from Jakarta, out over the ocean.

He looked around the helo again, noting that the gunman with the HK MP5 machine gun – the one he wanted to get his hands on – was sitting too far away. Even the two Uzis were well out of reach.

He focused his attention on the briefcase, and then on the helo itself.

There was another sliding door on the opposite side of the bird, but it was closed. He looked closer. It was closed but not locked, and possibly not even latched. It wouldn't take much to push it open.

There they sat, in silence, traveling over the open expanse of the ocean, for well over an hour. Savannah clung to his hand.

Finally, the appearance of an island dead ahead set off a flood of discussion in Russian. Unlike his friend Johnny Nilsson, Ken wasn't any kind of a languages expert.

But he did speak enough of what he called 'survival Russian' to get the gist of what they were saying. First they would drop the Americans, and then they would make the delivery. Then they would all go back to Jakarta and have dinner with someone named Benny who was either Large's brother or his cactus. Ken was betting they were brothers.

Savannah had had enough. 'Where's my uncle?' she shouted over the roar at Mr Large. 'Has he been kidnapped? Is that what this is about?'

'Actually, I don't know where he is,' Large shouted back.

'He missed an important meeting and . . . I took it upon myself to regain some of my losses. I make a good imitation of Alexi's voice over the telephone, no?'

'*You* called me?' She was stunned.

' "Hello, Savannah," ' Large shouted. ' "This is Alex. I'm sorry reception is so bad . . ." Alexi was gone, but he'd kindly left his palm pilot in his hotel room. He'd spoken of you most fondly, so I knew you were the one to call to deliver the funds.'

'Oh, my God,' Savannah breathed. 'What have I done?'

This whole thing was just a scam, a con job. Chances were Savannah's Uncle Alex was already swimming with the fishies. Ken guessed this was a botched kidnapping. And with the kidnappee suddenly deceased, Large and company had had to get creative to get their ransom money. They'd struck paydirt by calling Savannah.

'You got the money,' Ken shouted. 'You got what you wanted. Why drag us all the way out here?'

'Because it's not just about money,' Large shouted back. 'It's about maintaining the necessary respect.'

Oh, *fuck*. Those were not the words Ken had hoped to hear. The kind of respect Large was referring to was maintained through intimidation and fear. Through making examples of the poor suckers – or the poor suckers' nieces and family friends – who crossed him. Death was looking to be a real option here.

They were flying over the island now, heading over the lush jungle, climbing steadily in altitude as they headed farther into the interior.

Savannah was silent, shocked by the realization that she'd come so willingly into danger. Ken doubted that she'd made the connection that he had – that her uncle was probably dead, and unless they did something, unless they took action, they themselves had literally minutes left to live.

Ken estimated and counted the number of paces it would take him to cross the helo. To get to the guy with the HK MP5 machine gun. To get to Large. To get to the attaché case. To get to the handle of the closed helo door.

They flew for close to another hour in silence, until Large once again barked out an order in Russian.

'This is far enough. Give us sufficient—'

Ken didn't know the last word. It had something to do with flying. Ken had learned his Russian by painstakingly drumming vocabulary into his head. Apparently the chapter on flying hadn't took.

But the pilot sent the helo pretty much straight up, higher into the air. And Ken remembered. The word was *altitude*. Give us sufficient altitude.

Sufficient altitude for what?

And just like that, Ken knew.

Holy fuck. Drop the Americans meant *drop* the Americans. As in push them out of the helo at hundreds of feet above the jungle floor.

Unless he suddenly sprouted wings and learned to fly, he and Savannah were in serious trouble.

The missionaries' boat had an air mattress and a canopy across the bow to keep out the sun.

Or any prying eyes.

Jones couldn't remember the last time he'd been this nervous. Or this aroused. It was not a good combination.

By some kind of unspoken agreement it was understood that any sex that was going to happen today wasn't going to happen until Molly had paid her visit and they were on their way back down river, heading for home.

But now here it was. Lunch was over, goodbyes were said. And they were alone again on the boat.

All the way up river, Molly had spent the time telling him about her childhood in Iowa, about her mother, about her sitcom perfect, sainted father who'd died when she was only ten.

She told him detailed, personal stories that made him envision her as a child, and he knew she'd wanted him to do the same in return.

He'd managed only a few sentences, scattered haltingly throughout their conversation.

'I grew up in Ohio,' and, 'I used to love playing baseball,' and, 'I haven't seen my mother in at least ten years.'

She hadn't pressed him for more information. She'd just smiled at him as if he'd given her a precious gift.

Jones reached down to start the outboard motor, but she stopped him. 'Let's just drift.'

He couldn't speak, so he nodded. Drift. Right. Good idea.

'You want some lemonade?' she asked. She sat down right there in the sunshine, on one of the benches that lined the stern of the boat.

All morning long he'd fantasized about this moment. She'd lead the way beneath the canopy, taking her clothes off as she went, smiling that smile that made him rock hard. Then she'd lie back against the air mattresses, completely naked. He'd just look at her for a good long time before he joined her there. Before he sank down into her and . . .

'I'm going to have some,' she told him, reaching for the cooler. 'I'm a little nervous in case you didn't notice. It's been a while since I've tried to seduce anyone. Particularly someone so much younger than I am.'

'Chronological age means nothing,' he said. 'I was older than most people I've ever met when I was twenty-five.'

She looked up at that. 'What happened when you were twenty-five?'

Jones shook his head. 'Let's not go there. I shouldn't even have brought it up.'

He could see from her eyes that she knew it had to do with his scars. She didn't press. 'Okay.'

Molly had some scars of her own – even more faded than his, pencil point thin on both of her wrists. He'd first noticed them last night, when he'd come to her tent for the second time. But if he wasn't going to talk about his, it didn't seem fair to ask about hers.

Molly opened the container of lemonade and poured them each a cup. She handed one to him and took a long drink from the other. 'However, there *is* something you need to know about *me* before we go any further.'

Jones was silent, knowing that she would tell him whatever it was she wanted to tell him if he just waited long enough.

'True confession time,' she said.

He waited.

She wasn't done stalling. 'Before we, you know, pass the point of no return.'

She took another slug from her cup, then, balancing it on her knee, she put the lemonade back into the cooler. The boat was drifting close to the river's edge, and the sun was streaming through the trees, the dappled light playing games with her face. Jones just watched her and waited and tried not to worry about what she was about to say.

She was married, she was dying of cancer, she was really a man . . . Christ, he knew. She was a *nun*.

'I need to tell you that . . .' Molly took a deep breath. 'I've recently become a grandmother.'

He laughed in relief. He couldn't help it. 'No shit?'

'Nope.'

'Well . . . congratulations.'

She was looking at him as if she expected him to do or say something more.

'Boy or a girl?' he asked.

'Girl,' she said. 'My . . . daughter had a little girl. Caroline.'

'That's great.'

But that still wasn't what she wanted from him. So he said, 'I didn't know you had a daughter.'

'Yes,' she said. 'Yes, I do.' And still she looked at him expectantly.

Jones gave up guessing. 'Molly, if there's something I'm supposed to do or say, you're going to have to give me a bigger hint. This is kind of out of my realm of experience. Children, grandchildren . . . What am I supposed to say here that I'm not saying?'

'Nothing,' she said. 'You're not supposed to say anything. It's just . . .'

Here it came, thank God.

'Isn't it a total turn-off?' she asked. 'Knowing I'm . . . Lord, I'm someone's *grand*mother.'

Jones had to use every one of his poker-playing skills to keep a straight face. 'Gee,' he said. 'I don't know. But maybe if you promise to keep your teeth in while we're doing it . . .'

She laughed. 'Dave. I've just exposed myself to you. I've

shared one of my biggest insecurities, and you're making *fun* of me?'

Jones put his cup down. He stood up, took her cup from her hands and put that down, too. Pulled her to her feet. 'Give me your hand.' She did. God, he loved her hands with those long, graceful fingers. 'Promise not to be offended?'

She nodded.

He brought her hand down to his package. Placed it right there, right on top of him, so she could see for herself that he was far, *far* from being turned off.

'Oh, my,' she said, but she didn't pull her hand back. On the contrary, she wasn't at all shy about exploring what was beneath her fingers.

For a few seconds, he couldn't speak. He had to clear his throat to get his voice to work. 'Say "I'm a grandmother",' he instructed.

She laughed. 'I'm a grandmother.'

'I don't know,' he said, gazing into her eyes. 'I think that might've made me even harder. Kind of tough to tell if it's knowing more about you or if it's your touch that turns me on the most.'

The smile and the kiss that Molly gave him was right out of his wildest dreams.

'Do you know what I've been fantasizing all morning?' she whispered as he held her close, as he ran his hands up beneath her blouse and touched her incredibly smooth skin. She was so soft.

'No,' he said, 'but I'm praying it involves me.'

'I fantasized that once we headed down river, I wouldn't have to say a thing. We'd both just know it was finally time to make love. I'd just smile at you and go under the canopy, and I'd take off my clothes.'

He had to laugh. 'I was thinking almost exactly the same thing.'

'And you'd look at me that way you always look at me.' Her voice was husky. 'As if I'm the most desirable woman in the entire world.'

'And then you'd lie back on the mattress,' he continued, 'and let me look at you some more—'

'While you take off your clothes for me,' she finished, 'and let *me* look at *you*.'

'That wasn't part of what I was thinking,' he said. 'But I can work with it.'

'Good,' she said as she pulled out of his arms and headed for the canopy.

Her sandals came off and she shook her hair free from its braid.

She watched him, a small smile playing about the corners of her mouth as she worked the buttons open on her blouse, giving him only the briefest glimpses of what lay beneath. Black lace. Pale skin. Full breasts.

The combination of all three together was heart-stoppingly erotic.

Finally the last button was opened, and her blouse slid down her shoulders and onto the deck. Her skirt followed with a swish of silk and there she was, Molly Anderson, in the black lace underwear that he knew – he *knew* – she'd put on just for him.

She unhooked her bra, slipped out of her panties and . . .

Granny was not the first word that came to mind.

She was overweight by America's foolish standards, but not by Jones's. To him, she was perfection. Soft and smooth and completely, lushly, provocatively female.

She was Mother Nature, Mother Earth – with beautiful,

full breasts peaked with generous dark nipples and womanly hips that could cradle and comfort and take a man to heaven without him fearing he'd snap her in two.

She laughed. 'I love it when you smile like that.'

'I love it when you're naked like that,' he countered.

'I'm not feeling nervous anymore,' she told him. 'Just . . . really ready for some of that full penetration sex that you've spoken of so often.'

She settled down on the air mattress, arranging herself back on the pillows so that she was half sitting up, hair spread out around her. Gravity did amazing things to her breasts, accentuating the taut erection of her nipples. With her eyes heavy lidded and that little smile on her face, she was a picture of total female arousal.

It was all he could do to walk slowly toward her, to keep himself from tearing off his clothes and lunging into her.

He kept his movements controlled, deliberate, as he pulled his T-shirt over his head, as he kicked his feet free from his sandals.

He hesitated for only the briefest fraction of a second before he unfastened his shorts, but then he remembered. This woman had already seen him naked. She knew about his scars.

All of them.

And she'd even promised not to ask him about them.

Jones pushed off his shorts and Molly's smile widened. 'Still no underwear,' she said. 'I'm curious, Dave. Is that by choice, or from the lack of a reasonably priced department store in the neighborhood?'

'By choice,' he told her. It was bizarre. She was naked and he was naked, and they were having a conversation about his lack of underwear. 'Although, I got used to not wearing any back when I didn't have much of a choice about anything. Now wearing it makes me feel like I have too much clothing on.' He paused. 'You're unbelievably beautiful, by the way.'

'You are, too,' she said. 'Come over here.'

'Not yet. I'm not done looking.'

'I want to touch you.'

'Yeah, well, the feeling's mutual. But too bad. I'm taking my time. I've been waiting months for this.'

'Months?'

Jones smiled at her. 'I've been walking around in this state ever since I first saw you. A few more minutes isn't going to hurt too much.' It was the day he'd gone to the village to hire men to help him clear the airfield. Everyone had been so suspicious of who he was and where he'd come from – except Molly, who'd given him a warm smile. 'I'm a fan of anticipation, so if you don't mind, I'm just going to sit down over here for a little while and anticipate.'

She laughed as he did just that. 'You are such a liar. You're the King of Immediate Gratification. You just want to hear me beg. That's what this is about, isn't it?'

It was remarkable how well she knew him. He'd barely told her anything about himself, and yet . . . 'Begging would put a really nice spin on this particular fantasy, yeah.'

Molly didn't say a word. She just held his gaze, smiling that smile that made his blood run hot as she let her legs fall open.

'Or not,' Jones said, up and heading toward her. 'Not begging also works for me.'

She reached for him, sitting up to kiss him as he knelt between her legs, as he took her in his arms and lowered

185

himself on top of her. She wanted him inside of her, and God, he wanted to be there, too, but he hadn't yet put on a condom. Besides, he wanted to touch her first. To touch her and kiss her and taste her, to breathe her in.

But she was naked beneath him, and all that soft, smooth skin against his felt too damn good.

And when she pulled away from his kiss to gasp, 'Okay. I'm begging. Please. *Please*—'

It was a long ride home. There'd be plenty of time for foreplay after they got it on.

She had a condom waiting for him. He covered himself in record time, and then . . .

He'd always prided himself on being good in bed, good with women. He'd always had willpower to spare and could pleasure a woman for hours, giving her exactly what she wanted, without ever losing his own control.

But with Molly – the one woman in the world he was willing to die to be with – it was as if he were seventeen again.

A woman liked the first time to be meaningful. She liked eye contact and acknowledgment – a certain amount of reverence – that this, his very first moment inside of her, was special and unique.

But Jones crashed his way inside of Molly as if she were a hooker at one of the assembly line whorehouses in Jakarta. He was completely out of control even before he buried himself inside of her, and once he did, he couldn't have stopped if his life had depended on it.

She was ready for him, thank God. She was hot and wet and oh Jesus so tight, and the sound she made was sheer pleasure, and that word she was crying was *more*.

So he gave her more. Hard and fast and deep as she

sucked his tongue into her mouth and gripped him tightly, her legs locked around him. He fucked her – there was no other word for it – with absolutely no finesse.

It was sheer luck that she climaxed before he did. All he knew was that he was on the verge, and that it was going to happen too goddamn soon whether he slowed down or not. Not even the potential humiliation was enough to act as a damper.

'God, Molly,' he gasped. 'I can't keep from—'

But then she shattered around him, the power of her release making her shake.

That was all he needed. He was right on her heels, shouting her name in a rush of mind-blowing pleasure.

She still clung to him, so he let himself stay right there, on top of her, his heart still pounding, his face buried in her fragrant hair.

They drifted. It might've been two minutes, it might've been twenty. All he knew was that he wanted to stay right there, just like this, for the rest of his life.

But then Molly laughed. 'Good Lord,' she said. 'You certainly do deliver, David.'

David. Dave. Maybe it was frustration that, despite her words of satisfaction, he knew he should have made the sex better for her.

But whatever the cause, he knew that he didn't want her to call him Dave. Not now. Not ever. But especially not while they made love.

'Call me by my real name.' Jones lifted his head and looked down into her eyes. 'Call me Grady.'

'Shhh,' she said, skittering away from him, forcing him to pull out of her. 'Are you crazy?'

'Yes,' he said. He was. Definitely crazy. 'Come on, Molly.

Do you know how long it's been since someone who doesn't want to kill me has called me that?'

'Too bad,' she said. 'It's because I *don't* want to kill you that that name is never going to cross my lips. *Never.*'

She was serious, but he was, too.

'Please.' It was his turn to beg. He gestured around them at the boat, at the river. 'It's not going to get any safer than this.'

'I don't want to get into the habit,' she told him. 'I won't risk your life that way.'

'Please.'

'Don't ask me to do this!'

'Just this once.' Jesus, why was this so important to him? 'Just today. Let Molly Anderson make love to Grady Morant, not some lowlife loser named Jones.' His voice broke. '*Please.*'

Molly had tears in her eyes as she reached for him. As they sank back on the air mattress, he didn't know if he was holding her or if she was holding him.

She kissed him – sweet kisses – as she ran her fingers through his hair.

'You're a dangerous man, Grady Morant,' she said in a voice that was softer even than a whisper. 'You have the power to make me want to do things I know damn well I shouldn't do.'

He kissed her – her mouth, her throat, her breasts – and she sighed. 'Maybe we should just stay out here on the river forever.'

'I don't know,' Jones murmured. 'Something tells me people would miss you and send out a search party.'

'No search party for you?' she asked.

'No. A lynch mob, maybe. But only because they would all assume I'd kidnapped you.'

'Oh, come on.'

'I could disappear,' he lifted his head to tell her, 'and unless you disappeared, too, no one would even notice I was gone.'

Molly touched his face. 'Not anymore.'

Jones kissed her, filled with a curious mix of emotions. Elation. Dread. Anger. Sooner or later, he was going to leave. Sooner or later, if he stayed too long, the past would catch up with him. He'd have to disappear before that happened.

He *would* disappear before that happened.

He tried to remember what it felt like to be missed, but Molly whispered, 'Make love to me again, Grady.'

Grady.

It felt better than it should have to be someone he'd long since buried in the past, and he kissed her again, angry both with himself and with her for making him feel things he shouldn't need to feel anymore.

He wanted to put on another condom, to lose himself in her again, hard and fast and rough, but he stopped himself. He slowed himself down, got back in control.

This time, he was going to do her really right.

Yeah, this time, he was going to make her miss him for the entire rest of her life.

Savannah would have been convinced that Ken was moments from falling asleep – if it weren't for the fact that he gently disengaged his fingers from hers.

His head was back and for the past hour he'd been staring blankly out the open door at the sameness of the jungle below as if hypnotized. He looked as if every muscle in his body were completely relaxed.

So she was caught off-guard as he suddenly launched himself across the helicopter's cabin. The men with the big guns were caught off-guard, too, and before anyone could do anything, Kenny opened the chopper's second sliding door – she hadn't even realized it was there – grabbed her briefcase and the crate that was holding it in place, and threw them both out of the chopper.

From where she sat, if she craned her neck, she could see both the crate and the case, tumbling toward the ground. The sun reflected crazily off the briefcase's metal surface.

The bigger of the gunmen – the Russian man who seemed to be in charge – was furious. He gave an order, and all four of the guns went up, aimed at Ken, who seemed to be inches from following the briefcase out the door, holding tightly to some kind of net attached to the wall.

'Kenny!' Savannah knew he'd gone too far this time. She didn't speak Russian, but it was obvious that in a matter of seconds Ken's bullet-riddled body was going to plunge toward the ground.

And it was a long way down.

'If you want that money, you better keep both of us alive,' Ken shouted at the big Russian. 'That briefcase doesn't just have a combination lock on the outside. There's also an interior lock that's voice activated – and it won't open unless the commands are given by both Savannah *and* me. Do you understand? Kill us – kill just *one* of us – and you won't get a dime of that money.'

One of the gunmen shouted something in Russian.

'No, I'm not lying,' Ken countered. Did he speak Russian? Savannah realized that there was so much she didn't know about him, so much she wanted to know. Please God, don't let him die!

190

'The lock's got a built-in security device,' he continued. 'The money inside's been treated with a chemical that'll cause it to burn very quickly at a very high temperature upon exposure to oxygen. Yeah, I know what you're thinking, but you don't actually believe I could make this shit up, do you?'

Yes. Savannah knew he was making it all up. She'd bought the case herself just a few days ago and there was no interior lock. But the Russian didn't know that, and Ken's delivery was so convincing, she nearly found herself believing him.

'If the case is tampered with, or if you try to override or bypass the lock in any way,' he warned them, 'it'll fail to trigger the release of an agent to counteract that chemical, and your two hundred and fifty K will be ashes. This is SOP – standard op – for traveling with sensitive documents. It's not usually done for money, but we wanted an insurance policy.'

The gunmen were having a heated argument in Russian. The tall man shut them up with a single hand in the air. 'Why did you throw the briefcase from the chopper? Why not simply show us this second lock?'

'And have you force us to open the case right here and now?' Ken shook his head as he laughed. Four guns were pointed at him, and he was *laughing*. Yes, there was a *lot* Savannah didn't know about this man. 'No, this way we land, and you and I and Ms von Hopf here can discuss alternative solutions to all of our problems while the four Stooges take a few hours to find the money.'

The Russian looked to the front of the chopper and shouted something. The pilot shouted something back.

Again, Ken spoke as if he understood. 'Yes, there is,' he

shouted. 'There's a river about five kilometers back the way we came. I saw a clearing big enough to set this helo down. It'll be tight but if your guy's any good, he should be able to do it.'

The Russian didn't look happy.

Ken shrugged. 'Either that, or forget about the money.'

The Russian shouted a command to the pilot, and the chopper – or *helo* as Kenny called it – headed back the way they'd come.

Ken looked at her then, for the first time since he'd released her hand. He looked her in the eyes, then looked at her shoes, then back into her eyes.

He was obviously sending her a silent message, and it could only mean one thing.

Those stupid-ass shoes . . . weren't designed for running . . .

Heart pounding, Savannah slipped off first one shoe and then the other.

And Kenny nodded at her. It was almost imperceptible. But she saw it. And she knew for sure.

As soon as this helo set down, it was going to be time to run.

Eight

'*I turned to see exactly what her idea of a 'Euro-God' was this week. And nearly dropped my champagne flute.*

It was Heinrich von Hopf. Right here in Manhattan,' Jones read aloud. He looked over the top of the book at Molly. '*Needless to say, he wasn't wearing his SS uniform. Dah, dah dum!*'

He sang what was supposed to be dark, suspenseful music, and Molly had to laugh. 'Don't stop there,' she said.

'It's the end of the chapter.'

'So turn the page. I want to find out what happens next.'

Jones put the book down and pulled her into his arms. 'Guess what? She survives the war.' He kissed her. 'She lives to the ripe old age of eighty-something and writes a book. And oh, yeah, her name – on the cover – is Ingerose Rainer *von Hopf*. I hate to break it to you, but that's a pretty large hint about how things are going to turn out between her and old Hank. It kind of kills the suspense, don't you think?'

'Can you imagine being an American spy during World War Two and actually marrying a man you knew was a Nazi spy?' Molly asked as he skimmed his hands down her body. For a man with such big, roughly callused hands, he had a remarkably soft touch.

'Is that really what she did?' Jones countered, far more interested in the curve of her waist than their conversation.

Molly pulled back from him and sat up. This deserved his full attention. 'I don't know because – gee – even though I do know she survived the war and married Hank somewhere down the line, I don't know the details because I haven't read the entire book. Was she still in love with him when they got married, or did she do it purely out of love of country? I think she must've loved him on *some* level, don't you? I mean, she lived with him as man and wife, so . . .'

'You said they were hot for each other right from the start,' he pointed out. He'd propped himself up on one elbow, the better to look at her. His gaze was almost as palpable as his touch, and hardly less distracting. 'Lust at first sight.' He smiled into her eyes. 'I know what that feels like.'

He was so beautiful and completely relaxed lying there. Dark hair, dark eyes, rugged features, hard body, open mind . . .

As long as she couldn't see the scars on his shoulders and the backs of his legs, she could pretend he was no different than any other man she'd found attractive enough to make love to. She could ignore his other scars as well – the emotional ones that had turned him into a grim, angry, defensive man who claimed he was more comfortable when he was alone.

A man who didn't have friends because – he said – friends could get him killed.

Without her friends, Molly would've shriveled up and died years ago.

'I think you better keep reading,' she told him.

'I can think of better things to do while naked and floating on a boat in the middle of nowhere.'

'Really?' she said. 'Because I was going to start a naked floating readers' group and see if you wanted to join. You know, hold regular meetings here on the boat . . . ?'

She was teasing, but he answered as if she'd spoken seriously. 'You know, I was actually wondering if . . .' He cleared his throat, and she realized he was working hard to come across as nonchalant. She had to wonder if his entire relaxed pose was also just an act. 'If this – today – was just, uh, a one time thing.' He made himself smile. 'A bout of temporary insanity.'

He was trying hard to hide it, but she saw it anyway. A flash of hope in his eyes. Hope that this thing between them – their friendship, their relationship, whatever it was – was something real.

No doubt he didn't realize exactly what she was feeling. If he did, he'd run away so fast, she wouldn't see more than a blur before he vanished for good. No, if she wanted him to stick around for a while – and she did – it wouldn't do to tip him off to the fact that somewhere between the day he'd first appeared in the village and this incredibly precious moment, she'd managed to fall in love with him.

Not that that was such a big surprise. Molly knew herself well, knew she had the ability to find something to love in everyone she knew. But her feelings for this particular man were heart-stoppingly intense.

He honestly hadn't understood why her having a daughter who'd just had a daughter might've been a potential problem. Some men – some people – were so overcome by their fear of aging, all she had to do was whisper the word *grandmother* and they would've dived overboard to get away from her. But Jones – dear, sweet Jones, who tried so hard to be the tough guy, who'd actually shamed himself in his attempt to take the intimacy out of their physical relationship by making it purely monetary – probably wasn't going to give it a second thought.

Molly was far too practical to hope their relationship would last. How could it? She wasn't going to stay on Parwati Island forever. In fact, her job here was nearly done. She was going to leave. And he was going to leave, too. Probably first.

Instead of wishing for what couldn't be, she was resigned to cherishing her memories of this day, and all the beautiful days with him yet to come, long after they both were gone.

He was waiting for her to respond, so she laughed. Keep it light, Molly. Don't scare him.

'It's definitely insanity,' she told him. 'But I was thinking this was – to be embarrassingly cliché – the start of a beautiful friendship.'

His smile was much more real now. 'Okay,' he said. 'Yeah. That's pretty much what I was thinking, too.'

'Now would be a really good time for you to invite me to your place for dinner,' Molly suggested.

'Dinner? Jesus, you don't want to come for dinner. I can't cook for shit.'

'I won't be coming for the food.'

His eyes got even hotter. 'How's tomorrow?'

'What time?' she asked.

'As soon as you can get there because I know that by six A.M., I'm already going to want to fuck you so bad I'll be half blind.'

She had to laugh. 'You know, forget about the name

Dave. I think from now on I'm going to call you Mr Romance because you have such an elegant way with words.'

He grinned. He actually *grinned* as if he were having fun with their banter, and Molly's heart turned to total mush.

'You wanted honesty,' he said. 'I'm just being honest.'

'I think you need to borrow a few of my romance novels,' Molly told him, 'to learn how to be honest and confess your secret ardent desire for me in a less . . . *earthy* manner.'

'My ardent desire's not too much of a secret at this particular moment.'

No, indeed, it most certainly wasn't.

Molly handed him the book he'd been reading to her. 'Where were we?'

Jones snorted. 'For a do-gooder, you really get off on torture, don't you?'

She smiled happily at him. 'I remember. Rose and Hank meet for the first time in years.'

'You're pretty twisted. Of course, I happen to really love that about you.'

He loved that about her. It was crazy the way her heart leapt at his words.

'You said you enjoyed anticipation,' she countered. 'I, on the other hand, love it when you read aloud to me. This way we should both be completely happy.'

Jones crawled closer. 'I was lying, remember?'

She kept him at bay with her foot. 'You have such a sexy voice. Hearing you read makes me . . . hot.'

'Yeah, go on, devil woman. Look at me like that and lick your lips. You think I don't know you do that just to torment me? We both know that driving me crazy is what makes you hot.'

'Either way,' she pointed out, 'after five, ten pages – tops

– I'm going to want to fuck you so bad I'll be half blind.' She smiled at him as sweetly as possible. 'Did I get that right, Mr Romance?'

Jones laughed. 'Jesus, Molly, I—' He stopped laughing, stopped speaking. He just looked at her with the funniest expression on his face.

'What?' she pressed, wanting to know what he could possibly be thinking.

But he shook his head and opened the book. *'Did you come here tonight with your husband?'* he read aloud.

It was the first thing Heinrich von Hopf said to me. It had been three and a half very long years since I'd seen him last, and he didn't even start with hello.

At first I didn't know what he was talking about. 'I'm not married,' I told him before I remembered exactly what he was referring to.

Shortly after my return to New York in the summer of '39, I'd started receiving letters from him. Love letters reminding me of our dreams of travel and adventure. Passionate letters proclaiming his love and devotion, telling me how much he missed me, just what he would give to kiss me again.

I would read his letters, and my heart would break all over again. I knew his words were nothing but lies.

So I finally wrote back to him, and I lied, too. I told him that I was very sorry, but my love affair with a young man I knew from college had been rekindled, and we were engaged to be married.

After that, his letters stopped.

'It didn't work out between me and . . .' I couldn't remember my fictional intended's name.

'Charles.' Heinrich actually knew it.

'Yes,' I said. 'Because he . . . well, he *died*. In the war. At Pearl Harbor. It was horrible – shocking. I've tried hard to forget him – I guess it worked.'

Jones stopped reading, looking up toward the canopy that stretched over their heads.

Molly pushed herself up on one elbow. 'What—'

'Shhh,' he cut her off and she realized he was listening, intently.

And then, just as she could begin to hear something rumbling in the distance, he said. 'Chopper. I heard it earlier, heading east, off in the distance, but now it's coming back and it's coming right this way.'

He put down the book, and reached for his clothes, tossing her skirt and blouse toward her as well, as the noise from the approaching helicopter grew steadily louder.

Molly didn't bother with her underwear. She just hid it under the air mattress, along with the condom wrappers they'd discarded.

Jones had taken his gun from wherever he'd been hiding it, and was checking to see that it was properly loaded.

'You don't really think you're going to need that, do you?' she couldn't keep from asking.

'Only people I know on this island who have access to a chopper are the gun runners, the drug lords and crazy-ass General Badaruddin's troops. None of them are the type I'd want to have so much as a phone conversation with, without being armed.'

The boat was drifting close to the middle of the river. They had reached one of the spots where it was wide and relatively shallow.

Jones started the outboard motor with a roar and quickly

steered them to the shore where the trees and brush of the jungle bent over the water. Cutting the engine, he pulled them under the canopy of low hanging branches.

They would be hidden from anything flying overhead, but they could still be seen from the river.

'Get over here and get down,' Jones ordered tersely.

Molly looked at him, eyebrow raised.

'Please,' he added. 'Please come here so that I can please keep you safe. Please. Jesus H. Christ, next you're going to tell me to smile.'

She went to him, under the canopy.

'Whoever they are, they're going to fly overhead without seeing us,' Molly told him. 'In three minutes – less – they'll be gone. And then I'm not going to *tell* you to smile, I'm going to *make* you smile.'

He stopped looking so grim. In fact, he even almost smiled as he kissed her. 'Forget the reading aloud. Forget the torture. I think you really get off on being rescued.'

She smiled into his eyes. 'I must confess, the Han Solo, man of action, thing is impressive. Can I be Princess Leia?'

But Jones wasn't looking at her anymore. He was looking upstream. He swore softly.

About three hundred yards away, in a small clearing by the edge of the river that the boat had passed just moments earlier, the helicopter came in for a landing.

The mistake was the large Russian's. He was clearly in charge of this abduction and in command of the men on board the helo. He was the boss, and as the boss, he should have made sure that the crates of cargo this Puma was carrying were secured to the bulkhead.

That way they couldn't slide around.

Or be used as a weapon.

As soon as the helo touched down, Ken heaved one of the heavy crates at the Russian, who, just like a cooperative head bowling pin, knocked over both Uzi One and Uzi Two and the lucky dude with the HK MP5.

'Run!' Ken shouted at Savannah, who, bless her, took off through the open door like an Olympic sprinter.

Except, god *damn*, she ran across the open area, along the river, instead of heading for cover.

'Toward the jungle!' he shouted at her, as he grabbed for the Uzi that had – in a surprising show of good luck – skittered across the metal deck and almost directly into his hands.

It wasn't perfect luck, though. He would have preferred to have the HK, but beggars couldn't be choosers.

He grabbed the weapon and ran.

Boom. Magnum .44 was firing at him, and Ken felt the giant bullet whizzing past his head, like a softball traveling at thirteen hundred feet per second.

Uzi Two had regained his hold on his weapon, and he fired, too – the staccato, tearing sound of modern death.

The shots were meant to frighten and to stop him – or to hit him in the legs – which meant they'd bought his story about the interior lock on the attaché case.

The Russian and his gang couldn't risk killing them. If they did, they might lose all that money.

This was going to be a piece of cake. Ken caught up with Savannah, grabbed her and pulled her toward the jungle.

He would hide Savannah – he could tuck her someplace dark where these clowns would never find her – and make them hunt for him.

And Ken, he'd take them out one at a time until it was

just him and the helo pilot. And then it would just be him. He'd never flown a Puma, but he was smart enough to be able to fly Savannah back to that little town he'd seen on the coast of this island. Four hours, five tops, and he'd get her to safety and be on his way home.

But first he had to keep these bozos from following them so he could get Savannah stashed away. He glanced back and saw that Uzi One and Magnum .44 were jumping out of the Puma, ready to give chase.

He opened fire, trying at least to drive them back to cover, at best to take them out. These assholes had been planning to push him and Savannah out of that helo at seven hundred feet. And as soon as they found the attaché case and discovered Ken's bluff, they, too, would be trying to do more than shoot them in the kneecaps.

Uzi and Magnum dove back into the bird, and Ken kept on firing, riddling the damn thing with bullets, even as he continued to run with Savannah for the jungle.

And then, holy Christ, it shouldn't have happened. Not even a one in a billion lucky shot should've done it.

The Puma fireballed.

One minute it was there, and the next . . . boom.

Ken grabbed Savannah, trying to surround her with his body as the shock wave from the explosion sent them flying.

He rolled as he landed, attempting to keep his weight off of her, cushioning her as best as he could, which sadly wasn't very well.

Ears ringing, he didn't take the time to check to see which parts of him hurt like hell and why. He just grabbed the Uzi, dragged Savannah to her feet and pulled her the last few dozen yards to the cover of the jungle brush.

Jesus, the Puma was gone. Black clouds of oily smoke

mushroomed up into the sky, and all that remained of the helo – a metal skeleton – blazed.

'Are you okay?' he asked Savannah.

He didn't wait for her to respond; she was probably in shock. He wasn't a hospital corpsman like Jay Lopez, but he knew enough to get by. He ran his hands down her arms and legs, checking for broken bones.

Her designer suit was ruined, her pantyhose shredded and her feet bruised and scraped, but nothing was broken, thank God. Amazingly, she was still clutching her handbag.

'You're bleeding,' she said, and he realized that her gaze was clear, her eyes focused. She wasn't in shock. She was just badly shaken.

'I'm all right,' he told her. It was only half a lie. His elbow was thrashed. The good news was that it wasn't broken. The bad news was that he'd scraped the shit out of it, and in this bacteria-loving climate, an infection could be a serious threat.

He'd packed antibiotics, but they were in his knapsack – which he'd last seen beneath Uzi Two's feet on the deck of the helo. Unlike Savannah, he hadn't managed to keep his pack or his duffle bag with him.

She peeked out of the brush at the flaming remains of the helo. 'They're all dead.'

It wasn't a question, but he answered it anyway. 'Yeah.'

'They were going to kill us, weren't they?'

'Yup. And when they don't show up wherever it was they were going next, someone's going to connect their disappearance to this smoke signal here, and send another helo to check it out. We need to find your money and be far from here when they show up. We need to hope they didn't send a message to their home base reporting that you and I made a run for it. If they did, a second helo's going to be out here that much sooner. They'll definitely be looking for us, *and* they'll be pissed.'

Savannah nodded, her blue eyes clear and steady as she gazed at him. 'You think they sent a message.'

'Yes,' Ken said, 'I do. The large guy – the Russian – was getting and receiving radio messages all throughout the flight.'

'This is all my fault,' she said. 'I should have known Uncle Alex would never have asked me for that much money. In cash. How could I have been so stupid? He's dead, isn't he? Alex?'

'I think there's a good chance that he is.' Ken went for the cold hard truth before thinking it through. Her eyes filled and he realized his mistake. They didn't have time for her to dissolve into tears.

But she managed not to cry. Instead, she pulled herself to her feet. 'I nearly got you killed, too, but that's going to change right now. We need to get moving, get somewhere safe – get you back on a plane for Hong Kong.'

Out on the river, an engine – an outboard motor – started.

And Ken yanked Savannah down on top of him. Who the hell was out there?

And then he saw it. Holy Jesus, how could he have missed it? It was more like a raft than a real boat, with a wide, shallow hull and a faded fabric canopy shielding the bow. It moved out from the shadows at the edge of the river – that's how he'd missed it. Whoever they were, they'd been trying to hide. And he hadn't been looking for a boat. He hadn't been thinking of much besides getting Savannah away from the men on the helo.

Senior Chief Wolchonok would've smacked him upside his head. Because in this part of the world, danger was everywhere. God *damn*, he better make sure she wasn't sitting on a poisonous snake.

No, she was sitting on him.

'Stay down,' he told her, pushing her off his lap and making sure the Uzi was locked and loaded.

Jones pulled out from the overhanging branches and vines, and pointed the boat down river. For something with the aerodynamics of a floating shoebox, this thing could move when coaxed.

'What are you doing?' Molly called over the roar of the outboard motor.

'It's called getting the hell out of here,' he shouted back.

'We can't just leave! Those people need help!'

She was serious. World War III had started just up river. Machine guns had been fired, and a helicopter had gone up in a pyrotechnics display he'd never before witnessed the likes of.

And now Molly wanted to do her Good Samaritan thing.

'Here's how it works,' he told her. 'Group A fires their guns at Group B. Group B fires back, and Group A's chopper explodes, killing everyone on board, everyone within twenty feet. At least.'

'You don't know that for sure,' she countered.

'Yes,' he said. 'I do. Meanwhile Group B's still out there with their big, bad guns. And Group A's chopper is going to be noticeably absent – wherever it is that it belongs. And someone else from Group A is going to come looking. When that happens, *we* are going to be far, far away from here.'

'Dave,' Molly said. 'Grady. Please. I can't just run away

without checking to make sure someone didn't survive that. If they did, they surely need help.'

And Jones knew that if he didn't turn around now, she'd come back later. Without him. And then she probably would run into whoever had lost that chopper. And they would be furious and out for blood and revenge.

He spun the boat around.

'We'll get as close as we can,' he told her. 'But you're not getting off this boat. Do you understand?'

Molly made a sound that might've been agreement.

But fortunately – or unfortunately for these poor bastards in the chopper – as they went past the inferno, it was more than obvious, even to Molly, that no one could have survived.

'They were probably bad men. Killers and thieves,' Jones said, after he turned the boat around again and headed for home. After they'd gone some distance he'd cut the motor. 'The world's probably a better place with them gone.'

'No one's so bad that they can't turn their life around,' Molly said quietly. 'Everyone deserves a second chance. They won't get theirs now.'

Was that what she was doing with him? Giving him a second chance, thinking he had both the motivation and inclination to 'turn his life around'? If that was what she thought, she was going to be bitterly disappointed.

They were still a few miles from the village, and he reached for her, needing her desperately, hating her for making him want things he couldn't have, for making him want to be someone he could no longer be. Hating her for making him realize that, after all this time, he still had a heart, and that he hadn't forgotten how to dream.

*

The boat finally disappeared around a bend in the river, but when Savannah shifted, about to stand up, Ken motioned for her to stay put.

It didn't make sense. They were out here in the middle of the jungle, in the middle of nowhere. Ken seemed convinced that in a very short time another helicopter filled with gun-wielding men would be out searching for them, with every intention of killing them and taking her briefcase of money.

They should have been jumping up and down to get the boat's attention, to ask for a ride back to a place where people didn't shoot other people. To hell with the money. Let the men in the helicopter find it and keep it. It was as good as gone anyway; it didn't seem possible that she and Ken would be able to locate it. Talk about a needle in a haystack. She wouldn't even know where to start to look, wouldn't know in which direction to walk.

And the money seemed insignificant considering all the lives that had just been lost.

She felt sick just thinking about it, about Alex. How could he be dead? He was so full of life. Unlike her father, Karl, his twin, who in many ways acted as if he'd been dead for years.

Ken finally stopped scanning the river, searching for God knows what, and turned to her. 'Give me your jacket.'

She hesitated. She was soaked with perspiration both from fear and this oppressive heat. Quite frankly, she stank, and her jacket did, too.

'Come on, come on,' Ken was impatient. He put his gun down and fished in his pocket for something. 'We have to get moving.'

'It's . . . extremely ripe,' she apologized as she slipped her arms free.

'Join the club.' He took it from her. And promptly, with the use of his pocket knife, tore it in half. Right up the back. He threw it back to her in two pieces. 'Wrap your feet.'

She stared at him.

'We're going to be heading through some pretty dense brush. I'd offer you my sandals, but they'd be like snowshoes on you.'

Savannah sat down. She didn't have a clue how to do this. Her feet were sore and scraped. She didn't even want to touch them. But he was waiting for her, watching.

First things first. She wriggled out of her pantyhose and he stopped watching. She tried slipping her foot into one of the sleeves and gasped at its contact with her poor scraped toes.

He sat down then, too, muttering something – curses, probably – under his breath. He took off his sandals. 'Maybe I'm wrong. Maybe you should try these on.' He held them out to her.

She didn't take them. 'If you gave me your sandals, what would you wear?'

'I'll make you carry me piggyback.'

He'd actually managed to make a joke, but Savannah was the one now who couldn't laugh. She just grimly kept wrapping her right foot. 'I got you into this mess. No way am I taking your sandals, too.'

Ken crouched down in front of her, gently lifting her other foot. It was bruised, battered and bleeding from a cut on her heel. 'I'm sorry about this.'

She pulled her foot free, wrapped that one, too. 'Yeah, well, like you said, I should've had sneakers on. And it's better than being dead. Just think – every step I take, I'll be reminded just how very alive I am.'

Ken picked up one of his sandals. 'Maybe I can somehow adjust these—'

'Please,' she said. 'Don't. Let's just get out of here.'

He put his sandals back on. 'Maybe what we should do is get you hidden someplace. Let me go after the money by myself. We're going to want to head back this way – to stick relatively close to the river. Chances are it'll lead us directly to that little town on the coast.'

Panic made her heart pound. She'd as much as told him to ditch her while they were on the helicopter. But now, faced with the very real possibility, she was terrified by the idea. And even if he didn't *mean* to ditch her, how on earth would he ever find her again if he left her here?

'Okay,' she said as evenly as she could manage – which wasn't very evenly at all. 'If that's what you want to do.'

'On the other hand,' he said, 'maybe it's better to stick together until we know what's up. I mean, if they send in four different helos to search for us, I'm going to want you near me.'

Savannah took a deep breath. 'Kenny, maybe you should just forget about the money, forget about me, and get out of here. They may not even know about you – *I'm* the one they'll be looking for.'

He laughed, but it wasn't because he thought she was funny. It was with contempt. 'Jesus. You must really think I'm an asshole. That I'd just walk away from you? Leave you out in the middle of the freaking jungle?'

'You don't even like me.' She tried to make him understand. 'And you almost died. Those people did die because of me today, and you very well could have been one of them.'

Savannah caught herself trying to tuck her silk blouse

209

neatly back into her skirt, then realized how ridiculous that was, considering she was sweaty and smeared with jungle mud. Her footwear was designer, but she was pretty sure Donna Karan hadn't meant for her jacket to be worn quite that way.

Don't cry, don't cry, don't cry.

She clung to her handbag as she turned away, afraid if she so much as looked at Kenny, the floodgates would open. She'd been holding so much in for so long, if she started to cry, she might never stop. 'I will *not* put you in danger again. And if being with me means that you're in danger—'

'I don't know what Adele told you about me.' Annoyance rang in his voice. 'But here's the deal, babe. I'm not going to freaking ditch you in the freaking jungle. That's number one. Number two. We should go collect that money. As cavalier as you are about leaving it for the locals like one big-ass tip, the fact is, we might be able to use it to buy our way out of here.'

'I'm not *cavalier* about losing a quarter of a million dollars,' she protested. 'I just don't think it's worth dying—'

'Number three,' he interrupted. 'If the people who are looking for you are anything like the men in the helo, they're amateurs. You stay close to me, you do what I tell you to without question, and evading them will be a breeze. I'm a SEAL, Savannah. You and I can live off the land and hide from these guys forever if we have to. This isn't going to be any more dangerous than any other camping trip you've ever been on.

'Number four,' he continued. 'Those assholes didn't die because of you. They died because they were greedy. Because taking your money wasn't enough – they had to prove to the world how bad they were by trying to take your life, too. They got what they deserved, do you understand?'

She nodded, wanting to believe him.

'Good. Let's move. Let me know if I'm going too fast, okay?'

She nodded again, and he headed confidently away from the river. How did he knew which way to go?

Savannah followed. 'I've never been camping,' she told him.

Ken turned back to look at her, his expression incredulous. 'Never? Not even when you were a kid?'

'If we live through this,' she told him, 'I'll introduce you to my mother and you'll realize what a completely absurd question that is.'

'You don't need to,' he said. 'I see more than enough of her in you.'

Savannah stopped following him. There wasn't a young woman alive who didn't dread the idea of turning into her mother. 'I think that might be the rudest thing anyone's ever said to me.'

He didn't stop walking. 'If the truth is rude, that's not my fault, it's yours, don't you think?'

'I'm *nothing* like my mother.'

'Yeah? Then why are you wearing her clothes?'

She hurried to catch up to him, ignoring the pain in her feet. 'These are *not* my mother's clothes, thank you very much. There are *my* clothes – clothes I wear to work. To court.'

'They suck,' Ken said. 'They make you look ugly and they suck. I bet you don't even own a pair of jeans.'

'I do so,' she retorted, stung. He thought she was *ugly*? What happened to *you are so fucking beautiful*? Or was that

211

just something he'd said to get her naked? 'I bet *you* don't own a pair of pants that doesn't have fifty different pockets. I bet you don't even know what size jacket you wear. I bet you can't even tie your own tie.'

'Guilty, guilty, and guilty.' He moved through the jungle without hesitation, as if he knew exactly where the money was, and was intending to lead her directly to it. 'Ask me if I give a damn.'

Savannah closed her mouth, unwilling to give him the satisfaction.

'I bet I spend way more time comfortable and far happier than you,' Ken told her.

She didn't say a word. She just grimly marched on, on her painful feet. But she would probably bet that, too.

'Whoa,' Ken said as he found the broken crate not far from where the briefcase was half buried in the soft dirt.

'What is it?' Savannah asked, shuffling closer to look over his shoulder.

'Dynamite,' he told her. There were fuses here, too. It was a regular little do-it-yerself demolition kit.

'That's why the helicopter blew up,' she said. Smart woman.

'Yeah.' It was, indeed why the helo had fireballed. His bullets hadn't miraculously hit some vital part of the engine to make that puppy blow. No, they'd merely hit the cargo, created the right amount of friction to cause a spark and . . . Blam.

This had been one crate of maybe three dozen on board that helo. Whoever had ordered this from Death and Destruction-R-Us wasn't looking to do some little home project, like blasting a new hole for the family latrine. No, there had been enough explosives on the helo to clear a big enough patch of the jungle to build Disney-Indonesia. Or, far more likely, to grow acres and acres of cannabis or poppies.

'Whoever was waiting for this delivery isn't going to be happy,' Ken said.

That would make a crapload of unhappy people wandering around this part of the jungle – including him. The good news was that the money had survived its plunge to the ground thanks to the quality of the metal attaché case. The bad news was that he now had a battered metal attaché case filled with money to drag around with them as they traipsed through the brush trying to stay hidden.

Not only would it be a bitch and a half to carry, but it was made of shiny metal. Ready to reflect the sun and act as a signal beacon to the rest of the world. Here we are! Come and blow our heads off!

Yeah, perfect.

Ken dragged the broken crate and the dynamite back toward Savannah, who was not sitting on the money. Savannah, who was camping challenged, who was the second part of this perfect equation, dressed in just about *the* most inappropriate clothes anyone could wear in the jungle.

Okay, maybe that was an exaggeration. A nun's habit, an evening gown, a stripper's tassels and g-string all would have been worse.

No, strike that last bit. The tassels and g-string would have at least given him inspiration.

She'd taken off one of the pieces of jacket she'd wrapped around her foot and was examining a nasty looking cut on her big toe when she heard him coming and quickly covered her foot back up again.

He'd been able to tell from her breathing that every single step she'd taken had been painful. But she hadn't said a word. Not one single complaint.

He'd been about to offer to carry her more than once, but each time, she'd given him such a venomous look – as if she could read his mind – that he hadn't dared.

'You wouldn't happen to have a duffle bag or a backpack in your handbag would you?' he asked her now. 'Large enough to hold both the money and all this dynamite?'

He was only half kidding. Adele had managed to carry some pretty amazing stuff in her purse. Of course, Adele had carried a bag that was twice the size of Savannah's. Come to think of it, it made sense because Adele was twice the size of Savannah.

Savannah shook her head, no.

'What have you got in there?' he asked. 'Maybe we should take a minute and do a quick inventory, see what we've got, see if we can somehow lighten our load.' He went through his pockets, pulling everything out and dumping it in a relatively dry spot in front of her. 'Knife, keys, wallet, passport, a coupla squished power bars – that's good, we're bound to get hungry – and . . . oops.'

Condoms.

He was carrying around a half a dozen. He stuffed them back into his pocket, but not before she saw them.

He gave her a weak smile. 'I just, you know, always carry 'em.'

That was a lie and she knew it.

'If we get bored, we can use them to make balloon animals,' he added.

She was not at all amused.

'All right,' he said. 'So I'm not here purely because I'm a

nice guy. You're a lawyer – sue me. What have you got in your bag?'

Still silent, she handed it to him.

He unzipped it. It was neat and clean – no two-year-old receipts or stale, loose M&M's to be found. In fact, the contents read like an anal retentive neat-freak's checklist. Leather wallet with credit cards carefully arranged and, Jesus, more cash than he made in a month – half in American dollars, half in Indonesian currency.

The money was neatly arranged, too, every bill facing up, ones to one hundreds in crisp, perfect order, like she was ready to play real-life Monopoly.

Ken had been one of those kids who'd kept his Monopoly money in one huge chaotic pile. Orange five hundreds mixed in with the yellow tens and the pink fives. No doubt about it. Their relationship had been doomed from the start.

Savannah von Hopf wasn't really the hot chick with the messy hair dressed in his clothes on his patio and naked in his bed. She was the designer attired, perfectly put together, absolutely in control young woman who'd scared him to death back at the Hotel Del Coronado. The woman he'd spent the night with hadn't really existed.

And that was a goddamn shame.

He kept unloading her purse.

Cell phone. *Cell phone!* Please God, let there be some wealthy drug lord set up nearby with a satellite dish . . .

He flipped it open. He'd call Sam Starrett. Or Johnny Nilsson if Sam wasn't around. Or the senior chief. Yeah, he'd call the senior first. He'd have a helo from the nearest US military installation out here in a matter of hours. There would be one hell of a roaming charge for the call but who the hell cared.

Except nothing happened. No 'searching for service' message. Nada. Zip. Zilch.

'I didn't get a chance to recharge it,' Savannah informed him. 'I do it at night, every night, but . . .'

But last night she'd been otherwise occupied. Yeah, he remembered. A little too well.

He snapped it shut. 'Yeah,' he said. 'Right. Well, that would've been too easy, huh?'

She looked so miserable, he added, 'It probably would've been out of range anyway. It's not worth getting your panties in a knot.'

'I've charged my phone battery every night for the past nearly ten years,' she told him. 'I swear to you, I haven't missed a night. Except for last night and the night before.'

She was serious. She probably went to bed at the same time every night, too. 2330 on the dot. Time to charge the cell phone and then climb into bed.

Scary.

He dug deeper into her purse.

Keys, passport, mini tin of Altoids, nice pen, change purse containing some coins – heaven forbid they float around loose and create unnecessary chaos, a small pack of tissues, a little bottle of hand sanitizer in a ziplock baggie – to prevent leakage no doubt.

He tossed that to her. 'Put this on your feet. And anywhere else you've got broken skin. Try to use as little as possible.'

She unwrapped her feet and he dove back into her bag.

There were some zinc lozenges, probably in case someone sneezed on her on the airplane, a granola bar – one of the health food varieties that tasted like gravel and twigs – a little plastic bottle of painkiller, a travel sewing kit, a match book, the paperback book he'd seen her holding

216

but never reading on the plane, a spare pair of pantyhose, and – excuse me?

What was this? A demure little pink plastic case that held . . .

Tah-dah! Three foil-wrapped condoms.

'Well, well,' he said. 'Is this what you meant when you said you wanted to *start over*? You want to start over with my condoms, honey, or yours?'

She didn't say anything for a full thirty seconds and then, 'You're an unbelievable jerk,' she informed him.

He was aware of that, aware the moment the words had left his mouth that there would have been a far better chance of them actually using one of those condoms if he just kept his big mouth shut. But his jerk gene – highly dominant – had kicked in.

Still, it was probably for the best. He was ashamed of himself for still wanting her, even after knowing that she'd set out from the start to manipulate him. She wasn't his soulmate – as he'd had the stupidity to hope. Man, he was an idiot. Soulmate. Christ. Talk about fairy tales . . .

But the truth was, even though his chance of living happily ever after with this woman was nix, he still wanted another chance to make her come. And come.

And come.

God *damn*.

It was shallow, it was wrong, he'd end up *way* in over his head, but Ken knew the truth. If he could go back in time, he'd travel straight to her hotel room at the Del. He'd let her tell him that she'd come to San Diego specifically to find him, and – like she'd said she hoped he'd do – he'd force himself to laugh at the irony and at her resourcefulness in grabbing his interest.

And then he'd take off her clothes and bury his interest, so to speak, deeply inside of her.

If he had been just a little less stupid, he could've gotten it on with her in the Hong Kong airport and on the airbus flight to Jakarta. They could have shagged their way around the world. They could've been making use of one of those condoms he'd brought right this very moment as she showed him how much she appreciated his saving her life.

Instead, she was sitting there with her hair a mess again, streaks of mud on her face and clothes, giving him a baleful look with those incredible eyes.

He turned his attention back to the broken crate, wondering for the twenty-fifth time how the hell he was going to manage to carry that dynamite *and* the attaché case of money. Maybe there was some room in the case for some of the dynamite. Maybe . . .

'That's it?' She stood up. 'Conversation over? You have no response?'

'What's to respond to? You think I'm a jerk,' he said. 'This is not earthshaking news. Lots of people think I'm a jerk. What, do you want me to argue? No, I'm not a jerk? I'm a jerk, okay? I know it. You know it. Everybody and their flipping Uncle Fred knows it. *Shit.*'

Savannah laughed. She actually laughed.

Of course, that only served to piss him off even more. 'Good,' Ken told her. 'Great. Laugh at me, babe. You want someone to be polite, to come to whatever tea party you want to throw? Don't call me, okay? But if you need your ass saved, if you want to stay alive when other people want you dead—'

'I know,' she said. 'I'm sorry. I didn't mean to—'

He heard it before she did. 'God *damn.* Helo's coming.'

Christ, they had to get to cover. He looked around. Nearby there was a particularly dense growth of some kind of giant funky fern-type plant under an equally dense growth of trees. He pointed to it. 'Help me get the attaché case and the crate over there.'

She carried the case, he dragged the crate, and he covered them both with extra branches and dirt. 'Help me,' he said, and she helped him damn near bury the metal case.

He could tell just from listening that the helo was flying in a spiral search pattern, coming closer and closer each time. Next pass it was going to be overhead. And suddenly the patch of foliage didn't feel quite so thick. Particularly with Savannah dressed in light-colored clothes.

Ken grabbed her. 'Get down,' he ordered, pushing her under the ferns.

Shit, it was coming. She sat down.

'Lie down,' he ordered. 'On your belly.'

'Oh, God, I hate bugs,' she said, but she obeyed his command. 'And spiders. And snakes . . . Oh, God, do you think there are any snakes?'

She was really going to hate this, too, but . . .

He lay down on top of her, covering her with his far more jungle appropriate colors. From the sky, there'd be no one here at all.

Fortunately, she didn't misunderstand his reasons for this undeniable intimacy.

Still, 'Is this *really* necessary?' she whispered.

'I'm sorry,' Ken apologized. 'If I'd had more time, I could've taken off my clothes and covered you that way.'

'Then what about you?'

'I would've dug myself into the ground. Or used the dirt as an impromptu way to cammy up.'

'Cammy up?' she whispered.

'You don't need to whisper,' he said. 'There's no way they can hear us. Remember how loud it is on board a helo?'

'I am so completely freaked out,' she whispered. 'I think there's something crawling around underneath me.'

'Think about something else.' Kind of like the way he was trying to think about something besides the fact that *she* was underneath *him*. Jesus, he could still smell her perfume. He didn't know what it was called or how expensive it was. All he knew was that it should be sold in a big bottle with three letters printed on the outside – S, E, and X.

'What's cammy up?' she asked again.

'It means to get camouflaged – to put greasepaint on our faces so no one will see us. The SEAL teams usually use black and green in this kind of jungle environment and will you *please* lie still?'

The helo was directly overhead. Now was not the time to leap away so that they could both pretend that lying on top of her wasn't giving him one giant boner.

She stopped moving, but it was too late. She shifted once more, then froze.

Yes, indeed, babe, that there was him.

The fact that his body part in question was pressed right up against her sweet little tush wasn't helping the situation any.

Yeah, if she had any remaining doubts about the fact that he still burned hot for her, they were now gone. He was such a loser, wanting her so badly even after being duped by her, and now she knew it, too.

But even the waves of humiliation and anger – at himself, at her, at his parents for giving birth to him in the first place

– that swept over him weren't enough to subdue his body's extremely physical reaction to her nearness. No, his dick definitely hadn't yet caught on to the fact that he wasn't going to have sex again – at least not in the near future. And probably never again with Savannah.

He'd fucked up his chances of that ever happening but good.

Which was a goddamned shame. It was both a shame that it wasn't going to happen, and that he wanted it to happen again.

Ken closed his eyes, trying to focus on a programming problem he'd been working on in his spare time over the past few weeks, trying to think in code, praying that would counteract his rampant libido.

But her perfume cut through. It floated over the scent of the jungle, the dank earth, the rotting leaves, the plants, his own less than fresh aroma.

That perfume was going to make it impossible for him and Savannah to hide, he realized with eye-opening intensity. If the men in the helo started searching for them on foot, they were going to be in trouble.

One whiff and they'd be found, no matter how well Ken dug them into their hiding place. Jesus, even her hair smelled of it. And it wouldn't take a genius or a specially trained tracker to sniff them out. Just men with guns and noses.

The helo was finally far enough away, so he pulled his own nose out of her hair and lifted himself off of her. She got to her feet before he got the chance to give her a hand up.

She wouldn't meet his eyes. Of course, he wasn't trying very hard for eye contact himself.

'Sorry,' he muttered, figuring he should probably say something.

'You should probably work on your self-control,' she said much too sweetly. 'Considering that you think I'm ugly and that I dress like my mother your reaction was a little, well, unexpected and unwelcome.'

Ugly? 'Whoa,' Ken said. 'I never said—'

'Unless, of course, you have a secret thing for my mother.'

'—that you're ugly. I said—'

'Which I find extremely icky.' She was furious with him.

'—that your *clothes* were—'

'Stop,' she said. 'Just . . . just *shut up*!'

Ken shut his mouth, aware that Miss Too Polite had probably never told anyone to shut up before in her entire twenty-something years of life.

Talk about self-control. If he needed more – and he probably did, he'd grant her that – she needed less. There was real irony here that someone who was wound so tight, who liked everything in its prelabeled, predetermined slot would become so completely out of control during sex. Multiple orgasms. How freaking untidy. It probably scared her to death every time it happened.

Her entire night with him had probably scared her to death. Grease on her neck. Clothes that didn't fit. Tableware that didn't match. Sex that didn't end.

'I would rather you leave me alone in the jungle,' she told him now, 'than ever touch me again.'

That was a crock of shit. He had to laugh. 'No, you wouldn't.'

'Yes,' she said through clenched teeth, 'I would.'

All right. Fine. Let her think that she would. He wasn't

going to leave her, and he wasn't not going to touch her if touching her meant saving her ass.

'I'm sorry,' he said again. And he was. He was sorry he'd upset her. Sorry he'd given himself away. Sorry none of this had been as easy as she'd hoped it would be.

He was sorry for himself, too – sorry that she wasn't the woman he'd fallen so hard for last night. Last night? No, there'd been another night in there somewhere, but they'd been on a plane or in airports, so it didn't really count. His last real night had been spent in bed with her. Or maybe just with someone who looked a whole lot like her. 'I don't think you're ugly, Savannah. Let's just get that straight. I happen to think that you're unbelievably—'

'Enough already!' She looked ready to cry. But Ken knew absolutely that she wouldn't. Tears wouldn't help matters any, and even if they would somehow make her feel a little better, she wouldn't let her emotions get that crazily out of control. She would rather die first.

'—beautiful and extremely hot,' he said, finishing his sentence just to see what she'd do. What would it take to get her to throw something at him? Which would happen first? That, or her busting into tears?

Or maybe her head would just explode.

She turned away, her mouth a tight line. 'You always have to push it just a little farther, don't you?'

'It needed to be said.' He took off his shirt, took off his undershirt, put his shirt back on. What would she do if he grabbed and kissed her? Probably kick him in the balls. He decided not to try it and find out. He was still sore from being tossed by that explosion. 'Is there any extra room in that briefcase?'

'I don't think so,' she said tersely.

'Open it for me, will you?' Ken could still hear that helo in the distance. Judging from the sound, it was searching an area about seven clicks to the west.

He knew that there was room in the case. He'd seen when she'd opened it for him in her hotel room. There was an entire top section that covered, and hid, the money. There had been a few files, some loose papers in that top part, but that was it. He was betting he could get almost a quarter of the dynamite and all of the fuses in there.

The rest he'd carry in a bag he'd make by tying closed the end of his undershirt.

She opened the lock and sure enough, quite a bit of the dynamite would fit. It would make it even heavier to carry – something he wasn't looking forward to.

He took out the papers and files. 'Anything here irreplaceable?'

Savannah shook her head. 'No, those are copies. One's for Alex – was for Alex. The other's . . . not important. Something I was working on. I have it on my computer back in New York.'

'Bury it,' he ordered.

'Shouldn't we save it?' she asked. 'Won't this paper come in handy when we try to start a fire?'

A *fire*? She was serious.

'Rule number one for not letting the bad guys find us – no fires.' Ken loaded the briefcase with dynamite. Dynamite and money – what a combination. 'Smoke can be seen from miles away. Have you ever even been outside of the city before?'

'My grandmother had a summer house in Westport,' she said. 'In Connecticut. When I was little, I used to go there all the time. I haven't been up there in a while, though.'

Westport. To Savannah, fricking *Westport* was the rolling countryside.

'Actually we might want to save some of those papers – if you've got room in your bag.' Ken glanced up, wanting to watch her face as he added, 'It could come in handy as toilet paper.'

Nine

As I stood sipping champagne at the party at Jonathan and Evelyn Fielding's Manhattan penthouse, I realized that Heinrich von Hopf was the man I'd set out to locate.

He was surely the top-level Nazi spy, code name Charlemagne, of whose imminent arrival in New York City I'd heard whispers.

His face was more angular than it had been the last time I'd seen him, his aristocratic cheekbones more pronounced. The rest of him was thinner, too. Leaner, harder. His hazel eyes, however, were exactly the same. Beautiful and luminous, he still had the eyes of an angel.

'You've grown even more beautiful,' he told me. 'I wouldn't have thought it possible.' He took me by the elbow. 'Let's go out on the balcony. There's much I wish to say to you. Privately.'

Oh no, I did not want to go onto the balcony with this man, who knew I'd seen him as the Nazi he truly was – in his SS uniform, no less. He may have had the eyes of an angel, but he was pure devil. He knew I could blow his cover – even send him to his death as a spy.

However, one swift push off the balcony would silence me forever.

Yes, I know what you're thinking, dear reader. If he were a Nazi spy, he should have known that I was also believed by the Nazis to be one of their spies, right?

Wrong.

The German espionage network was organized very carefully. As a lower level operative, I didn't know the names of hardly any of my superiors, although I was working all the time to find out as much as I could. And likewise, there were only very few in the *Sicherhietsdienst* command who knew that agent code name *Gretl*, working in New York, was actually me, Rose Rainer. This way, if one of us was caught, it didn't mean the entire network would go down, too.

Which was a shame for those of us at the FBI and the OSS who were tired of a war that had already been going on too long.

Naturally, I resisted as Heinrich pulled me toward the balcony, trying to slow him down without flat out slugging him and creating a terrible scene. Or even letting him know that I was resisting him.

I'm not sure exactly why I *didn't* simply slug him and start shouting that he was a Nazi spy. All I know was that I didn't say a word.

Perhaps it was the shock of seeing him, of being this close to him again.

Maybe it was the realization that, although I'd tried to convince myself otherwise, I had not forgotten him. Despite all that he'd done, despite who he was – my enemy – I still found him to be the most attractive, most desirable man I'd ever known.

And on some level, I must have realized, too, that I was still in love with him, although I did not admit that to myself until later.

But as for now, I could see Jonathan Fielding heading toward us from across the room, ready to pretend to stake out his territory, the way he would if I truly were his mistress and another man had his hands on me.

'It's cold out there,' I told Heinrich, stalling for time. 'I'm going to need another glass of wine to keep me warm.' I quickly chugged my champagne in order to have an empty glass to wave at him.

He didn't release his hold on my elbow as he took the glass from me and exchanged it for a new one from a tray, somehow gracefully juggling his own champagne flute at the same time in a way that only European aristocracy or Cary Grant could successfully pull off.

But then Jonathan was there, thank goodness, taking hold of my other elbow. For a moment, I felt like the rope in a game of tug-of-war, but then Heinrich released me.

'Well, von Hopf, I see you've met my Rose. Quite the looker, isn't she? But watch out, there's a brain in that pretty little head, too.'

Evelyn would've smacked him if she'd heard that one. Of course, just like her frosty greetings to me, Jon's male chauvinist attitude – although all too common at that time – was pure make-believe on his part. One didn't woo and marry a woman like Evelyn while actually *believing* that kind of drivel. I think, however, that Jon enjoyed saying such things while we had no chance actually to smack him.

'She's been my secretary and all around gal Friday for . . . how long has it been?' Jon turned to ask me.

'Nearly two years,' I replied. 'Six since I started working in your office.'

'Six years,' he mused, letting his gaze linger on my low-cut neckline. Later he'd chide me for wearing that dress. Too risqué, he'd say. It gives the wrong kind of man the wrong kind of ideas. To him, I would always be eighteen and pure as the driven snow.

'Has it really been that long?' he continued. 'It seems just like yesterday . . .' He pulled his attention back to Heinrich. 'I'm a very lucky man, don't you think, von Hopf? To have such a lovely and talented secretary?'

Heinrich was smiling, but I saw him watching as Jon's hand moved from my elbow to my back and then lower. A muscle jumped in his jaw.

As if on cue, Evelyn appeared, stepping between Jon and myself. 'Ah, Rose.' Her voice dripped with ennui. 'I see you've met Heinrich von Hopf.' She turned to her husband. 'Have you introduced these two properly?'

'Rose, Hank von Hopf,' Jon did the honors in his traditional straightforward, New Yorker manner. 'Hank, Rose Rainer.'

Heinrich was looking at me, no doubt waiting to see if I would admit to having met him before. In Berlin. While he was wearing the uniform of the Nazi SS.

'Pleased to meet you, Mr von Hopf, I'm sure.' I held out my hand.

Heinrich took it and kissed it. It was a more intimate kiss than many I'd received on the lips. He gazed at me and I couldn't have looked away from him if my life had depended upon it.

'*Hank* von Hopf?' Evelyn scolded her husband. 'I'm sure Rose would appreciate a *little* more information. His name is *Prince* Heinrich von Hopf,' she told me grandly. 'He's from Austria. He fled after the annexation – after the Nazis took control, isn't that right, Prince Heinrich?' She turned back to me. 'He's been forced into exile, because of his opposition to the Nazis. If he'd stayed, they would have killed him or sent him to one of their horrible camps. He's fighting on our side now.' She turned back to Heinrich. 'What is it exactly that you're doing for the war effort, Prince?'

He finally stopped looking at me, and turned his attention to Evelyn. 'I'm afraid I cannot say,' he told her with one of those charming smiles that still managed to make my heart turn over. 'And please. I do prefer to be called *Hank*. Particularly while here in America.'

I found my voice. 'How long will you be staying?' If he *was* Charlemagne – and I was nearly convinced he was – this would be useful information. Of course, he could well lie. But I'd been given a crash course in Nazi spying techniques before leaving Berlin. We were urged to stick to the truth as often as possible. Chances are he would, too.

Heinrich looked back at me. 'I'll be here for just a few weeks. Then it's back into the thick of things.'

'How thrilling,' Evelyn breathed.

The band had started playing in the other room. Can you imagine? An apartment in New York City large enough to hold a band? The money of course was all Evelyn's. Her grandfather had invented some kind of gasket that was essential for sewer pipes, which brought a new meaning to the phrase *filthy rich*.

One didn't make all that much money working for Grumman – unless, of course, one was also subsidized by the Nazis. If I'd kept the money I'd received from the Germans since 1939, I'd've been able to move into the apartment next door. But I turned that money around, putting it all back into the war effort. I got a certain grim amusement in knowing that the Nazis were helping fund the creation of the OSS – the American spy network that would be essential in bringing Hitler's Third Reich to its knees.

'Since you're not going to be in New York for long,' Evelyn said to Heinrich, 'you must get in all the dancing you possibly can while you can. I'm sure Rose would love to dance with you.'

She was playing a dual role here – a woman who saw the opportunity to throw her husband's mistress at a very attractive man (and therefore getting her away from her husband), and a woman who was so happy in her own marriage that she couldn't believe the entire world didn't want to walk two by two, and was forever trying to set up her good friends with anything in pants.

'Rose did mention that she couldn't stay long,' Jon pointed out.

'Rose can surely stay for one dance,' Evelyn countered, reaching for another glass of champagne. 'Prince Heinrich appears to be smitten. Sir, you've hardly taken your eyes off our little Rose since she walked in. Perhaps you should just sweep her off her feet and abscond with her to Maryland. Marry her before midnight. Knock her up before dawn.'

That was going too far – even for outrageous Evelyn. But she was pretending she'd had too much to drink.

Jon had a sudden coughing fit.

And Hank – Heinrich – handled it with his usual charm, somewhat unfortunately for me.

Instead of asking Evelyn if she were completely out of her mind or stiffly excusing himself and walking away insulted, he smoothly said, 'Surely Rose deserves better than a husband who will disappear in two weeks time, and perhaps never return. She's already lived through that with her fiancée. She doesn't need for it to happen again.'

'Fiancée?' Evelyn looked at me and laughed. 'Since when have you had a fiancée? Really, Rose, what stories have you been telling this poor man?'

The jig was up, as all the famous gangsters used to say, at least in the movies. I'd been caught in a bald-faced lie. I glanced at Heinrich, and I'm sure my guilt was all over my face.

He grimly took my hand. 'Why don't we dance?'

Dancing with Heinrich von Hopf was only slightly higher on my list of things I wanted to do than having him push me off the balcony.

But I let him lead me into the other room and on to the dance floor. And then there I was. In his arms again. The band was playing a slow song, and he held me inappropriately close.

It was all I could do not to run away. Or weep. He smelled so good, so familiar. Even after all that time. Even though our time together had been so short.

'Why did you lie and tell me you were getting married?' he spoke to me very softly, and in German, right in my ear.

I didn't know what to say. I couldn't answer. It was the most hideous torture to have his body pressed so close to mine – to want something, *someone*, that I knew I shouldn't, couldn't want.

And yet I did. Oh, how I longed for him to kiss me, longed to run my fingers through the softness of his hair.

It was then that I realized I loved him still. It terrified me. How could I love a Nazi?

'Was it because of him?' he demanded. 'Is that when you started—' He used a phrase of German that I had never heard before. 'Besides the obvious, what did he offer you that I couldn't?'

I had absolutely no idea who or what he was talking about and I stared at him.

'Jon,' he clarified angrily. 'Did you end things with me because you wanted to be with him?'

He was serious, and I continued to stare up at him in total surprise.

He must have thought I still didn't understand, because he said again, 'I'm speaking of Jon Fielding. Your lover?'

Something must've flickered in my eyes. Or some expression must have crossed my face, because his eyes narrowed as he looked at me.

'Or the man you want people to *believe* is your lover,' he added softly. 'Perhaps because it's essential for your cover?'

'No,' I said. 'Jon is my . . .' But I couldn't say it. I had become an expert liar over the past few years, but I knew I wouldn't be able to get that one past Heinrich. Instead I tried to laugh. 'Essential for my cover? I don't know what you're talking a—'

'It's okay,' he said, pulling me even more closely to him, so closely, I could feel his heart beating. 'It's all right. Rose, don't you know we're both on the same side?'

Yes, but everyone thought I was on their side. So which side did that put him on? Again, I saw him in my mind's eye, dressed in that Nazi uniform. Could I really have any doubt?

'How long has Fielding been helping you?' Heinrich asked me.

I shook my head. 'Please, we must not talk of this. Not here. Not anywhere. Not at all.'

'You're right, of course. Forgive me.'

We danced in silence as I prayed for the song to end. But the band segued right into another slow number. And Heinrich didn't release me. He just kept right on dancing.

My mind was going a million miles an hour. He believed we were on the same side. That gave me a certain amount of power and control, since I knew that we weren't. I also didn't have to worry about him throwing me off the balcony any longer – unless of course, he was lying, too. In which case I was the one with a serious disadvantage.

I looked up at him, directly into his eyes.

And I found him looking at me with such naked desire, I knew at last that one thing he'd told me in Berlin hadn't been a lie. He really had wanted me.

And if I actually had found the courage to ask him up to my hotel room that night all those years ago, he would have gone not just because it was his duty as a good Nazi, but because he wanted to.

That had haunted me for years – the thought of how close I'd come to giving myself to a man who would have seen loving me as just another chore for the Fatherland.

'Why did you lie to me?' he whispered again. 'Why did you tell me you were to be married when it wasn't true?'

As I gazed up at him, I knew what I had to do. I had to make sure he would keep me with him for every minute that was possible of the two weeks he'd be in New York. I had to gain access to his room at the Waldorf-Astoria, search for whatever information he might have hidden there. I had to be with him, glued to his side while he met with his various contacts in the area. I would get one of those miniaturized cameras from the FBI office and take pictures, make lists of names. And then, when those two weeks were up, not only would the FBI apprehend Charlemagne, we would have uncovered much of the upper level of the Nazi network in New York as well.

The thought of Heinrich being brought into custody and facing charges of espionage, facing a death sentence, made my stomach hurt.

I didn't think I could actually do it. But the alternative would be equal to treason. And I knew I couldn't do that, either.

Still, before I did anything at all, I had to ensure that I would be with Heinrich for these next two weeks.

Around the clock, if possible.

My virtue flashed before my eyes, but I took a deep breath.

And I told him the truth.

'I lied because I was in love with you.'

He exhaled as if I'd punched him in the stomach, and tears actually came to his eyes.

'But I don't understand,' he said. 'You knew I loved you, too. I couldn't have been more straightforward in my letters.'

'I couldn't believe you were serious.'

'Oh, I was. Utterly.'

'It seemed . . . impossible,' I told him. 'We're so . . . different.'
He shook his head. 'We're exactly the same.'

I didn't have to force my voice to tremble or my own eyes to grow moist. Was it possible he truly had fallen in love with me in Berlin? 'I meant, we came from such different worlds. And, you – you were on the other side of the ocean.'

'Not anymore.'

His eyes held such a mix of hope and desire, it made me ache. Did he really feel all that, or was it just part of his game? I knew the desire was real. Even as inexperienced as I was, he was holding me far too close for me to be unaware of his physical reaction to me.

And then I whispered the truth that not only threatened to undo me, but that I believed virtually guaranteed that he would try to take me to his hotel room with him tonight.

'I still love you.'

Heinrich smiled at me. It was the strangest smile I'd ever seen. 'Let's get out of here,' he said. 'Before everyone wonders why I'm weeping.'

He pulled me off the dance floor and grabbed our coats. We were in the elevator heading down before I realized he was serious. He dropped our coats onto the floor and took me in his arms. 'Say it again,' he breathed. 'Please, darling . . .'

I knew what he wanted to hear. I touched his face, marveling at the tears that hung in his eyes, ready to escape. 'I love you. I think I'll always love you.'

'I thought I'd lost you forever,' he whispered as those tears rolled down his beautiful face. And then he kissed me.

He was not the only one who cried.

*

Alyssa closed Rose's book as the plane began its descent into LAX.

I thought I'd lost you forever.

Oh, God. She knew what that felt like. To lose someone. Forever.

She closed her eyes, but then all she could see was Sam Starrett. Sitting in her kitchen. Telling her he was going to marry someone named Mary Lou, whom he'd gotten pregnant four months earlier. Telling her that he loved her, but he had to do the right thing.

Telling her he was going to work to make it a real marriage. That, even if Alyssa had been willing to share him with this other woman, he wasn't willing – no matter how badly he still wanted her – to make his marriage vow a lie.

Alyssa knew that it had damn near killed him, but Sam had walked out of her apartment that day. Out of her life.

And she had lost him forever.

Just like Hank had believed he'd lost Rose.

Only unlike Rose, Sam *had* married Mary Lou.

'You okay?' Jules asked.

Alyssa nodded. 'Yeah, I just . . . got an eyelash or something in my eye.'

God, *what* was that smell?

Savannah couldn't believe it as Ken set down the sack he'd made from his undershirt and filled with dynamite, and untangled himself from the vines he'd used to strap the attaché case onto his back.

They were stopping here? In the land of stink?

'May we please go a little farther before we take a break?' she asked as politely as possible. She'd asked him about ten minutes ago if they could stop and share her granola bar, but hungry as she was, there was no way she was going to eat anything surrounded by this incredible stench.

'There's something we have to do before we go any farther,' he told her. 'Before we take any kind of break.'

'Do we have to do it right here?'

'Yeah,' he said, 'we do. You're going to hate this, but . . . You need to take off your clothes.'

Polite. Just be endlessly polite. She couldn't let him get to her even though she suspected he was purposely baiting her now. She would *not* lose her temper again.

'No, thank you.' She even managed to smile. 'I'd rather not.'

'Yeah, well, here's the deal,' he said. 'You smell like the perfume counter at Lord and Taylor's.'

She had to laugh at that one. 'I know what I smell like and it's more like a men's locker room after a football game.'

'Yeah, you got a little of that funk, too, but the perfume still cuts through.'

'So . . . what? You want me to wash in the river? It's hot enough out. I'll go in in my clothes.'

Ken shook his head. 'We've got to ditch your clothes anyway. The key to hiding is blending in. In case you didn't notice, yellow doesn't exactly blend in this particular environment. If someone comes looking for us . . . No, *when* someone comes looking for us, we're going to be at a serious disadvantage with you dressed the way you are.'

Her clothes had to go . . . ? It was hard not to get defensive about *that* one.

'My underwear's yellow, too,' she told him. 'I guess I better just walk around naked, huh?'

'As thrilling for me as that would be, your skin's a little

237

too pale, and we don't have time for you to get an all-over tan,' Ken told her with his usual charm. 'You're going to have to wear my shorts and shirt.'

'Oh,' she said. 'So *you're* going to be the one to go naked.'

'Boxers and sandals, baby,' he said. He smiled at her. 'Do you think you can stand it? You know, manage to control yourself around me?'

Savannah held out her hand. 'Just give me your clothes and go away while I change.'

'Yeah, well, not so fast there, Roadrunner. We've got to do a little perfume removal first.'

She didn't like the look of his smile. He was enjoying himself a little too much.

'What?' she asked. 'I need to wash in the river, but first you need to teach me the secret Navy SEAL method for keeping the piranhas at bay?'

'No,' he said.

'No piranhas or . . . ?'

'No river – well, not exactly.' He sat down on the attaché case as if he didn't particularly mind the fact that it held enough dynamite to blow him into millions of little pieces. 'See, here's the thing about perfume. It's oil based and it doesn't just rinse off when you jump in a river. So what we – you – have to do is mask the scent.'

Mask the scent. She knew where he was going with this. And, oh no. No way.

'What you smell,' Kenny told her with just a little too much glee, 'is nature in action. This part of the jungle probably flooded last time the river rose, and something happened to trap the water – maybe a tree fell, it doesn't really matter. What matters is that the water didn't recede, and as a result of that, all the native flora, i.e., the plants and trees and shit, in this part of the jungle, have drowned.

'What you smell, honey, is rot. It's that same unmistakable aroma you get when you leave a dozen roses sitting in a vase of water four weeks after they've died. I'm sure you do that all the time.'

He was being sarcastic. He knew quite well that she never let anything sit four weeks.

But Savannah shook her head. 'No,' she said. 'No. There's got to be another way.'

'The other way,' Ken told her, dead serious now, his mouth grim and all amusement completely gone from his eyes, 'is called *death*. The other way is me going to a whole hell of a lot of trouble to hide us, only to have some asshole with an AK-47 catch a whiff of Chanel Number Sixty-Nine or whatever that stuff is that you're wearing, and turn both of us into hamburger with a twitch of his trigger finger. Or maybe we'll be found by someone who doesn't like to waste ammo – he'll use his machete on us instead. He'll kill me first, figuring I'm most likely to fight back.

'You he'll probably keep alive a little bit longer.'

She opened her mouth to speak, but he wasn't finished.

'No, I'm not going to leave you,' he told her, somehow reading her mind. 'Learn this now, Savannah. Pay close attention – read my lips – because here it comes. Until we are both safe and on a plane heading for home, whatever happens to you is going to happen to me, too. So. Tell me. Are we going to live or are we going to die?'

Ken actually felt sorry for her.

Savannah didn't say a word as she stood in her underwear and coated herself with stagnant water and rotting plant slime. She didn't curse, didn't complain, didn't cry, didn't make a sound.

She just silently did what he'd told her to do.

He buried her skirt and blouse in the mud, slipped out of his shirt and pants and hung them over a branch where she'd be sure to see them. The less time she spent in only her underwear, the better.

As far as his underwear went . . .

He'd lucked out. He was wearing one of the pairs of boxers Janine had given him last year as kind of a joke – boxers in every different camouflage print. These were urban patterned. They weren't perfect for the jungle, but they were better than the light tan desert print. And way better than his usual utilitarian white.

'Don't forget your hair,' Ken called to Savannah.

'I don't have perfume in my hair,' she called back tightly.

'Yeah, actually,' he said. 'You do. What do you do – spritz a whole lot into the air and then walk through it?' That was the way Adele had put on perfume. It had seemed like a waste to Ken. And it got perfume on anything and anyone within range. He'd learned to duck and run for cover or guys would look at him funny when he got back to base.

She reached up and gingerly started sliming her hair. 'When can I rinse this out?' Her voice shook only slightly.

'I don't know,' he admitted. 'We'll have to play it by ear.'

She turned to look at him, apparently forgetting her attempt to keep her back to him at all times, particularly while wearing only her underwear. Which was, indeed, gloriously yellow and much too skimpy.

'Do you even know that this is going to work?' she asked.

'Absolutely,' he said.

Her eyes narrowed. 'Are you lying?'

'Just a little,' he lied, just to see if maybe that would get a rise out of her.

And eyes. It certainly did.

'You *son* of a *bitch*!' She was holding a handful of slime and stink and she just hauled back and threw it at him. It hit him directly in the chest. *Whack*.

'Good throw,' he said admiringly. He'd done it. He'd actually made her angry enough to lose her cool. But still no tears. She was incredibly tough for a cream puff.

She was livid. 'If you just made me put that . . . that . . . dreck on myself just so you could get your jollies . . . You are *such* an asshole, Kenny!'

Her next shot would have hit him square in the forehead, but he saw it coming and moved slightly to the side. Close, but no cigar. Still, what an arm.

She rushed him. Scooping up a double handful of Eau de Disgusting, she came straight at him.

Time to come clean – in an attempt to *stay* clean.

'I was kidding,' he said. 'I *do* know that this works. I just . . . when I learned about it, I didn't pay attention to the part about when it can be washed off, because, frankly, bad smells don't bother me.'

She was intending to coat his hair with the rotted plant crap in her hands, but he could see that she'd managed to do a pretty halfhearted, half-assed job on not just her own hair, but her entire body.

It didn't take much – she *was* a cream puff, after all – for Ken to divert what she was holding onto her own head. But that still wasn't enough to get rid of her fancy scent.

He threw her over his shoulder and carried her back to the pit of slime as she kicked and proved that she had both a great set of vocal cords and the ability to invent some really creative compound words even with her limited Miss Manners PG-13-rated vocabulary.

Fart-face. He liked both fart-face and asshole-bastard.

It cracked him up, which unfortunately didn't help ease her transition back to a better, less angry place.

When he set her down in the glop and, holding her with only one arm, proceeded to properly slime her with his other hand, she made a very admirable attempt to knee him in the balls. But he twisted his hips and she probably ended up bruising her knee on his thigh. He spun around, so that her back was to his front, pressing her against the old family jewels so there was no way she could reach him and do him any real damage.

Thankfully, this time he wasn't aroused.

At least not yet.

'Let go of me!' she said through gritted teeth. 'I mean it Kenny! Let *go*!'

'Yeah? What are you going to do? Beat me up?' He tried not to think about where he was touching her or how smooth her skin was. He just started at her neck and went methodically southward.

'I'll . . . I'll never forgive you,' she said wildly.

'Yeah, well, I'll never forgive you either, so we'll be even.'

The fight went out of her at his words, and for a moment Ken thought he'd finally made her cry.

But no, she didn't burst into tears. She didn't say anything else, didn't try to get away from him. She just stood there. Submissive.

Which, of course, made it a hundred times harder to touch her the way he was touching her. Her breasts. The smooth softness of her belly. He got it done, got it over with by making his touch as impersonal as he possibly could. Then he released her.

Savannah scrambled away from him, up onto the bank.

'It'll probably smell a little better when it dries,' he told her.

'Yes,' she answered politely. 'I'm sure it will.'

He followed her out of that stinkhole. 'Savannah—'

'Let's just get out of here,' she said quietly. 'Let's get this over with. As far as I'm concerned, there's nothing more that needs to be said.'

'Actually, there is,' Ken told her as he wiped the plant slime from his scraped elbow. She shook out his pants – ever vigilant about spiders and bugs – and stepped into them as he fished in her purse for the antibacterial gel. 'You should put some of this on your feet again, too,' he told her.

She nodded, zipping his zipper and tightening his belt to the new hole he'd punched into the leather with his pocket knife. Without that belt, his pants wouldn't have stayed around her waist.

'There are some ground rules we've got to set,' he told her as she rolled his pants legs up. 'No drinking any water that you find, no matter how fresh it looks. In fact, no eating or drinking anything unless I give it to you. Understand?'

'Yes.' She finished one leg and started another.

Ken squeezed a dime-sized drop of the antibacterial gel into his hand and – 'Jee-zus!' He hopped around in pain. 'You didn't tell me this stings like a *bitch*!'

'It's got alcohol in it,' she informed him coolly. 'Of course it'll sting.' The look she shot him was pure 'what a baby.'

She'd put it all over her busted-up feet without so much as a sound.

'I just want you to know,' Ken told her, 'that I've noticed how tough you are. I've noticed – and appreciated – the fact that you don't complain about anything. I apologize for yanking your chain about the plant slime. It really does work. We really did have to do that. But why don't we give it a couple of hours and then try washing it off. I'll see if I can still smell any perfume and—'

Ken saw it happen.

He was talking as he watched her take his shirt from the branch of the tree where he'd hung it, and he knew – he absolutely *knew* before it even happened – that she was going to shake the shit out of it to rid it of any spiders or creepies that might've crawled onto it.

'Don't!' He dropped the bottle of gel and lunged for her, but it was too late. She shook the shirt like a fricking hurricane.

'Oh, *fuck*!'

And Ken watched the miniaturized tracking device he'd put in his pocket back in San Diego go flying into the stagnant pool of plant crap.

He thought he saw where it went and he dove after it, but Jesus, it was so fucking gone. He sifted through the slime, searching for it for longer than most people would have. Finally giving it up for lost, he slapped the water.

'*Fuck!*'

Savannah was staring at him as if he'd completely lost his mind. Of course, she had no clue. She probably didn't even see the MTD fly out of his pocket. She'd just seen him randomly dive back into this shithole and act like a flipping lunatic.

Now what? Tell her what she'd just done or not?

He wiped slime from his face, slicked back his hair as he

slogged back out of the swamp – with an added bonus of a couple of leeches on his leg. 'Shit!' He quickly got them off by using a fingernail to break the suction of their mouths.

Savannah looked like she was going to hurl, and he added leeches to her hate list of crawling things and made a note to himself to keep her out of the slower moving parts of the river.

As he wrung out his boxers the best he could while he was still wearing them, he knew that he had to tell her. She would feel like shit, but she deserved to know. She wasn't some child that needed to be protected from the truth.

She knew something major was up. 'What did I just miss?'

He told her as calmly as possible about the MTD, about his tracking software, about the fact that it was just a matter of time before Sam or Nils went to his house to see if he'd activated the program, about how he'd been banking on the fact that if he and Savannah didn't get out of there on their own, within a week or so, some branch of the US military would come looking for *them*.

'The MTD'll keep working for only a few more hours,' Ken told her. 'At best. See, I still haven't developed a completely waterproof device.'

Savannah looked stricken. 'I am so sorry.'

'It's just as much my fault,' he said. 'More. I should have told you about it before this. I just . . . I don't know, it was my ace in the hole, you know? My Get Out of Jail Free card.' He sighed, rubbing his forehead. 'I don't know, maybe I was afraid that it wouldn't work – and it won't unless someone's got a satellite dish, or unless they bring some kind of system in – and I didn't want to get your hopes up. Or maybe I thought it would impress you more if a Navy helo just suddenly made the scene, with all my buddies inside.' He looked up at her. 'Savannah, this really isn't your fault at all. It's my fault.'

'You've already impressed me,' she told him. '*And* you've pissed me off, but . . . mostly you've impressed me.'

'Yeah, well, not this time, huh?' Ken blew out a laugh of exasperation. What a freaking loser.

'I've decided to forgive you,' Savannah told him.

As he sat there, as he looked at her dressed in his clothes again, her hair a wild riot of wet, slimy curls around her face, as he gazed into her eyes, those incredible eyes, he was the one who almost broke down and cried.

She looked like his Savannah again, like his fantasy, like the woman he'd fallen so hard for in such a short amount of time. But that woman didn't exist. Instead, there was only this woman, her evil twin.

Except, maybe she wasn't so evil after all. She was an incredibly tough, strong-willed woman, who maybe wouldn't have been his first choice of a companion to be stranded in the jungle with, but who certainly wouldn't have been his last.

At least not anymore.

He cleared his throat. 'Thanks,' he said. 'I don't deserve it, but . . . thanks.'

Max Bhagat himself met them at the airport in Los Angeles.

'Mrs von Hopf,' he greeted Rose with a handshake, helping her down from the airline cart that George had insisted was provided to take them from the gate to the waiting limo because they were in a hurry – not because anyone thought she was too old to walk. 'I'm sorry we have to meet again under these circumstances, ma'am.'

246

She was about to ask if there was any news, but he beat her to it, in tune with the fact that she was anxious about Alex's safety.

'No word on the whereabouts of your son,' he reported as he helped her into the limo. 'I'm not going to lie to you – that's not particularly good news. The earlier the ransom request comes in, the better the chances are that we're dealing with rank amateurs. People who know what they're doing tend to wait, play mind games with the victim's family, let them get good and worried before they make known their demands.'

'But isn't it also more likely that the pros – the people who know what they're doing – will ensure that the victim is safely returned?' Rose countered. 'It's got to be bad for business if they don't return their victims in good health.'

'That could be important, yeah, if our intentions were to negotiate. I know I don't need to remind you that the US government doesn't negotiate with terrorists.' Max climbed into the limo next to her, but then switched to sit across from her. And next to Alyssa Locke. Now, wasn't that interesting?

'*You* may not be willing to negotiate,' Rose told him, 'but I am. If it comes down to it, if it seems as if that's the safest way to go, I will pay whatever it takes to get my son back. I expect you to honor my decision, Mr Bhagat.'

'Yes, ma'am. But we won't be able to help you with either the negotiations or the delivery of the ransom.' He looked at George, Jules, and then Alyssa, giving her a different sort of smile than he gave the other two. Wasn't *that* interesting? 'Flight okay?'

'Yes, sir.'

'Your flight to Jakarta leaves first thing in the morning,'

Max told them. 'I've got you rooms at the airport Hampton Inn.' He looked at Rose. 'If you need anything at all, ma'am—'

'Is there a reason why we aren't flying out tonight with you?' she asked. 'I assume you are flying out tonight.'

Max looked her straight in the eye. He was a good-looking man, with dark hair, melting chocolate brown eyes, and a somewhat swarthy complexion that told of his part Indian heritage. He had told her, last time they'd met, that his father's father had come to America from Raipur right after World War II. He had been an engineer, quite a brilliant man, and had gone to work, interestingly enough, for Grumman.

'Mrs von Hopf,' Max said. 'With all due respect—'

'Please call me Rose,' she interrupted. 'If you're going to be painfully honest, we may as well be on a first-name basis.'

He laughed. 'Okay. Rose. You're eighty years old. You've just taken a six-hour flight from New York to LA. Now, I don't care if you can still run an eight-minute mile and bench press two hundred pounds. I'm not putting you on another endurance test of a flight across the Pacific Ocean until you get some time to rest. You'll be stopping over in Hong Kong, too.'

Hong Kong. Just what she needed. A night in Hong Kong, of all places.

Max started to ring. 'Excuse me.' He fished in his jacket pocket and flipped open his cell phone. 'Bhagat.' Pause. 'Who?' Pause, this time looking across the car at Rose. 'I need more information. Was she traveling with anyone or alone? Did she declare anything to customs? See if you can find out if she made any major withdrawals from any of her bank accounts over the past few days.' Pause. 'Yeah, and do it fast. I want answers.'

He snapped his phone shut. 'It seems that one Savannah von Hopf was aboard a recent flight to Jakarta via Hong Kong.'

'Savannah?' Rose was completely taken aback.

'Her granddaughter,' George informed Alyssa and Jules.

'My son Karl's daughter,' she told them. 'His only child, as a matter of fact. We used to be quite close, until her ninny of a mother insisted they move back to Atlanta.' She was still convinced Priscilla had forced Karl to move to Georgia to get Savannah away from Rose's 'bad' influence.

Now she saw Savannah only once or twice a year, despite the fact that she'd returned to the New York area after attending law school. Rose had made little attempt to reestablish their relationship because it appeared the girl had been artfully molded and shaped into a Priscilla clone.

She never – not in a million years – would have expected Savannah to come within two thousand miles of someplace as far from the big-hair and matching-shoes-and-handbag crowd as Indonesia.

'She made it to Hong Kong,' Max reported. 'The airline insists that she boarded the flight to Indonesia, but once she hit Jakarta, she dropped off the map. She didn't pick up her luggage, didn't check into her hotel.'

Alyssa looked at Max. 'And you think Savannah . . .' She didn't finish her sentence, she just gazed into Bhagat's eyes and apparently read his mind.

He read hers, too. 'Yeah,' he said.

'You think Savannah what?' Rose had to ask.

Alyssa answered. 'It's possible your granddaughter was

249

contacted by the people who took Alex. And that she came to Jakarta to make a ransom drop.'

'Oh, dear God,' Rose said.

'Do you think that's possible?' Max asked. 'Would she do that without notifying anyone? Without even telling *you*?'

'I'm ashamed to say that I don't know her well enough to answer that.'

Max's phone rang again. 'Bhagat.'

He listened to whoever was on the other end, and they all watched him. George – bless him – reached over and took Rose's hand.

'Son of a b—' Max started to say then looked up at her and stopped himself mid-bitch. 'Yeah,' he said into the phone. 'Right. Thanks. Good work.'

He snapped the phone closed. 'Savannah took a total of a quarter mil from various bank accounts on Wednesday. Thursday, she flies from JFK to San Diego. Saturday night, she's on her way to Jakarta.'

'San Diego?' Alyssa interjected. 'Why the delay in San Diego?'

Max had already picked up the telephone that connected him to the limo's driver. 'Turn around. We need to go back to the airport. Find out which airline has an hourly shuttle to San Diego and head for that terminal.' He hung up that phone and addressed Rose. 'Does the name Ken Karmody mean anything to you?'

Rose shook her head, no.

'WildCard Karmody?' Alyssa said.

Jules was sitting forward, too. 'What's he got to do with this?'

'He's not Savannah's boyfriend or significant other or . . . ?' Max asked Rose.

'Her mother told me she was seeing some Romanian man. Vlad somebody,' Rose said. Priscilla had imparted the news with a certain amount of smugness. Vlad apparently was a count or a duke or something equally ridiculous in this day and age. How could her son have married this ninny?

'Apparently Savannah didn't travel to Jarkarta alone,' Max informed them. 'She also bought a ticket for one Kenneth Karmody, who according to the info on his passport, is absolutely the Ken Karmody we know from SEAL Team Sixteen.'

Savannah had gone to Jakarta to make a ransom drop for her uncle, and had had the presence of mind to take along a US Navy SEAL. It was possible the girl had a few cells still firing in her brain.

'I need you to go to San Diego,' Max said to Alyssa. 'Right now. Talk to Tom Paoletti. Talk to Nils and Starrett. See if they know where Karmody went, where he was heading once in Jakarta. Find out who's got a spare key to his apartment or wherever he's living and check the place out. It wouldn't surprise me one bit if he intentionally ditched their luggage and checked into a different hotel.'

He looked across the limo at Rose. 'This is a good man,' he told her. 'Chief Petty Officer Ken Karmody of SEAL Team Sixteen. He's nicknamed WildCard partly because he's something of a wildman – which isn't necessarily a bad thing in this situation – but mostly because he's really good at thinking up unique solutions to problems.'

'He's a computer specialist,' Alyssa volunteered. 'Absolutely brilliant. A little unconventional—'

'Understatement of the year,' Jules muttered.

'But someone – a SEAL officer – once told me that having Karmody on your team is like playing poker with a wildcard in your hand,' Alyssa told Rose. 'That's why he got the nickname. When WildCard Karmody's around, he'll come up with more options for winning. If he's with your granddaughter, Mrs von Hopf, she's as safe as she could possibly be.'

Rose nodded. 'That's good to hear.'

Jules leaned forward, addressing Max across Alyssa. 'Excuse me, sir. But I'll go to San Diego instead of Locke.'

Max just looked at him, eyebrow raised. It was a look meant to terrify, but Jules didn't back down.

'It's all right,' Alyssa murmured to her partner.

'No, it's not all right,' he whispered back to her. 'At least let me go, too,' he said to Max. 'Sir. We'll be back in time for the morning flight.'

Max still didn't say a word.

'Please,' Jules said, his gaze still locked with Max's death glare. 'Believe it or not, sir, I'm friends with Sam Starrett. I can go talk to him while Locke meets with Lieutenant Commander Paoletti.'

The limo pulled up to the terminal and stopped.

'It's all right,' Alyssa said through clenched teeth.

But Jules didn't back down. 'Sir. If I go, too, we can gather the information we need in half the time.'

Finally Max nodded. 'All right.'

Jules nodded, too. 'All right.' He smiled, obviously nearly faint with relief. 'Thank you, sir.'

'If you're going, get out of the limo,' Max ordered him.

The young man nearly tripped in his haste to do just that.

'No wonder you keep him around,' Max murmured to Alyssa as she slid across the seat, following Jules. 'He's ferocious.'

'He's not going to be around much longer, because I'm going to kill him,' she said. 'I *could* have done this alone.'

'Yeah, I know that, but why should you if you don't have to,' Max said as he followed her out of the limo. He stuck his head back in. 'Excuse me for a minute.'

'Of course.' Rose turned to George. 'What was that about?'

He shook his head. 'I don't have a clue.'

Ten

'What's your husband like?'

Husband? Molly turned to look at Jones. She was still shaken by the destruction they'd witnessed, and at first his words didn't make sense.

Like her, he'd put his clothes back on as they drew closer to the village, but it didn't matter. He looked as good dressed in shorts and a T-shirt as he did naked.

Well, maybe not. But it was certainly close.

'I don't have a husband,' she told him.

'Your ex-husband, then.'

'I don't have an ex-husband.' She understood what he was asking about. She'd told him she had a daughter and a granddaughter, and he'd made some assumptions. 'I've never been married.' She had to work not to call him Grady. That wasn't good. 'Dave.' Dave, David, Davy. Anything but his real name, which she never should have used in the first place. Lord, she was a pushover.

'Oh. Sorry. I just thought . . . I mean, of course, that's fine with me,' he backpedaled furiously. 'I'm not . . . I don't—'

'I know,' she said, amused at how flustered he'd become. 'It doesn't quite fit with the do-gooder stereotype, does it?' She purposely used the phrase he'd used to describe her.

254

'No, but not much of you does. I guess what I should ask is what your daughter's father was like.'

Molly sat down across from him on the bench at the stern of the boat. 'Well, that's another one I can't answer. I don't know precisely who her father was.'

Again, she'd surprised the heck out of him.

Dear Lord, saying it aloud like that made it sound seedy and awful. This was not something she spoke of very often, and she looked away from Jones, suddenly afraid of the disapproval and censure she might see in his eyes.

But he surprised her by coming to sit next to her. By taking her hand in his. 'Sounds like there's a story there.'

She tried to laugh, but his sweetness flustered her. 'Oh, there is.'

'Can you tell me? It's okay, you know, if you can't.'

He pushed her hair back from her face so gently, she was a little afraid if she opened her mouth, she'd blurt out how much she loved him. Wouldn't that change the mood fast? He'd probably jump out of the boat.

She looked at him out of the corner of her eyes. 'It's pretty ugly.'

He just waited.

So she took a deep breath, sat up straight, looked him in the eye and told him. 'When I was fifteen, I met Jamie. He was eighteen and already out of high school, and you know that expression "all that"?'

Jones nodded.

'He was all that. And more. Handsome, athletic, intelligent, kind. Very sweet and sincere, too. Kind of like if Jesus had decided to become a rodeo rider. Of course there weren't too many rodeos in our part of Iowa, so Jamie did a lot of traveling. But he came home an awful lot, and I knew that was because of me.

'At first he made all this noise about me being too young, and us having to wait to, you know, get physical, but I'd made up my mind, and, frankly, he didn't have a prayer.'

Jones laughed. 'I can imagine.'

'My mother disapproved, so she took me to see one of his shows. We actually flew down to Kansas City, without telling him we were coming. I think her plan was to make me see the kind of carrying on Jamie did while he was on the road. But we got there, and as we were asking around for where he might be, we found out that his nickname was the Priest – on account of him never, ever sleeping around. Word was he could come back to his trailer, find it filled with naked women, and he'd apologize, shut the door and go off to sleep in his truck. It seems all he ever talked about was me.

'I will never forget the look on his face when he saw me there in KC. If I doubted before that he loved me, I didn't doubt it after that. And Mommy – she never again said another word against him, never tried to talk me into breaking things off.'

Molly took a deep breath. 'Long story short, he was killed in a head-on with a drunk driver about a month later, coming home to see me.'

Jones swore. 'I'm sorry,' he said.

'I lost it when he died,' Molly admitted. 'I seriously went mad with grief. I tried to kill myself – took a razor to my wrists. I say that now, and I'm ashamed, but at that time, I couldn't see my way out of the darkness.' She turned her hands over, showed him the scars, long faded, almost invisible.

Almost.

Jones traced them with one finger. 'Yeah, I noticed them yesterday. I wasn't going to ask, because, well ... But I definitely noticed.'

She knew he hadn't asked because he didn't want her asking about his scars in return.

'When that didn't work,' she said, getting to the part of the story that was, oddly enough, easier to tell. 'I tried to kill myself in other ways. By drinking. Drugs. I spent a whole month tripping. Anything to avoid the reality of life without Jamie, you know?'

She took a deep breath, and said it. 'I used sex, too, to – I don't know – maybe to try to regain at least some of what I'd had with Jamie. A ghost of the closeness and love we'd shared.

'Again, long story short, I pretty much fucked my way through every boy in our school and plenty from the neighboring towns, too. I don't remember much of it, but I do have this one hideous memory of me being stoned and naked in the back of some guy's van and servicing the entire Howardville football team, one and, Lord help me, sometimes even two at a time. I was just so *desperate*, I—'

Jones was still holding onto her hand. 'Molly, you don't have to make yourself feel bad all over again by telling me this.'

'I do,' she said. 'I think I do. Have to tell you it, I mean. I know there were things I did that were even worse, things I can't remember now, things I've blocked. But the memories that weren't blocked – I'm pretty sure they were left intact to keep me humble.' She took a deep breath, let it out in a rush. Then she looked him in the eye. 'The woman I am today was born from that desperate girl, as surely as my daughter was. Obviously, because of my promiscuous behavior, it wasn't too long before I got pregnant.'

'You must've been just a kid yourself when your daughter was born.'

'Sixteen and a half years old,' Molly told him. 'When I found out I was pregnant, there wasn't too much anyone could do. I mean, what? Hold a town meeting? I suppose we could have found the father through DNA testing, but wouldn't that have been fun? Okay, everyone between the age of sixteen and twenty-five in this and the next three counties line up to give a DNA sample so we can find out the father of the town slut's baby.

'No, instead, my mother did something that changed my life forever. She used the money she'd saved for my college education, and she put me in a drug rehab and counseling center specifically for troubled pregnant girls. It was an organization run by a couple of women who'd been in my shoes, and through their kindness and understanding, I finally began to come to terms with Jamie's death. With their help, I focused on the baby that was growing inside of me, focused on life instead of death. I started a new relationship with my creator, and discovered that I truly wanted to go on living. I met a woman and a man who wanted to adopt my baby, and I knew they could give her things that I couldn't give her. Even though I wasn't running crazy anymore, I knew I still had a long hard journey ahead, so I signed the papers, and I gave her away.'

'That must've been hard for you to do,' Jones said quietly. 'My mother didn't have the strength to give me up. She got pushed into marriage with my father and we all suffered for it. She tried, but . . .' He shook his head. 'Take it from me – you did the right thing for your kid.'

'Thank you for saying that.' He'd just told her more about himself than he ever had before. It wasn't a lot, but it was certainly a start. And he'd shared that with her to try to give her comfort. She touched his cheek. 'You're a good person.'

He laughed. 'Yeah, dream on. *You're* the good person.'

'I like myself just fine these days,' she told him. 'But I'm glad you think so, too. Some people might not after hearing my tales of my wicked past.'

'What's that saying about "he who casts the first stone . . ."? Believe me, I'm in no position to look down on anyone, let alone you.'

Molly laughed. 'David Jones, are you actually quoting the bible?'

'I don't know,' he countered. 'Is that where that's from?'

He was smiling at her again, with that look in his eyes that told her if they only had more time, he'd very soon be starting to undress her.

'I realized as I was telling you about the football team that maybe this was something I should have mentioned before you and I became intimate,' Molly told him. 'I was so freaked out about the grandmother thing, it just never occurred to me that you might be put off by the crowds of men who had come – no pun intended – before you.'

'How many guys have you slept with since your daughter – what's her name?'

'Chelsea. I let her adoptive parents name her. It seemed only fair.'

'Since Chelsea was born?'

Molly chewed on her lower lip as she thought. 'Well, it's been twenty-five years . . . I guess . . . three? Yes, three.'

He laughed. 'Three men in twenty-five years?'

'What can I say? I happen to really enjoy sex.'

'Yeah, I noticed, but, Molly, three men in twenty-five years is *not* a lot. You don't want to know how many women I've been with. Add a zero – or two.'

'But I didn't even start having sexual relationships again until I was thirty – that was kind of a landmark year for me. It was the year I got the letter from the adoption agency, saying that Chelsea wanted to meet me. So it's really only been twelve years.'

'So am I four?' he asked.

'No, you're three.'

'Jesus, you *are* a nun.'

'I don't think so.' She smiled, remembering what they'd just spent the afternoon doing, and he laughed.

'That smile of yours is going to kill me. If we run into each other and you smile at me like that, I'm not going to be responsible for my actions.' He kissed her, and she felt herself melt.

They just sat there, then, kissing like a pair of teenagers. It was unbelievably sweet.

'I hope we do run into each other more often,' Molly finally whispered. 'I like talking to you. You're a good listener.'

That embarrassed him and Molly had to smile. At times, he was such a man.

'I also really like it when you let me be on top and you push yourself way deep inside of me,' she added.

That, of course, did not embarrass him one bit. He actually laughed at that. 'Yeah, okay, great. I spend the entire afternooon having the best sex of my life, and still you're determined for me to walk off this boat with a hard-on, aren't you?'

'I just want you to plan to stick around this part of the jungle for a while,' she admitted, praying that by saying this she wouldn't make him run away. Best sex of his life . . . 'And I wanted you to have something to think about tonight.'

'I would have done just fine on my own, thanks.'

She smiled at him. 'But now you'll know what I'll be thinking about.'

'Jesus, Molly, you make me—' He cut himself off, shook his head. Pulled himself out of her arms, stood up and moved to the outboard motor. He shook his head again, as if to clear it, the way men sometimes did when they got punched in the face. 'Look, we're almost to the village dock. I better get off before we round the bend. Anyone who sees us together – sees this stupid grin I can't keep off my face – is going to know what we've been up to.'

'Maybe they'll think I converted you – that you've found God or been born again,' she teased.

He pulled the cord to start the outboard, then turned to look at her. She couldn't hear him over the initial roar of the starting motor, but she could see his lips move and she would've sworn he'd said, 'Maybe I have.'

He steered the boat to the side of the river, kissed her quick, grabbed his pack, and vanished into the underbrush.

Only to appear two seconds later.

'Can you come for dinner *tonight*?' he shouted.

Oh, my. She cut the engine so they wouldn't have to shout. 'I'm sorry – I've been gone all day. I can't be away all evening, too.'

Jones nodded. 'Yeah, I wasn't thinking – that was stupid.'

'No, it was sweet. I'd love to, really, but . . .'

'Tomorrow, then,' he said as the boat started to drift downstream.

'Definitely,' Molly said. 'Tomorrow.'

But he still didn't leave. 'You know, I really liked talking to you, too. And reading to you. I liked it all – except maybe the part where that chopper blew. That I could have done without. But the rest of it was . . .'

'I had a wonderful day, too,' she called back to him.

He was still standing there, looking after her, his hand lifted in a wave, as the boat drifted around the bend.

Ken hadn't said he'd forgiven her.

Savannah knew that that wasn't the worst of her problems, since she was stranded in a tropical jungle somewhere in Indonesia, on some island of which she didn't even know the name, with men with big guns in a helicopter searching for her because they wanted to kill her.

The helicopter had come back. Twice more. Searching for them relentlessly.

Still, she couldn't stop thinking about Kenny. *I forgive you*, she'd said to him. And all he'd said in return was *thanks*.

He'd marched her silently along the river, stopping only to rinse off at a place where the water was running rather briskly.

'No leeches here,' was all he'd said, and she'd gone in with her – his – clothes on.

After she'd come out, he'd resumed the fast pace. She'd had to struggle to keep up. There was no way she could maintain that pace and try to talk to him at the same time, so they'd walked in silence for hours, stopping only during the sudden occasional cloudbursts, when the rain got too heavy to see their feet, or when the helo passed overhead.

As they walked or waited out the rain or hid from the helo, she'd brooded over the fact that if he hadn't forgiven her back by the slime pit, then he probably was never going to forgive her.

But now he set down the sack of dynamite. 'We'll stop here for the night.'

He was kidding. He had to be. It was still early, wasn't it?

Her watch was set to Hong Kong time. She had no idea what time it was here. Wherever here was.

'Now would be a really good time to relieve yourself,' Ken told her. 'Don't go too far, and bury whatever you leave behind. Really bury it – don't just kick around a little dirt. Then get back here. When it gets dark out here, it gets dark fast.'

'You're serious,' Savannah said, blinking at him. 'I thought . . .'

He was trying to untie himself from both the vines and the attaché case, and he only glanced briefly over at her. 'What, that we would make it all the way to that town on the coast in one afternoon?'

'Well . . . yes.' She started toward him. 'Can I help you?'

'*No.*'

His response was so vehement, she took a step back.

'At the slow pace we were moving, it's going to take us a couple of days, at least,' he told her.

That gallop they'd done all day was *slow*?

'Think about it,' he said. 'How long were we on the helo after we hit land, heading up into these hills?'

These mountains were *hills*?

'I don't know,' she admitted. 'I wasn't paying attention.'

'I was. It was close to an hour. Fifty minutes or so. And we were probably moving at . . . Well, cruising speed of a Puma is about a hundred and sixty miles an hour.' Ken finally got out his knife and cut himself free. 'God *damn* it.'

And Savannah could see why he'd had such trouble getting free. The vines he'd used to tie the case of money to his bare chest and back had rubbed his skin raw in places. 'Kenny, my God, why didn't you tell me? I could've helped carry something.'

'I didn't want to slow us down.' He shrugged it off. 'It's not that big a deal. While we were walking it was a little annoying. And now it stings. Nothing more. Really.'

'And what happens tomorrow?'

He was already moving, already organizing where they would sleep. On the ground, with the snakes and bugs. Oh, joy.

'I'll tie the case on in a slightly different spot,' he said shortly.

'And you'll get rope burns there, too.' She fished in her bag for the antibacterial gel. Who could've known it would become her most precious possession? If she had to choose between leaving behind the gel or the case with the money, she'd leave behind the money, no doubt about it. 'Tomorrow you can have your shirt back.' She brought him the bottle. 'Do you want me to help you put this on?'

He'd already started cutting branches that he was no doubt intending to use to camouflage them once they settled in for the night. Although, if the jungle were as dark as he'd described, it seemed kind of unnecessary. As she moved closer, he stopped and looked directly at her, the strangest look in his eyes. 'I still smell your perfume.'

She took a step back. 'You couldn't possibly.'

He came toward her and sniffed her hair, her neck, her throat. He pulled her shirt – his shirt – out from her body and actually took a whiff down the neckline.

Savannah yanked the shirt away from him and took another step back. '*Excuse* me.'

'Take off your underwear,' he said. 'It smells like perfume. What did you do, put it on before you got completely dressed, while you were in your underwear?'

'Yes. That's the point of perfume – to make *you* smell good, not your clothes.'

'Take it off and bury it,' he ordered, back to cutting branches. 'And, by the way, now I'm really looking forward to you giving me my shirt back in the morning.'

He was purposely being rude. Savannah gritted her teeth as she headed for the underbrush. But then she turned back. She couldn't keep herself from saying *some*thing. 'I thought we were over the pouting phase. Aren't you getting just a *little* tired of—'

'I wasn't kidding about the way it gets dark out here. I don't know when moonrise will be. I do know it's only a crescent tonight – waning – so it's not going to help much in the night-light department even when it is up. So if you want to be able to see where you're walking after you answer the call of nature, you better go now.'

The light was definitely fading. It was spooky how fast it was going.

Savannah turned and walked into the jungle on feet that stung. Still, it was nothing compared to the way Ken made her feel with his unhidden disdain.

Savannah came back out of the jungle pissed off at him.

Good. Ken was okay when she was pissed. It was when

265

she got all doe-eyed and soft and vulnerable that he had trouble being around her. Or when she stood around in her underwear, or when she touched him or talked to him or smiled at him or . . . Crap. It was only when she was tight-lipped and angry that he *didn't* want to pull her into his arms and tell her everything was going to be okay. That not only was he going to get her safely out of here, but he was also going to be her personal slave for the rest of his natural days.

Jesus, he was mad at himself for wanting her like that. He didn't even fricking like her – well, at least not very much. After the slime fight, and after practically running her along the river for hours without a single complaint, he really had to work at not liking her.

They had five, maybe ten minutes of light left – tops – and she came marching over to him and threw her underwear at his head. He hadn't been expecting that, and she got him dead on.

Good aim. It was hard not to like someone who had such good aim.

'My underwear does *not* smell like perfume,' she insisted.

Her bra and panties dropped into his hands after they banked off his face. They were still warm from the heat of her body, all slippery satin and yellow lace. God, God, God. He held them up to his nose and breathed deeply. 'Yeah, actually, Savannah, it does. You're just used to the scent.'

She was staring at him like he'd just grown a second head, and he realized he was sitting there, sniffing her panties. Perfect, Karmody. Way to go. Nothing like confirming the fact that he was a raging pervert.

'Sorry,' he muttered. 'I'll, uh, bury this for you later.' He dropped it behind him and handed her one of the coconuts he'd cut and bored a pair of holes in with his pocket knife. 'Drink.'

'Thanks.' She sat down, her eyes widening as she caught sight of tonight's main course.

Plenty of people around the world ate bugs and insects for protein. As a SEAL, Ken had eaten more than his share in the past. Some people enjoyed what he thought of as the clam-and-oyster effect – eating something that was still alive. He personally preferred not to eat things that wiggled, particularly if, like tonight, he wasn't in a hurry to get moving again.

He'd found a fine collection of edibles under a fallen tree trunk – it wasn't really enough to feed them both, but then again, he doubted Savannah would be joining him.

He popped one into his mouth. 'Some of 'em have a nasty aftertaste, but this one isn't half bad,' he told Savannah.

She just looked at him expressionlessly. It was actually pretty amazing that she managed to completely hide her revulsion and shock, especially knowing how freaked out she got by bugs.

'If you don't eat,' Ken told her, 'we're going to have to slow down even more tomorrow.'

Savannah shook her head and laughed. It was a pissed off kind of laugh. 'What's the response you're looking for from me here, Kenny?' she asked. 'Am I supposed to faint? Or maybe start to cry?'

She picked up a particularly plump-looking slug. 'I bet this tastes a lot like escargot. It could probably use some butter, but what can you do?'

She ate it. She freaking ate it. Now he was the one gaping in amazement. He managed to get his mouth shut.

'You hate bugs,' he said inanely.

'I would also hate cows if they were an inch long and tried to crawl up my pants leg,' she told him. 'But that wouldn't keep me from enjoying a nice steak.'

Ken laughed. Well, what do you know?

'When I was little,' she told him, 'Uncle Alex used to take me to these exotic little ethnic restaurants in New York City, where they served God knows what. We tried it all. I was probably eating bugs years before you were, back when I was five. Then, after my mother made us move to Atlanta, he started sending me chocolate-covered grass-hoppers. I didn't particularly like those – I'm not a big fan of the crunchy ones – but I used to eat 'em – I still do – to annoy Priscilla.'

Priscilla was her mother.

She was silent for a moment, no doubt thinking about the fact that her uncle wouldn't be sending her anything anymore.

But before he could think of anything remotely comforting to say, she shook herself out of it and pulled herself back into the here and now.

'I was thinking about the shirt thing,' she told him as she helped herself to another slug, washed it down with some coconut milk. 'How about we cut these pants you're letting me wear into shorts, use the legs to make a couple of sacks to carry the dynamite? That'll free up your undershirt. I can wear that, and you can have this shirt back – it's thicker and it has sleeves. It'll keep you from getting more rope burns.'

It wasn't a half-bad plan. Except, 'I was going to dig you in here, get you settled for the night, then do some scouting. Roam around this part of the jungle. See if I can find where that boat came from, maybe snag some supplies and a few more clothes to wear.'

'Snag?' she said, her eyes widening. 'You mean *steal*?'

Oh, Jesus.

'I'd leave money in return,' he told her, 'but that could lead the bad guys with the big weapons right to this part of the jungle. I mean, imagine if you were living out here, and your extra shirt disappears and there's a hundred American dollars in its place. Aren't you going to talk about it? Pretty loudly, too?'

She definitely saw his point, but she still wasn't happy.

'Look, if it really bothers you, we can make sure we send money or food or clothes or whatever we take back to this island after we're safe.'

'How about if you leave behind Indonesian money?' she asked.

That's right. He'd forgotten she had a wallet full of the local currency. Still . . . 'Don't forget the thank you note with the smiley face,' he said. 'We better leave one of those, too.'

She didn't back down. 'What if you steal – not snag, Kenny, *steal* – someone's *extra shirt*, and it turns out that bad guys with big guns are after them, too? What if they need that shirt more than we do?'

She was back to calling him *Kenny* all the time, damn it. As if she didn't particularly care that it annoyed him.

So he wouldn't let it annoy him.

Except, God damn, it annoyed him.

And then, like an anvil from the sky, the last of the light vanished and darkness fell.

'Oh, my God,' Savannah breathed. 'You weren't kidding.'

'Freaky, huh?' he said. The devil in him wanted to sit absolutely still and be completely silent – let her think he was gone. See how long it took her to panic. But even he wasn't enough of an asshole to do that to her.

'I can't even tell which way is up.' Her voice shook.

'Are you claustrophobic?' he asked. Gee, maybe if she was, he'd have to sleep with her holding on to him, to help her ground herself. That would be too bad, wouldn't it?

She laughed nervously. 'I never thought so before, but something tells me I will be after tonight.'

He could hear her moving toward him, felt her touch his leg. She sat next to him, close enough so that she could hold onto his ankle.

He reached down and took her hand, pulled her so that they were sitting shoulder to shoulder, leaning back against the trunk of a fallen tree, touching at the hips as well.

'Please,' she whispered, holding tightly to his hand, 'don't go anywhere tonight.'

Ah, crap. 'Savannah, you've got to trust me to find my way back here. I can move around much faster without you – I'm not saying that to insult you or anything, so—'

'No,' she said, 'I know it's true. It's just—'

'I'll get you settled, take a short nap myself, then take a few hours and find the quickest route out of here. It'll be a big advantage in the morning.'

She was silent, and he knew she truly didn't want him to leave her alone – and that she probably wasn't going to say another word about it.

'Ah, Christ,' Ken said as it started to rain again. It was the rain forest, after all. This one was less furious than the cloudbursts they'd endured throughout the day, but probably wouldn't be over as quickly, either. Son of a bitch.

Savannah was so tense next to him, he could almost feel his own shoulders tightening in sympathy. Clearly she wasn't looking forward to a night spent trying to sleep in mud puddles with snakes and bugs. But she didn't say a word.

'How come you never complain about anything?' he asked. 'Are you some kind of Zen master or something?'

She exhaled a laugh at that. 'What's the point of complaining? It just makes the people around you feel bad, too. Besides, if I ever feel really awful and pathetic, I just . . . think about my grandmother.'

'What, did she beat you with a big stick every time you whined?' Ken asked.

Another nervous burst of laughter. Man, she was unbelievably tense. Still, she was talking to him. That was a good sign that her head wasn't going to explode. Yet.

'No, she was a special agent for the FBI and the OSS – she started working for them during World War Two. The Nazis thought she was one of them, but she wasn't. She was a what-do-you-call-it. A double agent.'

No shit?

'If she had been found out,' Savannah continued, 'they would have killed her – killed all of her mother's – my great-grandmother's – family still living in Germany. She took risks I can't even imagine, and spent every day of her life for years looking over her shoulder. These past few days are the closest I've ever come to knowing what she must've lived through. I think about her and suddenly I don't have too much to complain about, you know?'

Yeah, he did know. 'I bitch and moan all the time.' Ken felt humbled. 'You must think I'm a real jerk.'

'Yes, well, I think you're a jerk but not because you complain all the time. I actually haven't noticed that. Probably because your other jerkishnesses are so prominent.'

'Ha ha,' he said. 'Very funny.'

'She's still alive,' Savannah told him. 'My grandmother.'

'No kidding?'

'Yeah, she's in her eighties and she just wrote a book – an autobiography. Of course, it made the *Times* list when it first came out. She doesn't do anything halfway.'

'That's the book you've got in your bag,' he realized.

'Yeah. I've been carrying it around for months because I haven't read it yet. I feel like I should, but I already know the story so well. Family legend, you know? I grew up hearing about her. And, well, nothing like inducing feelings of inadequacy. I haven't been able to crack the book. I mean, imagine if you were Wonder Woman's granddaughter, except you had no superpowers. Oh yeah, and you were skinny and kind of squinty, too.'

'You're not squinty.' He knew the moment the words left his lips that it was the wrong thing to say.

'Gee, thanks, Ken.'

'I didn't mean—'

'I know.' She was quiet for a moment. 'If Alex really is dead . . .' She sat in silence for several long beats before going on. 'It's not going to kill her – sometimes I think she's immortal – but it's really going to hurt. I think much more than if it was my father who died. There's a lot that's been left unsaid between Rose – my grandmother – and Alex.'

Ken sat there in the darkness, letting her voice flow over him, kind of like the warm rain.

'I always told him that he should just invite himself to her apartment, go into her living room, and just say it. "Hello, Mother. I'm gay." Did he really think she would stop loving him? Her own son?'

'I don't know,' Ken said. 'This isn't a problem I've ever had to deal with, so . . .'

'What's your family like?' she asked.

Oh, no. No, he *so* didn't want to go there.

'You said your father died a while ago, right? But your mother's still alive?'

Shit, she had a good memory. 'Yeah,' he said. 'She's still living in New Haven. You know, there's a question I've been wanting to ask you.'

'About the money, right?' she asked.

'Not exactly. But now that you mention it . . .'

'My father owns seventeen different companies. No, eighteen now. Everything from manufacturing plumbing supplies to high tech. I own stock in practically all of them.'

'So you're like . . .'

'Obscenely rich?' Savannah laughed, but it wasn't because she thought it was funny. That little disparaging laugh was, interestingly enough, the closest he'd ever heard her come to complaining. 'An heiress? You bet. Like me any better now?'

'No.'

She laughed again, more genuinely this time, as she squeezed his hand. 'I actually believe you.'

'Money's just not that important to me,' Ken told her. 'I mean, it's nice to be able to pay your bills on time, but . . . if you're not doing what you love to do, what good is it, you know?'

Savannah was silent – he could practically hear the wheels turning in her head. 'But . . . this is what you love to do, right? What we're doing right now? Sitting in the mud, getting rained on. Eating bugs? Crashing around in the jungle?' She started to laugh.

'I don't crash,' he said, wounded. 'I slink.'

She laughed even harder – just on the verge of hysterical. 'Either way, you are one seriously sick man.'

*

Jules turned to look at her as he pulled their rental car up in front of Sam Starrett's house.

'No,' Alyssa said. 'I am not waiting in the car.'

This sucked. She had no excuse not to be here. WildCard Karmody's friend John Nilsson was out of town on a training op, and his CO, Lt. Comdr Tom Paoletti, was in a meeting until late this afternoon. Tom could see her at 1630, maybe a few minutes earlier, if she didn't mind showing up and waiting. In between now and then, there was nothing to do except find and talk to Sam Starrett.

Sam and Nils and WildCard were like the Three Musketeers or maybe the Three Stooges of Team Sixteen – she wasn't sure which exactly, although she suspected it was the latter. If anyone knew what WildCard Karmody was up to, it would be Sam. Or Nils. But Nils wasn't around to interview. Just her luck.

Jules sighed. 'Look, sweetie—'

'Don't fucking *sweetie* me, Cassidy,' she snapped, then closed her eyes. 'God, I'm sorry. I'm just . . .'

Jules put the car into park and turned it off. 'A little tense, huh?'

'Yeah.' She looked out the window. Sam's truck wasn't in the drive. Instead, there was a white minivan. No way on earth would Texas-born and -raised Sam Starrett drive a minivan, let alone one that was white. 'I don't think he's home.'

Jules nodded, opening the car door. 'Let me go find out.'

Alyssa opened her door, too. '*We'll* go find out.'

'Have you met her before?' Jules asked as they went up the neatly kept path. The house was tiny, but it – and the postage-stamp-sized yard – were immaculately kept.

'No,' Alyssa said, knowing he was speaking of Mary Lou, the woman who had popped back into Sam's life – four months pregnant – literally hours after he'd told Alyssa that he loved her.

Jules stopped walking. 'You know, there's a shopping mall about a half a mile away. How about I drive you over there, drop you off, let you buy some new hiking boots so you can kick Max Bhagat's ass for even *suggesting* you come here—'

Alyssa went up the steps to the front door and rang the bell.

'Shit.' Jules scrambled to be standing next to her as the door began to open. 'Let me talk, okay?'

What did he think she was going to say? 'Hi, you don't know me, but I used to have incredible sex with your husband back before he was your husband . . . ? And if he weren't so damned honorable, I'd be messing around with him still, because as disgusting and hurtful as that would be to both you *and* me, I am and have always been completely unable to resist the man.'

The woman standing on the other side of the screen was short and dumpy and exhausted-looking. And wearing . . . maternity clothes? Dear Lord, was she pregnant again?

'Mrs Starrett?' Alyssa asked.

'Yes?' At one time, Mary Lou had probably been rather pretty. But right now she looked as if life had drop-kicked her. She hadn't showered yet today – or maybe not this week – instead she'd just scraped her brown hair back into a ratty looking ponytail. Her eyes were blue, with big gray bags beneath them. Her mouth was tight, as if she didn't spend much time smiling or laughing.

She *did* have boobs that rivaled Dolly Parton's, although

right now she wasn't blessed with the rest of Dolly's figure. Her blouse was stained with food – probably from the baby, but come on. After it gets *that* bad, change it, for God's sake.

'Agents Jules Cassidy and Alyssa Locke from the FBI, ma'am,' Jules said, no doubt when it became apparent to him that Alyssa was going to do nothing but stand there and stare at Sam's wife. 'We have official business to discuss with Lieutenant Starrett. Is he at home?'

'I'm sorry,' Mary Lou said with an accent that hailed from *way* south of the Mason-Dixon line. 'Who did you say you were? Jules Cassidy and . . . ?' She turned to look at Alyssa.

'Special Agent Alyssa Locke,' Alyssa told her, and now Mary Lou was staring at *her*. Oh, shit. Sam wouldn't have been so stupid as to tell his wife about her, would he?

No, that was ridiculous. Sam had been definite when he'd ended their relationship. He had absolutely no reason to say anything at all about her to Mary Lou or to *any*one. He wasn't cruel – and he'd insisted he was going to try to make his marriage to Mary Lou work.

'Is Sam home, ma'am?' Jules asked again.

From somewhere in the house, a baby began to cry.

'He is,' Mary Lou said, looking over her shoulder, distracted by the baby. 'I'll get him.'

But she didn't have to, because there was Sam, coming out of one of the rooms in the back of the house. Blue jeans, T-shirt, cowboy boots, and baseball cap. Tall, golden brown, and handsome, fluid and graceful even just in walking down the hall of a little suburban house.

'Baby's awake again,' he said to Mary Lou in his familiar cowboy drawl, annoyance in his voice.

'Yeah, I hear her,' Mary Lou said shortly.

He squinted at the door. Apparently, he couldn't see clearly through the screen. 'Who's here?' His hair was down to his shoulders, his face clean shaven. His lack of mustache and goatee meant he'd been doing a lot of diving lately with the teams. He'd told her once that the seal on his mask didn't work so well with facial hair.

'FBI,' Mary Lou said shortly, heading back toward the crying baby. 'For you.'

'Well, don't even invite 'em in, for chrissake.' He shook his head in exasperation as he came toward them. 'Sorry, she's—'

Then he saw them. Saw her. He stopped short, but then made himself keep going. He pushed open the screen.

'We're here on an official visit,' Jules said.

Sam shook his hand, giving him a ghost of his usual megawatt grin. 'How the fuck are you, you little faggot?'

'I'm great, you giant rednecked homophobe,' Jules said, grinning back at him.

'I love the hair,' Sam said.

'Yeah. I figured it was about time to go back to my natural color.'

'Looks good.' Sam turned to look at Alyssa. He held out his hand, his blue eyes carefully neutral. 'Alyssa.'

She put her hand in his, bracing for the contact. His hand was warm, and – one of his fingers had a Band-Aid on it – dinged up as usual.

'Roger,' she greeted him. *Sam* was just a nickname. His given name was Roger, but not even his mother called him that anymore. Only Alyssa ever did.

He smiled, and she saw it in his eyes. He was just pretending that the sight of her standing on his front step

SUZANNE BROCKMANN

wasn't making his heart beat like crazy – the way hers was
going, too. He wasn't any more over her than she was over
him. She wanted to cry. And here he'd gone and made
Mary Lou pregnant again.

He dropped her hand and stepped back, still holding the
screen open. 'What's up? Come on in. What some coffee or
lemonade, or . . . Shit, I don't even know what all we have
in the house.'

Jules looked at Alyssa and she shook her head, just the
teeniest of movements. Please don't make her go into that
house and sit in Mary Lou's living room or kitchen. *Please*.

'We're all set. How about we talk out here?' Jules
suggested as if it were his preference.

'Okay.' Sam stepped outside, and they moved away
from the front of the house, over to their car at the curb.
'What's this about?'

'Do you know where WildCard Karmody is?' Alyssa
asked him.

Sam laughed. ' "It's ten o'clock, do you know where your
children are?" No, I can't say that I do. What'd the Card get
himself into this time?'

'We were kind of hoping you could tell us,' Jules said.

Sam leaned back against their car, folding his arms
across his broad chest. 'He met a girl.' He glanced at Alyssa.
'Woman. Sorry. Took two weeks leave. It seemed to be
completely out of the blue. He didn't tell me where he met
her or even what her name was. Just that . . .' He laughed
again. 'Apparently, it was lust at first sight. I'm . . . not
comfortable saying anything more.'

'Did he tell you where he was going?' Alyssa asked.

'Nope.'

Jules sighed. 'He didn't mention Indonesia?'

Sam straightened up and stared at Jules and then Alyssa. 'You're telling me WildCard's in fucking Indonesia?'

Alyssa looked at Jules. He nodded. 'We're not sure, but we think he was approached by a woman named Savannah von Hopf and possibly hired to accompany her to a ransom drop for her uncle who's been missing from Jakarta since last Monday.'

Sam was shaking his head. He pushed himself off the car and started to pace. 'No. No way. Whoever she was, this woman he took leave to be with – she was not paying him. Jesus, at least not in cash. He didn't mention Indonesia to me, didn't mention anything except . . .' He shook his head again.

'He's gone missing,' Alyssa told him, hoping that would make him tell them whatever it was he was leaving out. 'He and Savannah vanished almost immediately upon reaching Jakarta. They were carrying a quarter of a million dollars. That's missing, too.'

'Holy fuck! What'd the idiot do, rob a bank before getting on the plane?'

'Savannah von Hopf's father is worth eight hundred million,' Jules told him. 'The money's hers. She probably pulled it from her "What to do on a rainy day if your uncle is kidnapped" account.'

'Shit,' Sam said. 'But why didn't he tell me he was going to Jakarta? It doesn't make any sense. Best I can come up with is that he didn't know he was going out of the country when he talked to me and Nils – which was . . . Saturday, late morning.' He turned to look at Alyssa. 'What's she like? This Savannah?'

'I've never met her,' Alyssa told him. 'She's a lawyer, lives outside of New York City, in her late twenties. Blonde, blue eyes, short. Everything I know about her is superficial. She's rich, she's got a terrific grandmother, but they aren't close.' She shrugged. 'Sorry.'

'Is she the kind of woman who'd use sex to make a man do what she wanted?'

'I honestly don't know,' Alyssa said.

Sam closed his eyes. 'Ah, Jesus, if she's just some insincere bitch doing a number on Ken, I swear to God, I will find her and make her wish she'd never laid eyes – or anything else – on him. He does *not* need this.'

'You're certain he slept with her.'

Jules hadn't asked it as a question, but Sam answered as if it were one. 'I'm positive.' He closed his eyes and exhaled. 'Look, don't write this in some fucking report, all right? But apparently this Savannah is like some kind of multiple orgasm queen.'

'Excuse me?' Alyssa said.

'Jesus, Alyssa, make me say it to you twice.'

'I heard you. I'm just . . . horrified that he actually told you about it.' She couldn't believe that this was the first conversation she was having with Sam since he walked out of her life. And it was about sex. It had to be about sex, didn't it?

She wondered if he ever thought about her. About them . . .

He wouldn't look at her. 'It wasn't locker room talk, I swear. He didn't even tell us her name, he wasn't bragging, he didn't give any details. He just wanted information, like, what do you do when she just keeps coming, three, four times in a row. Stuff like that.'

'Oh, God,' Alyssa said. 'That's something I didn't particularly want to know about Savannah von Hopf.'

'Yeah, well, you know WildCard.' Sam glanced up at her. 'He was just . . . being WildCard. Collecting all the data he could. To do the best possible job he could.' He laughed. 'So to speak.'

'What did you tell him?' Jules asked. Alyssa smacked him. 'Ouch. Hey, I'm just curious.'

'We've got all the information we need,' she said. 'At least about this particular aspect of Karmody's relationship with Savannah von Hopf.'

'Please don't put what I said into a report.'

Alyssa met and held Sam's gaze. 'I won't write it down,' she told him. 'But I am going to mention it to Max.'

'Max.' Something shifted in Sam's blue eyes. 'How *is* Max?'

'Fine.' She turned away, knowing just from looking into his eyes that he'd heard the rumors that were circulating about her and her boss. Despite her efforts to quell them, or maybe *because* of her efforts, those rumors just wouldn't die.

'You wouldn't happen to have a key to Ken Karmody's apartment, would you, Sam?' Jules asked.

Sam went back into leaning mode. 'You've told me everything you know, right? There's nothing lurking back there that you've forgotten to mention, like impending charges against him for . . . God knows what . . . ?'

'We think he's in trouble,' Alyssa said, 'but trust me, it's not with us. We want to find him so that we can help.'

He gave her a long look, then nodded. 'I do trust you.' He pushed himself back off the car. 'I've got about an hour before I have to get to the base,' Sam told them. 'If WildCard went to Indonesia, he'd have set up his tracking program, made sure he took along an MTD – miniature tracking device. Let's go to his house, see if we can't find him. That is, if you don't mind dropping me in Coronado after . . . ?'

'No problem,' Jules said. 'We're heading over there ourselves.'

Sam went toward the house. 'Just let me grab Ken's key and my gear and tell, you know, the wife that I'm leaving.'

He went into the house, but was back out the door in a matter of seconds. 'I'm outta here,' he shouted as the screen door slammed behind him.

Mary Lou came to the door, baby in her arms. 'When will you be back?' she called.

'Late. Don't wait up.' Sam threw his gear into the back seat of their car and climbed in after it.

He directed Jules across town, and they drove in a silence that was slowly driving Alyssa mad. She could smell him – his scent was so familiar.

She shot Jules a look, begging him to say something. To make some kind of noise. Small talk. Anything. Break this blasted silence.

He gave her his *what?* face. Great. Perfect time for him to lose his telepathic powers.

So she turned slightly in her seat to face Sam. 'I guess congratulations are in order.'

He looked at her blankly and responded with his trademark directness. 'For what?'

'Isn't . . .' Mary Lou's name caught in her throat. '. . . your wife pregnant again?'

He stared at her. Then laughed. 'Fuck, no. Jesus, that's all I need – two babies screaming day and night.'

'I'm sorry,' Alyssa said. 'I thought . . .'

'Yeah,' he said. He leaned forward slightly to direct Jules. 'Left at the light.' He settled back in his seat and briefly met her eyes. 'I know what you thought. But the baby's not exactly easy to handle. Mary Lou hasn't had the chance to get off all the extra weight from the pregnancy. She doesn't fit into any of her old clothes, but she doesn't want to buy anything new. I keep telling her to, but she won't – like that would be admitting defeat or something. I don't know. Next right,' he said to Jules.

'I'm sorry,' Alyssa said again. 'I didn't mean to . . .' She shook her head.

'Yeah, well, welcome to my life. I didn't mean to either.' He looked out the window, the muscle jumping in his jaw.

She looked at the lines of strain on his face, at the grim set of his mouth, remembering how he had always been so quick to smile. She watched him for as long as she dared, feeling awful for him and for Mary Lou, too, remembering the way Sam had been so eager to get out of his house. *I'm outta here.* Alyssa wasn't the only one who'd been injured here. That was easy, sometimes, to forget.

She turned back around and caught Jules's eye. He gave her a look that she read quite easily – it was an 'oh my God, did you have to ask him *that*' look. But then he made a sympathetic face and down near the seat, where Sam couldn't see, he made the ASL sign for 'I love you.'

Alyssa sent him back a more international sign that meant something rather different.

Jules tried his best not to smile.

So much for her attempt at small talk.

'Try to sleep.'

Savannah ungritted her teeth to say, 'I can't.' Her heart was beating too hard. She could feel it pounding in her chest, almost shaking her body.

She heard Ken sigh in the relentless darkness inside of

283

SUZANNE BROCKMANN

the blind he'd built around them. 'If you close your eyes it won't seem so dark.'

'But when I open them, I get dizzy.'

Silence. And then another sigh. 'You know what I'm going to say to that, right?'

'So keep them shut. Yes. Thanks so *very* much. It's not that easy. Oh!' She sat up, but nearly fell over because she couldn't see even her hand in front of her face. 'We never put antibacterial gel on your rope burns.'

Ken sighed again. Very deeply this time. 'Savannah, I'm fine.'

Oh God, it was dark. She had to brace herself with both hands on the ground on either side of her to keep from losing her balance. Her heart was racing as if she'd just run a mile. Her chest hurt, and her head was pounding, and it was hard to breathe. 'You said it was easy to get an infection out here because—'

'Yeah, yeah, yeah. I know what I said. Just—'

'Kenny,' she gasped, 'I'm so sorry, but I think I'm having a heart attack.'

She heard him moving toward her in the small space, felt his hand connect with her leg. 'Okay,' he said. 'It's okay, just try to breathe slowly, all right? Deeply. Come on, I can hear you – you're hyperventilating – that's not a heart attack. You're just getting too much oxygen because your breathing got all messed up.'

He touched her other leg, then felt his way up to the rest of her, pulling her against him and settling back onto the ground with his arms around her, her back to his front. 'Shhh,' he said. He cupped one hand loosely around her mouth and nose. 'Just close your eyes and breathe as deeply as you can.'

284

'I'm sorry,' she said. Hyperventilating. How embarrassing. Her grandmother had gone one on one with Nazi spies without flinching, and Savannah freaked out because it was too dark.

'You're doing great.' Ken's voice was right in her ear. 'I know I'm not supposed to ever touch you again, but is this helping a little?'

It was. His hand smelled like the jungle dirt and the plants he'd cut to create a canopy of branches above them. His body was so solid and warm.

He shifted and she clung to his arms. 'Don't let go of me!'

'I'm not,' he said. 'I'm just . . .' He shifted again. 'There was a rock right under me. It's gone now.'

'I'm sorry,' she said again. Don't cry, don't cry, don't cry.

'You're sorry that it's gone?' he said. 'That's pretty harsh.'

'No,' she said. 'I'm just . . . sorry.'

She was breathing more slowly now, and he took his hand from her face.

'Yeah,' he said. 'I've noticed – you've said that about two million times.'

'I'm . . .' She stopped herself from saying *sorry*.

'I can feel your heart,' he told her. 'I think what you're having is a panic attack. It's not going to kill you. It's just a little scary though, huh? Does this happen to you often?'

'Never,' she said. It was starting to get hard to breathe again. 'God! How do I make it stop?'

He covered her mouth and nose again. 'Have you ever been underwater at night? This is the same kind of darkness. If you let it, it can feel nice – kind of like being at the bottom of the pool. The water surrounds you in the same way, you know?'

Savannah nodded. She did know.

'Hey, there's something I've been wanting to ask you and now seems to be a pretty perfect time since you're not sleeping and I'm not sleeping,' Kenny told her. 'It's about the other night. When we, you know, got it on?'

'No,' Savannah said, her voice muffled beneath his hand. 'I'm not having sex with you ever again, remember?' Although, right now, it might just be the distraction that she needed. If he kissed her, she wouldn't push him away.

But he didn't kiss her. It was almost a shame.

'Believe me, you made that perfectly clear. I'm just wondering . . .' His laughter sounded embarrassed. 'Maybe this is a really stupid question, and forgive me if it is, but you're like a walking orgasmatron. I mean, I've never been with a woman who, you know, detonates upon . . . I was barely inside of you and . . . It's like you've got a hair trigger or something. Touch it and, bam.'

Savannah could not believe he was talking about this. She was back to gritting her teeth, but for an entirely different reason now. 'Yes, Ken, this is a really stupid question.'

'Well, wait. I haven't even gotten to the question yet. What I want to know is, when you're out walking around, if you accidentally bump into something, do you, like, have an orgasm?'

She laughed in surprise. 'What?'

'I just wanted to know.' He was actually serious. 'This is a brand new one for me and—'

'Oops,' she said, 'you just bumped me. Oh! Ooooh! Unh!'

'Sure,' Ken said. 'Mock me. Go ahead. I'm genuinely interested because it was . . .'

She waited.

'Great,' he finished quietly. 'It was fricking great, all right? To have you do that was . . .'

She waited again. He'd succeeded in completely distracting her with his ridiculous question, but now her heart was beating harder again for an entirely different reason.

'I mean, what's the most number of orgasms you've had at any one time?'

Oh, brother. Typical of a man to turn it into a contest. 'I don't know. I don't keep score. It's not about that.'

'It's not?' he asked. 'I mean, baby, if I could do what you do, I'd be, like, running all kinds of tests to see—'

Tests? She laughed. 'How would you do that? Would you get a vibrator and lock yourself in some room for days on end?'

He was actually considering her question, as if she'd asked it seriously. 'Well, I think I'd probably prefer a human partner, but—'

'For a woman, sex isn't really so much about the mechanics as it is about . . .' She searched for the right words. Love was definitely not one she wanted to use. Not with Kenny. Not now. She started over. 'It's not just a physical thing. It's mental and emotional, too. For me, it's not about "oh, if someone touches me right there, in that exact spot, I'll come right away," like it's some kind of magic button or something. It's about *who's* touching me, and how badly I want them to touch me, and what I see in their eyes when they touch me.'

Ken was silent, which she'd learned meant that he was thinking about what she'd just said. And probably getting ready to ask her more hideously embarrassing questions.

'Can we not talk about this anymore?' she asked somewhat desperately.

'How about we stop talking and just have sex instead?' His mouth was so close to her ear, she could feel the heat of his breath. If she turned her head, she could kiss him.

'Go to sleep,' she said instead. 'You're such a—'

'Jerk,' he finished for her. She could tell from the sound of his voice that he was smiling. 'Yeah, I know. Still, I had to ask. You know, 'cause maybe you changed your mind, right? But, sleep – that's a good idea, too. Not as much fun, but definitely my second choice for this evening's activity.'

He was quiet for several long seconds, and then he asked, 'You okay now?'

She was. As long as he kept her arms around her. 'Don't leave,' she begged him. 'Please.' He'd told her he was going to go out and scout the surrounding area. If she woke up in this darkness and he was gone . . .

'I won't,' he promised. 'Not tonight, okay?'

Thank God. 'Do you mind sleeping like this?' she had to ask, not sure what she would do if he said yes.

Kenny laughed softly. 'Yeah, right, I mind it a whole lot. But somehow I'll muddle through.'

Eleven

'What are *you* doing here?'

It was a damn good question – and one that Jones had an easy answer for. He held up the book that had managed to find its way into his bag yesterday afternoon on the boat.

'This is Molly's,' he said. 'I'm returning it.'

He'd found it this morning, in with his stuff. She'd probably missed having it to read last night before she went to sleep. It didn't seem right to make her wait until tonight to give it back.

Billy Bolten's voice was loaded with hostility. 'She's in the middle of a class right now.'

Jones knew. He could see her with about a dozen little kids in the shade of a tree.

Billy reached for the book. 'I'll give it to her when she's done.'

Jones stepped back. 'No, that's all right. I'll wait.'

He glanced over at Molly again and at that exact moment, she looked up and saw him. And smiled.

It was like being struck by lightning.

Yeah, right, he was here to return the book. That was just a lame excuse. What he'd really wanted was to see Molly. To see that smile. To try to sweet-talk her into running with him all the way back down the trail to his camp, so he could pull her into his arms and kiss her, pull up her skirt and lose himself inside of her soft heat.

Jesus, he wanted her. He'd woken up wanting her, just as he'd known he would.

Billy laughed with derision. 'You're totally wasting your time, man. She is *so* out of your league.'

'Ain't *that* the truth.' She looked over at him again, and this time the warmth and – Jesus – admiration in her eyes pissed him off.

She thought he was some kind of hero. She thought he was special, that he was good and kind and just like her.

But she was wrong.

He was a liar and a thief, and as soon as he got tired of her, he would take what little she had and never come back.

The thought of never coming back made his chest ache. But it would happen. When he left, it would be because he wanted to.

'Don't mistake her friendliness for something that it's not,' Billy warned him.

'I know,' Jones lied. 'She's already told me she just wants to be friends.'

'Really?'

'Yup.'

'Yeah, that's what she told me, too.' Billy warmed considerably toward him at that news, just as Jones had expected. They would now bond in their mutual misery.

Billy sighed. 'I know she's older but there's something, I don't know, *magical* about her. When she smiles . . .' He lowered his voice and leaned closer. 'You know, you can't help but look at her and imagine just what she could do to you with a mouth like that.'

Jones kept his own voice low, his tone easygoing. 'If you

ever say anything like that again – no, if you so much as *think* those thoughts, I will come into your tent in the middle of the night while you are sleeping and cut your balls off.' He smiled at the younger man. 'Got that, junior?'

Billy blinked at him. He opened his mouth as if to speak, apparently thought better of it, then turned and quickly walked away. So much for bonding.

Across the clearing, Molly was watching, curiosity in her eyes. She shook her head at him and, as he watched, scribbled something on a piece of paper. She folded it in half and in half again, then handed it to a little girl, turning to say something and point at him.

And here came the little girl, trotting towards him. Note from Molly in hand.

She handed it to him with a giggle, and dashed back to her class.

Jones unfolded the note. Molly had bold, messy handwriting. He had to work to make out the words.

'You're distracting me,' it said. It was underlined, with three exclamation points. 'Wait in my tent and I'll be done here more quickly.'

It was an invitation into her tent. Jones practically ran all the way there. He knew she had rules about what could or couldn't go on in there, but in his experience, rules were made to be broken.

It was cool inside, even with the flaps down. Cool and dimly lit.

He looked around, breathing in her scent. She'd washed out some clothes and hung them on a line she'd stretched across the middle of the room. Underwear. It slid cool and damp and soft through his fingers.

A notebook was open on her table. 'Dear Chelsea,' he

read, 'I have met the most incredible, wonderful, inspiring man . . .'

This was a letter to her grown-up daughter, dated last night. He knew he had no business reading it, but he couldn't resist hearing what Molly had to say about him. Inspiring. Jesus. She was a lousy judge of character.

'. . . and I finally know where I am going, what I'll be doing in a month when my time here on Parwati Island is through.' What the hell was she talking about? She was leaving Parwati in a *month*?

'His name is . . .' *What?*

He read it again.

'His name is Father Benjamin Soldano, and I met him purely by chance at a church in the city. A child from our village got terribly sick, and I wrangled a ride to the hospital via airplane from one of the American ex-pats living in these mountains. (The very man you warned me about in your last letter, Chel!) He was quite the hero – you have nothing to fear. I don't know where he's been or what he's done – or what's been done to him. Lots, I think. Lots of luggage, very private stuff. But he's a kind man, a gentle man beneath that "don't touch me or I'll kill you" facade. I can tell you this: I would trust him with my life without hesitation.'

Wrong. He was not to be trusted – how could she write that with such conviction? A few conversations, an afternoon spent fucking, and she thought she knew enough about him to trust him with her *life*? What was wrong with her?

'I can't tell you much about him here,' her words continued, 'but I'll fill you in in a few weeks when I come visit.

'Let me tell you instead about Ben. You would love him as much as I do. We met because he was also staying at Nadine and Ira's house that night after I brought Joaquin and his mother to the hospital, and it was amazing! We were two old friends who had never seen each other before – we clicked instantly and talked almost all night long.'

That was the night she'd taken Jones out to dinner. She'd said good night to him, then gone and stayed up all night with this Ben.

Jesus Christ, he was actually jealous. Jealous that she'd *talked* with another man. A priest no less. He had no right to be jealous of that, but he was.

'He's convinced me to come join his mission in Africa, so that's where I'll be heading next. It will help ease the pain of leaving this place and these people – so many of whom I've come to love. *Too* many of whom I've come to love. Oh, Chelsea, I wish I could tell you about this absolutely stupid thing I've done, but I don't dare write it down.'

That was it. The letter was unfinished and that was as far as she'd gotten.

Of course, he knew *he* was the stupid thing she'd done. He didn't have to be a genius to figure that out.

Jones backed away from her table, more disturbed by the fact that she was leaving the island and going to Africa where she'd talk night after night with some priest named Ben than the fact that she considered her affair with him to be stupid.

It *was* stupid of her to have anything to do with him. He knew that and was actually a little relieved that she knew it, too. Maybe on some level she honestly knew that he wasn't this hero, this 'kind' and 'gentle' man she'd written about in her letter.

He sat down on her bed, then lay back, his feet still on the floor. Her sheets and the bright-colored spread smelled like Molly. He stared up at the inside of the tent, the news that she was leaving rolling around in his head, making him feel things he didn't want to feel.

Angry.

Hurt. Why hadn't she told him she would be leaving soon?

Yeah, like *he* ever told a lover that he wasn't planning to stick around.

Except she was *Molly*. She was supposed to be here, in this village, working tirelessly to help these people forever. Wasn't she?

He was the one who was supposed to leave.

Fuck.

He sat up and opened the book that he was still holding, opened to the place where Molly had used a leaf as a bookmark and started to read, willing to do damn near anything to silence his disturbing thoughts.

We danced until four A.M., and I pretended to drink too much champagne.

That was my big mistake, I realized far too late. And the truth was, I didn't just pretend to drink too much. I actually did imbibe somewhat more enthusiastically than I usually did, hoping it would give me the courage I needed to look up at Heinrich von Hopf as we danced at the Supper Club, and whisper, 'Take me home with you tonight.'

It didn't. I couldn't get the words out.

He brought me to my apartment in a taxi, saw me to my door, and quite gracefully eluded my clumsy attempt to pull him inside.

That was the best I could manage in the seduction department.

'You've had too much champagne. I'll see you at lunch tomorrow,' he murmured before he sweetly kissed me good night and practically ran down the steps to the waiting cab.

I didn't sleep at all that night.

I paced. I cursed. I gnashed my teeth. I groaned, imagining what it would be like when Hank was charged with espionage and brought to trial. I imagined seeing pictures in the newspaper of him hung, a black hood on his head, his body limp and lifeless.

God, I didn't want that to happen. I didn't want him to die.

But if I didn't turn Hank in, if I continued to let him work for Nazi Germany, God knows how many American lives would be lost.

Yet I loved him. I still loved him. The words I'd told him just a few hours ago had been the truth, bitter as it was.

I put on a pot of coffee and drank it all.

By the time the sun came up, I knew what I had to do.

It was the most difficult decision I'd ever made in my life, but I was an American.

And this was war.

I threw on my evening coat and, still wearing my gown from the night before, I went out into the cold morning air and took the subway – an indirect route as usual, in case anyone was following me – to the FBI headquarters in Manhattan.

Ken opened his eyes, instantly alert in the ghostly light of the predawn, with an awareness prickling the back of his neck, telling him that he was not alone.

Yeah, duh, obviously he wasn't alone. He was sleeping in a camouflaged blind, invisible to most of the world, with his arms around Savannah von Hopf. She'd turned toward him in the night, nestling her blond head beneath his chin, throwing her leg across his. But she wasn't why he'd woken up.

Snick.

There it was again. The barely discernible sound of someone or someones trying to move soundlessly through the jungle.

Scuff.

Pop.

Yeah, there was definitely more than one person out there. Probably three. And as far as moving soundlessly went, they pretty much sucked at it.

He saw one, two, yeah there were definitely three men in complete jungle cammo gear. He watched through the holes in the brush he'd cut to hide them while they slept. The uniformed men were almost on top of them.

Snick. Pop. Crshh. The sounds were louder – Ken couldn't believe Savannah didn't wake up.

He *did* move soundlessly, then, shifting Savannah in his arms, so that one hand was free. He used it to cover her mouth. God forbid she start talking in her sleep.

Of course, his hand over her mouth made her jerk awake, but he moved her head so that she could see him, so that she was looking directly into his eyes. His mouth was close enough to hers so that he could press his finger against his own lips in the universal gesture for silence.

She nodded, her eyes wide, and he took his hand from her mouth, pointed out toward the jungle. Held up three fingers.

There was a flare of fear in her eyes as she nodded again. She understood what he was telling her. She looked out through the branches that hid them, got a glimpse of an AK-47, then closed her eyes, tucking her head back against his chest.

He could hear her work to keep her breathing slow and steady – no doubt she was remembering how loud her breathing had been last night when she'd started hyperventilating.

Savannah was smart and she was tough, and damn, he was proud of her for somehow knowing that she should breathe steadily, for having the instincts to look away from the men who were searching for them.

Ken had absolutely no doubts that those three Rambo wannabes were hunting Americans. Hunting *them*.

He held onto Savannah for a long time after they'd vanished into the jungle to the north, finally letting her go when he was sure there was no one else out there, and that these clowns hadn't doubled back.

She untangled her legs from his, lay back in the dirt, and exhaled a long, shaky breath. 'I think I was hoping they wouldn't ever get out of their helicopter.'

'I don't think those guys were from the helicopter.'

She looked at him. 'Then who were they?'

'I don't know yet.'

She pushed herself up onto her elbows, her face brightening. 'Maybe they can help us.'

'Yeah, those weapons they were carrying were standard Welcome Wagon issue.' Ken unfastened the side pocket of the cargo pants she was wearing and took out his knife, putting it into her hand. 'While I'm gone,' he told her, 'take off these pants and cut the legs off like you said last night – so we can use 'em to carry the dynamite. Use that little sewing kit you've got in your bag to stitch up the bottom ends and—'

'Wait a minute,' she shifted around to face him. 'While you're gone . . . ? Gone where?'

'I'm going to follow these guys. See where they're going, hopefully see where they came from. It could take a while. As in hours. Maybe even all day. You need to stay here, stay hidden. Don't leave this blind for anything. Do you understand?'

'Yes, but—'

He pulled the Uzi toward her. 'I'm leaving this with you. Here's what you need to do to fire it.' He showed her. 'Squeeze this – but not unless you really mean it, all right?'

She didn't look happy. 'Ken—'

'Try not to kill me by mistake when I come back.'

'You mean it's okay if I kill you on purpose?'

'Very funny.' The fact that she was able to joke made him feel better about leaving her there alone. With the sun coming up and the light getting stronger every minute, she would be fine. He reached around to the other pocket in the pants she was wearing, took out the power bars. 'Eat these if you get hungry. Give me a sec, and I'll get you a couple coconuts so you have something to drink.'

'You know, Kenny, maybe you should just keep going,' Savannah said, turning slightly to face him.

He glanced at her, and she was watching him with those eyes, her face completely serious.

'I'm going to pretend I didn't hear that,' he told her tightly.

She didn't let it drop. 'You can go get help and then come back for me.'

'Nope.' He made an opening in the branches and wriggled out into the jungle, taking a few seconds to admire his handiwork. He was a computer specialist and he didn't consider building blinds – places to hide in the forest or jungle – as one of his strengths, but this one was damn fine. You really had to know what you were looking for to find it.

Savannah poked her face out of the hole in the branches. 'Ken—'

'Nope,' he said again, handing her first one and then another coconut. 'If I'm going to follow those guys, I better move.'

'Be careful,' she said, her eyes and mouth worried, her hair a mess of curls around her face.

Ken leaned over and kissed her. It was a stupid thing to do, but he didn't really think about it. He just did it. He'd just spent the night holding her, and it somehow seemed appropriate to kiss her before he walked out of their bedroom – so to speak.

It was kind of like kissing a fish, though – she was completely caught off guard. Okay, it was like kissing a sweet, warm fish that he wanted to have sex with more than just about anything.

The worst of it, though, was right afterward, when what he'd just done lay there between his realization that he shouldn't have kissed her and her expression of complete surprise.

'Sorry,' he said shortly, then covered her up with the branches. He got the hell out of there before she could tell him for the seven thousandth time that he was a jerk.

That he already knew.

'Bhagat.'

'Sir, it's Locke,' Alyssa said into the telephone. She was standing in Senior Chief Stan Wolchonok's office in the Team Sixteen building in Coronado. He'd shown her there so she'd have privacy to make her phone call, and then vanished.

'What'd you find out?'

'A little too much nothing,' she told her boss, who was now on the other side of the Pacific. 'We've interviewed Paoletti and Starrett and just about all of the other SEALs in Team Sixteen with the exception of John Nilsson, who's out of the country. But no one here even knew Savannah von Hopf's name. Only Starrett knew that Karmody had recently – and I mean extremely recently – met someone and begun an intimate relationship.'

'Intimate?' Max interrupted.

'Sexual,' she defined. 'Karmody also didn't mention Indonesia to anyone – not even Starrett, whom he spoke with only hours before leaving San Diego. I don't think he knew he was going until the last minute because he was completely open with Starrett about certain other details of his relationship. My guess is that Savannah used sex to make sure Karmody'd be willing to follow her anywhere.' She paused. 'With your permission, I'm going to withhold that theory from Rose von Hopf.'

'Good idea.'

'I've called the Los Angeles office.' There was a framed

picture of a pretty, dark-haired, dark-eyed woman on the senior chief's desk. It was his wife, Teri, who was a helo pilot for the Coast Guard. In the photo, she was leaning over the edge of a hot tub, looking directly into the camera's lens. The look in her eyes and on her face was a mixture of desire and pure love.

Alyssa had to move to the other side of Wolchonok's desk. Looking at that picture made her acutely aware of everything that was missing in her own pathetic life.

'They've sent a couple of agents to LAX to talk to the airline personnel,' she continued. 'See if anyone recalls Karmody and Savannah getting onto the plane. See if there was anything unusual about them in any way, see if he seemed at all coerced, or maybe drugged, or . . . I know I'm reaching here, but—'

'No, that's good,' Max said. 'Reach away. Did you get into Karmody's apartment?'

'Sam had a key.' Alyssa silently cursed herself for slipping and calling him *Sam*. Starrett. She had to call the man *Starrett*. Make it sound as if he were just another source of information for this case. 'Karmody's got a house – two bedrooms, one of 'em filled with computers. He's the team hacker, you know. A real gear-head.'

'I'm familiar with his talent. What'd you find?'

'He's got a prototype of a tracking system running on one of his computers. He'd activated it before leaving San Diego. We managed to get a fairly accurate readout of his trail through Hong Kong, into Jakarta. He left the Jakarta airport either via boat or helo. But we lost him shortly after that, over the open ocean. At first we were thinking this wasn't good news – that he was thrown over the side of the boat or something, but Sam—' *Shit.* '*Starrett* messed around

SUZANNE BROCKMANN

with the program – came up with some kind of satellite error message, which hopefully means Karmody's still alive. We've got the general direction he was heading, though – which could really help. I've downloaded everything, including the program. A copy's already on its way to HQ, I gave a second to Tom Paoletti, and I'll be hand delivering a third to you.'

'Good job,' Max said. 'The New York office just got access to Savannah's phone records – she received a call from Jakarta on Wednesday. It's likely that was the ransom request – except the call was made from Alex's hotel room. We're sifting through hotel security tapes – see if we can't ID whoever went into that room and made that call.'

'Wow,' Alyssa said. 'Is this going to turn out to be easy?'

'Please God, I hope so,' Max said.

'Commander Paoletti has already called in a team,' she told him. 'They're ready to go wheels up at your go ahead. He thinks it would be worthwhile to get some men who know WildCard Karmody out into that jungle. He's probably trying to call you right now.'

'Actually, I've just been told Paoletti's on hold. Is there anything else you need to tell me before I take his call?'

'Not over the phone.'

'Uh, oh,' Max said. 'Seeing Starrett was that bad?'

She had actually been thinking about the intimate details of WildCard and Savannah's relationship. 'No, sir. That was no problem at all,' she lied smoothly.

He laughed. 'You know, I almost believe you.'

'Sir,' she said stiffly. 'Commander Paoletti's waiting for you.'

'I know,' Max said. 'Alyssa, I'm sorry I had to ask you to go there.'

'Sir, I'm a professional and—'

'Yeah,' he said. 'I'm still sorry. Now get your ass on a plane back to LA. I'll see you when you get to Jakarta.'

With a click of the connection, he was gone.

Alyssa hung up the phone and went looking for Jules – and came face to face with Sam and Mary Lou Starrett out in the hall, outside of Sam's office, which was several doors down. Neither of them noticed her and she ducked back into Wolchonok's cubby hole.

'What are you doing here?' Sam said. Alyssa could hear him quite clearly.

Mary Lou had managed finally to change her shirt. She sounded nervous, her voice a little wobbly, as if she were really upset. 'When you called, you said you weren't sure how long you'd be gone and I . . .' She cleared her throat. 'I wanted to see you before you left. I thought you might want to say goodbye to Haley.'

Alyssa peeked around the corner – sure enough, there was Sam's little baby, tucked into one of those carriers that doubled as a carseat.

'She's asleep,' Sam said flatly.

There was silence for a moment, but then Mary Lou said, 'Yes, she is. Just like you usually are the few hours you're actually ever home.'

Sam sighed deeply. 'I got things to do before we go wheels up. This is not the time for—'

'You talk in your sleep,' Mary Lou interrupted him. 'Did you know that?'

'*Shit*.'

'Do you know what you say?'

'Jesus, Mary Lou—'

'You say, *Alyssa*,' Mary Lou said, and Alyssa cringed.

Oh, Sam . . . ' "Oh, Lys . . . Don't go, Lys . . . Alyssa, oh, God . . . oh, yes . . ." '

'Aw, *fuck*.'

'Yes, I believe that sums up what you're dreaming about quite nicely.'

'I'm sorry,' Sam said quietly. 'I can't help what I dream. If I could, I'd stop. I swear to you, I have not been unfaithful since that day we agreed to get married.'

'She's black,' Mary Lou said.

And Alyssa, who'd been about to back away from the door after hearing that Sam called out for her in his sleep, froze. She waited to hear what he would say in response to that.

'She's at least part African-American, yes.' Sam's voice was a little less quiet now. 'Why, is that some kind of problem for you?'

'I can't believe it wasn't a problem for you,' Mary Lou countered. 'Unless it was just about the sex.' She must've seen something on Sam's face, because she added, 'Oh, my dear Lord, what did you think – that you were going to *marry* her? You actually think that would've worked? A white man and a black woman? You know, a woman like her never would've married someone like you! And even if she did – where would you live? Can you imagine her living on our street? Or maybe you'd prefer living in one of the black neighborhoods across town?' Her voice rose. 'Don't you walk away from me!'

'What do you want from me?' Sam asked, his voice low, intense. 'How can you be so angry with me for something that never happened – something that's only a might-have-been? I *didn't* marry Alyssa. I married you. I come home to you and Haley every night. I'm working my ass off to pay for that house and the things you want to put inside it. What else do you want?'

Alyssa felt like crying. She knew she should close the door and plug her ears so she didn't hear any of this. This was private between Sam and his wife. She shouldn't be listening. But she couldn't make herself stop.

'She wouldn't have married you,' Mary Lou told Sam. She was really upset. She wasn't the only one. 'She was just playing you, Sam. You really think you meant anything more to her than a good-looking man with a big—'

Sam cut her off, from the sound of his voice, he was walking away. 'I've got to go. Take care of the baby – and yourself, too, while I'm gone.'

'I'm not finished here!'

'Well I fucking am!' He took a deep breath, spoke more quietly. 'I don't want to fight with you. Especially not here. Jesus, Mary Lou.'

'Instead you're going to go off and save the world – with her, right? She's going, too. And I'm supposed to be okay with that?'

'Don't let this craziness make you start drinking again,' Sam said. 'Call your AA sponsor when you get home, okay? Promise me. Tell her I'm out of town for the next few weeks at the least.'

Mary Lou followed him. 'Maybe you should take advantage of seeing her again,' she said shrilly. 'Maybe you should go to her and finish what you started. That way when she drops you, it can really be over. That way you don't have to spend the rest of your life wondering about those might-have-beens.'

Sam turned to face her. 'Are you telling me to go have an

SUZANNE BROCKMANN

affair with Alyssa Locke? Because if that's really what you want, I will *gladly*—'

'Of course that's not what I want!' Mary Lou was in tears now.

'Then tell me what you want,' he said again. 'Do I need to open a vein and bleed for you? Will that help, Mary Lou? Because, frankly, I don't know what the fuck else to do.'

'I'm sorry,' she sobbed, and Alyssa peeked around the doorway to see her clinging to him. 'I know you're trying, I do. I'm sorry I got so upset. I was just so jealous and . . . and . . .'

And a mean-spirited racist bitch.

'And *shocked* when I saw her. She's so beautiful and I'm fat.'

'You're not fat,' Sam said tiredly as if they'd had this conversation too many times before. 'You just had a baby. Give yourself a break.'

'I don't want you to open a vein, Sam,' Mary Lou told him softly. 'I want you to open your heart. You loved me once. Couldn't you love me again?'

'Jesus, I'm trying my best,' he said, as if this were killing him.

And Alyssa knew. Whatever he'd once felt for Mary Lou, it hadn't been love. And it would never be love as long as he was still dreaming about what he'd found with Alyssa.

She knew what she had to do. She had to talk to Sam.

Lucky for her – yeah, right, her luck was really holding here – they were both about to leave for Jakarta.

When Kenny had been gone for three hours, Savannah ate both the power bars, one right after the other.

She'd done as he'd asked and carefully used his knife to

306

make the pants she was wearing into shorts. She'd sewn up the ends of the cutoff legs and made odd-looking sacks large enough to carry the dynamite, feeling vaguely like the Martha Stewart of the jungle as she worked.

Ken's undershirt, which had been holding the dynamite up to now, was badly stretched out of shape. She tried it on – wearing it was as good as going naked. The armholes were too large, the cotton awfully thin. But if Kenny came back – *when* not *if*. *When*. He'd need to wear the shirt he'd first given her or else risk getting more rope burns from the vines—

Savannah dug through her purse and found her extra pair of pantyhose. God, why didn't she think of this yesterday? Martha Stewart, indeed. Uses for pantyhose number 43,516. It wouldn't take the attaché case's full weight, but they could use it along with the vines to tie the case to his back. It would certainly help so that he could – as he continued to insist was vitally important – keep his hands free and his Uzi at the ready.

She glanced at the gun that he'd left behind; it had been her sole companion for all of the hours he'd been gone. She knew Ken had left it so she'd feel more secure, but in truth it made her uneasy. She didn't want to shoot anyone. She wasn't going to touch it. He should have just taken it with him.

Thoughts of the Uzi invariably led back to thoughts of the way Ken had kissed her right before he'd left. For the past four hours, everything she'd done had led to thoughts of that kiss.

What did it mean?

She honestly didn't know. Ever since he'd shown up at the airport he'd alternated between icy silence and rude disdain.

And yes, okay, to be fair, there had been plenty of moments when he'd laughed or been impossibly kind, and he'd turned back into the man she'd found so irresistible that night at his house. That night she'd broken all of her personal rules and slept with him.

He'd kissed her on the helo, but that had only been to shut her up. She knew that.

Was that kiss he'd given her this morning more of the same?

She would ask him. She'd just look him in the eye and confront him, right when he got back.

Until then, there was nothing to do but drowse in the heat. Or finally to read her grandmother's book.

What would Rose do? It was the question she'd asked herself repeatedly, ever since this fiasco began.

According to family legend – and God knows she'd heard the story so many times she really didn't need to read about it in a book – Rose was just one step down from Superwoman. Because, of course, she couldn't fly. But aside from that, she was strong and unstoppable. Determined and invincible.

Rose would eat bugs if she had to. Rose wouldn't complain about covering herself with slime. Rose would refuse to believe that Alex was dead, would find him and bring him to safety. And everyone – both good guys and bad – would fall completely in love with her along the way.

Those were pretty intense footsteps to follow. And so far Savannah was failing miserably. She'd managed to make Kenny dislike her. She was a pain in his butt, a problem that needed taking care of, someone to slow him down.

He'd probably kissed her because he knew she'd obsess

about it. No doubt he'd figured it would keep her occupied until he got back.

Savannah opened Rose's book to a chapter in the middle, determined not to think about Kenny Karmody for at least the next fifteen minutes.

Okay, *five* minutes. She'd start small.

'I need to borrow some money.'

'Of course.' Evelyn Fielding set down her cup of tea and reached for her pocketbook.

'No, Evelyn.' I stopped her with a hand upon her arm. 'I need to borrow eight thousand dollars. I can't tell you why. And it might take me years – decades – before I can pay you back.'

She laughed, but her eyes were dead serious. 'Well, when you put it that way, how could I possibly refuse? Can I write you a check?'

She was going to lend me the money! Elation didn't keep me from being cautious. 'No, you better not.' In case something went wrong, I didn't want my name showing up on one of Evelyn's bank checks. 'Thank you so much.'

'I'll get you the cash right now if you want to take a ride to the bank.'

I nodded. 'Please.'

We gathered up our coats and she didn't say another word until we were in a taxi and heading across town.

Then she turned to me and said, 'If you're in some kind of trouble, Rose, I might be able to help. And if you don't want to talk to me, there's always Jon—'

'I know.'

'He told me you've asked for the next two weeks off – emergency medical leave.'

The words hung between us. She knew that was the code we

309

used when I had to give one hundred per cent of my attention to my FBI job.

'Yes,' I finally said. I coughed and tried to make it sound good.

Evelyn laughed softly. 'I hope you know what you're doing.'

The taxi pulled up in front of her bank, and she got out. 'Wait here,' she ordered us both – the driver and me.

I hoped I knew what I was doing, too.

I'd gone to the FBI early that same morning and announced that I'd been contacted by someone I'd met while in Berlin. That got me in to see not just my immediate superior, Anson Faulkner, but his bosses, and their bosses, too.

They brought me coffee, and, still dressed in my evening gown, I told them that this man was a high-level Nazi, and that if he so much as suspected he was being investigated, he'd vanish. But he wouldn't suspect me. I told them that he thought I was in love with him.

I didn't tell them he was right.

I sketched out my plan to play along, to gain access to his room and his personal papers, to meet everyone he talked to and find out who was working for him. I told Anson and the others that I didn't just want to bring this man down, I wanted to take out his entire network of spies.

They seemed to think this was a good idea, but they weren't so keen that I should be the one to do it.

I tried to convince them otherwise. I told them all I would need to pull this off was some of that money I'd given back to the war effort. I told them I wanted eight thousand dollars to make this man believe that I'd been working for the Nazis for years.

They didn't like *that* very much at all.

It was then that I told them Hank's name was Dieter Mannheim. That was, of course, a lie, but I was convinced if they knew his real name, they would start following him, he'd become aware of it, and run.

They told me I'd done my part. Now I was to play it safe, to let them run an initial investigation. I was to make myself scarce, to take several weeks off from work, to make it hard for Mannheim to find me.

I demurely agreed. They weren't going to give me the help that I needed, but despite what I told them, I *would* go through with my plan. I'd borrow the money from Evelyn.

Before I left the building, Anson Faulkner pulled me aside to say, 'Don't do anything stupid.'

'I won't,' I said, and he knew I was lying. He was a young man, and he'd later told me that, at the time, he'd fancied himself more than half in love with me.

'You're willing to take this Nazi as a lover?' he'd asked. 'Because that's what he'll expect, Rose.'

I'd looked him in the eye, trying my hardest to be cool as that proverbial cucumber. 'There are a lot of people making sacrifices to win this war.'

The door opened and Evelyn climbed back inside the cab. She handed me an envelope. 'It's all there.'

I hugged her. 'I'll pay you back.'

'I know,' she said. 'I have faith in you.' She paused. 'Are you sure you can't tell me what this is about?'

I nodded. 'I'm sure.' What could I say? I'm about to attempt to pull off the impossible. I'm about to take the biggest risk of my life, to try to win a no-win situation. I don't have a clue how I'm going to manage this, and I've never been so terrified in all of my life. I've been alternating between feeling sick to my stomach and wanting to burst into tears. If I tell you what I'm going to do, you'll try to talk me out of it, and I can't risk being swayed from this path. 'Wish me luck,' I said instead.

'Women make their own good luck,' Evelyn hugged me, too, 'by being smart and careful. And unafraid to ask for help. I'm here if you need me. For anything. No questions asked.'

Well, that was it for me. We just sat there then, hugging each other and crying.

I have faith in you.

I realized in that cab that I had faith in me, too. I would do this. I would not back down. I would not quit.

I would not fail.

I hoped.

Twelve

The three men in camouflage gear took forever, but finally made their way back to a camp where about eight other men were gathered.

Ken watched from the cover of the jungle as his three guys checked in and gave some kind of report to a man who was wearing a black beret. A frickin' wool beret in this heat.

He didn't even come close to speaking their language, but he listened to the tone of their voices and read their body language. His guys didn't have any good news for Beret, who was clearly their boss. Beret wasn't happy, but he sent them over to another man who gave them something to eat from a pack.

Holy shit, they actually had US issued MRE's – Meals, Ready to Eat, food rations given out to soldiers during times of war or conflict.

Ken's stomach rumbled. Imagine that. He actually longed for an MRE.

Beret paced, hands behind his back, deep in thought, as Ken checked out the rest of the camp. It was a temporary resting place, that much was obvious. There was a single tent – for Beret, no doubt. The rest of the men slept in the open. There was no fire lit, and no sign that there had been

SUZANNE BROCKMANN

one last night, either. Obviously these guys didn't want to draw any attention to themselves.

There were at least two guards hiding in the brush, guarding the camp's perimeter. Ken had spotted them right away, but it had been ridiculously easy to keep them from seeing him. He suspected there were at least two others, maybe more, on the opposite side of the camp.

Beret had the military leader walk down pat. He paced back and forth with just the right amount of revolutionary swagger. But his troops left something to be desired. They wore the right clothes and carried big weapons, but clothes and arms didn't an army make.

Whoever they were, they weren't the ABRI, the Indonesian armed forces. They had no flags, no identifying insignia of any kind. When Ken had first started following them, he'd guessed they were part of some rival gun runner's staff. Or maybe hired guns brought in by the men in the helo.

But Beret didn't have the look of a man who was in this for the money. This group was political or maybe religious. Or both.

Ken wished he were wrong. He could handle gun and drug runners scampering around the jungle. He understood their bottom line: money, revenge, power. He could predict their response in most situations. But religious or political zealots weren't quite so easy to second guess. They were often willing or even eager to die for their cause.

As Ken moved even closer, he saw that these men had had some training of some kind. But that almost made them even more ineffective than people with no training at all. These soldiers *thought* they were hot shit. They thought they had things under control. And maybe, if their targets were civilians, they did. But pit 'em against the SEALs or the guys from Delta ...

They made the same mistake that people who had guards with big weapons stationed around the perimeter of their camp usually made. They assumed that as long as *they* weren't on guard duty, they could relax. Close their eyes. Drowse in the afternoon heat.

Because of this, Ken waltzed right up to the bag with the MRE's and helped himself to about a half a dozen of the packets and a canteen filled with some kind of liquid before blending silently back into the underbrush.

He could have taken a uniform shirt, too, but he suspected that might be missed. He didn't want to tip these guys off to the fact that he was out here.

It was then that Beret stopped pacing and gave an order, and the camp came to life. They were moving out.

Ken got ready to follow, taking the opportunity to chow down on one of the packets labeled 'chicken with vegetables.' Not his favorite, but he was hungry enough to love every gooey, body temperature mouthful.

As he ate, he thought about Savannah, waiting for him back in the blind. He'd already been gone for hours. Even without having to trail the three very slow tangos, even moving at his own top speed, it would take him close to three hours to get back to her. She was probably already worrying about him, probably starting to wonder if he'd decided to take her suggestion and leave her behind.

Shit.

It pissed him off that she still kept bringing that up as a possibility. What did he have to do to prove to her that he wasn't going to ditch her?

He had to start by coming back. Preferably before the sun went down. And then maybe in a few days – by the time he got her to safety – she'd finally realize he'd meant what he'd said about not leaving.

But right now he wanted to see where these guys were going. It would be smart if he could at least get a sense of the direction they were heading, smarter yet if he could find out where they came from and what the chances were that there'd be more of 'em creeping around this part of the jungle.

Still, he kept imagining Savannah, alone in that blind as the sun started to set.

Worse yet, he imagined her assuming he wasn't coming back and striking out on her own.

Jesus, he had to get back there right away before she did that.

Ken was out of there and halfway down the hillside before he stopped and forced himself to take a deep breath and think this through.

He was doing the very thing to Savannah that pissed him off so much when she did it to him. Just as he'd promised her he'd come back – it might take a while, but he'd definitely return – Savannah had promised him that she'd stay in the blind. And as long as she was hidden there, she was safe.

So why was he rushing back?

Because he didn't trust that she'd do as she'd promised.

Do unto others as you would have them do unto you. If he wanted her to trust him, he had to start by trusting her.

Ken headed back toward Beret and his camp, and when they finally moved out, he followed.

*

Molly went back into her tent after lunch, and Grady – *Jones* – was still asleep on her bed.

He'd brought her *Double Agent*, and it lay beside him. He must've been reading it before he fell asleep; his finger was still marking his place.

She let herself look at him – her lover.

In a few hours, just before sunset, she would go to his camp, and they would make love again. All evening and into the night. She couldn't wait – she ached for the day to end.

Lucky Jones – he was sleeping it away.

She loved his eyes, she realized, as she gazed down at his face. As he slept, he looked so peaceful, so young and pure with those eyes closed, his eyelashes thick and dark against his cheeks. He was exceptionally handsome, with a mouth that looked decadently good no matter if it were arranged in a grim line, or stretched into a full grin, or relaxed in sleep. His chin was sheer perfection, and he'd shaved it again this morning.

For her.

Molly reached out to touch the smoothness of his face, just lightly, and he moved, reaching up to grab her wrist with one hand.

Just like that, he was awake, eyes open and completely alert, gazing up at her.

'I'm sorry – I didn't mean to wake you,' she said, losing herself for a moment in the midnight of his eyes. He was gorgeous when asleep, but when he was awake and looking at her with those incredible eyes . . . He had the power to make her heart pound.

'What time is it?' he asked, his voice rough from sleep.

'It's nearly one. I let you sleep,' she explained with a

smile that she hoped hid the way her pulse was jumping. 'I figured you needed it after I wore you out yesterday.'

He laughed that little laugh that she'd come to love and tugged her down so that she was sitting beside him on the bed.

'I couldn't wait to see you,' he murmured. 'I couldn't wait to . . .'

Molly wasn't quite sure how he did it. One second she was sitting above him, the next she was lying beside him, partially beneath him on the bed. He was kissing her – slow, deep, impossibly erotic kisses. He brought her hand down to his male parts and pressed her palm against him – a very grown-up version of the show and tell she'd done with her youngest class just this morning. He was hugely aroused – so much so that despite her rule of what could and could not go on in her tent, she didn't want to let go of him.

She did this to him. It was an unbelievable turn-on.

'I've been walking around like this since I got off the boat yesterday,' he whispered as he pulled up her shirt and pushed aside her bra, his mouth hot and wet and desperate as he suckled her hard. Almost too hard.

Molly clenched her teeth against the sound – that of sheer, mind-blowing pleasure – that threatened to escape from her throat.

Stop. She had to tell him to stop. They couldn't do this here.

But she was still clinging to him through his shorts, and he unfastened them, pushing them down and out of the way so that she was really touching him – hard and smooth and hot and large.

Her door was unlocked. Even if she did want to break her rule – and, Lord, she didn't – she would *never* do this with her door unlocked.

But he roughly pushed up her skirt, pushed aside her underpants and touched her. She was slick from wanting him, and he filled her with his fingers, making her gasp. God, she wanted him inside of her. But they could not do this here.

'Grady! I want . . .'

'I know,' he said. 'I'm almost . . .'

He was covering himself with a condom using only one hand, and she found herself helping.

'Please,' she breathed, 'I can't do this here!' But she wanted to. She wanted him more than she could ever remember wanting anything or anyone. All she had to do to make him stop was to pull away. Instead of wrapping her legs around his waist she had to get off the bed, rearrange her clothes and tell him that, really, they had to wait for later.

But she didn't want to wait.

'Stop,' she said frantically, even as she pulled him toward her. 'Please! You've got to stop because I can't!'

He did stop – pulling his head up from the hedonistic things he was doing to her nipples with his mouth to look down at her in amazement. 'You want *me* to be the one to stop this? You're kidding, right?'

'No!' She could feel him, heavy and hot against her and her hips moved up, seeking more of him. 'My rule. It's the right thing. Don't make me—'

'Screw your rule,' he told her, pushing himself just a little bit inside of her, but pulling back out as she opened herself to him, as she lifted her hips toward him again.

She heard herself make a sound not unlike a whimper and he laughed.

'Yeah, right, I'm going to stop when you do that. What

kind of hero do you think I am, Mol? I only do the right thing when there's a payoff in my favor. Don't ever forget that.'

'Please,' she breathed, but she didn't really know what she was begging for. He just kept teasing her, pushing himself a fraction of the way into her and then pulling out of reach.

'It's your rule,' he told her. 'You want to follow it, you're going to have to do it yourself. Here's my rule – to come inside you as often as I can before you fucking leave.'

He slammed himself into her, and she heard herself cry out. Yes. Oh, *yes*. He muffled the sound she made by kissing her, his tongue hot and thick in her mouth.

She clung to him, matching the slam-bam urgency of his pace, her fingers in his hair, digging into his back. He didn't slow down and she didn't want him to.

She forgot about her rule, forgot about the unlocked door. There was only Grady and his need for her – and her insatiable need for him.

His hands and mouth were rough as he drove himself harder and faster inside of her, again and again and again.

'Come now,' he breathed into her ear. 'Come with me – oh, Christ, Molly!'

She exploded, too, waves of pleasure making her shake. Yes. Oh, *yes*!

'Shh,' he said, laughing a little, pressing his hand down over her mouth. 'Shhh!'

And then there they were, in her tent, in her bed, breathing hard, having just broken her biggest rule. Lord, it was really her *only* rule.

One of them should've been able to keep their wits about them. And it just wasn't fair that it should always have to be her.

Grady – Jones, damnit, she had to start thinking of him as *Jones* – sighed. It sounded just a little too satisfied and smug.

So Molly bit him on the finger. Hard.

'Ouch! Jesus!' He pulled out and slightly off of her, and she took the opportunity to scramble off the bed and onto her feet. To quickly rearrange her clothing. Damn it, he'd given her a hickey on her breast. She quickly checked her mirror to make sure he hadn't marked her any place that showed.

Her hair was a mess, and her face looked . . .

Like she'd just had outrageously wild sex in the afternoon in her tent in the middle of a missionary's camp in a village where she and her coworkers had been preaching safe sex and restraint from the moment they first arrived. She closed her eyes, cursing her weakness.

Jones came up behind her. 'You all right?'

Molly opened her eyes and looked at him in the mirror.

He was genuinely concerned. 'I didn't hurt you, did I? I didn't mean for it to get that rough. It just . . . And then you seemed to like it, so . . .'

'I asked you to stop.' It wasn't a fair accusation, and she knew it. She'd asked but she hadn't really wanted him to stop. Not at all. This was her fault, entirely.

Her eyes filled with tears, and he cursed and pulled her into his arms. 'I'm sorry,' he said. 'Jesus, I swore to myself that I wasn't going to apologize for this. Just tell me I didn't hurt you. I'd rather die than hurt you.'

'You didn't,' she whispered. He hadn't. Not yet anyway. But she was in much further over her head than she'd thought, if she was in a place where she'd so casually throw her rules out the window to share a cheap and easy quickie with this man, in the middle of the afternoon.

She couldn't get enough of him. What was going to happen when she left? She was leaving in a few short weeks. Of course, he'd probably leave Parwati Island first.

How was she going to deal with that if she didn't even have the power to push him out of her tent?

'Will you still come tonight?' he asked her.

Molly managed a smile. 'Gee, I hope so.'

He smiled, too, but it was halfhearted, and it occurred to her that he might be as shaken by this as she was. As much as he would try to deny it, this wasn't just about sex for him, either. And if the emotions that ran together whenever their eyes so much as met scared the hell out of *her*, what did it do to him?

'That is, if you still want me to,' she added quietly. She gave him an easy out. 'I understand if you need to make a delivery or something in your plane. You've kind of killed the morning and half the afternoon by coming over here.'

'The Cessna's down again,' he told her. 'I'm waiting on a part. Jaya – a guy I know's – working on getting it for me. I could probably rig something to get into the air if I really had to, but it would be pretty risky. And these past few days – it's funny, you know? My death wish hasn't been quite so strong.'

Molly felt the tears return to her eyes. She suspected that that was the closest thing to a declaration of love she was going to receive from this man.

She reached for him and he took her into his arms again.

Please God, she prayed as Jones kissed her so gently, so sweetly, so tenderly. Please give me the strength to accept this man's love for what I know it to be – just a temporary gift.

*

'What's in New Jersey?' Heinrich asked in the cab on the way to my apartment.

It was day five of my self-assigned mission, and I had gotten nowhere. Five whole days, and I still hadn't learned anything about his network of Nazi spies. I'd set foot in the man's hotel suite exactly once – for about fifteen seconds before we left for dinner two evenings ago. I was a failure at being a Mata Hari because I couldn't get up the nerve to seduce the man and he, apparently, had no intention of compromising me.

I did, however, use some of the money I'd borrowed from Evelyn Fielding to take a room at the Waldorf myself, right across from Heinrich's room – although he didn't know it. Every night, he dropped me at my apartment, and I would go inside. But as soon as his taxi pulled away, I'd follow. And every night, he always went straight back to the hotel.

Taking care that he didn't see me, I would follow him inside as well, watch as he went into his room and locked the door. Once he was in for the night, I would creep out into the hall, and put a thread across his door. I'd wake up early to check it, before breakfast arrived, and every morning that thread remained unbroken. That was how I knew that Heinrich von Hopf hadn't gone anywhere nor let anyone into his room.

It was frustrating. As much as I enjoyed our time together – and Nazi or not, I *did* enjoy nearly every minute I spent with the man I loved – I'd found out very little.

He often had meetings during the morning, but try as I might to follow him, I repeatedly lost him in a matter of a few city blocks. He was as good as I was at losing a tail.

I knew he had a notebook, a small pad, that he kept in his inside left jacket pocket. I'd only gotten a glimpse of it, but was certain it contained a list of names. I'd seen him jotting notes into it while we were out in society, at a club or a party, and I was growing more and more desperate to get a look at it.

I was going to have to be brazen. There was no way around it. If he wasn't going to invite me to his room, I would have to invite myself.

'New Jersey?' I said now, stalling. Light from the streetlamps shining in through the cab windows moved across his face as we headed for my apartment. He was seeing me home. Again. No matter how I kissed him, he never suggested I go back to his hotel with him.

He held something in his hand. 'This fell out of your coat pocket back at the club.'

I looked more closely. It was my bus ticket to Midland Park, New Jersey. Dated yesterday. I'd gone out to finish up work on a project that I hoped would be the solution to many of my current problems. But I couldn't tell *him* that.

'It *is* yours, isn't it?' Heinrich asked.

Spy rule number one: Stick as close to the truth as possible. 'Yes,' I told him. I smiled. But don't be afraid to lie when you have to. Keep it simple, easy to remember. 'Didn't I tell you? Lorraine, my best friend from college, had a baby a few months ago. You'd said you were busy all day, so I went out to see her.'

'No, you hadn't mentioned it,' he said.

'It's one of those topics an unmarried woman tends to avoid when with a man. Happily married friends with new babies.' I shook my head in mock disgust. 'Even if it's brought up innocently enough, it's perceived to be a giant hint. Hurry up and put a ring on my finger. Snap to it and put a baby in my womb. What are you waiting for? I hear it can be fun.'

The cab driver did an obvious double take in the rearview mirror, and Heinrich leaned forward. 'Let us out up ahead, just at the next corner here, will you please?' He looked at me. 'You don't mind if we walk for a bit, do you?'

I shook my head.

He paid the driver and we got out of the cab. The night was cold, but not bitterly so.

'He was a little too interested in our conversation,' Heinrich said as the cab drove away.

'Did I embarrass you?'

'No,' he said, then laughed. 'Well, yes, a little. But I wasn't embarrassed so much by you as by the driver. I'm not used to America where the servants listen and even join a discussion. In Austria, they maintain a distance.'

'They're listening in Austria,' I pointed out. 'They're just pretending that they're not. It's an illusion.'

'Maybe so,' he said. My apartment was about two blocks away. He offered me his arm as we began to walk. 'But it's an illusion I prefer.'

I didn't take his arm. 'Should I stop talking then, Hank?' I asked. 'Because I'm a servant.'

It was a stupid thing to say – to antagonize him that way when in a matter of a very short time we'd be standing on the steps to my apartment. This time, there would be no cab waiting for him to climb into and drive away. If I played it right, Heinrich would come inside with me. And once there, I wouldn't let him leave.

It would not be quite as effective or potentially rewarding as seducing him at the hotel – among whatever papers he might have there. But it would be a step toward getting into his room. And I knew he had his notebook with him.

He stopped walking and turned me to face him, his face so serious. 'Is that really how I make you feel?'

'No, of course not,' I admitted. 'Not usually. But honestly, it is what I am. I mean, if you think that cab driver is a servant . . . What's the difference between him and me? We both work for a living, providing a service to other people. He drives a cab. I'm a secretary.'

'Forgive me,' he said. 'I didn't mean to offend you. I just wanted . . .' He smiled ruefully. 'Some privacy. Although I know right now there's no such thing. There's so much we mustn't talk about.'

Like his network of Nazi spies living here in New York City? I had to try to get as much out of him as I possibly could.

'Surely no one can overhear us here on the sidewalk,' I said. 'You can tell me anything. You know that.' I moved toward him – any closer and we would be embracing. Even with our winter coats on, it was shockingly intimate.

'We both know why I'm here,' he said quietly. 'I really can't discuss it – not even with you, darling. We just don't know the extent of the enemy's ability to listen in to conversations.'

'But—'

He kissed me, the way he always did when he wanted to end a difficult discussion. Oh, how that man could kiss. By the time he was done, I was ready to beg him to come inside with me. I opened my mouth to say just that, but he spoke first.

'How do you feel about children?'

His question didn't make sense, and I stood there, blinking at him like a ninny, I'm sure.

'Do you want to have a family some day?' he asked again.

'Some day,' I said. 'Of course. Where did *that* come from?'

'I was curious,' Heinrich said. 'You'd mentioned your friend's baby, and it occurred to me that we'd never talked about it. Them. Children.'

'Doesn't *every*one want children? I mean, as long as they can afford them?' Back then, even though I thought otherwise, I was young and naive.

He tucked my hand into his arm and we started walking again. 'Actually, no.'

'Oh.'

We walked in silence for a while, and then suddenly there we were. In front of my apartment building. And I had to ask.

'Are you one of those people who doesn't want children?'

Heinrich looked at me, and I couldn't read the expression on his face. 'Actually, I was just thinking that there was nothing I would rather do than have a baby with you.'

It was a shockingly forward thing for him to say – especially since, for all this time, he'd been so painfully polite.

I laughed, half embarrassed, half terrified. This was it. If he wanted to have a baby with me, then, 'Before you *have* a baby, you have to make one.'

Heinrich nodded, his eyes never leaving my face. 'Yes, then there's that. I would definitely love doing that with you, too.'

'Come inside,' I breathed. The words were almost inaudible, but I knew he heard them.

His heart must've been pounding as much as mine, because he was suddenly breathing as if he'd run a mile. 'Rose, I'm leaving in just a few more days.'

'I don't care,' I told him recklessly, and suddenly it wasn't about getting access to his papers. It was real. I wanted him to come inside.

'I won't be back.' He gripped my shoulders and all but shook me. 'Do you understand? Maybe not ever – certainly not until the war is over.'

'Then you really better come inside.' I kissed him, and I knew from the way he kissed me in return that I had won. I would not be going inside alone. Not tonight. 'If this is all the time we've got – oh, Hank, I love you – let's make it perfect.'

His beautiful eyes filled with tears. 'Yes, let's.' But instead of coming up to my apartment with me, he pulled away. 'Tomorrow,' he said, backing down the stairs. 'Meet me for dinner at my hotel?'

I was standing there staring at him, I'm sure, with my mouth wide open. He was . . . *leaving*? After that kiss? After all that I'd said? After . . . ?

'I have something I must do all day, but I should be back by around half five. Is that all right?' he asked.

Dumbly, I nodded my head.

'It *will* be perfect,' he said. 'I promise. I love you desperately, Rose.'

He turned and ran to flag down a taxi.

And just like that, he was gone.

Alyssa closed Rose's book, knowing that she should take advantage of the long airline flight to get some sleep.

But every time she shut her eyes, she saw Sam's face. *I'm trying.* He was trying to be Mary Lou's husband, but it wasn't easy because he was still dreaming about Alyssa.

She was human. She couldn't deny that knowing Sam dreamed about her at night made her feel electrified. He loved her. He may have married Mary Lou, but he loved *her*.

But unless Sam was willing to divorce his wife, that wasted love wasn't doing any of them one bit of good.

George came and sat next her. 'You okay?'

Alyssa nodded. Compared to him, she felt wrinkled and grimy.

'You look exhausted,' he commented. 'What did they do to you in San Diego? Make you run the BUD/S obstacle course?'

She smiled politely at his joke. The tough obstacle course

used for SEAL training *would* have been easier than seeing Sam again. Seeing him with Mary Lou . . .

From the window seat to her left, Jules roused. 'Aren't you supposed to be with Mrs von Hopf? If you don't want to sit up in first class, *I* will.'

'The stewardesses just found out who she is,' George told them, 'and she's signing autographs. Holding court. I figured now was a good time to brief you on some information that came in this morning.'

Alyssa watched George Faulkner as he spoke. He had a lean face that was classically handsome. It was a Yacht Club face – slightly weather-beaten from golf and sailing, a face that would just keep on getting better looking into his fifties, sixties and even seventies.

'Are you married?' she asked him.

'Divorced.' A true FBI agent, he didn't assume she was asking simply because she was curious. He was looking at her a little more closely now, wondering why she wanted to know, wondering if maybe she was interested.

'Don't worry, George,' she told him. 'You're not my type. I really was just curious.'

He didn't believe her. Men were so stupid. 'I spoke to Max this morning,' he said, watching for her reaction to their boss's name.

Alyssa resisted the urge to roll her eyes. Obviously, George thought there was something going on between her and Max – just like the rest of the world. If an attractive single woman worked with a group of men, one of them had to be sleeping with her, right?

'And?' she asked.

'We've got an ID on the man who made the phone call to Savannah von Hopf. His name is Misha Zdanowicz. Born in Smolensk in 1953. He and his brother, Otto, run a black market operation specializing in guns and drugs.

'Apparently, the main security cameras were taken out by his people before he came into the hotel, but his security chief was recognized in the lobby about forty minutes before the call went through. And there was one hidden camera in Alex's room that he missed. We've got him on tape. It was definitely Misha Zdanowicz. Apparently, he's a very tall man with some girth.'

Jules leaned forward. 'There was a hidden camera in the hotel room?'

'Yeah, probably for blackmail purposes.' George laughed. 'Apparently, it's not uncommon. So don't do anything in your hotel room in Jakarta that you don't want to see on the Internet.'

'We'll keep that in mind,' Jules said, shooting a meaningful look at Alyssa.

And just what was that supposed to mean? Alyssa sent Jules a serious dose of disbelief and disgust. Did he really think she was going to invite Sam Starrett back to her hotel room now that he was married?

'There's more,' George told them. 'Bob Heath – Alex von Hopf's personal assistant – told Max that up until about two months ago, Alex and Misha were pretty tight. It was both a business and personal relationship – a friendship. Misha's got a wife. As far as we know, he's not, you know . . .'

'Gay.' Jules had no trouble saying the word.

'Right. But then, Heath said, about two months ago, Alex found out that Misha's import-export business was just a front for smuggling weapons and drugs. Apparently Misha wanted Alex to use his own business in a similar way. Alex refused, and cut all ties with the Zdanowicz brothers. Heath was ordered to refuse Misha's calls. Alex wanted nothing to do with him. Bob Heath was adamant about that. And apparently, Misha was pissed.'

'Has Zdanowicz been located and brought in?' Alyssa asked.

'That's where it gets a little murky,' George told them. 'According to the word on the street in Jakarta, *Otto* Zdanowicz is on some kind of revenge rampage, searching for something or someone. Money. There's a rumor about a whole lot of money somewhere in the jungle, which fits since we know Savannah had taken a quarter of a million dollars from her bank account.

'There's also a rumor that Misha's dead. His helicopter allegedly went down in the middle of nowhere, killing everyone on board. We've confirmed neither the fact that the chopper went down, nor the location of the alleged crash. But from what we've been able to gather – of course these are rumors we're working with – if it really happened, it happened just hours after Savannah's flight landed in Jakarta.'

Oh, God. Alyssa looked at Jules, who put into words what she was thinking. 'So Max thinks Savannah and WildCard Karmody were on board when the chopper went down?'

'It's certainly a possibility.' George looked abashed. 'I, uh, haven't managed to tell Rose that part yet.'

'Except,' Alyssa pointed out. 'Who's Otto looking for? *Some*one's still alive if he's spending his time searching for them. If you don't tell Rose, I will. But I'll tell her, yes, there's a possibility her granddaughter is dead, but in my opinion, there's a bigger possibility that she's not. And if she's not, WildCard Karmody is with her. He *will* keep her alive. I have no doubt about that.'

'Thank you, dear.' And there was Rose. Standing in the aisle, listening in. The ambient noise of the jet in flight had kept them all from hearing her approach. She gave George a scolding look. 'Shame on you for withholding information.'

George refused to apologize. 'I was going to tell you, but not until we were about to land in Hong Kong. I figured there was a chance we'd have more information then. I didn't want you to sit here worrying. What good would it do?'

Rose addressed Alyssa. 'Why don't you come and sit with me,' she said. 'I'd like to hear more about this WildCard Karmody.'

'Yes, ma'am.' Alyssa slipped out of her seat as George moved his legs to the side to let her pass.

'See what being nice gets you?' George muttered to Jules. 'Banished to coach.'

When dusk fell, Savannah finally gave up and let herself get good and worried about Ken.

She was more than halfway through Rose's book after having gone back and started at the beginning, but this jungle was shadowy and dim even at the brightest hour of the day, and soon it would be too dark to read.

And no matter how fascinating her grandmother's story was, Savannah couldn't stop thinking about Kenny.

He'd been gone for hours and hours. What if he'd been captured? Or shot? What if he were lying out there in the jungle, right now, bleeding to death? What if he were already dead, his eyes wide open, staring vacantly up at the canopy of leaves that filled the jungle sky?

Oh, God.

Or what if he were still alive, and being tortured to reveal her location?

He'd never tell them where she was. He'd die first. She knew that with a certainty that was unsettling.

Ken Karmody would die for her.

I'm not going to leave you. Whatever happens to you happens to me, too. So are we going to live or are we going to die?

The fact that he was gone, that he'd followed those soldiers, was mostly her fault. If she'd been honest with him, if she'd looked him in the eye and said, 'Please don't leave me. Not even for a minute. I'm scared to death and I'm afraid I'm going to lose it, big time, if you're not here to hold onto,' he probably wouldn't have gone.

He definitely wouldn't have gone.

Beneath his lack of tact and his high intensity, in-your-face attitude, was an extremely sensitive and caring man.

Whom Savannah had badly hurt by failing to be completely honest when she'd had her flat tire.

Yes, if she'd been honest about who she was and why she was there, she probably wouldn't have spent the night in his bed. At least not right away. But she would've gotten there eventually. And once she did, she probably never would've left.

If she'd been honest with Kenny from the start, she probably could've made him fall in love with her.

God, what it would be like to have him love her! A man like that would love her forever, unswervingly, completely. The way Heinrich had loved Rose.

Please God, don't let Kenny be dead. Let him be lost. Let him be detained. Let him have followed those men so far that he wouldn't make it back until morning.

She would be okay here alone until then. Even though night was falling – that blanket of darkness that completely terrified her – she would be okay.

She would get through it. She could do this. She'd go to sleep. And when she awoke in the morning, Ken would have returned.

Savannah lay back, aware that there was a rather large hole in the blind right above her. Kenny had told her not to leave for any reason, but surely he hadn't considered the fact that she'd have to go to the bathroom.

Not that she'd found a bathroom in the jungle.

Still, she'd gone several dozen yards away, and then come right back. But she'd been unable to repair the blind – at least not the way Ken had managed to do it.

She closed her eyes, sending him a telepathic message. 'Wherever you are, stay safe. I'm okay. Don't get into any trouble trying to get back here to me.'

Crackle, crunch.

Savannah sat bolt upright. *Ken*.

But outside the blind, nothing moved.

The light was fading fast. Wasn't this the time of day when animals emerged from their hiding places to get food and water? She'd watched endless episodes of *National Geographic* as a kid, but she couldn't, for the life of her, remember the types of animals that lived in the Indonesian jungle.

But . . . wasn't this where Bengal tigers came from? Relatively speaking, Indonesia was pretty close to Bengal, wasn't it?

It was certainly closer than New York.

Crunch, crack.

There was definitely something in the brush right outside

of the blind. One large plant in particular moved slightly.

Savannah pulled the Uzi closer with one hand, while reaching for one of the sacks of dynamite with the other, her eyes never leaving the tiger's hiding place.

She drew a plastic-wrapped stick of dynamite from the bag, and threw it at the brush in question through the hole she'd made. But it caught on the top of the blind, and tumbled silently and impotently to the ground.

Shoot.

But a tiger didn't come leaping out at her, eager to make her his dinner. So she reached for another stick of dynamite and, this time reaching her hand out so that she was clear of the hole, she threw it – hard – and hit her target plant dead on.

A big, colorful bird flew up, squawking its displeasure.

A bird, not a tiger.

Weak with relief, Savannah sat back, alternating her prayers to keep Ken safe with a plea to keep all tigers – Bengal or other – far from this corner of the jungle.

And again, just like yesterday, night fell. Bang. Pitch darkness.

Savannah had been about to leave the blind to reclaim the sticks of dynamite, but there was no way she could find them now when she couldn't even find her own hands in front of her face.

Oh, *shoot*. Throwing the dynamite had seemed like a good idea at the time, but now it seemed outrageously stupid.

The good news was if she couldn't see them in the darkness, no one else could see them, either.

But she'd have to wake up, right at the very first light, and find them.

*

Jones met Molly about an eighth of the way down the trail as the sun was about to set.

It was definitely weird. He'd dressed up in his best clothes and had shaved again. Twice in one day. It was a new record for him.

'You're early,' he said.

'I know.'

She was wearing a sarong – a full-length dress that wrapped under her arms, leaving her shoulders bare and him dying to unwrap her. Her hair was down, and even without makeup on, she looked like a million bucks.

He'd been afraid that she wouldn't show after this afternoon. He'd been coming to get her, to carry her back to his camp if necessary.

She kissed him hello. It was warm and sweet and over far too soon, but he loved it. It was a girlfriend kiss – possessive, familiar and filled with promise. It had been a long time since anyone had kissed him like that.

'You look very nice,' she said.

'So do you.'

'Thank you. Are we going to stand here all night?' she asked, with one of those killer smiles. 'Or are you going to take me back to your place and read to me?'

As he took her hand and led her back toward his camp, he saw that she was carrying the book he'd given her. 'If that's really what you want, sure.'

Molly laughed. But then she stopped laughing. 'You're serious, aren't you?'

'Yeah. Tonight's all yours. You want it, we do it.'

The corners of her mouth started to move upward. 'Oh, really? *Whatever* I want?'

He took the book from her hand, carrying it for her, loving that smile. 'Yup.'

'You'll cook pancakes for me – naked?'

He glanced at her. 'I told you, I'm a lousy cook.'

'But you're very good at being naked.'

Jones had to laugh. 'So are you.'

'Yes, I am, thank you for noticing.'

They'd reached the door to his Quonset hut and he pushed it open, letting Molly go in first.

'Good heavens,' she breathed.

He'd filled the room with hundreds of candles from a crate that he'd added to his cargo a few months ago by mistake. It had taken him an hour to set them out and light them all, but it was worth it now, seeing the look on Molly's face.

He'd covered his table with a piece of lacy cloth – also from a shipment that he'd never been able to unload. He'd set it with plastic plates – the best he could do.

He closed the door behind her then crossed to his tape player and turned it on, wasting precious battery time. He couldn't think of a better use for it, though.

He set her book down next to the tape player. 'May I have this dance?'

'This is incredible.' Her expression was everything he could have wanted as he took her into his arms. He wasn't a very good dancer, but his only tape was Greatest Country Hits of 1993, and most of them were slow songs. All he had to do was hold her and sway. 'You did all this for me?' she asked.

'I figured that since I couldn't cook, if I invited you up here for dinner, I'd better make it memorable in other ways.'

She looked around at all the candles. Looked at the flowers he'd put by his bed. Looked at the floor space he'd cleared so that they could dance. Looked at the mosquito netting he'd rigged over his bed, figuring the candles would draw bugs.

'This is because of what happened this afternoon, isn't it?' she asked.

Jones laughed. 'What? No.'

'You feel guilty,' she said. 'You're trying to make it up to me.'

'I don't feel guilty about anything,' he told her. 'I don't do guilt.'

She wouldn't let it drop. She gestured grandly at the candles and flowers. 'So all this is because . . . ?'

'Because I wanted to . . . make love to you by candle-light.'

Molly's eyes softened and she relaxed a little more into his arms, her fingers playing with the hair at the back of his neck. Christ, it felt good.

'Thank you,' she said, 'for not using that other word.'

He'd been about to. 'I'm trying to make this romantic,' he admitted.

'It is,' she said. 'Very much so. But . . . Why?'

Jones didn't know how to answer that without sounding like a complete fool.

'You got me,' she continued. 'I'm hooked. I couldn't stay away from you if I tried. You don't need to romance me.'

He didn't dare tell her that he wanted her to remember this, to remember him after she left for Africa. 'I want to.'

She seemed satisfied with that answer. 'You are the sweetest man on this earth.'

'Yeah, you are so wrong about that.'

'I beg to differ.' She kissed him, pulling him with her, toward his bed.

She was wrong and he was right, but now was not the time to argue.

'Savannah.'

Silence. Oh, please God, let her still be here. Ken spoke a little louder, a little more urgently. 'Savannah.'

Still nothing. He took a major risk and lit a match, blowing what little night vision he had and exposing their location to who or whatever might be out there in the darkness, simply because he couldn't wait another minute. Because, face it, he was scared shitless that she'd given up on him and struck out on her own.

But there she was.

Safe and sound, still inside his blind. Curled up, her eyes tightly shut, fast asleep.

He'd honestly expected to find her hyperventilating and frantic, maybe even in tears. But somehow she'd managed to make herself fall asleep.

He should have known Savannah would do anything to keep from crying. Except, as the flame from the match burned his fingers and he quickly doused it, he could have sworn there were streaks of clean on her face that could have meant only one thing.

He'd finally managed to make her cry.

Of course, maybe it didn't count since he hadn't been here to see.

Sightlessly and soundlessly, he joined her in the blind, making sure he completely patched the hole he'd made to get inside.

He found her in the darkness by touch, his hand

connecting with the smooth silk of her thigh, aware that she'd done as he'd asked and made his pants into shorts.

She stirred. 'Kenny?'

'Yeah, it's me. Are you all right?'

'Are you?' She sat up suddenly and managed to clock him right in the nose with, Jesus, it must have been her elbow.

'Ow! Christ! I was before you did that.'

'Oh, God, I'm sorry.' She touched his face more gently this time, as if she were visually impaired. It felt just a little too good, and he couldn't keep himself from putting his arms around her and hauling her up against him. And, what do you know? She didn't push him away.

'I'm the one who's sorry,' he said. 'I tried to get back by sunset, but—'

'It's okay.' Instead of smacking him intentionally this time, which he probably deserved, she held onto him tightly. 'I'm just glad you're safe.'

He laughed at that, enjoying the fact that if she held him any tighter, she'd be sitting on his lap. 'Of course I'm safe. Those guys were amateurs.'

'I was afraid—' Her voice broke, and she struggled to regain control.

'You know, Savannah, if you cry, I won't tell anyone,' Ken said quietly. 'I promise.'

'I was afraid I wouldn't get another chance to apologize to you,' her voice was very small, 'for being dishonest about who I was and why I was in San Diego. For letting things get out of control that night at your house. For wanting you so much that I completely ignored my normally good judgement.'

Well, shit, when she put it like *that* . . .

'Please forgive me,' she whispered. 'I'm afraid something terrible's going to happen and . . . And I don't want to die with you still mad at me.'

He had to laugh. 'Savannah, come on, I'm not going to let you *die*.'

'Please.' She touched his face again. 'Can't you forgive me?'

'Yes,' he said, thankful that it was impossible to see her gazing at him imploringly. God knows what he'd promise her if he could see her eyes. 'All right? I forgive you.'

'Really? You're not just saying that?'

Christ. 'Yes, really.' He could forgive her. He just wasn't ever going to forget. 'Do you need me to prove it by signing my name to something in blood?'

'I know you think this is really funny,' she said tightly. 'But I really thought that you were dead, and that I was going to get eaten by a tiger.'

'Jesus, you saw a *tiger*?'

'No, it was only a bird. But I *thought* it was a tiger. I was scared to death.'

She was serious, and Ken, in a burst of true genius, recognized that now would probably not be a good time for him to laugh.

'Look, I promise I won't leave you again,' he said instead, managing to sound very serious, too. 'Okay?'

'Thank you.'

'You're welcome.'

There was silence then. She didn't say anything more, she just breathed. And clung to him as if despite his promise, she was never going to let him go. Just in case.

He was very aware of the fact that she was soft and warm in his arms. Her head was against his shoulder, her

SUZANNE BROCKMANN

hair tickling his neck, and he knew exactly where her mouth was, even though he couldn't see her. It wouldn't take much effort on his part to lower his head and kiss her and see how far his saying he forgave her would get him, but it just felt too pathetic. He'd be taking advantage of her.

Over the past few days he'd intended to look for the opportunity to do just that – to use her the way she'd used him. But now that his chance was here, he couldn't do it. His body was more than ready, but his soul just wasn't willing.

He liked her too much. And wasn't *that* the stupidest reason he'd ever come up with for *not* trying to get into a woman's pants?

'How'd you manage to fall asleep?' he asked, mostly in an attempt to make himself stop thinking about sex and how amazing it would be to lose himself in Savannah's body right now.

'I'm not sure.' She lifted her head slightly, putting her mouth even closer to his. 'I just did it because I had to, you know?'

He did know. That was how he'd gotten through BUD/S training. By just doing it.

He could hear her waiting there in the darkness. He sensed her anticipation. Or maybe he was just imagining it. God, he didn't know anymore. He either had to kiss her or push her away.

He wanted to do both – and neither.

Her stomach growled and he remembered the MREs. 'Hey, are you hungry?'

'Yeah, I ate both of the power bars almost right after you left.'

No shit. Ken was sure she would have rationed them.

He'd expected to find that she'd had exactly one-third of one of them – no more, no less. He gently disengaged himself from her arms and found one of the MREs in the darkness.

'I have no idea what this is,' he said as he opened the packet, 'but it's way better than bugs. Don't squeeze it until you put the open end in your mouth.'

'What are you giving me?' she asked.

'The guys I followed had a camp a few dozen clicks from here,' he told her as he helped her guide the open end of the MRE packet to her mouth. Her lips connected with his finger, and he pulled his hand back, fast. 'They had some extra supplies. US issue MREs – Meals, Ready to Eat. It's what we give our combat troops when they go off to fight. It's pretty nasty. They must put it in a blender before packaging it. It's got a soft consistency – like room temperature baby food. I think that's so our troops can snarf it down quickly without choking while they're under fire.'

'It's wonderful,' Savannah said, almost reverently. 'I love it.'

'I'll keep that in mind next time I invite you to dinner,' Ken said. 'I'll skip the expensive filet and get MREs instead.'

She stopped eating. 'Is there going to be a next time?'

Bad topic to joke about, he realized too late. Her question was a tricky one. He tried to avoid answering it directly. 'Let's just get Stateside first, okay?'

'Why did you kiss me this morning?'

Ken laughed, surprised by her question. From the way she'd asked it was hard to tell if she was angry about it or not. It was gutsy of her to ask, though, he had to give her that much.

343

'I don't know,' he admitted. 'I temporarily lost my mind, I guess. I apologize.'

She was quiet for a moment, then, 'Why were you gone so long?'

That one he could answer. 'I followed those guys to a camp, right? They checked in with some guy with a beret who looked like he was in charge, had some chow, then the whole gang – there were about fifteen of 'em altogether – packed up and left. It was already late by then and I'd already gone pretty far, but I wanted to follow them, see where they were going. I trusted you to stay here, so I went for it.'

'Who were they?'

'I don't know, but they're not connected to the gun runners. I'm pretty sure about that. For one thing, their dress code is different. The guys in the helo all wore street clothes – flashy ones, too. Like they had money and they wanted people to know it from what they wore. These other dudes were decked out in BDUs – battle dress uniforms. Standard issue jungle print cammy gear. If I had to guess, I'd say these guys are revolutionaries. Maybe terrorists of some kind – although these days the line between the two tends to blur. Whoever Beret is, he'd have been far better off spending his money on training instead of uniforms. Clowns like that put on a uniform and think they're unstoppable. Kind of like your little brother playing dress up.'

'I don't have a little brother,' she said. 'I'm an only child. Want some?'

It took him several bemused seconds to realize she was talking about the MRE. 'No,' he said. 'Thanks. It's all yours.'

'So where did they go?'

Who? Oh, right. 'I followed them to a river – it wasn't our river, it was a different one, I'm pretty sure. There were three more soldiers there, guarding patrol boats and a helo outfitted with some pretty major artillery.'

'A helo,' Savannah said. 'So maybe they are the same—'

'Nope. Different kind. The Puma we were in and the helo that's been flying overhead looking for us are pretty close to state of the art. This was a dinosaur – it wouldn't surprise me if it had been rebuilt from various parts left over from Vietnam.

'Beret issued some orders and climbed into the helo,' Kenny continued. 'I don't know what language he was speaking, but everyone but the three guys I first followed got into the boats and were outta there. It was kind of obvious from how glum my guys looked that they'd been ordered to stay behind until they completed their mission.'

She shifted in the darkness. 'You think they're looking for us – for me – too?'

'I think it's possible they've heard about the missing money, yeah. A tango can do a lot of damage with a quarter of a million dollars. And maybe they think if they can get hold of you, they'll get even more.'

'Tango?'

'It's radiospeak for the letter t, which, in my business tends to stand for terrorist.'

'Terrorists and gun runners,' Savannah mused. 'Is there some way we can sic them on each other? Use them to cancel each other out? You know, if they're busy fighting each other, maybe we can sneak away without getting caught.'

Ken laughed. 'You think like a SEAL.'

'I think like a coward who will never, ever again

complain about the dullness of reading court transcripts day in and day out.'

He settled back on the ground, hands up behind his head. 'Is that what you do, you know, as a lawyer?'

'Yeah. Lots of reading and writing,' she told him. 'Not so much of the Perry Mason stuff. In fact, not any of that at all.'

'Really? I bet you'd be good at it.'

'What I'm good at,' her voice was as smooth as the darkness that surrounded him, 'is finding other people's stupid mistakes.'

Yeah, he could believe that.

'It's amazing how often prosecutors and even judges cheat the rules,' she told him. 'Our justice system only works if the rules are always followed and everyone – *every*one – gets a fair trial every single time. I've got to believe in that completely in order to do my job because, trust me, some of these people I handle appeals for are the complete scum of the earth.'

Ken tried to make himself more comfortable on the hard ground. 'Like, give me an example,' he said, curious as to whether he might fall into that particular subset.

'I did one appeal for a guy who was in jail for second-degree murder because he went target shooting when he was drunk. I'm talking completely tanked. He didn't go far enough into the woods; turns out he was near a campsite, and a ten-year-old was struck by a bullet and killed. Well, his whole trial was riddled with errors. The judge didn't read the correct instructions to the jury, the prosecutor included some information in his closing that was hearsay, *and* there was an incident in which the defendant fell and hit his head on the way into the courtroom and actually showed signs of concussion. He claims he was completely out of it, incompetent to stand trial, and yet it went on without him getting any medical attention, without him even being checked by a doctor. I had a whole list of reasons to appeal.

'And yet,' she continued, 'even though we didn't have a ballistics match because the bullet that killed the girl exited her body and was never recovered, we have testimony from forensics experts as to where the shooter was located when the girl was killed. And there was some extremely damaging proof in the form of shell casings found at that very spot – with my client's fingerprints on 'em – that match the ones he used in his rifle.

'He claims he didn't see anyone, didn't know that anyone had been hurt, but God, he was guilty of manslaughter at the very least, and here I was about to get him a whole new trial. That little girl's parents were going to have to go through hell all over again, and that really stank. But it would stink even more if we started slacking off on giving everyone a fair trial. Oh, you know, *he* doesn't need a fair trial. It's okay that he has a concussion and can't even focus his eyes while he's in the courtroom because he's guilty, right? Wrong. *Every*one gets a fair trial. It's the only way the system can truly work.'

'Wow,' Ken said.

'Sorry. I sometimes get a little too ... I don't know. Passionate, I guess.'

'I don't think there's such a thing as too passionate,' he countered.

'Yes, there is.'

'Not in my book,' he said. 'If you think otherwise, you've probably been hanging with the wrong people.'

He couldn't see her, but he heard her smile in the darkness. 'You're a SEAL, Kenny. It makes sense that you don't scare easily. But you should see the way people – men – run sometimes when I go off on a rant like that.'

'Really? They run? Because I was, like, getting really turned on.'

Savannah laughed. 'You know, just when I start to forget, you remind me exactly how much of a jerk you are.'

Ken smiled at the sound of her laughter.

'You do that on purpose, don't you?' she asked.

'Do what?' He played dumb.

'You probably got farther in life by playing the clown than you did from being a straight-A student. Am I right?'

'Savannah, Savannah, Savannah,' he said. 'Do not even *attempt* to psychoanalyze me. I assure you, many a seasoned professional has been stumped and even driven to tears by the magic that is me.'

She laughed again, just as he'd hoped she would. She had the sexiest laugh. Low and husky. 'You're not so hard to figure out.'

'Terrific,' he said. 'When we get back to the States, do me a favor and write up a report. I'll bring it with me next time I go in for a psych eval. That's kind of a mental health checkup that we all have to go through pretty regularly,' he added before she could ask.

'All right,' she said, around a yawn. 'I will.'

'Maybe we should try to sleep,' he suggested. 'I want to get moving as soon as it's light in the morning.'

'I'm sorry. Here I am blabbing away. You must be exhausted.'

'Don't apologize. I'm fine. I thought you were tired. But if you want to talk more—'

'I don't.'

'Well,' Ken tried not to sound disappointed. 'Okay. Good night then.'

'Good night.'

Truth be told, he was wired. And he couldn't remember the last time he so desperately wanted sexual release. He actually ached from it. If he were alone . . . But he wasn't. And he'd promised her he wouldn't leave her, so he couldn't even wait until she fell asleep again and then sneak off to . . . Ah, Christ. What was he doing even *think*ing about this? If she could read his mind, she'd be disgusted. He was disgusted with himself.

Doubly disgusted because she'd all but started this conversation by admitting how badly she'd wanted to sleep with him back in San Diego.

He'd managed to make her laugh – that was good – but he hadn't moved the conversation to a place where he could ask if maybe she wasn't still a little bit hot for him. Because if that was the case, he wouldn't be taking advantage of her, would he? Not if she wanted him and he wanted her.

'Ken?' Savannah whispered.

'Yeah.' Please, Jesus, don't let her ask him to hold her unless she wanted him to jump her, too.

'Will you . . .' She cleared her throat. 'Would you mind very much if I asked you to, you know, just put your arms around me?'

Fuck. She only wanted his arms.

But why not give her what she wanted? He couldn't want her any more than he already did. It wasn't going to hurt him any worse than he was already hurting. 'Sure,' he said, before he thought it all the way through.

Oh, *shit*. She was already coming over to him, feeling her way in the darkness. Her hand found his hip, and he nearly jumped a mile. 'Whoa, Van! Time out, okay? Are you familiar with the effects of adrenaline on the male physi—'

Ken cut himself off as she curled up beside him, her head on his shoulder, her hand on his chest, her legs not even touching him.

'Am I familiar with what?' she asked.

'Nothing.' Okay. This would work. As long as her hand didn't drift lower. As long as she didn't throw her leg across him in the night.

Oh, God, don't think about that. Don't think about how easy it might be to get her heated up while she was more than half asleep. Don't think about pushing off her shorts and pulling her on top of him and . . .

'Good night,' Savannah said again, her voice right in his ear.

'Okay,' he heard himself say. Jesus, what a loser. Good night – okay?

He heard her move slightly in the darkness, felt the coolness of her knee against his thigh, and almost screamed. She shifted even more and he turned toward her desperately. 'Savannah—'

She kissed him. Her lips were soft and warm and tasted faintly of the pseudo-tomato sauce mixture used in an MRE. She got him right on the mouth, which had to be an accident. If he hadn't turned his head, she would have kissed him chastely on the cheek.

'Sorry,' he practically shouted at her, pulling back from her, forcing himself not to grab her and jam his tongue down her throat. God, he wanted to kiss her. He made himself laugh instead. 'Christ. That's the last thing we need here, right? First you try to keep me up all night talking and then, well . . . Jesus.'

Jesus, indeed.

He'd always thought that a woodie should've been like Pinocchio's nose, but instead of growing with each lie, it should by all rights shrink with stupidity. But no. Despite his total flaming idiot comments, it raged mindlessly on, at full happy salute.

Savannah settled back down against his shoulder, thank God.

'Good night,' she said again.

'Yeah,' he said. 'Good night.'

As if he was going to get any sleep.

Thirteen

As usual, following Heinrich was an exercise in futility.

I lost him four short blocks from the hotel.

I must confess that I didn't go straight back there and finagle my way into his room so I could search it at my leisure.

No, instead I went shopping.

And it was in the dress shop, as I tried on an exceedingly gorgeous and very spicy red evening gown, that I realized I didn't need another dress to wear out on the town.

What I needed was a nightgown.

Something diaphanous and sexy. Something I wouldn't be able to wear outside of the privacy of a hotel room. Something that would broadcast my intentions loud and clear. Something Hank wouldn't be able to misread. Or ignore.

I squared my shoulders and went into the lingerie department. And I couldn't do it.

The prices were exorbitant, silk was scarce, but my biggest hurdle was *me*. I couldn't even get up the nerve to ask the salesclerk (who looked a little too much like my mother) to show me what they had in my size. Perhaps if I had a wedding ring on my finger . . . But no. Even then I think I would have been too embarrassed.

There was only one thing to do, one place to go for help.

'You want to borrow *what*?'

'You heard me.' I turned to face Evelyn, forcing myself to meet her eyes. I'm sure my face was flaming. 'You know I wouldn't ask if it weren't vitally important.'

I'd caught her coming back from lunch, and she set her hat down on a table just in the magnificent entry hall of her penthouse suite.

She was looking at me intently, studying me. It was quite a few moments before she spoke. 'Do you love him? Whoever it is that you want to borrow this dressing gown for?'

I didn't hesitate. 'Yes.'

Her expression softened then. 'Oh, Rose. All right then. For a minute there, I was afraid you were intending to seduce some suspected Nazi. I wouldn't help you do that, but for love . . .'

She led the way up the stairs to her dressing room, gesturing for me to follow. 'Who is he?' she asked.

'Would you mind very much if I didn't go into details?'

'Please tell me it's not the Euro-God. Hank what's-his-name?'

I followed her into her bedroom, toward the first of a row of dressing room doors. 'I really am quite uncomfortable discussing this.'

'Oh, dear, it is Hank, isn't it?' Evelyn turned to face me. 'Darling, he's some kind of prince. A man like that's not going to *marry* you.'

'I could really do without a lecture—'

'Sorry.' She threw open the door. 'But if you want the gown, you've got to take the lecture, too. It's a package deal.' She took a deep breath. 'Rose, sweetheart, I know it must seem horribly romantic. He's about to leave, to go fight the war, right? He may die, it's true. But live or die, either way, *this* one is not going to come back to you.'

It was a good-sized room, dedicated to holding clothes, and as she pulled me inside, I saw she had a selection of nightgowns

353

that would have put most of the major department stores to shame. Black, white, red, pink, purple, violet, blue, in various substances of silk and lace.

'Do you really want to be his American mistress?' she asked me. 'Is that honestly enough for you?'

'Yes.' I pulled a red one from the bunch and found that it was completely sheer. I gaped and Evelyn gently took it from me and hung it back among the others.

'Do you actually wear that? In front of Jon?' I couldn't stop myself from asking.

Evelyn laughed softly. 'Do you remember when we first met, and you were so worried that I might be afraid Jon would try to cheat on me with you?'

I nodded. Yes. I had known neither of them all that well at the time.

'Trust me when I tell you that I was never worried,' Evelyn said with a smile. 'I think white,' she decided. 'With your fair skin and blond hair, you'll look like an angel.'

'I'll look like a virgin,' I countered. 'And I don't want him thinking about that. He'll pack me up and pat me on the head and push me out the door. He's very good at that.'

'He's been keeping you at arm's length, has he?' Evelyn realized. 'Good boy, princey, I wouldn't've thought you had it in you. Rose, darling, hasn't it occurred to you that he's doing the right thing?'

'I want something red,' I told her. 'Or black.' I pulled out a black silk gown that was slightly more substantial, except for the back, which was completely open and held together by laces. It had a slit up the side that looked to go well past the wearer's hip. Dear me.

'Has it occurred to you that he might be right about doing the right thing?'

'He's not.'

'Rose—'

'I know he's not going to marry me,' I told her, fighting the urge to burst into tears. 'I know he's not coming back. These next few days are all the time we'll ever have together, and I want every *minute* of it. I want it *all*.'

There were tears in her eyes, too. 'Oh, Rose.'

I held the gown up to me, looked in the mirror. Willed myself not to cry. 'What do you think?'

Evelyn became brisk, businesslike as well. 'That one's way too hard to get out of. Kills the mood. And black's not your color, dear. It washes you out. I think royal blue, instead.' She laughed as she searched through her gowns. It was shaky, but it was definitely laughter. 'If Jon finds out I helped you, he'll *kill* me.'

'Not while you're wearing one of these.'

She held up a silk gown of the deepest blue. It was almost demure in its simplicity, and yet I could see light passing through it. 'This is the one,' she said. 'Trust me.'

She had slippers to match, of course, and we wrapped up both gown and slippers and I headed back to the hotel. I didn't try the gown on at Evelyn's house – I knew if I did, I'd chicken out. No, I had to put it on for the first and only time in Heinrich's hotel room. I had to have it on and be there, waiting for him to return from wherever it was he'd gone.

But first I had to get into his room.

It was simple enough to do. I used the house phone in the hallway to call down to the front desk.

'This is Mrs Sally West in room 5412.' I gave the false name under which I'd registered for the room across from Heinrich's. 'Silly me, I'm afraid I've locked my key in my room. Could you send someone up to unlock the door for me?'

A bellboy stepped off the elevator in a matter of minutes,

eager to help. (I'd tipped him most generously when I'd checked in.)

He quickly unlocked the door to my room with his pass key – except it was not my room. It was Heinrich's, right across the hall. But it was indeed the door I was standing in front of when the young man approached, and of course he didn't think to check the numbers.

'Thank you so much.' I gave him a smile and one of my few remaining five-dollar bills, and slipped into the room, locking the door behind me.

It was that easy.

The hotel suite was dim and cool with the curtains closed. It smelled like Hank – like the soap he used, like his expensive cologne.

The sitting room was undisturbed – the only sign it was being used was a copy of that morning's New York Times out on a breakfast table.

It wasn't a promising start, but then again, I didn't truly expect to find Nazi files and lists of informants scattered about the room.

Still, his bedchamber wasn't much different. His personal items were few. His clothes were hung in the wardrobe, shoes neatly below. A few toiletries were out on a dresser, everything precisely lined up.

I went through it all methodically, careful not to touch anything until I examined it closely. And yes, there were hairs strategically placed across dresser drawers, even across his leather toilet kit in the bathroom. I was careful to replace them all so that he wouldn't know his belongings had been searched.

Of course I found nothing. No miniature cameras, no great sums of money hidden behind mirrors or taped to the bottom of drawers. No intricate Nazi instructions to cripple the United States war effort. No list of underlings in Heinrich's spy network.

There was, however, a safe. It was in the wall, in the bedroom, beneath a rather dull oil painting of a meadow. The safe didn't have tumblers and a combination, but rather a lock that could be opened with a key.

I set to work immediately, attempting to pick it.

No, that's not as crazy as it sounds. Remember, my father was a carpenter and he had taught me a thing or two about installing (and getting past) all sorts of locks.

But this was not the kind of flimsy lock one could pop open using a hat pin. And I was still there, still trying rather futilely, some time later when I heard the sound of a key in the door to the suite.

Hank was back.

Early.

Jones turned to find Molly awake and watching him reading by candlelight.

'Good book, huh?' she said. That was all she said. She didn't tease him about it, didn't try to embarrass him. She didn't even ask what the hell he was doing still wide awake at this time of night.

'Yeah, actually, it's not what I'd normally choose to read, but . . .' He shrugged.

Molly stretched and reached out a hand to run her fingers through the hair on his chest. 'Maybe you should think about writing *your* memoirs.'

He laughed. 'Yeah, right.'

'I'm serious. There's got to be a reason a man changes his name, his entire identity . . .'

'Yeah, it's called survival of the smartest. If I *don't* change

357

who I am, I'm too stupid to live and deserve whatever they can throw at me.'

'Who's *they*?'

'Anyone's who's seen the wanted posters.' Jones kissed her. 'Want to fly back to Iowa first class? I'm your ticket, baby. Just whisper my real name into the right set of ears and—'

She sat up, all playfulness gone. 'That's a terrible thing to say.'

'Hey, I was just kidding.'

'Well, don't kid. Not about that. I would never betray you. *Never*. And if you think otherwise . . .' She started looking for her clothes. *Shit*. He didn't want her to go. 'What time is it?'

Jones's watch was on a crate next to the bed. He leaned forward to check the time. 'Oh-two eleven.'

'I have to get back to the village.' She slipped out from the mosquito netting and found her panties, pulled them on. Her dress was nearby. She'd wrap it around herself and be out the door before he could stop her.

'I double-crossed the biggest drug lord in Thailand.' Holy fuck, had he actually said that aloud? The look on her face told him, yes, he had.

'Nang-Klao Chai?' she asked.

'You heard of Chai, huh?'

'Yes.' She came back in, under the netting. 'Yes, I have.'

She sat on the bed and gazed at him, eyes wide, waiting for him to tell her more.

Jesus. Was he actually going to do this?

'This story starts a long time ago. When I was a medic with . . . Well, never mind who I was with. US Special Forces. That's all you need to know,' he told her, and he knew from looking into her eyes that she knew damn well he was going to tell her about the scars on his back. 'You want to hear it, you've got to promise to stay until dawn. Because I'm going to need about four hours of sex afterwards.'

She didn't crack a smile, didn't assume he was kidding, didn't hesitate. 'I'll stay as long as you need me to stay.'

Jackpot. But what was he going to do in a month, to keep her from leaving for good?

'Chapter one,' he said. 'In which I join the US Army, train to become a medic, get accepted into an elite special forces unit, train my ass off even more, and get sent overseas on clandestine operations designed to help the US fight the war against drugs. Which, by the way, I think we lost.

'If we didn't lose the war, we sure as hell lost the battle. I really don't know what happened on that particular day. I've played it over and over in my head and there's just too much chaos. We were ambushed. That I know. It was as if they knew who we were and where we were going. It was a bloodbath. Everyone died, Molly.'

She took his hand. 'You mean, everyone but you.'

He still wasn't so sure of that. 'Chapter two, in which I should have died, but didn't. It was the most fucking stupid thing – I spent five months in the hospital, healing, just so they could beat the shit out of me when I got out. I went from the hospital to a prison that might as well have been on Jupiter for all I knew. It was in the jungle, in the mountains, but the only thing that mattered was that it was some ancient stone fortress, with walls three feet thick and windows – holes, really. Way up high in the cells – too small to slip through. I had no prayer of getting out of there.

'Of course, I didn't believe it. I started digging, chipping at the rock, doing whatever I had to do. It was . . . It was . . .'

It was damp in those cells – during the rainy season the water had come up to his knees. He'd had to sleep sitting up or drown. But that wasn't the worst of it.

The worst was being so fucking alone. He'd tapped on the rock walls in Morse code, but no one had ever answered. Never. His only contact with other prisoners had been the screams he'd heard in a language he didn't completely comprehend. At least not at first. And his contact with the guards was limited to the expressionless men who led him in chains and at gunpoint to the room where they'd torture him.

Interrogation, they'd called it. Questioning. Christ. Each time they'd start the same way. By seating him at a table. By talking to him as if he were a human being, with courtesy and respect. It fucking blew his mind each time they apologetically stuck needles under his fingernails or administered electric shocks to his gonads, or whipped the skin off his back. And if that's all they did, that would be a good day.

'Grady.' Molly had her arms around him, the soft coolness of her bare breasts against him. 'You don't have to tell me about it. I can guess what happened there. I've heard about conditions in those prisons, about the torture that goes on.'

'It was bad,' he managed.

'God, I'm so sorry. And so glad you made it out alive.'

'They fed me on the days they took me out of my cell to torture me,' he told her. 'I think I might have started to associate pleasure with serious pain. If you think I'm fucked up now, you should have seen me back then.'

She pushed his hair back from his face. 'I don't think you're, you know, fucked up.'

'I am,' he told her. 'Be warned.'

'How long were you there?' she asked.

'Three years, three months, twelve days. And all that time those fuckers didn't break me because I believed that my country didn't know I was still alive.' He'd believed it with his very soul. 'I believed that all I had to do was somehow get word out to the rest of the world that I was there, that I was still breathing, and my teammates from special forces would come and kick down the prison walls and set me free.'

Jones laughed and it sounded brittle to his ears. 'But then Chai came in and he managed to do in twenty minutes what those fuckers hadn't done in over three years. He showed me documentation that proved that the United States not only knew I was still alive, but also knew exactly where I was. He showed me memos from the Pentagon that proved I was sacrificed for politics. And that was it. I broke. He flipped me as easy as that. I cried like a baby and told him everything he wanted to know. Of course, by then it was old news, but he got it out of me. Shit, I *wanted* to tell him. I begged to tell him. I even offered to teach his men all the tricks we used. He promised me he'd get me out of there, and two months later, he did, on the condition that I work for him.

'At that point, I would have followed him anywhere. I was with him for nearly two years, Molly.' He'd killed people for Chai. Worst of all, he'd done as he'd promised and taught SF fighting techniques to the men in Chai's private army.

'Chapter three, in which I find out Chai's about to sell

me back to the US, where I'll be charged with desertion and treason, and shit, I don't know what all else.' He could remember the day, the *minute*, he found out about Chai's betrayal.

'I could have just walked away,' he told Molly. 'I could have just disappeared into the jungle, but no.' He'd had to fuck the fuckers. He had to get back at Chai. And he did. He'd burned a warehouse filled with heroin, crippled Chai's entire fleet of ships, and completely fucked up the organization's computer systems – including their backup zip drives. 'I trashed his organization, and set it up so that he would walk right into the authority's hands. Of course, they managed to let him get away – fucking idiots.'

'And now he's after you,' Molly said.

'It's been years,' Jones told her. 'He's built himself back up again, and yeah, he seems intent on revenge to the tune of a five-million-dollar price on my head.'

'Why do you stay here?'

'Where would I go?' he asked.

'*Anywhere*. Grady, my God!'

'It's not so easy. All of my papers – my passport – it's forged. It's fucking badly done, too. If I had like a shitload of money, I could maybe get my hands on a better passport and then . . .' Still, he couldn't even *think* about going back to the United States. That was never going to happen in this lifetime. Besides . . . 'Maybe I want him to catch me.'

She was silent, just looking at him with those eyes.

'That was a joke,' he said. 'Believe me, I don't really want him to catch me.' Chai would make that prison stay seem like a kiddy carnival.

'Everyone you've ever trusted has let you down,' she said softly. 'Haven't they?'

What could he say to that?

'I won't,' Molly told him. 'I swear to God, Grady, I won't.'

When she looked at him like that, he could almost believe her.

'Ken?'

Ken took about seven seconds to decide whether or not to play possum there in the darkness of the blind. 'Yeah.'

'Were you asleep?' Savannah asked.

'No.'

'Can I tell you about something that happened today?'

The nights that Ken had spent with Adele had been few and far between, and when they were together, they hadn't done a whole hell of a lot of talking. Janine, his last girlfriend, had often spent the night, but they hadn't had a whole hell of a lot in common. She was a morning person, too, often falling asleep at 2200, so there hadn't been too many pillow talks in the dark in that relationship, either.

It was stupid. *He* was stupid. But it was something he'd always wanted. Someone who loved him, lying soft and warm beside him in the night, telling him about her day, sharing her secrets.

Well, here he was. And here Savannah was, too. And at least he got the lying beside him part right.

'Yeah. Sure,' he said. 'Tell me what happened today. You mean, besides the ferocious tiger, right?'

She laughed softly, shifting slightly in his arms. 'No, this is . . . Well, while you were gone, I read half of my grandmother's book. And guess what I found out?'

'That . . . she was an alien from outer space?'

Her laughter washed over him, warm and intimate in the darkness. 'No.'

'You asked me to guess,' he pointed out. 'You told me she was like Wonder Woman, and maybe I need to check my favorite comic book reference website, but didn't W-squared come from another planet?'

'But that's just it. Rose *wasn't* Wonder Woman. She was like *me*, Kenny.'

She sounded so excited by her discovery, he didn't have the heart to zing her for slipping and calling him *Kenny*. Fuck me again, Kenny. How many times had he heard *that*? Adele had believed in getting right to the point. And the two things she'd wanted most from him were sex and for him to do her homework, write her term papers. And with the clarity of hindsight, he realized now that it was probably the other way around. She wanted him to do her homework, and his reward for doing it, like a trained seal, was the sex.

Shit.

He hadn't wanted to go to Yale. And yet in a way, he had, through Adele. He'd graduated with honors, too. He'd gotten A's on every paper he'd written, every assignment he'd completed for Adele.

But those grades meant shit to him. He'd done it so that Adele would say 'Fuck me again, Kenny.' Which, in his youth and stupidity, he'd heard as 'I love you, Kenny.'

'I'd always thought of her as this enormously driven, self-righteous and absolutely confident person,' Savannah was saying, talking about her grandmother, the FBI double agent, Rose. Man, talk about pressure to follow in some freaking giant footsteps. Grandma kicked Nazi ass. What can you do to top that?

'I pictured her kind of like a female James Bond,' Savannah said.

Ken pulled himself back to the present, forced himself to listen. This was what he'd always wanted, wasn't it? Someone to tell him things that mattered in the dark.

'Cool and collected and always fearless,' she continued. 'But she wasn't. She was scared to death most of the time. She spends most of the book in tears. Uncertain. Terrified at heart.' She laughed softly. 'Maybe not so different from me after all.'

'That's very cool,' Ken said. 'But . . . You, like, haven't read the book before this?'

'I was avoiding it,' she admitted. 'I mean, I grew up hearing all these stories, so I thought . . .' She took a deep breath. 'I'm not saying I'm *exactly* like her. I'm not half as strong. I mean, I'm not about to run off and join the FBI when we get out of here.'

'When,' he said. 'Good.'

'What?'

'You said *when* we get out of here. Instead of *if*. That's good. You made up your mind that we're going to make it. That's important, you know.'

'Yeah, now if I only had a pair of ruby slippers so I could click the heels together and—'

'You don't need ruby slippers,' Ken said. 'You've got all you need to get back home. You've got yourself and you've got me.'

'I think it's more accurate to say that I've got you – and you've got the burden of me.' She was serious. He knew because her voice got very small. 'I'm sorry for all the trouble I've caused you. I really am. I know that you don't even particularly like me—'

365

'You think I don't like you? Why the hell wouldn't I like you? And you're way less of a burden than – okay – than I first thought. But Jesus, you're incredibly intelligent – a real creative thinker. I'd rather be stuck in the jungle with you than, say, Jerry Leet, my swim buddy during BUD/S training, who couldn't think his way out of a paper bag. He ran out on day one of hell week, by the way. I'm starting to think you would have made it all the way through.'

She made a noise that was halfway between laughter and exasperation. 'I didn't say that so you would try to convince me—'

'Yes, you're far more comfortable when you're completely in control, so the past few days have been something of a challenge for you and therefore for me, too, but—'

'—that this hasn't been anything short of awful for you.'

'Awful? Are you kidding? Jesus Christ, other than the fact that you're tense as shit, you don't complain! You don't think I appreciate that from the bottom of my heart?'

'Kenny—'

'"Fuck me, Kenny,"' he corrected her. 'If you're going to call me *Kenny* just like Adele, you've got to say it exactly the way she did. And she never said *Kenny* without saying *fuck me* first.'

That wasn't quite the truth, but it succeeded in shutting Savannah up.

'Here's the deal,' he told her. 'I do like you. Really. I'm not just shitting you because we're in the middle of the jungle and there's no one else to talk to. To be brutally honest, I didn't like you at first. I didn't like being used.'

She started to make noise, but he just talked over her. 'I still don't like it,' he said, 'but now that I know you a little

366

better, I can imagine where you were coming from. And I believe you – I do – when you say you didn't plan for it to happen. Truth is, I've managed to work my way around to being flattered about the whole thing. You couldn't resist me that night. Thank you. Maybe you're lying, but I've decided that I'll be a whole hell of a lot happier if I pretend that you're not.'

'I'm not.'

'I thought at first you were really this cold bitch, but then I realized that when you get all quiet and uptight, you're just freaking out about being out of control, about being, well, scared to death.'

'Which is all the freaking time,' she muttered.

'No, it's not.'

'Yes, it is. I've spent my entire life scared. I'm a total coward.'

'Savannah, you're one of the most courageous women – no, fuck women – you're one of the strongest, most courageous *people* I've ever met. Do you even know what courage is?'

She took a breath as if she were going to answer, but he didn't let her.

'It's when you're about to shit in your pants because you're so scared, and you don't back down. It's when you're terrified and you still get the job done. Fearless people aren't courageous – they're just too fucking stupid to know they're in danger. Or they're too crazy to care. Courage is all about being scared and sane and staying the course anyway. Do you know what I see in you?'

Again, he didn't let her answer. 'I see the same kind of strength that I saw in the guys who made it through BUD/S training, who made it into the SEAL teams. I wasn't kidding when I said that about you making it through. You're like the guys who made it easily – if such a word can be used to describe the process. They just kept going. They were just quietly strong. They just put their heads down and succeeded simply by not quitting.'

'Is that how you did it?' Savannah asked. 'Because I've heard about the training that SEALs have to go through and—'

'I'm an asshole, remember?' he said. 'I don't do anything the easy way. Nah, I was the guy who was targeted by the instructors. I was the one who was supposed to ring out right away. I got labeled a smart-ass and a screwup right off the start, and I got hammered. Every freaking minute of every day, I had one of the instructors breathing down my neck, telling me I wasn't good enough, telling me they were going to break me like a twig, telling me I was going to crawl away from BUD/S like the loser that I was.'

'But you didn't.'

'Yeah, you see, that's what's interesting about it. If they hadn't ridden me so hard, I probably would've quit. But the fact that they told me I was never going to make it . . .

'See, sometimes people's lack of faith in you, sometimes the way other people can build a wall or a hurdle and then tell you that you'll *never* get past it – sometimes that's the best possible gift. I mean, it was for me. I guess it was something I learned from my asshole of a father, but all you have to do is tell me that I'm not good enough, and it's like Popeye with his can of spinach. Suddenly, I've got the strength to go three times as far and five times as fast. Sometimes, *no* is the best thing to hear. Because then you've got to really think about how badly you want this thing, and whether it's worth busting your ass to turn that *no* into a *yes*. And when you finally get it,' he added, 'you know damn well what it's worth.'

Savannah was silent. 'Thank you for telling me that,' she finally said.

'Go to sleep now,' he told her. 'We've got a lot of ground to cover in the morning.'

'Good night,' she whispered. 'Kenny.'

Kenny.

She sighed and nestled against him, her breath warm against his throat.

Ken held his tongue. Stupid thing was, he was starting to like it when she called him that.

I swung the picture into place, grabbed the package I'd brought from Evelyn's and rushed into the bathroom, locking the door behind me.

This was it. The moment of truth, with no time to waste. My heart was pounding as I quickly shucked off my clothes – all my clothes – as I slipped the shimmering blue gown over my head. It slid, cool and slippery, down my legs, pooling slightly on the tile floor. I slipped my feet into Evelyn's slippers as I took all the pins from my hair, shaking it free to tumble down around my shoulders. With a trembling hand, I reapplied my lipstick, nearly smearing it down my chin as the doorknob suddenly rattled.

'Who's in there?' Heinrich's normally gentle voice was demanding, imperious. He repeated the question in harsh-sounding German.

I threw my lipstick back into my purse and stepped back from the mirror, attempting to get a look at myself before I opened the door.

Evelyn had been right – the gown was gorgeous. It fit almost perfectly, clingy yet not too tight. In a certain light it was quite opaque, but when I moved and the light hit it from a different angle, it was suddenly shockingly transparent.

I couldn't move. I couldn't do this.

Heinrich pounded on the door. 'Open up right now, or I'll call hotel security!'

'It's me,' I said through the door. 'Rose.' But he'd already gone into the other room, no doubt to use the telephone.

It was too late to back out. Too late to do anything but take a deep breath and open the door.

'It's just me,' I called to him, desperate to catch him before the hotel staff became involved. It would be just my luck if someone came up who proceeded to recognize me as Mrs Sally West from room 5412. I followed Heinrich toward the sitting room, conscious of the fact that he'd turned on all the lights. I kept moving, aware that as long as I did so, he'd only be able to catch glimpses of my body beneath that gown.

'I didn't think you'd mind,' I said, 'if I came here a little early. I wanted to surprise you.'

He was surprised all right. He had the phone in one hand, and a small but very deadly looking little gun in the other. I was surprised, too. I didn't know he had a gun. He hadn't carried it when he was out with me in the evenings.

He gazed at me, and I saw realization dawn as to what I was wearing, why I was there. It was the most amazing thing – he didn't try to hide any of what he was feeling. He just looked at me with his heart and soul right there in his eyes for me to see. I no longer felt as if I were the only one nearly naked in this room.

He put his gun back into a holster he was wearing underneath his jacket, and spoke into the phone. 'Yes, this is suite 5411. I need a bottle of your very best champagne, and I need it now.

There'll be a twenty-dollar tip awaiting the man who can deliver it within the next two minutes.' He hung up the phone, turning slightly to follow my flight around the room.

'Stand still,' he ordered.

'I'm afraid to,' I admitted.

'Please.'

I turned and faced him.

'You're mine,' he whispered. 'Completely. Am I correct in assuming this is the message you wish me to receive?'

My mouth suddenly dry, I nodded.

He took a step toward me. 'Say it. *Yes.*'

'Yes.' I lifted my chin slightly. 'I have to warn you, I'm tempted to lock you away from the rest of the world and keep you just for myself. Because from now on, you're mine, too, you know.'

He laughed with a hot smile and a sudden burst of pleasure that quickly turned to something else. Something softer, something warm. 'I do know. But don't fear – I've been yours since the day we first met.'

I started toward him, ready to fling myself into his arms, but a sharp rap on the door made me freeze. It was the champagne. I ducked into the bedroom, and Hank traded a very large sum of money for the wine and for the room service waiter's equally swift disappearance.

'Do you know where I went this morning?' he called to me as he set about popping the cork.

I emerged from the dimness of the bedroom, instantly on edge. 'No.'

He poured us each a glass of fizzing wine. 'No guesses?'

'None at all,' I admitted as he handed me a glass. 'I also don't have any idea where you went this afternoon.' How could he possibly carry on a seemingly normal conversation while I was dressed like this?

He waved that away. 'This afternoon was work. But this morning . . .' He laughed as he gazed at me. 'I'm having a very good day,' he said. 'Do you know the kind of day I mean, when absolutely everything goes smashingly right? I was nervous about, well . . . But then here you are, and *oh, here you are*, and I realize I've received my answer before I even asked my question. That's very reassuring.'

The look on my face must have been one of sheer confusion, because he laughed again. 'This morning I went out to get *this*.' He took a jeweler's box from his jacket pocket. 'Let's get sandwiches for the car. I borrowed a car, Rose, and enough gas ration coupons so we could get to Maryland tonight,' he said as he pulled me down next to him on the sofa, as he handed the box to me. 'Do you think I could convince you to wear this dress? Underneath my overcoat, so no one else could see you, of course. I'd just . . .'

I opened the box, and found myself staring at not just one ring, but three.

'I'd love to always remember that you wore this when you married me,' Hank said.

Those were wedding rings in that box. One for Hank and two for me – a plain gold band and an enormous sapphire in an elegantly simple setting.

And there was Hank, down on the floor, on one knee before me. He wanted to marry me. He wanted to whisk me away, tonight – right *now* – all the way to Maryland, where we could be wed on the spot.

Oh, dear God in heaven, I couldn't *marry* him. There were so many reasons why we absolutely couldn't rush right off to Maryland – one of them being that I wanted, I *needed*, to see the contents of that safe. If we went to Maryland, it would be a full day – possibly longer – before we returned.

And yet, Hank, my dear sweet, misguided Hank, actually wanted to *marry* me.

But how could I marry him – and then betray him? Because that was my plan. To keep him from forevermore assisting the Nazis in their efforts to win this terrible war. It was bad enough that I loved him, but the truth was, we were mortal enemies. And I was going to do whatever I had to do, to ensure that Heinrich von Hopf was no longer a threat to my country.

'I know what you're thinking,' he said as I stared down at that gorgeous blue stone.

Oh, no he didn't. At least I *hoped* he didn't.

'You alone know that my title means much more to me than I let on. You know my feelings about honor and duty – to my family, to my country. Needless to say, you are not the woman my mother has picked out for me, and there will be hell to pay. If I survive the war.'

'Don't say that! *If* . . . ?' I snapped the box shut.

'I don't want to lie to you, Rose. I've had a somewhat dire premonition for weeks now. A feeling of . . . impending doom.'

'Hank!' Did he somehow know what I had in mind for him?

'It's what kept me from asking you to marry me on that night we were reunited. But you seem determined for us to become lovers—'

'You don't have to marry me. I should think that would be rather clear to you at this point.'

'I won't cheapen what I feel for you by taking you as a mistress.' He was serious and so fierce about it. 'I love you. Please come with me to Maryland. Marry me, Rose. Tonight. Everything else – my title, my position in Austria – is nothing without you.'

With that, I was down next to him on the floor. There was nothing to do but kiss him, and promise him everything.

'Yes,' I said. 'Yes, I want to marry you.' It wasn't a lie. I did want it. It simply wasn't going to happen, though. 'But let's not drive all the way to Maryland tonight. Please, Hank? Let's go first thing in the morning.'

I kissed him again, and it was a good long while before he pulled back. But pull back, he did. He even managed to get to his feet, and to help me up as well. But he released my hand almost immediately, crossing to get his overcoat. 'I made a vow to myself that I would put a ring on your finger before . . .'

I moved toward his bedchamber, aware of the way the light hit my gown, and stopping to look back at him when it was just . . . so. He stopped moving, stopped talking.

I, too, had made a vow. I was going to get to spend at least one night in the arms of the man I loved. Come on, dress, don't fail me now.

With one last lingering look at him, I turned and went into the bedroom.

Before I even started walking, he'd already put his overcoat down and was following me.

But he brought the ring box in with him and insisted on putting both of those rings on my finger before he so much as kissed me again.

But he did kiss me again. And again.

And again.

And it came to pass that we both kept our vows.

Rose knew exactly at which point Alyssa Locke was as she was reading her book.

It was a little strange to sit near her, knowing that this young woman, this near total stranger, was reading her personal account of that night she seduced Heinrich von Hopf.

Of course, there was a lot Rose had left out. Details that the rest of the world didn't need to know. Details she didn't want to share with anyone.

The look of pure devotion and desire on Hank's face as he put his ring on her finger.

That had been so very hard to take. There was no minister or justice of the peace to make it official, but he was marrying her with that small act. *With this ring, I thee wed.* He didn't say a word, but she knew what he was thinking just from looking into his eyes.

And she – what a ninny – she'd actually started to cry. Which slowed things down quite a bit. Hank again tried to talk her into going with him to Maryland, and she finally took severe measures to stop him – by slipping completely out of the blue gown.

Evelyn had been right. That particular gown had been quite easy to take off.

But Hank was Hank, bless him, and he persisted until she climbed onto his lap and kissed him. It didn't take her long before she tugged him back with her onto his bed.

The sensation of his hands on her bare skin was such a powerful one. It was a tactile memory that she would carry with her to her grave. His clumsy haste in removing his own clothes still moved her – still made her smile, even after all these years. Suave, sophisticated, royally bred Heinrich von Hopf had fallen off the bed in his hurry to be one with her.

He was so beautiful, with winter-pale skin covering sharply defined muscles that he'd hidden quite well beneath his dapper business suits.

Her husband.

Despite her intentions not to, by letting him put those rings on her fingers, she *had* married him that night.

He'd loved her so exquisitely, so gently, so sweetly. But throughout each kiss, each caress, each softly whisered word of love, Rose couldn't escape the knowledge that, come the dawn, she was going to betray him.

Savannah awoke when Kenny put his hand over her mouth.

It was like déjà vu as she looked up at him in the ghostly early morning light.

'Someone's coming,' he breathed almost inaudibly into her ear. 'They're still pretty far away, and they'll probably miss us completely, but – Shit!'

She followed his gaze up to the hole that she'd made in the blind. In the misty light, it seemed to gape above them.

'I couldn't fix it right,' she told him. 'I tried, but—'

'I told you not to leave, not for anything!' He tried to adjust it, but there weren't enough branches to cover them properly.

'I had to go to the bathroom.'

'Not for anything means not for *anything*! For Christ's sake!' Short of going outside the blind, there wasn't much Kenny could do, and there was no time for that. She could hear voices. Whoever was coming this way wasn't making an effort to be quiet about it.

'I'm sorry,' she said, 'but what was I supposed to do, pee in the corner?'

'Yes.' He was serious. 'You stay hidden. You dig a hole and you – Jesus God, Savannah, is that a stick of dynamite out there? Holy fuck, it is!'

The dynamite. Oh, God. 'I threw some at the . . .' She cleared her throat. 'You know, the tiger?'

Ken picked up the machine gun and grimly checked it. Even though he was wearing only boxers and sandals, with his lean body and face streaked with dirt and mud, he looked like pictures she'd seen of men in Vietnam. Men who were hardened, experienced soldiers. Which was exactly what he was, she realized.

'How much did you throw?' he asked tightly.

'Just two sticks.' Just. One, bright red against the jungle foliage, was obviously enough. 'Let me go out there,' she said. 'You stay hidden, and—'

The glint in his eyes was hard, dangerous. 'How many freaking times do I have to tell you—'

'No,' she said, 'see, this way you could follow, and . . . and rescue me after—'

She didn't see him move, but somehow his hand was back over her mouth.

They – whoever they were – were coming closer.

Go past, go past, go past.

But there were excited voices in a language she couldn't comprehend, from over by the brush where she'd thrown the second stick of dynamite. More voices came toward the first voice, and then she could see them through the holes in the blind. There were at least five, maybe six men, all carrying guns, most hung by thick straps or ropes over their shoulders.

She felt Kenny tense, and she knew this was it. They were either going to find the blind or go past it. Right here and right now. These next few seconds were going to decide their fate.

A voice called out something, it was a command of some kind, and all the guns went up – aimed directly at their hiding place.

Another voice rang out, and although she didn't understand, she recognized it as being Russian. The language that the gun runners had spoken on the helicopter.

And in a flash, Savannah knew. They were going to die and it was entirely her fault.

Fourteen

Whoever they were – this pack of men with the weapons – their Russian was nearly as bad as his.

One thing was clear. They were asking something about the dynamite. That was one word Ken knew in just about every language.

Whoever they were, he doubted they were part of Beret's little army. They were too ragtag, too mismatched. There wasn't a scrap of jungle print camouflage on any of them.

Only three of Beret's soldiers had been left behind, and as far as he could tell, they weren't among this crowd.

It was possible, of course, these guys were mercenaries, locals of some kind, hired by the Russian gun runners.

As Ken scanned what he could see of their faces from the cover of the blind, he picked out the one who was the leader. An older man, with lines of experience on his leathery face, and a quiet watchfulness in his dark eyes. Someone said something in a different language – not Russian – and he answered, a brief, quiet command.

Wait.

Ken didn't need to speak the language to recognize a *wait* when he heard one. The old guy gestured to someone else.

And the question came again in Russian. Something

something dynamite. Something something something American something.

Huh?

Paid for. That was what Ken thought it translated to. They'd *paid for* it in American money. It being the dynamite.

Of course. These were the buyers – the people to whom that shipment of dynamite onboard that helo was intended to be delivered. Had to be.

Their faces looked grim, but if Ken could somehow communicate with them, he could negotiate their way out of this mess – a way that would keep him and Savannah alive and unharmed.

'Do you speak English?' he called out, and he could almost feel surprise radiating from Savannah.

Leatherface himself answered. 'English. Not good English. *Parlez vous français?*'

French? Not a chance, pal. '*Hablas español?*' His Spanish wasn't great, but it was better than nothing.

Leather looked at his men for a translation. Obviously no one here spoke Spanish, either.

'Okay,' Ken said, speaking slowly and clearly. 'Let's work with English here. I don't want to hurt you, do you understand?' His hand was still over Savannah's mouth, and he brought his mouth to her ear as the gang outside worked out a group translation.

'Dig yourself into the dirt,' he ordered her as quietly as possible. 'I'm going to stall until you get hidden. They don't know you're here, they don't need to know. I'll go out there, give 'em the dynamite, lead them away from you. If I'm not back here by daybreak tomorrow, start following the river. Do you understand?'

She nodded, her eyes wide, and he took his hand from her mouth.

'*Je parle un peu le français,*' she called out. In the stillness of the jungle, her voice rang clear and sweet and oh so very female. The double takes and reactions from the men outside the blind would have been comical if Ken didn't know from experience what groups of lawless and angry men could do to a helpless and unprotected woman in the middle of nowhere.

'Holy shit,' he said. 'Savannah!'

'This is *my* mess,' she whispered fiercely. 'I got us into it, I'm going to help get us out. I speak French, you don't.'

Blasting her for making a bad decision, for ignoring his direct order, was something that was going to have to wait until later. Right now he had to go to plan B – except he didn't have a freaking plan B yet.

Savannah said something in French, to which Leather-face quickly responded with a four-paragraph speech.

She replied.

'What are you saying?' Ken asked. 'What's he saying?'

'He's talking too quickly. I asked him to slow down. I haven't spoken French since college.'

There was another exchange of indecipherable French that drove him fricking crazy.

'I think he just asked if we worked for someone named Misha Zdanowicz,' Savannah reported. 'I told him no. That we don't work for anyone, that we didn't want to come here, but were forced. I said *made to*. I don't know how to say forced. I told him we were pretty unhappy about that and very mistrustful of everyone. I asked him to step back a bit, please – which obviously, he hasn't taken too seriously.'

Leather spoke again.

Savannah listened hard, narrowing her eyes as she struggled to understand. 'I think he said they're from a nearby village. He keeps saying something I don't understand – he's going on and on about it – about the road to the coast. I think. Yes. *La mer*. The sea.

Leather added something else in French. Freaking French. Why did it have to be *French*? Ken hated French. He hated France. Adele had dumped him for two months for some French exchange student named Pierre. Stupid people, stupid country, stupid language.

'He wants us to come out,' Savannah reported.

Yeah, right.

They weren't going anywhere, even though this blind was giving them only the illusion of safety. Ken knew they'd be hamburger the moment any one of those men opened fire whether they were inside the blind or out. Still, he wasn't moving.

'Tell him we have a semiautomatic weapon and we're not surrendering it.'

Savannah looked at him. 'With college French?'

'Yeah, isn't, like, *surrender* the first verb they teach you, in case while you're in France some other country attacks?' He was being an asshole. He knew it. He saw an echo of that sentiment in Savannah's eyes.

But he hated not knowing precisely what was being said. The fact that the conversation had gone on for so long was good. But he still didn't know who Leather and his men were and what they wanted.

Savannah said something to Leather, then told him, 'I asked where their village is. If they had telephones or a two-way radio. I told them we would pay them well for a hot meal, a shower, and a hotel room. At least I hope that's what I told them.'

Leather answered.

'No telephones, no radio,' Savannah translated. 'Shoot. And no hotel. But there's someone there – an American! – named Molly, I think, who speaks both English and . . . I don't know what. Indonesian, I guess. Her Indonesian is apparently better than my French, so . . .'

Leather spoke again.

'He's said he's already sent for her,' Savannah told Ken. 'She should be here any minute.'

And just like that, he had a plan B – wait for the American named Molly to come and save their asses.

It was hard to know whether the ache that drummed inside Molly's head was from last night's lack of sleep, or from the knowledge of leathery-faced village leader Tunggul's foolhardy attempt to buy dynamite from the scum-sucking, hideously dangerous lowlife Zdanowicz brothers, or from the heartbreakingly tragic story Grady – *Jones* – had told her, or – best bet yet – from the fact that her attempt to slip silently and unnoticed back into her tent this morning had failed miserably.

She'd been twenty minutes too late to slip anywhere unnoticed.

Rifki Rias had come pounding on her door, and she, of course, had not been home.

The entire village was in an uproar over her disappearance, about to send out a search party looking for her. Father Bob had taken one look at her, still wearing her brightly colored sarong – or rather, wearing it once again – and he knew if not exactly where she'd been, at least what she'd been up to.

He wasn't the type of man to judge, thank God, and he'd quickly pushed her into her tent to change into something a little less provocative, and sent out the word that she'd been safely found. He'd said nothing and would say nothing, but enough of the villagers had seen her. Word would spread – it no doubt already had – until everyone in the village knew that she'd spent the night with Jones.

So much for keeping their relationship hush-hush.

But right now that was the least of her problems.

The reason Rifki had hammered on her door at the very crack of dawn was because there were two Americans hiding in the jungle. Tunggul and his friends had found them while searching for dynamite – *dynamite?* – and needed Molly to come quick and help translate to end the Mexican standoff they'd gotten themselves into.

And so there she was. Sleep deprived, still shaken by all that Grady – *Jones*, damn it! – had told her, still shaken by the fact that he'd told her something so personal at all.

And suddenly, she was in the middle of an episode of *Gilligan's Island*.

Two American strangers didn't just appear out of nowhere. Not in this village, in this remote corner of Parwati Island. It was surreal.

But there they were. Ken and Savannah. Looking battered and bruised and not smelling all too fresh, but definitely American.

Molly had talked the safeties back onto the arsenal of weapons. She'd gotten Ken and Savannah to emerge from their hiding place, and they'd all trooped back to the village, where Father Bob had found some clothes for Ken to wear. Not that he needed them. He had the kind of hard male body that made clothing seem so unnecessary.

Now they sat at a table under the tent that was their makeshift house of God because the wooden church building was undergoing repairs.

Everyone was there. Tunggul and his two highest council officials, Molly, Ken, Savannah, and Father Bob. Billy Bolten lurked nearby, casting dark looks in her direction, which was probably just as good.

Not that the dark looks were so good, but as long as Billy was in sight, Molly knew he wasn't running off to Jones's camp to challenge him to a duel. *That* was just what she needed.

As the Americans ate what had to have been their first real meal in days, Ken told them he and Savannah had been brought to Parwati Island at gunpoint by a man who could only be Misha Zdanowicz. Zdanowicz intended to kill them but they managed to get the upper hand when the helicopter – filled with Tunggul's order of dynamite – exploded.

That had definitely been Zdanowicz's chopper she and Jones had seen burning by the river. All but a single crate of dynamite – which Ken handed over to Tunggul – had been destroyed, and everyone but Ken and Savannah had been killed.

But now Otto Zdanowicz – Misha's brother – was after them, angry and grieving and intent upon revenge.

Molly turned to Tunggul. 'Why?' she said. 'Why on earth would you contract to buy dynamite with the Zdanowiczs?'

Doing business with the gun runners gave them a virtual invitation to enter the village's airspace, so to speak. It had taken years to establish the village as a no-fly, no-enter zone for all the drug lords, gun runners, pirates, and political revolutionaries in this area.

And, dear God, there were a lot of them in this part of Indonesia.

It was especially important to keep Zdanowicz out because he was in the middle of a war with General Badaruddin, the most local revolutionary, who laid a claim to most of the mountains to the north on Parwati. If Badaruddin thought Otto Zdanowicz was taking over the village, he'd be here in a flash, and they'd find themselves smack in the middle of a territorial dispute. And wouldn't *that* be fun.

Tunggul was calm, as always. And he had a logical response, also as always. 'The alternative was to buy the dynamite in the port and bring it to the village on the mule train. During which time the Zdanowiczs' men would have robbed us. This way, we pay the Zdanowiczs a little more, perhaps, but we knew the dynamite would be safely delivered.'

Shaking her head, Molly translated for the benefit of Ken and Savannah.

'Ask him what the dynamite's for.' Ken asked.

He reminded Molly more than a little bit of Jones. He was younger by a few years, but there was something in his eyes – a quiet dangerousness, or maybe a self-assuredness – that was similar.

'Are you special forces?' she asked him.

He glanced at Tunggul who spoke enough English to recognize those two words. Then he laughed. 'I was in the Army a few years, but . . . No. Sorry to disappoint you.'

Lying. But okay. If she were special forces, she wouldn't want anyone to know either.

Savannah, with her wispy blond curls and her sweet face, was suddenly focused completely on the food on her plate. Was *she* special forces, too? It didn't seem possible, and yet . . . Why not? Charlie's Angels had a similar look – big eyes, fragile faces, completely adorable – and they kicked major butt.

'The dynamite's to clear the road from the village to Port Parwati, on the coast,' she told the two of them, whoever they were. 'There were a series of earthquakes about seven years ago, and the roadway was completely destroyed. What's left – dozens of miles – is blocked with rockslides. The only way into and out of this village is a trail that takes four or five days by mule. This causes a problem when someone gets sick and needs to get to a hospital, as I'm sure you can imagine. But the amount of dynamite we'd need to clear that road . . . I can't even imagine how much it would take.' She looked at Tunggul. 'We're working to get a grant. So that the blasting will be done professionally. So that the men in the village don't blow off their hands by accident.'

His English wasn't great, but she knew he understood what she was saying. They'd had this conversation often enough.

'There's no radio here in the village?' Ken asked.

'Every time we get one, it gets stolen. So, no. I'm sorry.'

'How about the people who steal 'em?' he asked. 'Where can we find them?'

Molly laughed. 'You don't want to,' she said. 'Trust me.'

'What I want, ma'am, is to get to a radio as soon as possible.'

Father Bob cleared his throat. 'Doesn't, ah, Jones have a radio?'

Molly refused to let herself blush. 'Not in his plane,' she said briskly.

'A plane,' Ken said, his eyes actually lighting up. 'A

plane would be even better than a radio. Can you take me to this guy? Jones, right?' He looked at Bob. 'Who is he?'

'A local. Ex-pat. Yes, his name's Jones. But his plane's out of commission again,' Molly said, suddenly afraid she'd told them too much. 'He's waiting for a part to arrive.'

'Can you take me to him anyway?'

What if both Savannah and Ken – neither of whom had volunteered their last names – were both special forces, and had been sent here to find and arrest – or kill – Grady Morant? A chill went down Molly's spine as all at once she truly understood the dark world in which Jones lived.

'I'll talk to him,' she said.

'Thank you,' Ken said. He turned to Tunggul. 'Now, about that dynamite . . .'

Jakarta was as hot as Alyssa had imagined.

The FBI had been given an entire floor of an office building that had seen better days. It was a large area, but it was wide open – no walls, just a series of poles holding up the ceiling, stretching on and on and on.

Laronda sat at an old metal desk that had been placed near the door, with a fan blowing on her, full force, looking none too pleased.

'Don't you go putting your handbag on the floor,' she said to Alyssa in lieu of a greeting. 'Not even for a second. There are bugs here, girl, that you *don't* want to be taking home.' She pointed down at the end of the big room, where Alyssa could see Max. And Sam. *Shit.* Sam was already here. She hadn't expected that. 'They're in the conference *room*. So to speak. Waiting for you. Max has asked for you only twenty thousand times in the past four hours. Like I had you hidden underneath this desk or something. The man needs to grow some patience.'

'Thanks, Laronda.' Alyssa took a deep breath and headed toward the far end of the room. The sound of her footsteps echoed in the cavernous space, and they all looked up at her. Max. Sam. The mighty trinity of SEAL Team Sixteen was there, too – Lt Cmdr Tom Paoletti, his executive officer, Lieutenant Jazz Jacquette, and Senior Chief Stan Wolchonok. There were about eight other men around the table, as well. A few more SEALs but mostly other FBI agents, many of whom she recognized.

They all stood up.

'Great,' Max called. 'You're here. Is Mrs von Hopf safely ensconced in the hotel?'

'George and Jules are taking care of that,' Alyssa raised her voice enough for it to carry to the end of the room. 'Gentlemen, please sit back down.'

They all sat but Max, who stood as he waited for her.

She could feel Sam watching, but she didn't so much as glance at him. She focused on Max, who really was very gleamingly handsome. Far more traditionally good-looking than rough-edged Sam Starrett. Max knew how to wear a suit, knew how to cut his hair, knew his manners.

And he sincerely liked Alyssa. Sam had hated her right up to the moment he claimed to have fallen in love with her, the bastard.

God, she still wanted him with an ache that made her stomach hurt.

'Rose was anxious for news, so I came straight over,' she said. And then she did it. She gave her boss a little something extra in her smile. A little more eye contact. A silent 'hey, it's *very* good to see you, babe.' She knew Sam would fill in the rest – the part that went, 'Can't wait until we get naked later.'

And Max, bless his soul and God help her, knew exactly what she was doing and sent a similar message right back at her.

Law enforcement genius that he was, he glanced slightly, just *slightly* furtively at Lieutenant Commander Paoletti as if Tom Paoletti – the highest ranking officer in the room – was the one person he didn't necessarily want knowing that he was getting busy with one of his subordinates. So that Sam wouldn't know this show was for his benefit, that he was being conned.

It was beautiful.

Sam shifted in his chair and cleared his throat.

Now he – and everyone in this room – suspected Max Bhagat was getting it on with Alyssa. In fact, it probably would have been considered a sure thing bet.

It was funny. Just a few years ago she would have died rather than let people think such a thing about her. Her reputation had been all that mattered. Now she found it very hard to care.

Max quickly introduced her to the people in the room she didn't know, and she shook their hands.

The only empty seats were next to Sam and across from Sam. So she sat across from him, careful not to put her handbag on the floor. God knows she had enough problems.

'Have you got something for me?' she asked Max, heavy on the attitude and big with the eyes.

Max's lips twitched and she saw him clench his teeth to keep from smiling as he sat down at the head of the table. 'Uh, yeah. Actually . . .'

Yes, okay. Her comment *was* a tad unsubtle. But as long

as she was doing this, she was going to leave no doubt whatsoever in Sam Starrett's caveman brain that he'd been happily replaced.

'We've had a ransom note,' Max told her.

'With proof that Alex is still alive?' Oh, please, God . . .

'There's a photo of him, yeah. Taken with yesterday's paper – headline clearly visible.' Max gestured for Sam to pass the polaroid photo over to her.

He slid it across the table, and she took it with a nod of thanks, avoiding eye contact, trying to ignore the pack of peanut M&M's that sat in front of him on the table. The man was addicted to chocolate. She knew that first-hand.

Once, when she had been very drunk, she and Sam had gone wild with a bottle of chocolate syrup. To this day, she couldn't so much as smell chocolate without remembering.

And breaking into a sweat.

She focused on the picture.

Alex von Hopf was in his late fifties and slightly over-weight. He had a thick head of gray hair, a goatee, and a slightly round, friendly-looking face. He was lying in bed, his eyes half-open, clearly ill or drugged.

'Who's got him?' Alyssa asked. She looked down the table at Max. 'Do we have any leads besides the note?'

'We're working on that,' Max said. 'We've got about five local groups who top our list of usual suspects.'

'Any thefts of insulin reported lately?' She tapped the picture of Alex. 'He doesn't look too good.'

'Local authorities are searching reports of pharmacy break-ins by hand.' Max was disgusted. 'They're not computerized, and they won't let us near their files.'

'Any mention of Savannah or Ken Karmody?' she asked,

trying to predict the questions Rose would be asking her upon her return to the hotel.

'Not in the ransom note, no.'

'We've made an attempt to pick up the signal from WildCard Karmody's miniaturized tracking device – MTD,' Sam told her, and although she was forced to look at him, she met his gaze only briefly. 'So far nothing. Either the MTD's not working, or WildCard and the granddaughter are way outside of the area we're searching.'

'We've got a local warrant out for Otto Zdanowicz,' Max added. 'We're pretty sure he knows where his brother's chopper went down. As soon as we connect with him, we'll send a team to investigate the crash site.'

Alyssa held up the picture of Alex. 'Rose is going to want to see this. And the ransom note as well.'

'When we're done here, I'll head back to the hotel with you,' Max said with another of those smiles that by all rights should have made her insides flutter.

Instead, her stomach hurt as Sam Starrett cleared his throat again.

'So what are you really doing in Indonesia?' the American missionary named Molly asked as Savannah tried her best not to freak out.

Kenny was merely on the other side of the village, giving the man named Tunggul a crash course in using the dynamite they'd saved. As Billy the missionary translated, he was teaching the villagers the best way to clear as much of their road as possible with the limited amount of dynamite they had.

If there was any kind of trouble, he would be beside her in a flash. Savannah knew that. She knew *him*. And she knew herself now, too. Whatever happened, they would make it through.

But from here on in, she was going to make it through *clean*.

Molly had brought her to an outdoor showering area, where a bag of sun-warmed water hung over her head. It was heavenly to be able to wash her hair, but she would've enjoyed it far more if Ken had been in earshot.

'And what's in that case that Ken won't let go of?' Molly asked.

'Money,' Savannah told her, and Molly turned to look at her face above the makeshift privacy screen.

She looked closer. 'You're not kidding, are you?'

She shook her head. 'My uncle called. At least I thought it was my uncle at the time. Asking for money. Asking me to meet him in Jakarta. But when we arrived at the airport, these Russian men grabbed us, threw us into a helicopter and . . . They were going to kill us. I think because they were angry at my uncle.' As she said the words, the reality of their situation hit her like a punch to the gut. 'They're still looking for us. If they find us . . .'

'They won't.' When Molly said it, it sounded so definite. She was older than Savannah by at least ten years and was beautiful in an Earth Mother sort of way that Savannah herself would never be. 'Your Ken seems to know what he's doing. He's got the whole village on your side.'

Ken had made a very generous offer not just to show the villagers how to use the dynamite they'd salvaged, but to return in a month or so, with enough explosives to clear or reroute the road into town. The man with the weather-worn face, Tunggul, seemed to like and trust him. Which was really no surprise. Kenny was extremely likable. And his straightforward manner – which he described as being that of a jerk – was honest and refreshingly direct.

'Where exactly did you find him?' Molly asked.

'I met him while I was in college. I was afraid to come to Jakarta alone, and he . . . had some time off.' She rinsed the last of the soap from her hair. 'He's not *my* Ken, though.'

Molly nodded. 'But he came here because of you. He's not some Delta Force soldier on some top secret assignment, right? I mean, it's kind of obvious he's not your average tourist, but . . . He just wants to find a radio or a plane and get you both out of here, the end. Right?'

She was afraid of something, afraid of Ken. Savannah couldn't figure out why, but all of these oh-so-casual questions were not so casual after all. The last of the water dripped onto her head.

'He didn't even know he was coming to Jakarta with me until the day we left San Diego. Whoever or whatever you're worried about is safe.' Savannah wrapped herself in a beach towel and stepped out from behind the screen. 'I need you to help keep Ken safe by deleting the words *special* and *operations* from your vocabulary. Ken is just another tourist.' His very life depended on people believing that. He'd made that very clear to her, and now it was her turn to make it clear to Molly. She looked directly into the older woman's golden brown eyes. 'Do you understand?'

Molly smiled. 'I do.' But then her smile faded, at the exact moment Savannah heard it, too. 'Chopper.'

The throbbing sound was unmistakable. It was distant, but growing louder with each second.

Savannah grabbed her shorts and shirt, yanked them on while she ran toward the place she'd last seen Ken.

Get into the jungle. She knew Ken would want them in

the cover of the jungle, but she was smack in the middle of the village, and she had no idea which way to run.

And then, thank God, she saw him, running full tilt toward her, case in one hand, gun in the other. 'Savannah!'

'The church!' Molly shouted, and Savannah realized she was right behind her, running, too. The chopper was coming closer, just beyond the tree line. 'Go under the church tent. Services!' she called to the other people – villagers and missionaries alike. 'Quickly!'

She grabbed Savannah's arm and yanked her underneath the cover of the tent, as she continued to shout to the villagers, this time in the local dialect.

'Savannah!' Ken was beside her, out of breath. She saw him gauge the distance to the jungle, saw him accept the fact that running and hiding was not an option now, with the helo directly overhead. 'We're going to have to fight.' He looked around the village for the best place to have a standoff with the men in the helicopter. The church was undergoing renovations, but it was the only wooden structure to be found. He pointed to it. 'I want you and the other women and children in there. *Now!*'

But then Father Bob was there, holding out a long religious robe. 'How's your hymn singing?' he asked Kenny. 'Want to lead the congregation in a few tunes?'

Ken realized what Bob and the other missionaries were up to at the same time Savannah did. Villagers of all shapes and sizes had filled the benches beneath the tent. They were going to hide Ken and Savannah in plain sight.

Tunggul tugged the attaché case from Ken's hands as Bob helped him put on the robe, the strap of the Uzi still over his shoulder, the gun hidden by the voluminous fabric.

Several of the other men lifted the cloth and cross and

some candlesticks from the tent's makeshift altar, and Tunggul put the case on top of it. The cloths covered it and the candlesticks and cross went back on top, and it was gone. Completely hidden.

'But there's only one robe,' Ken shouted over the sound of the landing helo. It was coming down, right there in the center of town. 'There's no way Savannah can be passed off as a missionary. They know what she looks like!'

He didn't want to do this, she realized. He'd prefer to stand and fight. He'd rather take action, even if there was a bigger chance of getting himself killed.

'The robe will hide you both,' Father Bob said calmly. 'God knows, it's worked before.'

'I only know Christmas carols.' Ken was the closest to panicked she'd ever seen him.

'Then we'll sing Christmas carols.' Molly started the villagers in a rousing rendition of *Joy to the World*. 'If they ask, tell them we're planning to cut a holiday CD, sell it through the God-is-Love Project catalog.'

Father Bob led them both behind the pulpit, a carefully made wooden box with a slanting top. 'Stand just so,' he said, positioning Ken's feet and legs into a widespread stance. 'Come quick.' He pulled Savannah down so that she was sitting on the ground between Ken's feet. 'I know it's not the most comfortable thing for either of you, but the robe goes all the way to the ground and Savannah will be well hidden. Just don't forget and start walking.'

'They're going to take one look at me and know I'm not a missionary,' Ken said.

'Just smile,' Savannah suggested.

'Oh, great,' he said. 'Yeah, just smile. Sure. Thanks for the tip.'

'And don't swear.'

Father Bob zipped up the robe, but Ken stopped him halfway. She could see his face, looking down at her, tight with tension. 'I promised I'd keep you safe.'

'I am safe,' she told him quietly. 'As long as I'm with you, I'm the safest I've ever been.'

He stared down at her, as if she'd spoken to him in Chinese and he was having trouble translating.

'Here we go,' Father Bob's voice said.

'Just don't fart,' she added.

And before Ken zipped the robe closed, she saw his face relax into a smile.

It was long past midnight before Heinrich fell fast enough asleep for me to creep from his bed without waking him.

A light still burned in the sitting room of his hotel suite, so I had no problem finding the jacket that he'd tossed aside so carelessly many hours earlier.

His holstered gun was no longer on the floor. I assumed he'd put it back into the safe at some point – probably while I was in the bathroom. His notebook, too, was gone from his jacket pocket.

His keys weren't in the pockets of his pants. Of course not. He'd used them to unlock and lock the safe. But then what? Where had he hidden them?

I knew he wasn't sleeping with them in his pocket – he was sleeping without pockets entirely.

Trust no one. It was a motto handed out liberally by both the Nazis and the Allies. I'd gone through both of their crash courses in espionage, and it was one of the things upon which they definitely agreed.

Don't take chances. The people around you could well be

working for the enemy. Never let your guard down, not even for a moment.

When hiding something that others might be searching for, put it in the one place they would never think to look. Put it on their very person.

In their pockets – I, too, had none. Or within their luggage.

I slipped into the sitting room, and quickly found my purse. No keys.

The dinner we'd shared, sent up from room service, was still out on the table, the dessert barely touched as we'd eagerly returned to the bedroom.

I moved closer to the table, to take another bite of cheesecake. It was delicious and I was hungry.

And there they were.

Hank's keys.

Next to the champagne bucket. He'd come out to get us more wine, I remembered. He must have set them down then.

Trust no one.

Obviously, he trusted me.

My appetite was gone.

I took the keys, slipped back into the bedroom, waited a moment to make sure he still slept, and then opened the safe.

I took it all – his notebook, his gun, and a very thick stack of American money – and locked the safe back up.

The gun went into my purse after I checked to make sure it was loaded.

The notebook, as I'd suspected, was filled with names – mostly prominent New York businessmen and society women. Hank had written brief descriptions of these people, followed by comments. *Maybe. Definitely. Yes.*

Were these all people who'd agreed to spy for Nazi Germany?

If so, the United States was in deeper trouble than I'd thought.

There was no doubt about it, I had to get this notebook into Anson Faulkner's hands as soon as possible.

I put Hank's keys back next to the champagne bucket, and went into the bedroom to wake him.

I confess that despite my need for haste, I took my sweet time. He smiled as I kissed him, as he rolled me back with him onto the bed.

'God, how I love you,' he whispered and I kissed him harder, so he wouldn't see the tears in my eyes.

I loved my country, but I loved this man, too. And I knew this would be the last time we would be together like this.

Because in just a few hours, he was going to hate me.

Jones heard them coming – people trying to move quietly on the trail from the village – and he put down Molly's book.

Yeah, even if he wasn't about to have visitors, it was probably time to end his morbid fascination with Rose, with her 'I'm going to betray you, my darling, for a higher cause' mentality. Nah, he really didn't want to read her account of how she turned von Hopf over to the authorities.

Maybe he was a Nazi, but the fool loved her. That much was clear.

Love sucked.

Trust no one.

She got *that* part right. Von Hopf should have paid more attention to that rule, too. Trust only in yourself. Look out for numero uno. *You* were the only person in the world you could ever completely count on.

Jones had learned *that* the hard way.

Whoever was on the trail was getting closer, and he checked his handgun to make sure it was loaded.

He'd heard the chopper overhead earlier and guessed it was Jaya on the trail, coming to deliver the part for the Cessna. And as frequently and successfully as he'd done business with Jaya in the past, it was always a good idea to be armed and ready for anything. The man did, after all, work for General Badaruddin – who had connections with the Thai, who wanted Jones dead. Scum, after all, tended to float together at the top of a pond.

Trust no one.

Yeah, Rose, that was *his* motto, too.

'Jones.'

Shit, that was Molly stepping into the kill zone of his gun. He put the safety on and tucked his piece out of sight, into the back waistband of his shorts.

His fool of a body gave its usual enthusiastic leap of excitement at the sight of her, at the sound of her voice. His pulse quickened, blood rushed around, and he knew instantly how long it had been since they'd last made love. Five hours and twenty-odd minutes. Which under normal conditions was an acceptable length of time to go without sex.

However, nothing about his relationship with Molly was even remotely normal.

He'd told her everything last night.

And here she was, already. Back for more, evidently. Go figure.

Except, she wasn't alone. She had two people with her – a man and a woman. Both American.

The woman was blonde and willowy, mid-twenties. Pretty in a porcelain, highly fragile, high maintenance way. He didn't give her a second glance. She was not a threat.

But the man . . . Not particularly big in either height or

build, he was one of those lean, wiry guys who could keep going forever. His hair was dark, his face angular beneath a scruffy growth of jungle stubble.

But it was his eyes that made Jones wish he hadn't put away his handgun. They were hard. Intense. Whoever he was, this guy was driven. He was a man on a mission. He was definitely an operator, no doubt about that. Jones could tell within a half a second, just from the way he moved.

He would have reached for his weapon again, but the guy was carrying an Uzi that was locked and loaded and held in a manner that broadcast an ability to use it and use it well.

What the hell was Molly doing, bringing an operator up here to his camp?

'This is Ken and Savannah,' she told him. 'Otto Zdanowicz is after them. That was his brother on that helicopter that burned.'

So that was Zdanowicz's chopper he'd heard earlier, not the crazy, fucking General's. Crap. He hated being grounded – it made him itchy. Jaya couldn't get here with that part soon enough.

Or maybe it was just Molly who made him itchy.

'Do you have a two-way radio?' she asked him. 'I know your radio in the plane's not working, but I thought maybe—'

'No. Sorry.'

The operator – Ken – was staring out at the runway, at the Cessna, which was clearly in serious disrepair. In addition to the Uzi, he was also carrying a big-ass metal briefcase – the kind Jones used to see all the time in Washington, DC, handcuffed to couriers' wrists.

'What do you need to get the plane off the ground?' Ken asked.

'A miracle,' Jones told him flatly.

Ken looked at him, wheels obviously turning in his head. Apparently, his mission was to get the blonde away from Zdanowicz. Jones didn't blame him. Zdanowicz and his pals didn't play nice.

'We'll pay you ten thousand dollars – each – if you can fly us to Port Parwati,' Ken said. 'Is that enough for a miracle?'

Jesus H. Christ on a pogo stick.

Somehow Jones managed not to cry. Somehow he managed to actually sound bored as he replied. 'It's enough for me to sell you my firstborn child, but unless you know a way to take off and land without an alternator, I won't be flying you anywhere. Try me tomorrow.' *Please*.

Ken was sizing him up, trying to figure out if Jones was the type to send up a signal flare to Otto Zdanowicz the moment he and his little blonde disappeared back into the jungle.

'Make you a deal,' Jones said. 'If they approach me, looking for you, I'll give you a chance to make a better offer.'

Molly wasn't looking too happy with him at that, but Ken nodded.

Jones knew from experience that Ken would buy that sooner than if he'd told the truth and said, 'You're safe because my girlfriend would probably stop sleeping with me if I sold you out to the local thugs.'

Another good reason not to have a girlfriend.

'Molly says you're the equivalent of the local Wal-Mart. Can you set us up with some supplies? Food, water purification tablets, ammo if you've got it. A local map?'

402

'The mule trail to the coast is clearly marked,' Molly volunteered.

'We won't be using that,' Ken said at the exact same time Jones said, 'They won't be taking that route.'

Obviously, an operator would know enough survival tricks to stay far from the well-traveled trails.

'When do you expect the alternator to arrive?' Ken asked.

Jones shrugged. 'It's not exactly coming by FedEx.'

'Do you have the things we need?' Ken asked.

'Do you have money?'

Ken had apparently figured out a thing or two about Jones, because he correctly chose show over tell, and pulled a wad of currency – both local and American – from the pocket of his shorts.

It was a very thick wad, and – ding! – it was the right answer.

It didn't take a whole lot of effort for Alyssa to find out Sam Starrett's schedule.

With that knowledge in her pocket, she managed to be crossing the lobby of the hotel at the exact moment the SEAL lieutenant came in the front door.

He was dressed in civilian clothes – shorts, T-shirt, baseball cap, sneakers – in an attempt to keep the locals as unaware as possible that there was an entire US Navy SEAL team staying in downtown Jakarta.

There was a Starbucks-wannabe coffee shop right by the front desk, and she was aware that Sam watched as she got in line.

He stopped to speak to Senior Chief Wolchonok, but he stood facing the coffee shop, so that he could keep her in his line of sight.

Yup. Here she was. All alone in line for coffee. Jules wasn't around. Rose wasn't there. Max was decidedly absent. It was just Alyssa. All by herself . . .

'Hey.'

She turned to find Sam standing right next to her. He was so close, she didn't have to feign her surprise.

Up close he was big. All wide shoulders and long legs and broad chest. He smelled like sunblock and heat, and as she breathed him in, Alyssa felt a flash of panic. What was she doing? This was crazy. *She* was crazy to get within ten feet of this man.

'Hey,' she managed to say back at him. Just don't hold his gaze. Don't get lost in those pretty blue eyes. And – dear God – definitely don't touch him.

'You got a sec?' he asked.

'Sure. You want coffee?' She risked glancing at him, risked meeting his gaze. But his eyes were reserved, matching his careful politeness. They might as well have been strangers.

'That'd be great,' he said. 'Can we sit for a minute?'

'Sure.' They ordered their coffee, paid and took it toward the little tables scattered about the shop.

'You want to, uh, sit over there?' Sam pointed to one of the tables in the back where it was dimly lit and shadowy.

Alyssa put her coffee down on a table right there in the front, in full view of the entire lobby. 'This is fine.'

'I just thought . . . You know, in case you didn't necessarily want, uh, Max or someone to see you having coffee with me or something. Shit, I don't know.'

Polite Sam crumbled slightly, and real Sam shone through. Alyssa didn't dare meet his gaze now. She took a sip of her coffee instead, even though she knew it would scald her all the way down.

'Max isn't the jealous type,' she told him as soon as she'd recovered enough to speak.

He sat down across from her. There was no way his legs were fitting under that tiny table, so he sat kind of sideways and kept them out in the aisle. 'So you're, um, definitely seeing him, huh?'

Damnit. It figured Sam would ask her about Max, point-blank. She didn't want to lie to him. Not outright. So she didn't answer him outright. She managed a smile. 'He's a wonderful man. We've got so much in common. It's good. It's a good thing.'

'That's . . . that's great.' Sam nodded. 'I'm really happy for you, Lys. I'm . . .' He put down his coffee, ran one hand down his face as he made a sound that might've been laughter. 'I'm so fucking jealous I can hardly breathe.'

His honesty almost undid her. She nearly confessed the truth.

'I'm sorry,' he said, all the stilted politeness suddenly stripped away. His eyes were Sam's again, hot and intense and desperate. 'I know that's not fair. I know I have no fucking right – I'm the one who's married. And . . . Mary Lou, she's . . .' He shook his head. 'You didn't see her at her best. She's a good person. She works her ass off taking care of that baby. And she's doing it stone sober, too. She's been sober for nearly eight months now, and that hasn't been easy. Every day, she works harder than anyone I've ever met in my life, just so she doesn't take a drink. She impresses the hell out of me, you know?'

'You obviously care for her a great deal,' Alyssa said quietly. It was also obvious that he wasn't going to leave her. He was still determined to do what was right, even though it meant his own unhappiness.

'She really loves Haley. And, well, me, too. It's kind of nice – the trouble she goes to, to make sure there's always a hot meal waiting for me when I get home. And the laundry's always clean, you know?'

'I'm the one who should be jealous of you,' she said. 'Max never does my laundry. He makes a lousy wife.'

Sam laughed. 'I bet. He's probably . . . pretty good at other things, though, huh?'

Lord God. She stared at him in disbelief. He was serious. 'Are you really sure you want to go there? Because—'

He leaned toward her. 'Just tell me you know what I know. That together we were incredible. That what we had—'

Alyssa shook her head and closed and rolled her eyes. Egocentric fool. How could she possibly love this man as much as she did?

'What we *had* was too short to ever be compared to a real relationship. For God's sake, Sam. We didn't get a chance to move beyond the screaming sex stage. Was it good? Yes. Was it better than what I've got right now with Max?' Dear God, she was really lying now. 'No.'

She leaned forward, too. 'Would it have lasted more than a few months? I don't think so. I mean, come on, Starrett. You and me? It was fun while it lasted. And I'll be the first to admit I wish it had lasted a little bit longer. But in a way, we were saved. It didn't have to die a natural death. We didn't have to get sick of each other. And face it. I definitely would have gotten sick of you.'

He was silent for several long moments, just sitting there, completely still.

'No offense,' she said.

'No,' he said, and finally moved. He looked at his watch. 'Well . . .'

'You probably have to be somewhere,' she said for him, as desperate for him to get away as he was to leave. If she suddenly burst into tears, he might guess that everything she'd said was a lie, and that her heart had broken all over again for the way she'd just hurt him.

'Yeah.' He stood up. 'Thanks for, um . . .'

Alyssa managed to smile. 'Yeah. I'm glad we could talk like this – you know, be so honest with each other.'

'Right,' he said.

Sam walked away without looking back.

And Alyssa knew he'd never look back again.

Fifteen

'You,' Molly said to Savannah, 'are not allowed to do anything but get off those feet. You're making me hurt just by standing there.'

Ken was looking at the map that the man named Jones had sold to them for fifty dollars. Fifty *dollars* for a map. And that was after Ken had haggled.

Savannah watched him, remembering how tightly he'd held her after the gun runner's helicopter had left the village, after they were safe. She hadn't wanted him to let her go.

Ever.

He glanced up at her, and, afraid to be caught staring, she looked around.

Jones's Quonset hut was a warehouse. It held boxes of everything from toilet paper to canned food. The building itself was in far better shape than it looked from the outside. The heavy-duty bolt on the door was controlled by some kind of high-tech keyless entry. But the push-button panel was hidden beneath a rusting flap of metal.

One corner of the room had been converted into living quarters, with a bed covered with mosquito netting, a table and chairs. There were votive candles – the kind in the little glass cups – scattered everywhere, on every available surface. Most of them were burned completely down.

Jones may have been a black marketeer or even a drug runner, but it was more than obvious that he was a romantic. And completely hung up on Molly.

Who pushed the mosquito netting aside to make Jones's bed. 'Come on,' Molly said, patting the smoothed bedspread. 'Lie down.'

When Savannah hesitated, she added, 'I'd like to point out that I don't make a habit of inviting other women into Dave's bed. The fact that I'm doing this should make you realize how serious I am that you need to get off your feet.'

Savannah laughed, and Molly added, 'It'll be awhile before he gathers all the supplies you and Ken are going to need, so you might as well take advantage of this. I know I would.'

And so Savannah climbed onto the bed, wincing as she slipped off the sandals she'd bought from one of the villagers.

'Oh, honey, there's no way you're going to walk all the way to Port Parwati,' Molly said. She raised her voice so that Ken and Jones – Dave was apparently his first name – could hear. 'She should stay here. You both should stay here.'

'I could hide you,' Dave volunteered. Dave Jones, Savannah realized. Yeah, sure it was his real name. No doubt about it. He was the person Molly wanted to keep safe. 'You know, for a fee.'

But Ken was shaking his head. He was wearing a shirt again, and shorts that he'd gotten from one of the missionaries. It was a shame. The half-naked Tarzan look had suited him. 'This guy Otto will show up here sooner or later.'

'And you'll be hidden,' Jones said. 'He won't find you.'

'But he'll find you,' Ken countered.

Jones shrugged. 'Fair enough. I wouldn't trust me, either.'

'Oh, come on.' Molly was exasperated. 'Stop trying so hard to be dangerous,' she said to Jones. She aimed her absolute confidence at Ken. 'You can trust him. *I* trust him. He's not going to sell you or anyone out to Otto Zdanowicz.'

Savannah recognized the set to Ken's mouth, and knew he wasn't going to be convinced. But Molly was stubborn, too. 'Look, the part for the Cessna's going to get here sooner or later. Why make Savannah walk all that way when she could fly? She could stay here and, I don't know, Ken could go out in the jungle and lead Zdanowicz on a wild goose chase. If they think you and Savannah are out in the brush, they're not going to come looking here. I really think you need to consider it. Her feet are pretty badly scraped up.'

Ken was gazing at her now, across the open room, and Savannah tucked the feet in question beneath her. 'I'm fine,' she said. 'Really. It's not that bad.'

'I'm not so psyched about that,' Jones admitted to Ken. 'I'd need to be sure she stayed hidden, and if you were there, she'd be your responsibility, not mine.' He glanced at Savannah. 'No offense, but you don't strike me as the type to hide in a dark place all alone for days at a time without flipping out.'

'No,' Ken said, with another look in her direction. 'She's tough. She could do it. I don't doubt that for one second.'

Her first response to his words was intense pleasure. Ken thought she was *tough*. But then apprehension slammed into her.

'Ken, please, I want to stay with you.' Savannah spoke as calmly as she could manage, considering that her heart was about to pound out of her chest at the thought of him leaving her here alone.

He looked at her again, his face and dark eyes unreadable. But he nodded. 'Yeah, I think that's probably best. That we stay together.'

'Suit yourself,' Jones said.

Molly wasn't as easily convinced. 'Savannah—'

'It looks worse than it is,' she told the older woman. Thank God, thank God. Kenny wasn't going to leave her.

Molly shook her head, clearly not believing her. 'I'm going to go help. Yell if you need anything. And keep those feet up.'

'I'm fine.' And she would be, as long as Ken was with her.

Molly disappeared among the mountain of boxes, and Savannah settled herself more comfortably on the bed.

A real bed. She'd almost forgotten how lovely and comfortable a real bed could be, just to lie upon. Imagine how wonderful it would be to actually *sleep* in one. With Ken's arms around her.

Like *that* was ever going to happen again.

Her gaze was caught by the familiar cover of a book, tossed onto an upside-down crate next to Jones's bed, and she leaned closer. It was indeed *Double Agent*. Savannah couldn't keep from laughing. Didn't it figure? A tough-assed smuggler on a remote Indonesian island was reading her grandmother's book.

She reached for it, to see how far he'd gotten.

He'd turned down the corner of a page not too far from where she was, herself, in the story.

Ken was completely absorbed by the map and she knew he wouldn't leave without her, so she settled back and started to read.

I watched Hank as he shifted gears, well aware that if things went according to my plan, I would have to drive this car back into the city.

'Left here,' I commanded.

He glanced over at me in the predawn darkness as he took the turn onto what was little more than a dirt road. 'This definitely isn't the way to Maryland.'

'I told you,' I said. 'It's a surprise.'

'A surprise. All the way out here in the middle of nowhere?'

'It's a New Jersey surprise.'

To my relief, he was still in a good humor, willing for me to lead him probably just about anywhere. It was my first real lesson in the absolute power of sex. He laughed softly. 'You've got me completely intrigued.'

'That's because I'm completely intriguing.'

'Darling, you are.' He pulled me close and kissed me, one eye on the road.

I kissed him back, well aware that we had almost arrived, certain this would be our last kiss. Perhaps forever.

'After this, we'll go to Maryland?' he asked for what was not the first time since we'd gotten into the car in Manhattan.

And for what was not the first time, I avoided answering. 'Oh, it's right up here. Slow down! On the left. Pull into the drive.'

It was a house. An unassuming little two-story farmhouse, surrounded by woods and fields. The nearest neighbor was two and a half miles down the road.

Hank bent over slightly to look out of the windshield and up at the house. 'Whoever lives here isn't expecting visitors at four in the morning.'

'I live here,' I told him.

He laughed, but then he realized I was serious as I added, 'I recently bought this place. I'm fixing it up. Come and look.'

Hank followed me out of the car. 'You bought this house? On your salary?'

'Of course not on my salary, silly.' I laughed gaily as I unlocked the kitchen door, as if my very life weren't ending. 'Come inside.'

I flipped on the kitchen light.

Hank silently took in the disarray of my renovations as I went to the sink and filled the kettle with water for tea. My hands were shaking, but I set it on the stove, lit the gas, and gave him a bright smile.

'Shall I give you the tour? This is the kitchen, of course. At least it will be when I'm done. I started the renovations in the basement – I'm working my way up, floor by floor. And this, the sitting room.'

He followed me, his hat in his hands, his face so serious. 'Rose. Where did you get the money to buy and fix this place? Who exactly are you working for?'

He'd opened up the subject for me, quite nicely.

'You know who I'm working for,' I countered, praying this would work. Praying that here and now, in the middle of New Jersey, with no chance of anyone listening in, he would open up and tell me more about the Nazis' network of American spies that he had helped to build. 'I work for the same noble cause you do, Obersturmfuehrer von Hopf.'

His reaction was not quite what I'd expected. He stood there, staring at me, the strangest expression crossing his face.

'*Mein Gott*,' he whispered.

'*Ja*,' I said. '*Für Gott, und Vaterland.*' (For God and country.)

'Rose,' he said, but then he stopped. He shook his head, clearly upset. 'I have to think. I need to think.' He took the car keys from his pocket, and I realized he was going to leave. He was going to drive away.

I didn't understand what was so distressing to him. All I had done was speak aloud that which we already both knew. Unless – oh, dear – he feared that this was some kind of trap.

He was moving toward the kitchen door, but I couldn't let him go.

Heart pounding, I took the gun from my handbag and pointed it at him. 'Freeze. Drop the car keys on the floor, then keep your hands where I can see them.'

It was his gun I was holding – the one that I'd taken from his safe. I could see that he recognized it – his face had gone quite gray.

'This *is* a setup, then,' he asked. 'I suppose – of course – it's been a setup from the start.'

'Hands on your head and move slowly,' I ordered, both of my hands wrapped around that gun. There was no way I would ever shoot him, but I prayed he wouldn't realize that. 'Into the kitchen.'

'You're remarkably good,' he told me, his voice harsh. 'Last night, it was . . .' He laughed. 'I'm such a fool. I actually believed you.' The look he gave me was one of pure hatred.

I steeled myself to it. I could handle his hatred. I just couldn't handle his death.

'Open the door,' I told him in a voice that wobbled only slightly. 'That one, to the left. Do it slowly – with your right hand only.'

'The cellar,' he said. 'What a surprise. I'll tell you right now, I won't dig my own grave. You'll have to do it yourself, darling. Get your hands dirty.'

'It's not a cellar,' I informed him. 'It's a basement, with a concrete floor. I bought this place because of it. There's a light switch to the right of the stairs. Please turn it on.'

He did.

'Down the stairs,' I ordered. 'Don't move too quickly, please.'

There was a separate room down there, made with the same thick stone foundation, and he laughed as he saw what I'd done.

I'd installed a heavy iron gate so I could lock him in.

I'd put iron bars on all the windows, too. I'd boarded them up from the outside, too, but he wouldn't find that out until the sun came up.

'Isn't this cozy,' he said, taking in the bed and small table, the bookshelf filled with books, the cabinet stocked with about a week's worth of tinned food. There was a sink and toilet, too, in another small attached room. It had been some kind of servants' quarters. With the stone walls whitewashed, it was actually quite nice.

It was the reason I'd bought this house.

'Go inside,' I told him, and he went, looking with narrowed eyes at my construction. 'All the way, back against the wall.'

His gaze took in the solid anchors that held my iron gate. My father had taught me well. As I closed it and locked him in with the vast array of chains and locks I'd bought, he realized he was not playing with some amateur.

The stone foundation of the house was impenetrable. The floor was concrete, the ceiling fortified with two by fours – that had been some job to do. He wasn't getting out that way.

Once I was gone, he wasn't getting out at all.

He rushed me then, but it was too late. I'd locked him up tight. He hit the gate, and it didn't even rattle.

'Why don't you just shoot me now?' he spat.

I dropped his gun back into my purse. My hands were truly

shaking now that I'd managed to get him down here and safely behind my bars. 'I'm not going to shoot you, Heinrich.'

I was exhausted, too, but there was much yet to do. I had to take the car back to Manhattan – wipe it clean of our fingerprints and leave it somewhere far from the hotel. I had to clear Hank's things from his hotel room and check out of my room as well.

I had to go through the list of names from Hank's notebook, try to make some sense of it, figure out who on that list was part of his information-gathering network.

My plan was to contact some of those people on his list and tell them that Heinrich had been killed in an altercation with an enemy agent. Since I was his lover, I would tell them, he trusted me enough to take over for him. I would somehow get them to reveal to me their method for sending information to Germany. I didn't know how, but I would do it. And then I'd stop the Nazis dead in their tracks by taking what I'd learned and telling the entire story to the FBI.

The part about Heinrich dying would be a lie, of course. All this time, he'd be locked in the basement of my house in New Jersey, safe from harm.

'Why wait, Rose?' Hank raged. He reached for me from behind the bars, his fingers spread. I honestly think if he could have gotten his hands on me, he would have eagerly throttled me.

I had known this would happen. But I hadn't quite prepared myself for the depth of his hatred for me.

'Turning me in will kill me just as surely as pulling that trigger,' he pronounced. 'So do it. *Do* it.' He pounded on the bars. 'I want *you* to do it. I want you to shoot me in the heart!'

'There's food in the cabinet,' I told him as calmly as I possibly could. 'Enough for a week. I'm not sure when I'll be able to get back—'

'Shoot me, goddamn you! Shoot me, shoot me shoot me—'

I lost it then. I screamed over him, 'No. *No!* I'm *not* going to shoot you! I'm *not!*'

He just stood there then, watching me, breathing as hard as if he'd just run a footrace. 'Darling, you've already killed me,' he said quietly. 'You might as well finish me off.'

'No,' I said through my tears. 'You're wrong. All this is to keep you alive.'

I could see from his face that he didn't understand.

'After the war is over,' I told him, 'when Germany has been defeated and you can no longer do the Allies any harm, then I'll let you go. Until then, you'll be right here.'

He shook his head. 'The Allies . . . ?'

'I'm an American, Hank.' I wiped my eyes. 'I love you, but I love my country, too. I couldn't let you continue to spy for the Nazis. But how could I turn you in? If I did, you'd be executed. I couldn't allow that to happen, either. *This* was the only way I could think of to protect both my country and you.'

'You're locking me up – here – until the end of the war,' he repeated, as if he were still struggling to understand.

'Yes. I realize it could go on for quite some time, and I'm sorry for that. I'll get you books to read, paper and pens if you want to write – whatever you like to help pass the time.'

He started to cry then, sinking down to sit on the floor, face buried in his hands.

I took a step toward him. 'I'm sorry.'

He looked up at me and I realized he wasn't crying – he was laughing.

'Rose, for God's sake, I'm working for the Allies, too. I have been from the start – even back in Berlin, when we first met. But of course, you thought – Rose, *Rose*, I may have been wearing

417

their uniform, but I assure you, I'm no Nazi. I've been working against them since 1936.'

I stared at him as he pulled himself to his feet.

'That bit upstairs,' he said. 'You were pretending to be a Nazi sympathizer to get me to talk, is that it?'

I started for the stairs. 'I have to go.' Whatever his plan was, I wasn't going to fall for it.

'Wait!'

'Nice try, Hank, but it's not working. I'll be back in a few days.'

'My notebook,' he said. 'Do you have it?'

I turned to look back at him.

'If you don't, it's still in the safe in the hotel,' he told me, talking fast. 'The key's right here.' He tossed the ring with his hotel room key onto the basement floor, next to my feet. 'Go into the safe, and get that notebook and bring it to the FBI, to a man named Joshua Tallingworth. There's important information in that notebook, Rose. If it falls into the wrong hands – German hands – lots of good people fighting to end this war will die. But take it, and ask to see Tallingworth. Use the codeword *starling* and you'll be inside his office before you blink. Go on, darling. Take the keys.'

'I already have the notebook,' I told him.

'Good,' Hank said. 'Take it, and go. Tallingworth will tell you the truth about who I am – that I'm not any kind of a Nazi.'

I stared at him. Could he be telling the truth?

'Go on,' he urged. 'I'm not going anywhere. I'll be right here when you get back.'

I started up the stairs, suddenly numb. What had I done?

'And after you do get back,' he called after me, 'we're going to Maryland. Don't think I'm going to forget your promise.'

That stopped me cold. 'You still want to marry me?' I couldn't believe it. 'After what I've done? If what you're telling me is true . . .'

'It is true. And Rose . . . ?' I heard him laugh, very softly. 'God, I love you, too.'

'I have to get back to the village.'

'I'll walk you,' Jones said, just as Molly suspected he would. It confirmed her belief that there were some truly nasty people floating around this mountain today.

He looked at Ken, who was repacking the knapsack Jones had sold him with the food and other supplies. 'Don't fuck with my stuff. If you need anything else, take it, but leave cash on the table. If you leave before I get back, lock the door behind you.' He wrote a series of numbers on a piece of paper. 'This is the current combination. You need to punch in these numbers to secure the system. Don't get too excited about my giving you this, because I change these numbers daily.'

'Thank you,' Ken held out his hand, and the two men shook. Then he reached for Molly's hand. 'You really saved our butts back there.'

'It seemed a shame to let two such fine butts go to waste,' she countered. 'Good luck, Ken.' She glanced toward Jones's bed, where Savannah had curled up with a copy of *Double Agent*. She'd fallen fast asleep, book tucked to her chest, and looked to be about twelve years old. 'Try to take it slowly, if you can. Her feet must really hurt.'

He nodded, his eyes soft as he looked over at Savannah. 'She's really incredibly tough. I could take her on a five-mile run right now, and she wouldn't say a word.'

'Just because she doesn't say *ouch* doesn't mean that she's not hurt,' Molly reminded him. 'Take care.'

419

'You, too.'

Jones held the door open for her, closed it tightly behind him. And then he grabbed her arm, reeled her in close and kissed the very breath out of her.

'Mmm,' he said when he finally let her up for air. 'I thought they would never leave.'

'They didn't,' she told him. 'We did. And I have to get back. Right now.'

Jones kissed her neck. 'Right *right* now? Or more like twenty minutes from now right now? Because I want to show you something I found.'

He pulled her across the glaringly hot runway toward the jungle on the other side, even though she told him, 'This is not good. I cannot be returning to the village with my hair a mess and my shirt on inside out and backwards. And believe me, everyone's going to be checking. They all know that I was with you last night and that we weren't discussing your extremely procapitalist, anticommunist habit of overinflating the price of toilet paper.'

But then he was opening some kind of door built right into an outcropping of rock. And she followed him into a cool, damp, dim, narrow room, maybe twelve feet by three feet. There were narrow openings like you might find in a castle wall, obviously designed to shoot a gun through. Not much light came in, because it was nearly completely overgrown – except for one small area that had been strategically cleared.

'This was where I thought they could hide until the alternator came in – Ken and Savannah. But I don't blame him for saying no. He doesn't know me.'

She could see almost the entire runway from that spot, as well as the Quonset hut Jones called home.

'It was built by the Japanese during the Second World War,' he told her, his voice bouncing slightly off the concrete and stone walls. There was an air mattress in there, and a cache of food and water. 'It's some kind of pillbox. There's a bunch of 'em, all around the airstrip – you really have to search to find them. I think the plan must've been to pretend to desert the airfield, wait for the Americans to arrive, and then shoot the shit out of them. I don't think it worked – there's no evidence there was ever any kind of battle out here at all. In fact, I think we didn't even bother to invade Parwati Island during the war; it wasn't worth the trouble.'

'So the Japanese built these things and just sat here waiting for an attack that never came?' Molly laughed softly. 'Why do I find that so sad? I must be extremely twisted.'

'Yeah,' Jones said. 'I think we've already verified that.' He came up behind her and kissed her ear, her throat, that delicate place between her neck and her shoulder. She could feel him, hot and heavy against her, aroused again. She loved the fact that he was aroused again. 'What time can you get back up here tonight?' he asked.

His hands skimmed beneath her shirt, brushing the undersides of her breasts, and she heard herself moan. He took that as an invitation and filled his hands with her.

'I can't,' she admitted. Oh, Lord, what he was doing to her felt so good. 'Not tonight. I want to, Grady, God, I do, but everyone will be watching.'

'Let 'em watch.' He unfastened the top button of her shorts, slipped his hand down inside.

Oh, yeah . . . 'I'm supposed to be a role model for the women in the village.'

'You're a great role model.'

421

'I have to be careful,' she gasped. 'Really. I don't want to do anything that'll make Father Bob send me home early.'

That caught his attention. 'If I can't see you tonight, when *can* I see you again?'

'You can certainly come to tea, but the tent flaps will be up.'

'I'll come to tea. But let me rephrase the question – when can I make love to you again?'

'I don't know. I'll try to find some other excuse for taking out the boat and—'

'Now,' he said, his breath hot in her ear. 'How about right now?'

'I have to get back,' she said, but she sounded far less convincing than she had the first time, particularly when he unzipped her shorts and pushed both them and her panties down to her knees. And then, God, he was inside of her, and all she could say was *yes*.

Ken watched Savannah sleep.

Her feet were in really tough shape, she had to be exhausted, and he felt a twinge of guilt for having to wake her and get her moving again.

He didn't trust Jones, but he did trust Molly. He should have made an arrangement to leave Savannah with the missionaries. They would keep her safe. And he – he could do what Molly suggested. Lead the gun runners on a chase up farther into the mountains.

Except, he couldn't do it. Even though he knew Savannah would be better off, he couldn't let her out of his sight.

He had never been so scared in his entire life as he'd been in the village, when that helo approached. He'd never been the fastest man in the Team, but he'd broken Olympic records, racing to get back to Savannah.

Shitless. For the first time in his life, he'd been scared practically shitless and it was not a pleasant sensation.

Even now, when he thought about it, thought about what Otto Zdanowicz might have done had he come face to face with Savannah, it made him sick to his stomach.

Because Zdanowicz could well have taken out his sidearm, aimed it at Savannah's head, and pulled the trigger. Blam. Savannah could have crumpled to the ground, dead. Executed on the spot.

And Ken – way across on the other side of the village – wouldn't have been able to do a single freaking thing to stop it.

No, Savannah was staying with him. Close to him. Where he knew she'd be safe.

As for her feet ... He was going to lighten their load. Take a small chunk of the cash from the attaché case, and then hide the rest of it. After he got Savannah to civilization and safety, he could come back for the money.

Until then, he'd bury it. And what better place to bury it than in the backyard of the local smuggler? This cowboy, Jones, knew damn well that Ken didn't trust him. He'd never expect him to hide an attaché case filled with American dollars within spitting distance of his Quonset hut.

Then, with the case out of the equation, Ken would only have to carry the knapsack with their recently purchased supplies. That way, he could help Savannah – maybe even carry her part of the way.

Tunggul, the village elder – the old guy with the leather face – had told Ken that there were people who might sell him a boat if he headed up to the north side of the island – *away* from Port Parwati.

This was a doubly good plan, since Zdanowicz wouldn't expect them to head away from the city.

He and Savannah were going to head toward that river he'd seen when he'd followed Beret and his army. If they could beg, buy, borrow, or steal a boat, they could travel by sea around the island to the port.

There were two major obstacles, Tunggul had warned.

First, that part of the island belonged to the local rebels. Beret was none other than Armindo Badaruddin, a revolutionary who wasn't above using terrorist tactics when the mood struck.

Second, once they hit the open sea, they would be the potential target of pirates.

Ken, however, was confident in his ability to avoid Badaruddin's less-than-expert patrols. An additional bonus was the knowledge that Zdanowicz would think twice about crossing into Badaruddin's territory.

As for the pirates – yeah, just let them try to attack. Most of the pirates were poorly armed, Tunggul had admitted. Ken, however, still carried the Uzi and had enough ammunition now to start a small war.

Savannah murmured something in her sleep, and Ken couldn't bring himself to wake her.

Instead, he took the attaché case and quietly went out the door, taking care to lock it securely behind him.

Molly kissed him again, both amusement and chagrin in her eyes. 'What am I going to do about you? I tell you I have to go, or that I won't make love in my tent, and you just steamroll right over me.'

'Hey,' Jones said. 'You've got to give me some credit – I didn't mess up your hair.'

She laughed. 'Fair enough.'

She kissed him again, but he pulled free, his eye caught by movement outside of the Quonset hut.

What the hell . . . ? It was Ken. He was coming out of the hut, carrying that metal case in one hand, Uzi in the other.

Molly turned to look, too. 'What's—'

He quickly put his hand over her mouth, held one finger to his lips.

As they watched, Ken stood silently, watching the jungle as one minute became two became three became even more. And Jones knew what he was doing. He was making sure that they really had gone back to the village. Ken knew that Molly, inexperienced in the tricks of the special forces trade, wouldn't be able to sit in the jungle for long without giving away her position.

Except, of course, if she were safely hidden in an old Japanese hide.

When he was seemingly satisfied, Ken vanished into the jungle, just beyond the hut.

'Shit, he's ditching the blonde,' Jones breathed into Molly's ear. That was just terrific. What was *he* supposed to do with her?

'I think he probably just needs to pee.'

'With the case?' He snorted. 'No, he's outta here. I wonder what the hell's in there, anyway.'

'Money.'

Jones turned to look at her. 'Excuse me?'

'Savannah told me there was money in that case.'

'How much?' Jesus, a case that size must hold . . . Damn, it would depend on the face value of the bills. If they were hundreds . . .

'I didn't ask.'

Of course not. But probably more than twenty thousand dollars. Jesus Christ, if the Cessna had been able to fly, Jones could have walked away with twenty grand in cold hard cash. *That* hurt.

'Why didn't you tell me about the money before?' he asked her.

'It didn't seem important.'

'You thought if I knew about it I'd try to take it.'

Molly rolled her eyes. 'Actually, that thought never crossed my mind.'

'Well, maybe it should have.'

'I really have to go,' she told him.

'Hey,' he said, catching her by the wrist. 'No way. You're staying here with Blondie. I'm going after Ken to drag his ass back here.'

'Wherever he went, he'll be back,' Molly said. 'He's not leaving here without her. Didn't you see the way he looks at her?'

'You mean, like he wants to fuck her?' He said it just to get a rise out of her.

Being Molly, she didn't even blink. She just looked at him, and he was the one who caved.

'Sorry. Yes, I noticed. He's obviously crazy about her. You're right. But there's got to be close to a hundred grand in that case. Love's all fine and good, but money like that transcends human emotions.'

'He didn't take the knapsack with the supplies,' Molly pointed out. 'Just watch. He'll be back.'

'Ken!' The shriek echoed inside the Quonset hut, followed by the unmistakable sound of pounding on the door.

Jones swore. 'The son of a bitch locked her in.'

*

Savannah couldn't believe it. 'Kenny, you . . . you . . . *asshole!*'

He'd left.

He'd taken the money and left her here alone.

There was no note, no explanation. Just a serious lack of Ken.

He'd locked her in, the jerk. How could he do that to her? She threw herself again against the door, but it wasn't going to budge. And there was no other way in or out. All of the windows in this place were barred.

'Ken!'

Yes, her feet were a mess. But she hadn't complained, she wouldn't complain. She'd keep up – somehow.

'Kenny!' She was screaming in vain. She knew it, but she couldn't stop. Couldn't stop pounding on the door, either.

How could he have left her?

How could she have been so wrong about him? It didn't seem possible – like watching Gandhi kick a puppy.

Okay, so maybe Kenny wasn't Gandhi, but he'd been so careful to reassure her. He wasn't going anywhere. He was in this with her until the bitter end.

So why would he leave her now? Unless he somehow thought she'd be better off here, with Jones and Molly.

'Kenny!'

The door opened midscream. Just like that. And there he was. Standing in the sunlight on the other side. He *hadn't* left her.

'Whoa,' he said. 'You're pissed. Sorry about that. I was only gone for a few minutes. You were sleeping, so I—'

Savannah burst into tears.

*

It finally happened.

Savannah had a meltdown.

Ken had finally – although this time quite unintentionally – pushed her past her point of tolerance, beyond the edge of her usually tightly held control.

She launched herself, crying, into his arms.

'Don't leave me,' she sobbed. 'Don't ever, *ever* leave me!'

'Oh,' he said, completely nonplussed. 'No. Babe, I wasn't. Did you really think—'

She was crying with great huge, noisy sobs. 'I thought you were being an asshole and that you left me behind!'

He had to laugh.

She lifted her head to look at him accusingly. 'Don't you laugh at me!'

'I'm not,' he said quickly. 'I'm laughing at me. I'm . . . I should have written you a note.' He cupped her face with his hand and tried to brush away her tears with his thumb. But he couldn't do it. They were falling too fast. His heart clenched – he actually felt it tighten. It freaking hurt and he knew it was so over – his trying to pretend that he didn't give a shit about her. 'I'm so sorry, Van. Honest. I was hiding the attaché case so we wouldn't have to carry it. I would never leave you. Never. I swear to God. I would die first.'

Savannah kissed him.

One second she was gazing up at him with those eyes swimming in tears, and the next she was kissing him as if there were no tomorrow.

She was salty and sweet and ferocious. And she nearly knocked him right on his ass.

It was an amazing kiss. The heavens rumbled and the earth shook, and it wasn't until the second blast that he realized Tunggul and his posse had begun clearing the road to Port Parwati.

He pulled out of Savannah's arms. 'Motherfucking idiot! Not you,' he quickly added. The third charge went off. 'The villagers are blasting. I asked them to wait twenty-four hours – nothing like shaking the mountain to draw unwanted attention. Zdanowicz is going to be back in this neighborhood in a freaking flash. We better make sure we're good and gone.'

She was standing there staring at him, wide-eyed, her face still streaked with tears, her mouth all but begging him to kiss her again. But there was no time to do anything but grab their stuff and run.

'Savannah, I need you to be tough for me, okay?' Ken said, praying she had just a little bit more of that awesome control left in her. 'Can you do that? Can you hang on just a little bit longer?'

She nodded, quickly wiping her eyes and her face with the heels of her hands. 'I'm sorry. I shouldn't have done that.'

Which? Cry or kiss him? This wasn't the time to ask.

'Pay attention,' Ken said, 'because this is important. I buried the attaché case in the jungle, fifteen paces from the southwest corner of this Quonset hut. And they're *my* paces. They'll be longer than yours. You got it?'

'Fifteen,' she said. 'Paces.'

'Get your sandals on,' he ordered. 'We've got to move. As fast as we can.'

He grabbed the knapsack, and she was back beside him in a heartbeat.

'You know the drill,' he reminded her as he locked the Quonset hut door. 'I say get down, you get down. I say run—'

429

'I run,' she said. 'I know.'

Her nose was red, and several tears still hung on her eyelashes, but otherwise she was back together. Ready to run on feet that would have had half the big tough SEALs in Team Sixteen bitching and moaning.

'If you want, I can carry you—'

'I'm fine,' she said shortly. 'Let's go.'

He'd said that wrong. He should have said, 'I want to carry you.' Or, 'I'm going to carry you now.' She took orders amazingly well for a control freak – she might've actually let him carry her if he'd used the right words.

Ken led her into the jungle, trying to focus completely on heading north and hiding their tracks.

But his brain wanted to multitask, and he couldn't stop thinking of the look on Savannah's face as she'd finally melted down. Her words repeated over and over with the cadence of their feet. *Don't leave me! Don't leave me!*

And then, god *damn*, she'd kissed him. She'd freaking *kissed* him. It was a no hesitation, high power, heavy tongue action, full body slam kind of kiss. The kind that screamed, 'I want you, I need you.'

Ken stumbled over his own feet, somehow managing to thwack himself in the face with a low hanging branch. God, he was a freaking moron.

Yes, she wanted and needed him – to keep her safe.

After he successfully did that, then and only then should he start considering any of her other potential wants and needs. And *potential* was the big word here. So what if she'd kissed him. It might've been simply from intense relief.

If a helo carrying Sam Starrett and Johnny Nilsson were to suddenly appear overhead and lower a rope to pull them aboard to safety, he'd certainly give them each a big wet kiss.

'Are you okay?' Savannah asked.

'Yeah, I was just . . . thinking about how glad I'm going to be when this is over,' he told her.

'Me, too.' Her words were heartfelt and Ken knew that she probably couldn't wait to get out of here.

Don't leave me.

Chances are she wouldn't sing quite the same song once he got her safely back to Jakarta.

Another misstep, and another branch hit him in the face. And he made himself focus by thinking about Otto Zdanowicz finding Savannah and shooting her in the head.

'I'm going to carry you now,' he told her, 'so we can move even faster. I'm not asking you, I'm telling you. Any response from you is unnecessary and unwelcome.'

She didn't say a word as he picked her up. Her life was now literally in his hands. His focus was clear and his footing sure as he moved swiftly through the dim jungle.

It took ten minutes to find where Ken had hidden the attaché case.

Really, the only reason Jones found it so quickly was because he'd seen exactly where Ken had gone into the jungle, and because he was a lucky son of a bitch.

Digging it up took about two minutes, popping the lock – thirty seconds.

And then there it was.

Holy mother of God.

'See?' Molly said. 'Money. Savannah wasn't lying.'

No, she most certainly wasn't. The inside of the case was

slightly smaller than he'd imagined, still there had to be well over two hundred thousand dollars here.

Molly closed the case and began reburying it.

'You know, there's a finders-keepers rule in the jungle,' Jones pointed out.

'You said you wanted to dig it up to make sure Ken hadn't hidden something here that was going to bring the demons of hell down upon you.'

Yeah, those had been pretty much his exact words. Still . . . 'Do you know what I could do with that much money?'

She shook her head. 'It's not yours.'

Except she was just reburying it. Right where it had been. Right where he could easily come and *un*bury it after she went back to the village.

What did she think? That he would just sit here and ignore the small fortune hidden here on his land?

Well, sure, it wasn't really his land. He was just a squatter, but still . . .

'If they don't come back for it in, say, a month,' Molly told him, 'then you can keep it. But you *know* they're going to come back for it. People don't just forget about that much cash.' She wiped off her hands and stood up. 'Walk me back?'

Jones stood, too, glancing around, memorizing the place that the case was buried. 'Sure. I'm not going to go into the village, though. And I better skip tea. That blasting is going to bring Otto Zdanowicz back here, and it's better if people don't see us together.'

She didn't say anything, but he knew she was disappointed. And even though he'd given her more of an explanation than he'd ever given any woman as to why he couldn't see her, he kept going.

'See, I have an agreement with the Zdanowicz brothers – I don't fuck with them, they won't fuck with me. By selling those supplies to Ken, I was officially fucking with them, Molly. This is not a good thing. You need to return to the village and tell everyone that I refused to help Ken and Savannah, and that they pushed on. Then when Otto shows up and starts throwing his weight around again, you can let it slip that you sent them up to me. He'll come here, and I'll tell him I'm pretty sure they headed down the mountain toward the port.'

'But they didn't.'

Jones held up both hands. 'I don't know where they went, and I don't want to know. But I do know they didn't take the mule trail. That's a definite.'

'So you're planning to double-fuck Otto Zdanowicz,' Molly observed. 'First by helping Ken and Savannah, and then by pointing Otto in the wrong direction.'

She was looking at him like he was some kind of a hero, and he shrugged. 'It's not that big a deal. I fuck with everyone, every chance I get.'

She nodded, but he could tell just from looking that she knew he was lying. She kissed him. Sweetly. Tenderly.

He thought about that money buried back behind his Quonset hut. That money would buy him damn near everything he'd ever wanted.

Except the one thing he couldn't have.

Sixteen

'The word on the street is that there's an unusual amount of interest in Parwati Island,' Max Bhagat said, drawing a red circle around the island in question on the big map that lay on the FBI conference table. 'Talk is a large amount of money up for grabs – which makes us think if the money survived the helo crash, then Karmody and your grand-daughter probably also survived. We sent a SEAL team out there – dressed as tourists in one of those commercial rent-a-choppers – to see what they could find.'

'And . . . ?' Rose said.

'They'll be contacting us via radio, ma'am. They should be checking in any minute, at which point I'll be notified. I'll put the call on the speaker phone.'

'Thank you.' The frustration was nearly overwhelming. Rose had to resign herself to the knowledge that no matter what happened, Jakarta was as far as she was going to go.

Both Savannah and Alex might be running around on Parwati Island, but it would be up to the teams of professionals to find them. Her job now was to sit and wait. And waiting had never been her strong suit.

Her other son, Karl, and his wife, Priscilla, had finally been contacted. They were on their way and would probably

434

arrive by tonight. Just in case waiting for news all by herself wasn't fun enough.

'In the meantime, I thought you'd be interested in knowing that one of the recent pharmacy break-ins – one in which insulin was stolen – occurred right here,' Max tapped the map, 'at the hospital in Port Parwati.'

'All on the same island,' Rose said. 'That seems a little coincidental.'

'Maybe, maybe not,' Max replied. 'Port Parwati's like one of those mining towns in the Wild West. Like Tombstone, Arizona. Trouble and troublemakers tend to gravitate there. If I were going to knock over a drug dispensary in this part of Indonesia, I'd head for Parwati.'

'It hasn't been confirmed,' Alyssa Locke leaned forward to say, 'but a man named Jayakatong was seen in the vicinity of the Port Parwati hospital on the night of the break-in. According to our sources, he's Armindo Badaruddin's right-hand man.'

Badaruddin. Rose recognized that name from the short list of suspects in Alex's kidnapping.

'Badaruddin's primary camp is here.' Max made another X, this one on a different island to the north of Parwati, but definitely well within range by boat or helicopter.

From what she remembered, Badaruddin was politically motivated rather than financially driven. This was not good news.

George cleared his throat. 'If they stole insulin, their intention must be to keep Alex alive.'

God bless George. He could read her like a book.

The telephone rang, and true to his word, after a brief conversation, Max turned on the speaker phone.

'This may not be absolutely clear – Lieutenant Starrett's

coming to us via radio. We'll have to do the best we can.' He raised his voice. 'Go ahead, Lieutenant.'

'As I said, sir, we found what we believe is the downed helo here on Parwati Island.' The lieutenant had a Texas drawl. 'I'm standing right next to it now, and it definitely burned, but it doesn't appear to have crashed. It looks like it landed first in a clearing alongside a small river. We've got some shell casings in the area, too, that imply there was some sort of firefight. Over.'

Rose spoke up. 'Are there any tracks, Lieutenant? Any sign that anyone left the area?'

'Ma'am, this part of the island gets torrential rainfall two, three times a day,' Starrett said. 'Any tracks were probably completely erased within a few hours. But that's a good thing. Because we're definitely not the first people to have found this helo. Come back.'

'If you were Chief Karmody,' Alyssa asked, 'and you were with Savannah von Hopf, where would you go from there? Go ahead.'

Starrett didn't hesitate. 'Downstream, ma'am. And we'd like permission to try just that. Come back.'

'Karmody's two days ahead of you, Lieutenant,' Bhagat said. 'If he's even there at all. Over.'

'Oh, he's here, sir,' Starrett said absolutely. 'As we were approaching the island, there was a series of explosions in the mountains – three different sets of 'em. Some of the locals were clearing a road, but I swear, they must've had WildCard's help in cutting the lengths of the fuses, because they went off in a pattern. Shave and a haircut. Three patterns just like that – bump badah dump bump. Three in a row. It's WildCard Karmody, telling us he's here. We tried to talk to the locals working on the road, but there were language barriers. And, well, frankly, WildCard's somewhat unique. If he *was* dealing with these guys, they're not going to tell anyone. They're either scared to death of him or the new presidents of his fan club. One or the other. Excuse me, Commander Paoletti, are you in the room? Can you back me here, sir? Over.'

Lt Comdr Tom Paoletti had been silent up to this point. But now he shifted in his seat. 'I'd have to agree with Starrett. That sounds like the handiwork of our missing man. Come back in, Lieutenant,' he ordered, 'but be ready to pick up your gear and head right out again. Over.'

'Aye, aye, sir,' Starrett said. 'Over and out.'

'I'd like to send out two different teams,' Paoletti suggested in his calm, easygoing manner. Rose liked both him and his executive officer, Lt Jazz Jacquette, immensely. 'One to Parwati and one to Badaruddin's island.' He turned to her. 'They'll be dropped via boat – they'll swim in. There's no chance they'll be seen – they'll be no danger to either your granddaughter or your son.'

She smiled at him. 'I appreciate that.'

Max Bhagat nodded. 'Do it.' He looked at her. 'Anything you'd like to add, Mrs von Hopf? And don't ask me to send you to Parwati, because that's not going to happen.'

'Believe me, Mr Bhagat, there's a rule I learned a long time ago – before you were born, I feel inclined to point out. And that rule is to recognize not just your strengths, but also your limitations. Sometimes you've got to sit back and let the specialists make use of their expensive education and training. Therefore, I shall be at the hotel, awaiting any news.'

As she stood, the entire table got to their feet, as if she were the queen.

SUZANNE BROCKMANN

George and her two other FBI handlers moved with her toward the door. But she turned back.

'Oh. If this WildCard Karmody is as good as everyone says, wouldn't it be a smart idea to set up some kind of intercept team, some kind of official safety net in Port Parwati? On the assumption that he and Savannah may well find us before we find them? Of course, you wouldn't want to waste valuable agents on such a tiresome—'

'Nice try,' Max said. 'But you're staying in Jakarta.'

'If you had let me finish, you would have only heard me suggest that I not tie up three of your staff. I assure you, Mr Bhagat, one FBI handler is sufficient. I give you my solemn promise to remain at the hotel until directed otherwise. I'd far prefer having these bright young people on hand to assist my granddaughter.'

It was amazing. George, Alyssa, and Jules – bless their hearts – didn't move an inch. They didn't allow their expressions to change, and yet she knew, she *knew* just how eager they were to go out into the field. She'd been young once, too.

George, however, cleared his throat. 'I'd like to volunteer to stay in Jakarta with Mrs von Hopf,' the young man said.

Rose looked at him.

'I want to,' he lied. He was a remarkably good liar.

'Thank you,' she said.

Max looked at Alyssa and Jules, looked at Rose, then looked at George and nodded. 'Okay,' he said. 'But you'll need to watch her like a hawk. She's fast, so keep the doors locked. And be ready to tackle her to the ground if she runs.'

Rose smiled as she led George toward the door. 'Very funny, dear. Be careful,' she added to Alyssa and Jules.

438

'She thinks I'm kidding,' she heard Max say as she walked away. He raised his voice to call after her. 'That was your *solemn promise* you gave me. Somebody grab a pen and write that down.'

'So what you're saying is that Rose figured out how to win the lose-lose scenario,' Ken said.

Savannah nodded, even though she knew he couldn't see her in the darkness. 'Yeah, she conjured up a third option. Turning Hank over to the FBI meant that he'd be tried and probably executed as a spy. But letting him go back to Germany meant that the Nazis might gain access to all kinds of secret information. So you're right, with only those two choices it was a total lose-lose scenario for her.'

'But she stepped outside of the box.' He laughed softly. 'Building a private jail in a house in New Jersey – that's pretty fricking brilliant. Hank doesn't die, and at the same time he doesn't get a chance to divulge any more secrets.' He laughed again, clearly tickled by her grandmother's ingenuity. 'Most people don't think that way, you know. They see obvious choice A or obvious choice B, and they wring their hands a lot and end up picking the one that sucks the least.'

'You step outside the box a lot,' Savannah said. 'Don't you?'

'Yeah. I'm usually pretty good at it – at least when it comes to certain things. I'm a little embarrassed about what happened today, though. You know, when the missionaries hid us?'

She turned toward his voice, wishing she could see his face. 'Why are you embarrassed? You were great.'

'Yeah, right. I was scared to death – too scared to think

straight.' He was silent for a moment. 'I'm usually better than that, Van. But I got caught up in . . .' He stopped again. 'I don't know. I usually don't panic, but today I just couldn't see any options besides run or fight. I was trapped in that particular nasty little box. You know, what happened today is a classic example of why they don't let women on SEAL teams.'

'Why?' Savannah didn't understand. 'You mean, because I didn't know which way to run to get to the cover of the jungle? That's not fair – I haven't exactly had the kind of training a woman would get if she were to—'

'No,' he said. 'No, it's . . .' He exhaled loudly. 'Can we not talk about this, please? I shouldn't have brought it up in the first place.'

'Sorry.' Maybe he would prefer to talk about *her* most embarrassing moment of the day. He'd been a little tense in a scary situation. But later, *she'd* flipped out. Not only did she burst into tears, but she'd kissed him. After which he'd merely set her aside and methodically gone about making sure she was safe.

She'd hoped he'd bring up the subject as they'd settled in for the night. He'd built another of these blinds around them, but he never said a word about it. So, hey, about that kiss . . . ? No, instead it was as if it had never happened.

'You didn't finish telling me about your grandmother,' Ken said now, from the pitch darkness. He was only a few feet away from her, but he might as well have been on the moon. 'So she locks Hank in her basement, and he tells her no, she's got it wrong – he's working for the Allies. Of course, she's not going to believe him. Who would? Then what?'

'She took his notebook – this list of names he always

carried with him – and went to the FBI. He told her who to go and talk to. She did, and oops, turns out he was telling her the truth. He was an Austrian patriot – he hated the Nazis and he'd been working against them since 1936. He was a double agent, only he spent most of his time in Berlin. He was actually an officer in the SS – he worked his way that deeply into the Nazi organization.'

'Holy shit.'

'Yeah.' Savannah had to laugh, his words were so sincerely heartfelt. God, she loved that about him – his honest reaction to the world around him. 'After she found that out, Rose went back to New Jersey, and unlocked the door to his cell. And you know what? He took her to Maryland and married her.'

Ken was as tickled by that as she'd been. He laughed softly. 'I like this guy. He was smart enough to get why she did what she did. Some guys would've been too busy being pissed off that she managed to lock them up in the first place, you know? Bent out of shape – hurt pride – because she got the upper hand. They wouldn't be able to see past it to the reason why she did it. I mean, it was because she loved him, right? She risked an awful lot for him. Technically, what she did probably wasn't treason, but it was close.'

'My grandfather was a pretty amazing person,' Savannah agreed.

He shifted slightly in the darkness, and she held her breath, but he didn't come any closer. 'Did you get a chance to know him?'

'No.'

'I'm sorry,' Ken said. Also heartfelt.

Savannah wanted to cry. 'Me, too. Mostly sorry for my grandmother. Until I read her book, I never realized how much she must have loved him.' She cleared her throat, trying to make it stop aching, afraid she was going to break down again. Twice in one day. God, what would he do? She cleared her throat again. 'Anyway, they got married, and he was supposed to go back to Germany at the end of the month, and, well, my grandmother managed to convince him to take her with him.'

'Jesus, to Berlin? How the hell did she do that?'

She opened her mouth to tell him, but he didn't let her speak.

'If we were to wake up tomorrow and find ourselves transported to New York in 1943,' he said hotly, 'there's nothing you could do to convince *me* to take you to Berlin, you better believe that.'

'Yeah, well, you don't love me, so . . .' She'd meant it as a joke, a weak one, sure, but it lay there absolutely flatly since he didn't even pretend to laugh. In fact, he didn't say anything at all.

Savannah cleared her throat. 'She used, well, sex as a weapon – her words from the book. She's not shy in describing her relationship with Hank. I mean, she didn't go into details, but pretty much every time he started making noise about how dangerous it would be, she took him to bed and convinced him she'd be fine as long as they were together.'

Ken finally laughed. 'She brainwashed him. It probably didn't take long before he started to associate intense pleasure with even just the thought of her going to Germany with him. The poor sucker didn't stand a chance. Especially if she was anything at all like you in bed.'

Now there was a compliment – of sorts – that she didn't quite know what to do with.

'Thanks,' she finally said. 'Kenny.'

It was his turn to be quiet, and she held her breath, wondering if he remembered what he'd said to her last night when she'd called him that. *Fuck me, Kenny.* She was far too chicken, far too polite, to say those words aloud. But it was what she wanted. She didn't just want to sleep beside him tonight. She wanted to sleep *with* him. She wanted them to be lovers again.

Desperately.

The silence stretched on, and she felt compelled to break it. 'They set up a kind of a scam,' she told him. 'Rose and Hank. Rose's contacts in Germany – the ones she'd been sending all that false information to for years – were told that the FBI had cracked down on a number of Nazi spies, including Ingerose Rainer. When she later showed up in Germany with my grandfather, she told the Nazis that she'd escaped with his help. That he helped her make her way to South America. And from there, he took her with him to Germany.'

She paused, but he didn't say anything. So she kept going, mostly to fill the silence. 'They hid their marriage from the Nazis – no one would've believed it anyway because Hank was Austrian royalty. Someone in his position wouldn't go and marry some nothing American girl, right? But they pretended they'd become intimate friends during their travels, and Hank set her up in Berlin as his assistant-slash-mistress.

'They lived in Berlin and provided information to the Allies until early 1945.'

Ken finally spoke. 'Jesus God. That long?'

'Yeah. In '45, there was a serious threat from friendly fire as both the Americans and Russians approached

Berlin – along with the usual dire consequences from the Nazis if they were found out as spies. Hank took Rose to London – kicking and screaming, no doubt. She was pregnant with my father and uncle, although neither Rose nor Hank knew it at the time. The war wasn't over, so my grandfather went back to Berlin. And that's as far as I got in the book.'

'That's pretty amazing,' he said. 'And very cool that your grandmother wrote it all down. You must be proud. You know, knowing that this is where you come from. Having those kinds of people in your family.'

'Just because your grandmother's a hero doesn't mean you're automatically one, too.'

'You said last night that you thought she was probably a lot like you.' So he *did* remember at least some of what was said last night.

'Scared,' she told him. 'She was *scared*, like me. That's what I meant. Believe me, I wouldn't have gone to Berlin in 1943 to spy on the Nazis.'

'But you'd go to Jakarta in 2002 to help your uncle.'

She made a disparaging noise. 'Not quite the same thing.'

'Yeah, well, I know you don't see it,' he told her, 'but you really are like her. Your grandmother.'

Savannah snorted. 'I thought I was so much like my mother. Wearing her clothes . . . ?'

'Oh, yeah. Right.' Ken actually laughed. He had absolutely no shame. 'That's true, too. But that's easy to fix. You've just got to stop wearing those butt-ugly clothes.'

'And what, pray tell, would you have me wear?' she asked, far more comfortable discussing this than doing a point by point comparison of herself and Rose.

'I like you in *my* clothes,' he answered. 'Cutoff shorts. T-shirt with no bra – hey, it works for me.'

'Cutoffs and a T-shirt. In court?'

'Okay, then maybe you should wear the kind of dresses some of the women in that village wore.'

'A sarong? Oh, that would go over really well with the appellate judges.'

'They'll love it. Bright colors. Bare shoulders. No bra. Mmm hmm.'

'I'm sensing a pattern here.'

'You asked,' he said cheerfully. 'And while you're at it, you've got to lose the scary 'do.'

'The . . . what?'

'Your hair,' Ken explained. 'When I came to the hotel you were all . . . de-curled and neat. Throw away your blow dryer, babe. The Martha Stewart look is way not you.'

She laughed her disbelief. 'I do not wear my hair like—'

'Your hair is adorable. It's all curly and cute and shit. Why do you pretend it's not?'

'Some people might not *want* to be cute and *shit*, thank you very much. Other people – *male* people – don't take you seriously if you're cute and *shit*.'

'Your grandmother successfully made a career out of it – probably exactly for that reason,' he countered. 'Because no one took her seriously, think of all that she got done. You know, I think you should use the shower and shake method on your hair – just let it dry wild. That and a what's-it-called? Sarong. Oh, yeah. Or one of those gauzy, hippie-style dresses. The see-through ones. I like them, too.'

'Well, thanks for the fashion tips, Mr Camouflage Boxer Shorts. Jeez.'

'You asked,' he said again, laughing.

'So all I have to do is ask, and you'll just tell me whatever I want to know? That's very interesting. I've been meaning to ask you about your father.'

He stopped laughing.

'Maybe you should,' Ken said. He shifted so that he was leaning back more comfortably against the fallen tree that made up the back wall of their blind. 'What do you want to know about him? Besides the obvious – that he was a son of a bitch with a mean streak.'

He waited to see what she would ask. *Did he hit you? Did you ever fight back? Did you celebrate when you heard he died?*

He heard her move slightly in the darkness, heard the quiet sound of her breathing. She drew in a slightly deeper breath before speaking. 'Did you love him?'

Ken laughed his surprise. Of all the questions she could have asked . . . 'Yes.' The word hung there in the darkness, and he felt compelled to add, 'He was my father, you know? But I hated him, too.'

'Why?'

Shit, another unexpected question. She knew damn well that there was violence involved, but he suspected she didn't want to put the words in his mouth by asking *Did he* hit *you*? Or *did he* beat *you*? Which was it? Because there was definitely a difference. He'd lived through both, and he knew.

'He was inconsistent,' he told her. 'I hated him because he was so freaking inconsistent. One day he'd beat the shit out of me for not cleaning my room, and the next he'd beat the shit out of me because my room was too clean – that meant I was namby-pamby, you know, a mother's boy. If he'd given me rules, I would've followed them. Instead, he kept me guessing.'

'If he'd given you rules, then he wouldn't have been able to beat you up,' she said.

'Yeah, you're probably right. He was such an asshole. But he taught me a hell of a lot about pain management.' Ken laughed.

'That's not funny.' Savannah's voice was tight.

'No,' he said, sobering. 'You're right. It's not. He . . . he didn't know what to do with me. He was a football player – college ball. He coached the high school team in town. I was his only son, and this total freak.'

'In his eyes,' she pointed out.

'No, I really was a freak. I was skinny and kind of small for my age, which never helps when you're a kid. I also always knew exactly what *not* to say in any given situation and I was completely unable to keep it from coming out of my mouth. I still have that problem some of the time. You know, blurting out the first stupid thing that comes into my head?'

'That doesn't make you a freak.'

'It does when you're in high school. I was like the antithesis of cool. I was a gearhead without any money to buy the gear, which is a bad combination.

'I didn't exactly run with the football crowd, but my father was convinced that if I went out for the team, I'd somehow magically become the son he wanted. That was the first time I got in his face and told him no, I wouldn't do it. Up to that point, I'd never challenged him – at least not more than passive aggressively. You know, playing the punching bag – refusing to stay down when he kicked the shit out of me. Never letting him see me act hurt. I swear, I could've had a broken leg, but if he was in the room, I would've walked on it. No, I would've *danced* on it. But this time . . . I really didn't want to play football. It wasn't my game, you know? It wasn't that I wasn't athletic; I liked rock climbing. And for a while, I was into cross country running. I was good when it came to endurance. I still am. That's probably why I stayed with Adele for so long.'

Adele.

Holy God, he'd actually brought Adele into this conversation. He decided to strike first with the personal questions that were sure to follow. 'How well did you know her?'

'Not very well,' Savannah was quick to say. She was eager, apparently, to talk about this. He didn't know whether to be glad or afraid. 'She was a senior when I was a freshman. You know what that's like. She was everything; I was just slightly more important than a ball of dryer lint.

'We lived in the same dorm and she and her roommates took me and my roommates under their wing. Sort of. They bought us beer and took us to parties. That kind of thing. Adele was supposed to be a genius, but . . . Well, I was never particularly impressed by her scholarly brilliance. It didn't come across in conversations. I think I was more dazzled at first by her charisma.'

'Yeah, she had a ton of charisma. Good word for it.'

'I was pretending to be an intellectual – here I was at Yale, right?' She laughed. 'I managed to elevate her to goddess status when I found out that some of the papers she wrote got published—'

'No fucking way! *Published?*'

'She didn't tell you?'

'No.'

'That's weird.'

'Published where?' he asked.

'I don't remember exactly. Some prestigious English Lit. journal, I think.'

'English? Not math?' His head was spinning.

'It was definitely English Literature. I remember one of the papers was on Thomas Hardy. Very profound.'

Ken started to laugh. 'Well, fuck a duck.'

'I can't believe she didn't tell you.'

'She didn't tell me because I wrote those papers for her.'

'What?'

'Her strengths were in math and science. I handled all her history and English requirements pretty much from day one.'

Savannah was silent, absorbing that. He didn't blame her. He still couldn't quite believe it himself. One of his papers had been *published*. English Literature. Jesus, the guys were going to give him shit for that. He had to laugh.

'You were going to college yourself, plus you were in the Navy. Why would you do Adele's work, too?' Savannah finally asked.

Yeah, in hindsight, that didn't seem so smart. What could he tell her? That he'd been blinded by the sex? 'You must think I'm a real loser.'

'I think you're crazy, but . . . I think you must have loved her very much. I could see it, you know. It was in everything you did when you were with her. I know I only saw you a few times, but . . .'

'Can I ask you something?' he said.

'Did she sleep with other guys when you weren't around?' she guessed. 'Are you really sure you want to know that, Kenny?'

Did he? 'Yeah.' Without quite saying the word yes,

449

Savannah had just given him a great big affirmative to that question. And yet he felt . . . nothing. A slight sense of sadness as the final nail went into the coffin of the innocent dreamer he'd once been.

'Do you still love her?' Savannah whispered.

Ken laughed, suddenly scared to death. He wanted to be honest with her about Adele, but he wasn't sure if he could do that without telling her everything. And he wasn't ready to tell her everything.

'That's kind of a tricky question, Van,' he said slowly, trying for once to choose his words carefully, 'because I've had this, um, kind of new insight recently? And it makes me, well, believe that for all those years, I only thought I was in love with Adele.'

'You mean, you weren't really?'

'I don't know. It's possible I loved her, but on a scale from one to ten – assuming you can love in varying degrees – it was probably only about a three or a four at the most. You know, with ten being the kind of love that makes you, I don't know, ready to die for someone, I guess, but at the same time, ready to live for them, too.'

She was silent, so he kept going, hoping that something he said would make her understand. 'With Adele, it was . . . I don't know, I guess it kind of turned into an obsession. I definitely wanted her in every sense of the word. And I was in love with the idea of being in love, but . . . I do that a lot. You know – think I'm in the number ten kind of love when it's really something else entirely? Infatuation, maybe. Or it's lust. Or both. Usually both. Infatuated lust. I think it could have become, you know, like an eight or a nine even, if Adele had tried – just a little bit. But . . .'

'She didn't deserve you,' Savannah told him tightly. He could picture her face, so fierce and he had to smile.

'I don't know,' he said, trying to lighten things up. 'Maybe she did. I wasn't much of a prize at the time. I was pretty relentless. She called me her boomerang. She'd throw me away, but I'd come zipping right back. She came back to me, too, though. It was a very unhealthy relationship. Lots of high drama. Did you know she got a restraining order against me?'

'Oh, my God,' Savannah said. 'No.'

'It was the best thing she ever did for me,' Ken admitted. 'At the time, I was devastated. She didn't give me any kind of warning. And when she got the court order, our relationship wasn't any different than it had been in the past. See, she was always breaking up with me and telling me it was over for good, but she always, *always* came back. Why should this time be any different, right? So I did what I always did. I still went to see her when I got liberty. I called her all the time – definitely excessively, I admit that. But that's what had worked in the past, right? There was no violence, though. Not against her. Okay, I did deck her new boyfriend in the lobby of a movie theater. But he hit me first. I would never hit a woman. Never.'

'I know,' she said.

'Anyway, the boyfriend had a sister who was a lawyer. They couldn't press charges against me because about twenty people saw him go for me first. But Adele later emailed me and told me they had talked her into getting the restraining order. It wasn't really her idea, she said. But she did it, and that was it for me. Just like that, it was over. We couldn't play our game anymore without me breaking the law, and you know, even when you love somebody a

451

solid ten you don't do that. A restraining order is some serious shit. And this was only a three or a four, so . . . End of game.'

'I'm sorry.'

'I'm not. You know, she called me. After she emailed and I didn't write back, she called to say that the time limit on the restraining order had run out and she wasn't going to renew it – or whatever you have to do to keep a restraining order active. So it was okay if I dropped by some time. Yeah, right, huh? She said she wanted to see me because she was thinking about getting married. But I knew what she really wanted was to spend the next ten years jerking me around some more. So I declined her invitation, wished her luck and got myself a three-month OUTCONUS – out of the country – assignment.

'She finally did get married. She still emails me sometimes, but I don't write back. I couldn't, you know. And now I don't want to.'

Ken stopped talking, but Savannah didn't say anything. He was anxious, he realized, about what she was thinking after hearing all that. 'So. Kind of pathetic, huh?'

She breathed for a little while longer, and then said, 'No wonder you got so upset when I told you I got your address from Adele. I had no idea.'

Fuck it, he was just going to ask. 'So are you nervous now, being stuck in the middle of the jungle with some asshole who needed a restraining order to stay away from his old girlfriend?'

'No.'

He started breathing again. 'That's good.'

'She was the asshole.'

'Yeah, well, like I said, I'm glad – now – that she did it.'

'I used to get so angry with her,' Savannah told him. 'I remember meeting you, and, well . . .' She laughed softly. 'Infatuated lust, indeed.'

'Really?' Ken rolled his eyes in the darkness. Could he sound any more lame? *Really?* What an idiot. He had to just be cool and listen and maybe he'd learn something that would give him the nerve to move toward her in the darkness. To kiss her the way she'd kissed him out on the smuggler's airstrip. Ah, Jesus, he wanted to kiss her again.

'Really,' she said. 'Maybe it was because you were so different from the boys who went to Yale. But I met you, and it was so clear to me that Adele didn't have a clue. She didn't know what she had. God, I hated her from that moment on. But I never let her know, because I wanted to be invited to the parties she threw whenever you were in town.'

'No kidding?' It slipped out and he silently cursed himself. Just let her talk.

'I had these fantasies where you would come to visit,' she admitted with a soft laugh. 'I would somehow intercept you before you got to Adele's room, and I'd tell you the truth about what she did when you weren't around.' She laughed again. 'And then I'd comfort you and we'd end up naked and you'd never so much as think about Adele again.'

Ken had to clear his throat. 'Wow.' *Wow* was even more stupid than *Really?*, but he was floored.

'Sleeping with you was probably my longest-running fantasy, not counting going for a ride in Chitty Chitty Bang Bang, the flying car,' she told him. 'That's one of the reasons I couldn't resist making it a reality that night. I mean, imagine getting a chance like that?'

453

Imagine.

She was quiet, and he knew that it was his turn to talk. After admitting something like that, she needed to hear what he was thinking. So he opened his mouth and told her.

'That's a lot of pressure for a guy. I'm glad you didn't tell me before we made love that night, because I would've been intimidated. How do you live up to someone's hugely inflated expectations? That's pretty terrifying. Jesus.' He both wished he could see her face and was glad that he couldn't. What was she thinking? What did she want him to do? 'I suppose I shouldn't take it as a very good sign that after sleeping with me once, you decide never to sleep with me again, huh?'

He heard her move, but she didn't touch him. God, he wanted her to touch him.

'I was angry when I said that,' Savannah said. 'I didn't really mean it. You're the one who's still pushing me away.'

Ken laughed his disbelief. 'Yeah, I pushed you away because you kissed me while we were completely exposed. Anyone flying overhead could have seen us there. Anyone taking a stroll through the jungle could have, too. Holy Mary mother of Jesus. You want to try it again now that we're safely hidden? I can guarantee you'll get a very different response, because right now I'm dying to kiss you again.'

Savannah tried on a number of responses before she spoke. *Okay*. That was a good one. Brief and to the point. He'd be all over her before she closed her mouth. And then what? They'd make love. That was a given. But eventually the sun would come up and then what?

I love you. She could tell him that, giving him her heart and soul along with her body. But what an enormous risk *that* would be.

I don't want you to kiss me unless you're willing to make our relationship more than just about casual sex. Perfect. Make her love conditional. It wasn't even true. She wanted whatever he was willing to give her. Even if it turned out to be just one kiss, just one more night in his arms.

'I was wrong back in San Diego,' Ken said, his familiar voice sliding around her in the darkness. 'I wanted to fall in love with you – a number ten kind of love – and I pretty much convinced myself that I had. But that was stupid, because love doesn't work that way. You've got to be really lucky to get a ten at first sight. But that's what I wanted with you. I didn't even know you, though. I mean, I liked what I knew, but I just kind of filled in the blanks the way I wanted you to be, so that you'd be perfect. And of course, the sex was incredible, which made it even harder for me to see the truth – which is that whatever we had, it was just starting.

'So when you told me you'd come to San Diego looking for me, well, your having withheld that from me the night before didn't fit with the perfect Savannah I'd imagined you to be. What I should have done was hear you out, give you a chance to explain in a way that I would be able to understand. Jesus, people make mistakes, right? You made a bad judgment call because you were so hot for me.' He laughed. 'I don't know what I was thinking. It was definitely temporary insanity, because I find it very hard to get upset about that now.'

'You believe me?' she dared to ask.

'Yes, I do.'

SUZANNE BROCKMANN

'You're not just saying that because you want to have sex with me?'

'Savannah, I've been talking my ass off for more than an hour now, telling you shit no one's ever heard anything about, hoping that I'll say something, Jesus God, *anything* that will convince you to have sex with me. But everything I've told you is God's truth. I swear.'

'Do you think,' she said, 'instead of having sex, we could make love?'

'I'd love that,' Ken whispered.

But still, neither of them moved.

'Why are we waiting?' she whispered.

'Because we're scared?'

'What are you scared of?' she asked. Damn, he had to stop saying the first thing that popped into his head.

But he *was* scared. Of her. Of the way she made him feel. Of putting too much stake in hope. Of love. Yeah, he was scared of love, scared of loving her too much. Scared he'd find this really was a genuine ten, when all she felt for him was a wimpy little one point five.

'Everything,' he told her.

'I'm a little scared that once we start making love, we won't be able to stop and we'll eventually eat all our food and all the bugs in the area, too, and they'll find our mummified bodies locked together about fifty years from now.'

Ken laughed. 'We'll have to stop. We'll eventually run out of condoms.'

'That won't stop us. We'll just have oral sex.'

Giddy, he reached for her, finding her leg, the smoothness of her thigh, in the darkness. Oh, yes. 'Do you have an answer for everything?'

456

'Usually, yes.'

'I like that about you. It used to drive me nuts, but recently I've been finding that it really turns me on.'

Once he found her leg it took him almost no time to trail his fingers up, all the way up to her face. And then somehow she was in his arms, and he was kissing her.

She was liquid fire – he could feel her shaking with need. For him. After just one kiss and a whole lot of talk. He didn't blame her – he was like a rock for her, and had been, pretty much since she'd kissed him that afternoon.

She started tugging at both his clothes and hers, and he helped her out of her shorts, aware that the only thing between them and the bug-filled dirt were the bug-filled branches he'd cut. Instead of laying her down on those branches, he went onto his back, lifting her up and on top of him so that she was straddling his chest. He slid down and pulled her up at the same time and then . . .

'Oh, my God, Kenny,' she gasped, laughter in her voice as she struggled to get away. 'What are you—?'

He didn't waste his energy trying to explain. He just held her down and kissed her.

And with a moan, she stopped trying to pull away. In fact – oh, yes! – she moved closer.

God, she was so sweet. He'd been wanting to do exactly this for way too many days, but reality was twenty million times better than his wildest imaginings. Except for the darkness. He wished he could see her from this unique vantage point. He wanted to watch her come undone.

Which was going to happen very soon. She was making little noises, little sounds of intense pleasure in between gasps of his name, the sleek coolness of her thighs deliciously tight against his face.

He knew exactly where to kiss her to make her detonate, and sure enough, it happened instantly.

She exploded with a cry, and Ken laughed his pleasure as he just kept on kissing her, drawing out her orgasm as long as he possibly could.

Finally, gasping and laughing, she pulled slightly away and he let her go.

'Oh, my God,' she kept saying over and over. 'Oh, my God!'

She'd told him that it wasn't just anyone who could make her do this. It was him. She'd said he'd been her personal fantasy for years.

Which worried him a little – well, he was as worried about it as he could force himself to be at the moment, with her sitting on his chest and her scent on his face.

Truth was, he didn't want to be the object of her desire. To put it bluntly, he didn't want to be her fantasy fuck.

Like his daydreams of Sarah Michelle Gellar. They weren't based on anything more than infatuation and lust. He didn't know squat about Sarah Michelle. And for what he'd always imagined them doing together, well, he didn't particularly need or want to know. He liked the image that was in his head – part Buffy, part exotic Hollywood star.

It was all fantasy. It was never going to happen, not in a million years.

Except for Savannah, it *had* happened. She'd lived her fantasy, got it on with her fantasy man. So who was she making love to right now? Her fantasy Ken, or the real, flesh and blood man with all his flaws and imperfections?

She'd finally caught her breath, and made as if she were going to move off of him, but he caught her hips, and pulled her back to him.

'I'm not done here,' he said. 'Is it all right with you if I take it nice and slow this time?'

Savannah laughed her surprise. 'You're not going to do something really obnoxious and start counting my orgasms, are you?' she said breathlessly.

He stopped kissing her long enough to say, 'One.'

She laughed again. 'You're such a jerk!'

'Exactly,' he replied, pleased she should recognize that. Fantasy guys were never jerks. Therefore . . .

He returned his full attention to the long, slow kisses he was giving her, and he felt her shiver, heard her sigh. Her fingers were in his hair and she was no longer trying to pull away from him.

'Kenny, I could get really used to this,' she breathed.

'Gee, I hope so.'

Jones was still awake at 0230, otherwise he wouldn't have heard it.

A single soft rap.

He grabbed his handgun as he rolled out of bed and moved silently to the door.

He rapped twice on the sturdy metal, and got the correct response in reply. Three soft raps.

Weapon held at ready, he turned on the light and unlocked the door.

It was Jayakatong, just as Jones had thought, and he'd brought the part for the Cessna.

Jones opened the box, examined the alternator. It was what he needed. Come the break of dawn, he could fix the engine in his airplane and fly away.

'So many candles,' Jaya said. 'And flowers. If I didn't know you better, I'd think—'

Jones cut him off. 'Amazing what a man will do to get laid.'

'Amazing what a man who's in love will do,' Jaya countered.

'Yeah, well, I wouldn't know about that. What's news?' he changed the subject as, keeping his eyes on Jaya, he got the money – local currency only – to pay him.

'Couple of Americans lost in the jungle,' Jaya told him. 'A woman and a man. Seen 'em?'

He looked the other man in the eye. 'No.'

'Rumor has it they're carrying a lot of money.'

Jones shrugged. 'Rumors have been wrong before.'

Jaya smiled. With his skinny face, it made him look ghoulish. 'Rumor has it the woman is worth millions.'

Millions. Jones kept his face carefully expressionless. Perpetually disbelieving.

'General Badaruddin was told she's some kind of royalty,' Jaya said.

'Great, except America doesn't have royalty,' Jones pointed out as he slapped the money into Jaya's hand.

The Indonesian man counted it carefully. 'If you see them, the Americans, the general's offering a hundred-dollar reward.'

'I'll keep that in mind.' Jones unlocked his door again, and Jaya slipped out.

He relocked the door, but didn't turn off the light. He sat down at his table with a bottle of warm beer, thinking about the money that was no longer buried in the jungle outside. No, he'd dug up the attaché case this afternoon and took out the cash, putting it into a duffle bag – easier to carry – and bringing it into his Quonset hut for safekeeping. It was hidden inside the packing craft upon which the box with the alternator rested.

He'd counted it.

Inside that duffle, there was two hundred and seventeen thousand dollars.

As Jones drank his beer, he thought about what a man could do with money like that. He thought about how long it would take him – once there was some small amount of daylight to work in – to get the Cessna ready to fly.

And he thought about Molly.

Who was leaving for Africa in less than a month.

'We can't fall asleep like this,' Kenny whispered. He was running his hand up and down and up and down Savannah's bare back and it felt decadently delicious.

Her head was on his shoulder, her legs straddling his hips. It shouldn't have been all that comfortable, but it was. 'I'm okay,' she murmured.

'I'm still inside you,' he said.

'I noticed.'

'That's not good.'

'Speak for yourself.'

Ken laughed. She loved the sound of his laughter. 'Let me rephrase. It's dangerous, unless you want to get pregnant.'

'I do.' She paused. 'Someday.' She lifted her head and kissed him on the side of his face. 'Scared you for a minute there, didn't I?'

'I don't know,' he said. 'Not really. I'd love to have sex with you without a condom.' He paused. 'Want to get married?'

Savannah's heart skipped a beat, but she laughed because he was obviously joking. 'That would go over

461

really well with my parents. 'Hey, Mom and Dad. Meet my new husband – *WildCard* Karmody . . .' Do you have a tattoo?'

'Yeah.'

'Really?'

'No, I'm lying to you, Savannah. Jesus.'

'It's kind of dark in here.'

'I'm deeply hurt that you don't remember.' He kissed her, clearly not hurt at all.

'Where is it?' she asked. '*What* is it?'

'A two of hearts,' he told her. 'You know, like a playing card. A wild card. Upper arm. Right. And—'

'You have two?'

'Yes, Miss Highly Observant. Miss Capable of Four Orgasms in One Hour But Can't Seem to Notice Her Extremely Virile and Competent Lover's Physical Characteristics, I also have a frog. On my ass. Don't ask.'

She giggled. 'Excellent. 'Mom, Dad, this is WildCard Karmody and—' Do people really call you that? *WildCard?*'

'Yes.'

'Really?'

He laughed. 'Yes.'

'Is that weird?'

'No, I like it. I don't really think of myself as WildCard, you know, I'm still twelve-year-old Kenny-the-dork in my head, but if they want to call me that . . . It's a compliment that I'll gladly accept.'

' "He's got two tattoos," ' Savannah continued. ' "One's a frog on his ass – and we got married because he wanted to have sex without a condom." It's almost as good as the reason Priscilla wants me to get married – because dear Vlad has a title. He's actually a count.'

'Being a count is almost as good as having a frog on your ass,' Kenny told her. 'But not quite.'

Savannah laughed. 'Kenny, I—' She stopped herself, uncertain even what she'd been intending to say. *I love you?* She had no clue how he would react to that news. And what they had right now was so good, she didn't want to screw it up.

'What?' he asked.

'Can I see you when we get back home?' she said instead.

'Well, yeah, it's going to be kind of hard for you not to see me if we're getting married, right?'

She lifted herself slightly off him. 'No, seriously.'

'Seriously, I have to clean up, Van, because I will be goddamned if I get you pregnant without the complete whistles-and-bells, no-condom fun.'

Savannah scrambled off him, searching in the darkness for her clothes. 'Why is there a frog tattooed onto your posterior?'

He laughed. 'Because I went out drinking with some of my classmates right after we officially became SEALs, and we all got a frog tattooed onto our *posteriors*.'

She slipped into her shorts and shirt. 'Not a SEAL?'

'You can come back now,' he said, so she settled against him. 'Clothes?' He sounded disappointed.

'Bugs,' she explained.

'Frog because the granddaddy of the SEAL was the Navy Frogman. Our posteriors because believe it or not the Navy frowns upon tattoos and we figured the COs wouldn't notice 'em there. And seriously there's nothing I'd love more than to keep seeing you when we get back home. But this is probably where I should give my warning about how completely I suck at long-distance relationships and how I swore I'd never get involved long distance again.'

'Well,' Savannah said slowly. 'There are probably lots of options in between "we have a long distance relationship" and "we have no relationship at all."'

'Yeah,' he said. 'Sure. But . . . I'm a SEAL, so I'm gone a lot.'

Well, that was none too encouraging.

'It's not easy on girlfriends and wives. And it's not going to change. I mean, I'm not leaving the team. Not in the near future, anyway. You know, I've had job offers – good ones, too – but I love what I do and I'm going to do it for as long as I can.'

'I would never even consider asking you to do something like leave the SEALs,' Savannah said quietly. 'That's not one of the options I was thinking of.' She kissed him. 'What did your father think when you became a SEAL?'

'And she changes the subject,' Ken said. He sighed. 'Maybe *you* should consider a career change – from lawyer to therapist. Because you get me to tell you things I never tell anyone. And, like, I'm eager to tell you. What's up with that?'

'You like telling me things because you think that'll make me want to have sex with you,' she reminded him. 'And it works, remember?'

Ken laughed. 'Right. My father came to BUD/S graduation,' he said. 'All the way out to Coronado. And afterwards he comes up to me and he says, "How come you're not an officer?"'

'Oh!' Savannah said. 'Let me at him! Good thing he's dead, or I'd *kill* him!'

'It was okay.' Kenny kissed her. 'I'd realized a long time

before that, that this was *my* life. I didn't join the SEALs so that my father would be proud of me. I joined so that *I* would be proud of me. I did it for me.'

Savannah kissed him back, and the spark that was always right beneath the surface in everything they did leapt into flame. But all he did was kiss her and kiss her. Slowly, lazily, deeply. God, he was a good kisser. And just when she thought she couldn't take anymore, he took off her clothes and put on a condom and . . .

And then it wasn't much longer before they were right back where they'd been when they'd first started talking.

She heard him smile in the darkness.

'Five,' he whispered.

Seventeen

Ken awoke to find Savannah gazing down at him. 'Hey,' he said, smiling as a series of extremely vivid memories from the night before flashed through his head. He was instantly alert, instantly happy, instantly wanting more. Except he could see her face. He sat up. 'Shit, how long has it been light?'

'For a while, I think.'

They had to get moving. It was kind of weird, being able to see her, to finally be able to look into her eyes after everything they'd done last night. He knew he was grinning like a fool, and she was smiling back at him.

'Last night was amazing,' he said.

She nodded. She'd gotten dressed – in an attempt to keep the bugs at bay that was more psychologically effective than anything else. 'For me, too.'

He kissed her, looking into her eyes right until the very last split second before their mouths met. Oh, yeah. She wanted him again, nearly as much as he wanted her. And, God, the idea of making love in the daylight, while he could see her, while he could hold her gaze, was pretty damn compelling.

'I can't get enough of you,' she breathed.

Oh, *yeah*. 'We don't have to leave right away,' he decided.

'I mean, what's another thirty minutes, right?' He reached for the buttons on her shirt.

But she pulled away from him. 'I have to go to the bathroom.'

He gestured to the corner of the blind. 'I'll dig you a hole.'

He could see from her face that that was not the response she'd hoped to hear.

'I won't watch,' he told her.

'Oh, God, that's just too weird.'

'What's weird? Big deal. I did it – must've been right before dawn – while you were still asleep.'

'Kenny, it's a miracle I can go to the bathroom in the woods at all.' She started moving a few branches. 'I'll just slip out and find a nice big fern to hide behind and slip back in here. And then . . .'

She smiled and unspoken promises hung in the very air around him.

'Go,' he said. 'But be fast and stay close.'

Molly woke up alone and feeling blue.

It was stupid. She'd been sleeping by herself for most of her life. It didn't make sense that one night spent with Jones's arms around her should rattle her routine so completely.

She dressed quickly, humming while she did so, trying to lift her dragging spirits.

It was Angie's turn to cook, and Molly greeted her with a smile as she helped herself to a bowl of fruit. 'Where is everyone today?'

'Father Bob took the boat down river to the falls to perform a funeral service. One of the Montemarano children died. We think it was blood poisoning.'

Molly closed her eyes. 'I should have gone with him.'

'He left early this morning.' She opened her eyes to see Billy pouring himself a cup of coffee. 'He didn't want to wake you.'

'He should have,' she said.

'Guess he thought you needed the sleep after staying out all night, huh?'

Molly put down her bowl with a thump. 'If you have some problem either with me or with something I've done, Billy, talk to me. Don't passive-aggressive me to death.'

Billy put down his coffee. 'You slept with Jones.'

'Yes. Thanks for your concern, but I'm well aware of any potential complications.'

Angie pretended to be fascinated by the vegetables she was cutting for the lunchtime salad.

Billy took a step toward her. 'I *am* concerned, Molly. None of us know this guy—'

'I know him,' she said.

Billy wasn't concerned, he was jealous, but Molly let him pretend he was on the high road. It was just as well.

'He's a smuggler and a thief and God knows what else.'

'Yes,' she said. 'God *does* know what else. He's a good man, and I'm completely in love with him.' Well, that was much more than she'd intended to reveal to anyone, and Billy, bless him, somehow knew it. Maybe it was from the way her eyes suddenly filled with tears.

'Oh, Molly,' he said, and there was real sympathy, genuine kindness in his eyes. He held out his arms to her, and she went into his embrace.

'What am I going to do?' she asked. 'I'm supposed to leave in just a few weeks and I don't want to go.'

'So maybe you don't leave,' he suggested. 'Maybe you

stay.' He kissed the top of her head. 'I wish it was me. I'm sorry for being such a jealous shithead.'

She laughed. 'You're never going to make it through the seminary if you don't clean up your language.'

'I'm working on it.' He pulled back to look down at her. 'Have you told him? Jones, I mean.'

'That I . . .' Love him. Molly shook her head. 'No.'

'You should. He should know. Even if he thinks he doesn't want anyone to love him – he wants it. Believe me. There's not a man alive who doesn't. And love is such a precious and enduring thing. Don't forget that. Even if you tell him and he runs away, he'll still carry it with him, always. He deserves that gift, don't you think?'

'Thank you,' Molly said.

Billy smiled ruefully, picking up his coffee cup. 'Lucky son of a bitch. I hate his fucking guts,' he said as he walked away.

'Language!' both Molly and Angie said in a near perfect unison.

Savannah heard them before she saw them. A snapped branch, the rustle of thick jungle foliage.

At first she thought it might be Ken, coming to check on her, and she quickly finished up and fastened her shorts.

But then she realized there was more than one person making that noise.

It was some kind of patrol, and they weren't making much of an effort to be silent.

For a half a second, she stood there, frozen.

This was why Ken hadn't wanted her to leave the blind. If she hadn't left, she'd be in there right now. Safely hidden. Instead . . .

If they found her here, it wouldn't take much for them to look around more carefully and find Ken. And if they found Ken and realized he was a Navy SEAL, they would kill him. Immediately.

Sheer terror flooded her and she ducked down, close to the ground.

She had to be far enough away from the blind when they found her. And then she had to make them believe that Ken had ditched her in the night.

Savannah didn't want to move. She wanted to curl up right there, in the shadows beneath the fern and simply pray that she wouldn't be spotted in the dense brush.

Instead, she began creeping, on her hands and knees on the jungle floor, as silently as possible, away from the blind and Kenny.

One more minute and he was going out there after her.

Jesus God, how could anyone take so long?

Ken looked at his watch again. And then he heard it.

Holy fuck.

Sounds of movement. Someone, no, lots of someones were out there in the jungle.

With Savannah.

Ken grabbed the Uzi and the pack with the extra ammunition and silently left the blind.

Alyssa sat with Jules in an outside café in Port Parwati, in heavy wait mode. They were here, they were visible, they were ready to evacuate Ken and Savannah immediately to Jakarta should they appear.

On the surface Parwati was far from the dangerous Wild West-type town that Max had described. It was a charming little mix of ecclectic architecture, with bright-colored signs and consistently terrific views of an ocean that was beyond gorgeous.

Clean and inviting, it sparkled enticingly in the sunlight, and as Alyssa gazed at it, she couldn't help but think of Sam Starrett. He'd joined the Navy, choosing to join the SEALs over elite groups like Delta Force and the Rangers because of his love for the ocean.

'Shit,' she said and Jules glanced up from his crossword puzzle.

'If we're frustrated,' he said, 'think how Mrs von Hopf must feel.'

'No,' she said. 'I was . . .' Thinking about Sam. Again. Would she *ever* stop thinking about Sam? 'You're right, of course.'

She picked up Rose's book. She was getting close to the end, and had slowed down – dreading finding out how it all turned out. When she'd last stopped reading, Rose was in London, heavily pregnant with twins, with no word as to whether Hank was dead or alive.

Victory in Europe! May 8, 1945. It was a day for celebrating, and I was as joyful as anyone in London at the news. More so, for it meant that finally Hank might be able to come home.

One week passed. Then two. Still no word, but I was undaunted. Reports told of the chaos in Berlin and the surrounding German countryside.

May became June became July and, seven months pregnant, I began making arrangements to go to Berlin, despite the trouble with the Soviets.

But health conditions in Germany were terrible. Disease was rampant. High blood pressure had already put me in the hospital once, and my doctors threatened to lock me up.

Then the news came. Ivan Schneider, another OSS operative, had seen Hank in Berlin just before the German surrender. Hank had been wounded, and Ivan believed mortally so. I couldn't believe it. I wouldn't believe it.

But several days later, I received a telegram from the War Office, notifying me that Hank had been officially presumed dead.

I spoke directly to Ivan, of course. I grilled the poor man, but he was unable to give me any hope at all that Hank might still be alive.

No, the hope was entirely mine.

Two weeks later, I was sent back to the United States – I think in the hopes that my mother and father would be able to prevent me from going to Berlin as soon as the babies were born, as I'd been stating I would do. I was given a seat in a military transport carrying General Eisenhower, but I remember little of the flight, even less of my first introduction to that great man.

The twins were born early, in late August, in my little farmhouse in New Jersey. My mother wanted me to name one of the boys after Heinrich, but I refused. It would be too confusing, I told her, to have two Hanks in the house. I named them Alexander and Karl – royal-sounding names for my little princes.

Months passed. Karl suffered a bout of pneumonia that kept him in the hospital for weeks and terrified me. It was nearly a year before he was declared well enough to travel and I began thinking, once again, of making my way to Berlin.

And then it happened. October 17, 1946. Over seventeen months after Germany's surrender. I received a visit from Anson Faulkner, my former boss at the FBI. Heinrich von Hopf had been found in a prison hospital in the Soviet Union.

Oh, how I cried at the news. I knew it! I *knew* it! Hank was alive!

He'd been badly injured and taken east with German prisoners of war. He was still quite ill, and finally had been brought home to Vienna.

I was delirious with joy, and would have rushed off to begin packing up the babies, ready to leave for Vienna on the spot, but Anson stopped me.

'According to the report I read, Hank was found a month ago, Rose,' he told me.

'A *month*?' and I was being told about it only now? 'Why didn't you tell me?'

'We didn't know,' he said. 'Not until today.'

'But . . .' Why didn't Hank try to get in touch with me? Surely he knew I would be nearly frantic with worry. It had been more than a year.

Solemnly, Anson took a newspaper clipping from his pocket and handed it to me.

It was from an English publication. A society-type column, announcing the engagement between Elizabeth Barkham, the daughter of Lord Someone – I've forgotten his exact title – to war hero, Prince Heinrich von Hopf of Austria.

I had to read it three or four times before the words made any sense. And then they made too much sense.

The article went on to report that Heinrich von Hopf had recently returned home to Vienna. His parents were ecstatic at his safe return, and the entire city was giving him a hero's welcome for his part in defeating the Nazi menace. Prince Heinrich was currently convalescing in his family's summer home, but he was expected to come to London to claim his bride before the year's end.

'I'm so sorry,' Anson said.

I couldn't help myself. I started to cry again. 'Thank God, he's alive,' I said. It was all I could say. 'Thank God, he's alive.'

Hank had married me because he was so sure he was going to die in the war. I'd suspected that all along and now I knew it for sure. But now the war was over, he was still alive, and his regular life – with all its responsibilities – had returned.

I went to visit a lawyer that afternoon, and before the sun set, I signed the necessary paperwork for a divorce.

Savannah kept crawling. Every yard she was able to move farther out into the jungle meant that Kenny was that much more safe.

She'd already made it quite a distance, half crawling, half crouching, but it wasn't far enough. Not yet.

She heard the sound of a low voice, calling out in a language she couldn't understand. It came from back behind her, from the direction she'd just come, and she hit the dirt, burrowing more deeply into the brush.

Please God, go past her . . .

She could see the shape of a man through the branches and she held her breath. He was moving slowly, cautiously. And heading directly toward her.

He'd seen her. She could tell from the way he called out again, in that same low voice. She didn't speak the language, but his meaning was obvious. 'Hey, guys, over here! I need backup!'

Savannah's ears were roaring as her heart pounded. Was she far enough from the blind? If they caught her here, would Kenny be safe?

She didn't know.

So she bolted. She burst out from the underbrush.

The man who'd been tracking her screamed, startled, and fumbled his gun.

She screamed, too, and ran as fast as she could.

*

Ken heard Savannah scream and then heard shots fired, blasting through the stillness of the jungle.

He felt them with his entire body, as if he were taking the impact of the bullets himself.

Oh shit oh *shit*! He ran toward the sound, his fear for Savannah sharpening his senses. There were voices coming from the same direction and more movement – people running. Lots of people.

Please don't let her be dead. Please God . . .

He silently crept as close as he could, aware as hell that there were guards in the jungle all around him. Uniforms. These were Beret's men – General Badaruddin, according to the villagers and Jones.

Jesus, there were a lot of them. A full platoon, at least.

And there, in the middle, was Savannah.

He seriously compromised his position to get a better look at her.

She was on her stomach, on the ground, with her hands on top of her head, but as far as Ken could see she was unharmed. Alive. She was breathing hard as if she'd been running. Or as if she were scared to death.

No surprise there – right now, *he* was scared to death. She wasn't dead, but all it would take was one asshole with a twitchy trigger finger and she would be.

'Does anyone here speak English? Or French? *Parlez vous français?*' Her voice rang out clearly over the din of male voices. She sounded cool and collected and completely in control, as if she weren't a prisoner, but rather as if she'd called them all together for a meeting on her behalf.

This was the same woman who'd dealt so effectively with the bellhop in her hotel room. She'd been in the midst of an emotional crisis, yet she'd managed to communicate her needs and even smile.

Ken realized he was seeing her mother's daughter in action. It might've been amusing if he hadn't just had the crap scared out of him, and if he weren't scared of a million different dangers. Someone in this bunch of Rambo wannabes could hit her in the head with the butt of their rifle to put her in her place. Or notice how great her ass looked in those shorts and decide to take advantage of the fact that she was female and helpless.

'*Parlez vous français?*' she called again.

Oh, fuck, Van. Not French. Don't talk to them in French.

The crowd of soldiers argued among themselves. If there had been fewer of them, Ken would've silently taken out the guards around him, then used the Uzi on the rest to get her out of there. But there was no way he could win in a firefight against an entire freaking platoon.

A skinny man with a scarf around his throat approached, clearly, from his manner and attitude, the platoon's CO.

'Where's the money?' he asked Savannah in perfect English, as if he'd just stepped off a bus from Ohio.

'I don't have it.' Savannah lifted her head to look up at him. 'The man I was with – he took it and left me here last night.'

What?

'He's long gone,' Savannah continued, and Ken realized what she was doing. She was protecting him – making sure they didn't catch him, too. 'I have no idea which way he went.'

Skinny and the other platoon leaders had a discussion.

'Excuse me,' Savannah said. 'I have some questions for you, too. Who are you? And can you help me get to safety?'

Oh, shit, this was it. Skinny was going to give her a swift kick in the head with his boot.

'And may I please get up now?' she asked. 'This is a little uncomfortable.'

'No,' Skinny said shortly, clearly irritated, then went back to his discussion.

Keep your mouth closed. Ken tried to send the thought to Savannah telepathically. He also said a quick prayer to God to strike her temporarily mute. Don't piss this fucker off, Van. This is not a man you want to make angry.

Miraculously, she stayed silent.

And Skinny finally turned back to Savannah. He gave a command to several of his men, who hauled her to her feet.

She was covered in dirt, but there was definitely no blood on her clothes, thank God. One knee was scraped and bleeding, but that seemed to be the worst of her injuries.

Skinny, meanwhile, was looking her over in a way that made Ken's skin crawl. And now he tried to send a telepathic message in his direction. Touch her, and you will be so fucking dead, so fucking fast . . .

The rebel leader finally spoke. 'You don't look much like a princess.'

'Excuse me?' Savannah said. Obviously she'd misheard that, too.

'We have been ordered by General Badaruddin to find Princess Savannah von Hopf. Unless there's more than one American woman running around on Parwati Island, I've got to assume you are she. But perhaps I shouldn't assume. Allow me to ask – are you the princess?'

Okay, the general was a bona fide nutball. Just what the world needed – another crazy lunatic with aspirations for world domination.

But Savannah's answer stopped Ken short. 'Yes.'

Yes?

'I am.'

She *was*?

Holy fuck. She'd said her grandfather was Austrian royalty. Was he some kind of prince? And if so, yeah, that would probably make her a princess. Or at least, like, a *half* princess.

'How do you know who I am?' she asked, with a shitload of royalty in her attitude.

Skinny smiled. He had a ghoulish smile that wasn't very nice. 'You're very popular on Parwati. There are a lot of people looking for you on this island.'

'I'm aware of that,' she said. 'And I'm grateful that you're not Otto Zdanowicz's men. They tried to kill me. They *did* kill my uncle, Prince Alex von Hopf.'

Prince Alex? Jeez, this was weird, but yeah, it made sense in a very Lifestyles of the Rich and Famous way.

Skinny laughed, and Savannah got haughty. 'I don't see the humor in my uncle's death.'

Ken braced himself for a backlash, but interestingly, Skinny bowed to her slightly. 'Prince Alex isn't dead, your highness. He has been ill, but his health is improving.'

The information just didn't stop coming. Savannah was a *highness*, and Badaruddin had Alex von Hopf. No, he had *Prince* Alex von Hopf. Ken's head was spinning. Was it possible the general's private army had snatched Alex from the start, and the Zdanowicz brothers had been simply trying to get money from nothing – calling Savannah to capitalize on the fact that Alex had gone missing?

As much as Ken hated the Zdanowiczs, he had to admire

the motherfuckers for thinking way outside of the box on that one.

'Where is he?' Savannah demanded. Easy, babe. Highness or not, don't push too hard.

Skinny stepped closer to her. Too close, and Ken achieved a whole new level of cold sweat.

'Please, I want to see him,' Savannah said. 'If you take me to him, and then take us both to Jakarta, I'll see that you get a reward. Two hundred thousand dollars. At least.'

'The general has asked for far more than that for Prince Alex. Surely he can get even more for the pair of you,' Skinny said.

So there already had been a demand for Alex's ransom. This was good. Because as soon as Alex von Hopf had gone missing, US professionals had surely been brought in. With Rose von Hopf's clout in Washington, the folks at the Pentagon were probably in a screaming hurry to bring Alex safely home. They'd probably sent the FBI to Jakarta to assist either special operations or special forces – maybe even the SEALs. Yeah, it was even possible SEAL Team Sixteen's Troubleshooters had been called in.

But whoever was out here beating the brush for Alex was no doubt aware that Savannah – no, *Princess* Savannah, God *damn* – and Ken had been crashing around in the jungle, too, for the past few days.

He was willing to bet that if there had been a ransom note, the FBI had traced it to its source. There were probably already teams of operatives hidden around the perimeter of Badaruddin's camp, just waiting for the right moment to go in and snatch Alex to safety. What might come in handy was having an operative – like, say, *Ken* – on the inside.

An additional bonus was the money they'd hidden. As

long as Ken and Savannah knew where it was and Badaruddin's men didn't, they could use it as a bargaining tool.

Or maybe they could strike a private deal with Skinny. If Skinny made sure Savannah remained safe until the ransom money was delivered and she was released, they could deliver him a nice little bonus that General Badaruddin didn't need to know about.

There were guards patrolling the jungle, coming right toward Ken. With very little effort, he could prevent them from seeing him. With even less effort, he could make them think they'd apprehended an intruder.

He hid the Uzi – no use making them shoot him – and prepared to be found.

Molly shaded her eyes as the helicopter approached the village center and prepared to land.

'That's it,' she said to Billy who'd come to stand beside her. 'We're planting trees here tomorrow. Big trees.'

'Shit,' he said. 'It's Otto Zdanowicz and his hired guns.'

Shit, indeed. Dust swirled around them.

'What do they want?' Billy asked, raising his voice over the din of the blades.

'I don't know, but I think we can assume they're not here to attend church services.' It wasn't like her to be a pessimist, but Molly knew in her gut that whatever Zdanowicz wanted, it wasn't going to be good.

'It seems we found your friend,' the skinny officer with the bad breath said, and Savannah's blood ran cold.

She could hear shouting, and what sounded like a struggle, and then five men manhandled Ken into the clearing.

He was covered with blood, and he went down, hard. He lay face first and motionless in the dirt.

She ran toward him. 'Kenny!'

She was jerked back before she could reach him, held down by the two soldiers who'd held her before, and she fought, kicking and hitting, struggling to get free. She connected purely by chance with someone's sensitive part, a nose or maybe a lip, and got slapped for her efforts – a brain-shaking, ear-ringing blow that knocked her on her butt and made her cry out.

And Ken pushed himself up onto his hands and knees. His nose was bleeding, she saw, as he looked directly at her. 'Don't fight them!' he said.

'Excellent advice,' the English-speaking officer said. 'You might want to follow it yourself.'

'Tell them to let go of her,' Ken ordered.

'Tell me where the money is.'

The men holding Savannah pulled her roughly back to her feet.

She wouldn't have thought it was possible for a man who was covered with blood and unable to stand to look dangerous, but Ken somehow managed. 'First tell your fucking goons to get their fucking hands off of her!'

'Kenny, don't!' Savannah said, but she was too late.

The officer gave a nod, and Ken got kicked in the ribs hard enough to send him into the air. He landed with a sickening thud and a groan.

'Stop!' Savannah sobbed. 'Stop! The money's buried fifteen paces from the southwest corner of the Quonset hut on an airstrip that belongs to a man named Jones! It's near a village about a half day's walk from here!'

Ken rolled onto his back and, with one hand, wiped

the blood from his face. 'Perfect,' he said. 'Just fucking perfect.'

When the phone rang, George was sitting outside the hotel suite, on the veranda.

Rose picked it up as he stepped back into the room, through the gauzelike curtains. 'Hello?'

'Mrs von Hopf, it's Alyssa Locke. Good news,' the young woman said, without having to be asked. 'We've pinpointed Alex's location. He's being held in the guest quarters of General Badaruddin's estate, on an island just north of Parwati.'

'He's alive.'

'Yes, ma'am. Lieutenant Starrett reported visual contact.'

Thank you, God.

Rose reached behind her blindly for the sofa, and George was right there, helping her to sit. Fear often kept a person standing, while relief could make one's knees fail utterly.

'They've seen Alex,' she told George and he squeezed her hand. 'I was so afraid,' she admitted.

'I know,' Alyssa said, her voice warm over the telephone line. 'You didn't show it, but, he's your *son*. I have a niece and, well, I know it's not the same, but I can imagine what these past few days have been like for you.'

'I'm a little light-headed right now,' Rose admitted, with a laugh.

'Is George there?' Alyssa asked. 'Are you sitting down?'

'Yes and yes,' Rose told her.

'There's more if you can stand it,' Alyssa said. 'We think we've located Savannah as well. We intercepted a radio message from one of Badaruddin's lieutenants saying that he found her on Parwati, and he's bringing in her and her companion – and their money. Now, we haven't verified this, but this is very good news. This means we're going to have a Navy SEAL right inside the camp. If he can connect with Alex, he'll be able to prep him for the rescue. It'll be covert, of course, and it'll be helpful if he's expecting that. The SEALs will go into that camp and pull Alex and Savannah out without a single shot being fired.'

'That's if everything goes according to plan,' Rose interjected.

'I can't make any promises,' Alyssa said, 'but if *my* son were being held for ransom, I'd want Lieutenant Starrett and his team to be the ones to get him out. Have faith.'

Rose chuckled. 'If there's one thing I've learned in this life, it's don't bury your chickens before you're absolutely sure they're dead. I shall spend the afternoon looking forward to tomorrow's tedious airline flight home to New York with my son and granddaughter.'

'Jules and I are about to board a plane for Jakarta since we're not needed here anymore,' Alyssa told her. 'Why don't you have George take you over to FBI HQ, so you'll know what's going on as soon as it happens. Jules and I will meet you there in about an hour, hopefully slightly less.'

'Thank you, dear.' Rose hung up the phone and burst into tears.

George, bless him, was smart enough not to say a word. He just put his arms around her and let her cry.

'I thought they were going to kill you,' Savannah whispered.

'*I* thought I was going to be able to use that money as a bargaining tool,' Ken countered softly as they waited for the general's helo to arrive.

He'd already given Skinny and company his song and

dance about the special lock on the attaché case, and how both Savannah and Ken would need to be kept alive to open it. He'd also spun wildly about who he was, and his relationship with Savannah. He was Prince Kenneth from Coronado, he'd told them – the princess's fiancé. He'd told Skinny that Savannah was pregnant with his child, and that that would increase her ransom value, since his parents – the king and queen of Coronado – would no doubt pay an additional sum to ensure the royal fetus remain safe. But if Savannah were compromised in any way – in other words, curb your men and keep your freaking hands to yourself – both Austria and Coronado would declare war on General Badaruddin.

Out of all the things Ken said, that seemingly wild threat was the closest thing to the truth. If they hurt Savannah, if they killed her, he would come back and decimate them. One at a time, right up the chain of command.

Skinny was no fool, but royalty was clearly out of his realm. It seemed clear that his plan was to collect the money and deliver it, with them, to General Badaruddin. Let the big nutball sort things out.

'Why did you let yourself get captured?' Savannah asked as Skinny moved farther out of earshot. The helo was coming. He could hear it throbbing in the distance. 'I was purposely leading them away from you so you wouldn't . . . but then you went and . . .' She shook her head in total disgust.

'You're mad at me,' he realized. 'You gave up the location of the money – the one ace up our sleeve – and *you're* mad at *me*.' He laughed in disbelief.

'What was I supposed to do? Just stand there and watch them kill you?'

'It's going to take way more than a bloody nose and a kick in the ribs to kill me. Jesus, I wasn't hardly even hurt. I was just making it look good.'

'I didn't know that.'

'Yeah, I guess we don't really know each other all that well after all, huh? I mean, you'd think the fact that you're a princess might've come up once or twice in the conversation.'

She rolled her eyes. 'I'm as much a princess as you are Prince Kenneth of Coronado. My grandfather was born an Austrian prince. Except Austria stopped recognizing titles and royalty in 1918. So he's not a prince. Except some people get off on royalty, and make a big deal of it. Excuse me, it's been almost a hundred years! Time to get a grip on what's important. I'm an American with a few princess genes, which probably means I have a higher chance of having a son with hemophilia. What a bonus.'

She looked at him, and he saw she had tears in her eyes. 'I do know you really well, you jerk,' she whispered. 'But I couldn't stand there and watch them hurt you. I couldn't.'

'You should have come back to the blind,' Ken said, frustrated that he couldn't hold her. Frustrated that he'd even let her leave the blind in the first place. What the fuck had he been thinking? He couldn't keep himself from asking, 'Didn't you think I could keep you safe?'

She made a sound that was almost like a laugh, and one of her tears slid down her cheek. Impatiently, she brushed it away.

'I knew you could,' she told him. 'I just didn't think I would be able to keep *you* safe. I'd rather die than let anything happen to you, Kenny.'

The helo was landing, and Skinny was shouting orders.

The soldiers standing guard gestured for them to get to their feet. Time to take another helo ride.

He looked at Savannah. 'Be ready for anything,' he told her, hoping she'd be able to read his lips because she sure as hell couldn't hear him over the noise.

She nodded, wiping her eyes with both hands and then, enunciating clearly so that he'd be sure to understand from reading *her* lips, she said, 'I love you a ten.'

The guard roughly jerked Ken toward the helo, and he turned to look back at Savannah.

She had to be scared as she was pushed along, too, but she managed a smile as she met his gaze.

Ken laughed as the guard shoved him again toward the helo.

'I know you probably won't believe this,' Ken said to the guy even though there was no way he could have understood even if he *had* heard him over the din, 'but the past twenty-four hours have without a doubt been the *best* twenty-four hours of my life.'

Eighteen

'I'm sorry,' Molly told Otto Zdanowicz for what was probably the fourteenth time. She reached for Billy's arm and squeezed it, to keep him from saying something. That's all they needed, for Billy to get into a shouting match with eight heavily armed men. 'But you're wrong. The people you're looking for were never here. Would you like some mint with that?'

They'd come into the open-sided tent that was their kitchen and dining room, and Angie had even poured them each a glass of iced tea. She'd set it down alongside the enormous handgun Otto had put out on the table as a threat.

'Enough of this bullshit!' Otto swept all of the glasses onto the ground. It was less dramatic than it might have been, because they were all plastic and they bounced instead of shattered, but still Molly flinched, her shirt partially doused. 'My brother is dead!'

She reached across the table for him, instinctively going for his hand. 'I'm so sorry for your loss.'

He slapped at her and picked up the big gun.

Oh, Lord, had she pushed him into doing that?

'Where are they?' Otto demanded. 'Where's the money?'

'I'm sorry,' she said again, and he sharply brought the gun up and over, aiming it directly between Billy's eyes.

'You have ten seconds to decide if you are sorry enough, or if you want to be even sorrier,' Otto told her.

'I took them to see Jones, but he wouldn't help them,' she told him, just as Jones had told her to. 'They must have bought a map from someone in the village, though, because last I saw them, they were heading toward Port Parwati.'

'Molly, don't,' Billy hissed. Of course, he didn't know the truth – that Ken and Savannah had gone north instead. It was good. It added a certain realistic edge to her story.

She looked at Billy. 'I'm not going to let him shoot you for some strangers!' she lied. She turned back to Otto. 'Their plan was to travel parallel to the mule trail – near it but not on it.'

There was a flicker of something – recognition of a realistic-sounding plan, please God? – in Otto's eyes. But he cocked the gun as if he were going to shoot Billy anyway.

'Please,' Molly said, talking even faster. 'Please don't. I know where the money is. They hid it up at Jones's camp. Don't kill him and I'll take you to it.'

Otto nodded. 'Now we're getting somewhere.'

Savannah was kept on the opposite side of the helicopter from Ken, but she watched him as they lifted into the air.

Be ready for anything.

Please God, don't let him take any unnecessary chances. His nose was swollen and his shirt was covered with blood, but when he met her eyes, he smiled.

She wanted to cry.

I love you a ten. She couldn't quite believe she'd actually gotten up the nerve to tell him, but she was glad she had. Now if something happened – to either of them – at least she would know that he knew.

The sound of the helicopter's blades made her heart beat much too quickly. Or maybe it was the way Kenny was looking at her. He was thinking about sex. She could see it in his eyes, in the little smile that was playing about the corners of his mouth. They were sitting here, surrounded by men who would kill them without batting an eye, and *he* was thinking about . . .

Not sex. Making love. About the way he'd kissed her and touched her and filled her so exquisitely last night. About the way he'd made her laugh one minute and then gasp with pleasure the next. About the way he'd breathed her name as if she were all he'd ever want or need.

Savannah looked into Ken's eyes and smiled, too.

It sure beat worrying about what was to come.

Jones's Cessna was gone.

Molly didn't know whether to feel worried or relieved as she dug through the dirt, searching for the attaché case.

That engine part must have come. Jones had probably done the repairs first thing this morning, and headed out to take care of business.

He probably had quite a lot he needed to catch up with, since he'd been without transportation for so many days in a row.

Her fingers hit the metal of the case, and her relief was nearly overwhelming. It wasn't until she held proof that her suspicions were wrong that she even realized she'd had suspicions in the first place. Jones *hadn't* taken the money and run.

The guards dragged both her and the case back to Otto, who was waiting with Billy on the runway, in the shade of his helicopter.

Billy looked considerably relieved, since Otto had made it more than clear that he'd be dead if the money wasn't there.

Otto himself opened the case. He didn't finesse the lock the way Jones had. He just broke it open.

And threw the case onto the ground in disgust. Empty.

'No!' Molly said. 'Oh, God!'

Then everything started happening too fast.

Otto simply nodded to his men, who dragged Billy away from the helicopter. He raised his gun and—

'Wait,' Molly sobbed, catching his arm and pulling it down. 'Please! This is *my* mistake! The money *was* here, I swear. If you kill anyone, it should be me, not Billy!'

Fear and anger and outrage made her mouth taste bitter. She'd been wrong about Jones – so terribly wrong. Otto hit her in the face with his gun, and she went down, but the pain was nothing compared to the anguish in her heart.

'Please,' she begged, clutching at Otto's leg as he lifted the gun and aimed once again between Billy's eyes.

But Billy was fighting, and when Otto fired, he was hit in the shoulder, not the head.

It pushed him back and down. Molly screamed and Otto swore.

The men who had been holding Billy had let go and ducked when Otto fired, and now Billy pushed himself back, skittering on his rear end as he held his bleeding shoulder.

Otto moved toward him, dragging Molly, who was clinging to his leg. He aimed again, intending to finish Billy off.

Molly was sure she was going to throw up, but when she opened her mouth, 'Grady Morant!' came out.

It was as if she'd uttered the magic words.

Otto turned away from Billy and looked down at her. 'What did you say?' She'd gotten the attention of his men, as well.

'Don't shoot him, and I'll tell you how to find Grady Morant.' Her voice shook, but her eyes were suddenly dry as she did the one thing she'd sworn to Jones she'd never do. 'What he looks like these days, the kind of airplane he flies – a red Cessna. He's going by the name *Jones* and he's the one who took the money,' she told Otto and his men. 'Grady Morant was right here, on this airfield as of yesterday afternoon.'

They came up over a ridge, and then there was Jones's airstrip.

The Cessna was nowhere in sight, but – oh, fuck! – Otto Zdanowicz's helo was sitting out there.

And yet they were coming in for a landing. Weren't Badaruddin and the Zdanowiczs mortal enemies? What the hell were they doing?

Skinny was barking orders over the din, and Ken watched the soldiers assume what had to be battle positions at the open door of the helo. They weren't going to land, they were going to blast the crap out of what was looking to be a very pretty sitting target.

He dove across the helo to pull Savannah down, to shield her with his body as they attacked.

Molly felt a slap and heat in her arm and she knew she'd been shot.

It didn't hurt. Not yet anyway, so she dragged Billy farther away from the attacking helicopter, toward the welcoming shadows of the jungle, away from the ragged sound of automatic weapons.

It seemed impossible that she'd been hit only once.

She saw Otto Zdanowicz fall, his chest riddled with blossoms of blood and she tugged Billy even harder. How could he be so heavy?

'Molly, run,' Billy begged her. 'You can make it without me!'

'I'm not leaving you!'

The attacking helicopter was twice the size of Otto's. A great, huge war machine, it made another pass, and she threw herself on top of Billy as a line of bullets hit dangerously close and kicked up sharp little shards of concrete.

Savannah was screaming.

Ken didn't blame her. She hadn't been through BUD/S, hadn't lived through countless training sessions, hadn't ever experienced a battlezone up close and personal the way he had. He was a hardened warrior, and the sound of all those machine guns and automatic weapons going off was almost enough to make *him* want to scream.

He put his mouth up close to her ear. 'Savannah. Listen to me. Listen to me. Listen to me.' He just kept saying it until she quieted down. 'Are you listening?'

She nodded. Put her mouth up close to *his* ear. 'Kenny, I don't want to die. Not now that I've finally found you.'

'I'm not going to let you die,' he told her, and a bullet from one of the Zdanowicz gang's guns hit the bulkhead right above their heads.

She squeaked and he tried to make them an even smaller target. 'Get ready to run, okay?'

She nodded again.

'As soon as we touch down, most of these guys are going to exit the helo. If we're ready there might be an opportunity in the chaos to make a run for the jungle. Are you with me?'

She nodded.

'Take the shortest path. Do you understand?'

Another nod.

'Wait for me to say *go*.'

The helo made a tight turn, and Savannah clung to him as if for dear life.

All of Zdanowicz's men were dead. Or if they weren't, at least they'd stopped shooting. Molly saw one of them waving a handkerchief – a white flag, and she searched her pockets for something to wave, too, finally settling on holding her hands in the air in the international gesture of surrender.

'I'm so sorry,' she told Billy. 'This is all my fault.'

'Yeah,' he said, teeth clenched against the pain. 'You're definitely responsible for all the gang warfare in Indonesia.'

The helicopter landed, and uniformed men rushed out, efficiently making sure Zdanowicz's men were dead or disarmed.

The one with the white flag was talking, very earnestly, first to a soldier, and then to a very angular man who stepped down from the enormous chopper.

The flag waver talked and talked, and then pointed. Directly at her.

Four soldiers ran across the runway toward her and Billy, guns held at ready.

'Put your hands in the air,' Molly said. 'Show them you're not armed.'

493

Billy's hands were garishly bright with blood as he held them up.

The soldiers grabbed them both, hauling them to their feet.

'Be careful,' Molly said and then said again, in the two major local dialects. 'He's wounded.'

'You're bleeding, too,' Billy told her, and she saw that she was.

She'd been shot in the arm. There was both an entrance and an exit wound, but it looked fairly clean.

If she lived, she was going to have one hell of a scar.

Now. If it was going to happen, it was going to have to be now.

Ken took Savannah's hand and pulled her with him toward the door and—

Shit!

A guard with an AK-47 was standing right in front of them, his dark eyes alert. He gestured for them to move back. Away from the door. He moved slightly inside the helo so he could watch them.

'Isn't there a back door?' Savannah whispered.

'Not on this helo.' Ken smiled a happy howdy at the guard, who frowned grimly back at him. Didn't it figure? There was one vigilant man in Badaruddin's entire private army, and he'd been assigned to keep an eye on them.

'What do we do?' Savannah asked.

If he were alone, he'd overpower the guy. It wouldn't take much, one on one, to get possession of that AK-47. Problem was, this guy could get off a couple of shots before that weapon completely changed hands. Another SEAL would be able to avoid getting hit by stray bullets, but

Savannah's instincts were ... Well, the truth was, she wasn't going to make the Warrior Princess team any time in the next decade or so.

'We wait,' he told her. 'We just stay cool and we wait for the next opportunity.'

'This man needs medical attention,' Molly said, but the soldiers who were dragging her ignored her.

'We were being held against our will by Otto Zdanowicz,' she tried. She might as well have been talking to walking two-by-fours.

'We're missionaries – people of God. Please help me get this man to the hospital in Port Parwati!'

The soldiers didn't so much as change their facial expressions as they brought her and Billy over to the angular officer and the wounded white-flag waver – the last surviving member of Otto Zdanowicz's gang.

The gaunt officer spoke English. 'This man says you know the whereabouts of Grady Morant.'

Molly was sick to her stomach from the death and destruction around her and light-headed from loss of blood, but she shook her head. She'd betrayed Jones once already – and once was more than enough even if he was a scum-sucking lying son of a bitch. 'He's lying. We're missionaries. From the village just down the trail—'

'*She's* lying,' countered the flag waver. 'She said Grady Morant was right here yesterday, said he flew a red Cessna and went by the name Jones.'

'Please,' Molly said. 'I wasn't serious. I would have said anything to keep Otto from shooting Billy. I'd heard the rumors about this guy Morant, so I said I knew him.'

The officer looked around, looked at the Quonset hut,

looked back at Molly. 'Jones is Grady Morant.' He laughed. 'He never told this to me. But then again, he and I were not lovers. He never lit a roomful of candles for me.' He turned to his men. 'Put them all in the chopper.'

Jones hated Jakarta. Whenever he came here, it was only because he absolutely had to, and as a rule, he couldn't wait to leave.

But he'd been sitting in this dingy airport bar for over five hours, as if glued to this booth. His plane was refueled and ready to fly to Malaysia. That's why he'd stopped. To fuel up so he could make like dust in the wind and vanish for good.

So what the hell was he waiting for?

The dufflebag filled with money was beside him. The money that Molly had been so sure he wouldn't abscond with.

Well, honeychild, he'd absconded. He didn't know who she thought he was, but maybe she'd figure out the truth now.

He looked at his watch.

It would still be a couple of hours before Molly came up to his camp and realized he was gone.

It would probably be a couple of days or even weeks – knowing Molly – before she realized he wasn't coming back.

Knowing Molly.

That was his big problem here. It had all started with knowing Molly.

He finished his beer with one long swallow. He would get a new passport, he decided. There was enough money in this bag to buy him an entirely new identity – one with which he'd even be able to get back into the United States if he wanted.

Not that he wanted.

There was enough money here to keep him from working another day in his life, if he played his cards right.

He could go to some remote corner of Malaysia and buy a house. Sit around and do nothing all day.

And end up thinking about Molly.

Jones put his head in his hands. God damn it, he didn't want the money. He wanted Molly. Even if it was just for another month.

What a pathetic fool he was. He'd made it all these years without any complications. How could he be so utterly stupid as to fall in love at this point in his wretched life?

The waitress approached. 'Want another beer?'

'No, thanks.' *Thanks*. He'd never said thanks to anyone before Molly.

'You're pretty cute.' She sat down across from him, an Indonesian girl of about twenty, pretty despite a black eye, despite being a little worn around the edges. 'Want to fuck?'

Jones laughed. 'Where were you a week ago?' But he knew it wouldn't have made any difference. He hadn't started messing around just because he was horny. No, right from day one, he'd wanted *Molly*. He stood up, dragging the duffle out of the booth behind him.

The girl followed eagerly, but he put up one hand. 'No,' he said. 'You misunderstood. I'm not . . .' He shook his head and laughed. 'But thanks for the offer.'

She shrugged. 'Suit yourself.'

Jones pushed open the door to the bright afternoon and headed for his Cessna. Fuck Malaysia. He was going back to Parwati.

And if he was lucky, he'd get there before Molly even knew he'd been gone.

General Badaruddin's camp had a perimeter that was half rough ocean and rocky cliffs and half jungle mountainside.

There was one road, leading through the jungle to the compound.

Molly and Billy were both stable. Ken wasn't a hospital corpsman, but like all SEALs, he knew enough to be able to temporarily patch up both of the missionaries. Neither of them had been hurt all that badly, although in this climate, they both needed copious amounts of antibiotics to fend off infection.

They didn't need his attention anymore, and Savannah seemed to understand that he wanted to take a look at their destination, so he inched closer to the open door of the helo as they made their approach to the camp.

The general's house was about the size of an English manor. It was at the very top of the hill, poking its head out of the jungle. There was a tiny strip of lawn directly in front of it, and what looked to be a pool and tennis courts in the back. But then the jungle took over.

Slightly further down the hill, on either side of the road leading up to the general's house, Ken could see more utilitarian-looking buildings, presumably housing for the troops, warehouses for ammunition and supplies. Jails for containing hostages.

The whole setup was extremely feudal castle – no wonder the nutball had a thing for royalty.

The helo had a landing pad further down the hill, outside what looked to be a very secure and heavily manned fence with a heavy-duty gate. Ken bet the fence was electric. He bet there were lights and a full rotation of guards and even dogs, all to keep people out. And he bet the soldiers and other people in the compound never for one moment thought that they were anything but safe as long as those guards were at that gate.

And he also bet there was already a team of SEALs inside the compound. He bet they swam in and scaled the presumably unscalable cliffs – probably without even breaking a sweat.

As the helo landed, he and Savannah, Molly, and Billy were loaded into jeeps and brought through the gate. The road up the hill was steep at first, but it leveled off for quite a ways as it approached the main house.

As he got a closer look at the outbuildings, he realized they weren't so much utilitarian as ramshackle. Even the main house, from this closer distance, broadcast a sense of decay.

General Badaruddin needed a financial transfusion, and fast. But he wasn't going to get it from them.

Although this was a fairly decent setup, it was far from impenetrable. In fact, any kind of rescue operation would be almost laughably easy.

Ken caught Savannah's eye and smiled.

He would bet big money that they would be out of here and on their way home by tomorrow.

Uncle Alex was heavily sedated.

The building – the thin officer had called it *guest quarters* – where Alex was being held was pretty cushy as far as a hostage holding cell went. It had two rooms and a bathroom. But whoops, no running water from the sink. The toilet flushed, though – which Savannah thought was a major triumph.

The structure was made of cinderblocks, and had only one door to the outside, facing the road. The only windows were on that same side of the building – obviously to keep all of the 'guests' from escaping.

The lack of windows in the back made for poor air circulation, though, and it was hot as hell.

The officer who'd brought them here had informed them that they would have an audience with the general in the morning. Badaruddin was coming in from Papua New Guinea where he'd been meeting with leaders of the OPM – the Free Papua Movement.

Ken came out of the other room, where he'd given Alex a quick check. 'He looks okay. He needs a shower, but who doesn't in this heat? They're definitely giving him something to sedate him, though. Maybe through the food – so don't eat or drink anything.' He included Molly and Billy in that.

'How long are we supposed to go without drinking anything?' Billy asked.

'Until tonight,' Ken said. 'We're going to be taken out of here tonight.' He lowered his voice, probably on the off chance that the single guard at the door spoke English. 'There's a team of SEALs already inside the perimeter of the camp, waiting for the right moment to pull us out. They'll use stealth. This is not going to be a guns blazing firefight. It'll be a covert operation. What you need to remember is to be as quiet as you possibly can and to do exactly what they tell you right when they tell you to do it.'

Savannah shook her head. 'How do you know this? I don't mean how they're going to do it. I mean how do you know they're here? Did you see them?'

'No,' Ken said. 'I didn't see anyone. But not only do I know they're out there, I also know which team it is and who's in command. It's Team Sixteen, and the CO for this op is Lieutenant Sam Starrett.'

Kenny grinned, and Savannah knew that he was actually enjoying himself. She was still terrified, though, and it made her speak a little sharply. 'And this you know from the way the wind was blowing, or . . . the pattern of clouds in the sky . . . ?'

'I know this because Starrett's a chocoholic.' He laughed at the look she gave him. 'He never goes anywhere – even into the jungle – without a supply of peanut M&M's. And lookee what I found in the pocket of dear old Uncle Prince Alex's shirt.'

He held it out on the palm of his hand. *It* was a peanut M&M's wrapper.

Savannah's head was spinning. 'Are you saying that this Lieutenant Starrett came into this building, past the guard, simply to put a candy wrapper in my uncle's shirt? Why didn't he rescue him at that time?'

'Okay,' Ken said. 'Yeah, I can see how that sounds crazy, but you have to understand a couple of things. It probably wasn't Sam Starrett who brought the wrapper in here. It was probably Jenk or Gilligan or well, never mind. The point is, the wrapper was a message. To me. Sammy Starrett is my best friend, Van. We're really tight; I know him better than I know just about anybody, except maybe you now. He's the guy that, you know, when I get married, he's going to stand up for me and be my best man? That wrapper in Alex's pocket was not just to let me know that he was here. It was also to let me know that he knew *I* was going to be here. That's why they didn't just pull Alex out. They were waiting for us so that they could save all our asses at the same time.

'And Jenk or Gilligan or whoever came in here to deliver this message,' Ken added, 'didn't come in through the door. I checked the back room. There are four cinderblocks that are loose right behind the bed – the mortar's been removed. They probably put some kind of patch on the outside to make it look secure, but those blocks are ready to go. We could walk out of here – well, crawl – right now, if we wanted.'

'Why don't we?' Savannah asked.

'Well, darkness would be nice, for one. It'll be harder for them to see us if it's dark. Two, it's probably better not to tip our hosts off to the fact that we're leaving until we know where and when to meet the bus that'll take us out of here. Number three, out of five of us, two are wounded, one is an overweight almost unconscious man, and one is five foot four and a lightweight with feet that are probably so sore that she should get lumped into the wounded category.'

'They're not that bad,' Savannah said quickly.

Ken laughed. 'God, I love you,' he said. But then, as if he'd realized what he'd just said, he stopped laughing.

'I do,' he said quietly. 'I love you, Van. It's a ten for me, too. So trust me when I say we need to wait, okay? Trust me when I tell you that my teammates are out there, that they're going to bring us home.'

Mid-November, 1946, I received a letter from Hank.

It was too thin to be the divorce papers I'd sent – besides those were to be returned to my lawyer's office. It had been almost a month, though, and there'd been no response.

Until now.

I opened the envelope, I confess, with shaking hands.

Rose

502

No *Dear*. Just my name, written in his so-familiar hand.

> *I will be visiting New York on November the 12th and should like to see you. Please will you join me for dinner at the Waldorf-Astoria at seven o'clock p.m.*
>
> *Yours, Hank*

November the 12th was the next day. I tried somewhat desperately to talk myself out of going, but of course, in the end, I couldn't stay away.

I arranged for Evelyn to come out and watch the boys, and, wearing my best dress, I took the train into the city.

The Waldorf was just as I'd remembered it, the lobby perhaps more crowded than it had been, with reporters and newspaper photographers everywhere I turned.

I went toward the restaurant, stopping to ask a young woman in a big purple hat what the fuss was about. (Why do I remember that hat? But I do. As clearly as if I'd seen it yesterday.)

'Some VIP's in town,' she told me with a snap of her gum. 'A war hero – some European prince.'

Hank. She was talking about Hank. These reporters were here because of him.

I gave my name to the maître d', whispering that I was to be dining with Heinrich von Hopf, whispering for fear one of the reporters with particularly good ears might overhear me and start asking questions.

I was led into the main dining room, which surprised me. I was certain Hank would have arranged for us to dine in a private room where no one could see us and speculate on our relationship.

If those reporters only knew – but I was determined not to

let our secret slip. Not just for Hank's sake, but for my sons' sakes as well.

'I think there must be some mistake,' I told the maître d', but then I saw him. Hank.

He was already there, sitting at a table near the big window that overlooked the street. My heart lurched at the sight of him. He was thin and his color wasn't all too good, but oh, it was *Hank*.

He didn't stand as he saw me coming, and I stopped short – my heart doing another flip as I realized he was sitting in a wheelchair.

None of the articles Anson Faulkner had sent me – and there were quite a handful about Hank in both the London and Wien papers – had mentioned anything about a wheelchair.

He used his arms to shift his chair, pulling himself out from beneath the linen tablecloth. And I saw that Hank, my dearest Hank, had lost the lower half of his left leg.

'Oh, God,' I said.

'So you didn't know,' he said.

I wanted to run to him. To fall to my knees in front of him and run my hands over and across him – making sure that the rest of him was healthy and whole. But there were reporters just outside in the lobby.

'It was an infection,' he told me, as I sank into my seat across from him instead. 'The doctors couldn't shake it, it nearly killed me. They opted to amputate in late September.'

I wanted to reach for his hand across the table, but I didn't dare. 'I wish someone would have told me. I would have come.' I realized as the words left my mouth that if he'd wanted me there, someone *would* have told me. 'I'm sorry, I'm . . .' I cleared my throat. 'But you're over the infection now? You seem quite well.'

He nodded, the muscles in the side of his jaw jumping. 'Yes, the infection went with the leg.'

'Thank God.' I tried to smile even though I couldn't hide the tears in my eyes.

'I was quite ill – bedridden until just a few weeks ago. The doctors tell me I was taken out of the Soviet camp just in time. Another week or so, and I surely would have died. I don't remember any of it. I mean, I remember being brought to the camp of course. I remember being wounded. But the damn leg just wouldn't heal. It just kept getting worse and worse. I don't remember them taking me out of there at all. I just woke up one morning in Vienna.'

'That must have seemed like such a miracle to you,' I whispered.

'Yes, well,' he said, shifting slightly in his chair. 'It was somewhat lacking, particularly when I found they'd taken my leg, but I suppose one can't be picky about miracles.'

There was silence for a moment.

Then, 'Will you be fitted for a prosthetic?' I asked. 'I recently read an article about the new medical technology. They've come such a long way since the days of pirates with peg legs and hooks for arms, you know.'

Hank smiled. 'Count on you to cut to the bottom line. And yes,' he said. 'I've been told I'm a good candidate, although there are no guarantees. I should like to be able to walk again. I've been feeling rather short these days.'

'Once you get your strength back you should be able to swing about on crutches, don't you think? I know that's not the best solution,' I said, 'but it'll get you where you want to go. And to be perfectly honest, even if for some reason you have to spend the rest of your life in a wheelchair, you'll always have plenty of beautiful women eager to push you around.'

He laughed at that.

'You'll always be easily identified as a war hero,' I continued, 'and women will fall – no, swoon – at your feet.'

'Foot,' he interjected, but he was still laughing.

'Look around,' I told him. 'You've still got the eye of every woman in this room.'

Hank stopped laughing. 'Including you, Rose?'

I couldn't lie to him. 'Including me,' I said quietly, unable to look him in the eye. 'Always me. I'm the one who found you irresistible even when I thought you were a Nazi, remember?'

'Excuse me, sir. Madam. May I take your order?'

'No,' Hank said. 'Go away.'

'Indeed, sir.' The waiter vanished, and as I looked up, I realized that Hank had tears in his eyes.

He reached into the inside pocket of his jacket and took out a packet of papers. He placed them carefully on the table, and I saw that they were my petition for divorce.

'Okay,' he said. 'You didn't know about my leg. I thought you did, I thought you were repulsed by the idea of—'

'No!' I said. 'Oh, God, no!'

'Obviously a one-legged man isn't a problem for you,' he said. 'So why? Why didn't you come to me? God, how I needed you, and you sent me *this*.'

What was he saying? That he *wanted* me to be there with him in Vienna? I couldn't stop myself from reaching across the table and taking his hand. 'Oh, Hank . . .'

'I know how hard it must've been for you,' he said, gripping my fingers. 'You believed I was dead for over a year.'

'No,' I said.

'At first I thought you'd found someone new. That had to be the answer. But you haven't. Unless you've been extremely discreet . . . ?'

'There's no one,' I told him. 'And I didn't believe you were dead. I didn't believe it for a minute.'

'Then I don't understand,' Hank said. 'I need you to explain as simply as you can possibly manage, why you don't want to be married to me anymore.'

'You have an English fiancée,' I told him. 'Lord Someone's daughter. I thought . . .'

He sat back. 'You thought I didn't want you.'

'This was the real world,' I explained. 'The after-the-war world. You're a *prince*. I'm—'

'A war hero, too,' he said. 'Elizabeth Barkham was never my fiancée. That was my mother's wishful thinking – I wasn't even conscious when that notice went into the *Times*. You shouldn't believe everything you read in the newspapers, Rose. Good grief, what would I want with a fiancée when I've already got a wife? The only wife I've ever wanted. *You*, Rose.'

But I'd had months and months of talking myself into believing that even if Hank did still love me, our marriage would never work. 'Are you just going to come home with me, then?' I asked. 'To live in New Jersey? An Austrian prince in Midland Park?'

'How about Hong Kong?' he asked. 'I've always wanted to take you to Hong Kong.'

He was serious.

'Yes, it's going to create something of a . . . stir when the news of our marriage gets out, but I've been gone from Vienna for so long, it's not home for me anymore. This is home,' he said, squeezing my hand. 'Right here in the Waldorf. Or in Hong Kong. Or in Midland Park. Wherever *you* are.'

He brought my hand to his lips and kissed me, and about twenty-five cameras flashed. Oh dear! I pulled my hand away, but Hank didn't even blink. I realized with some shock that the

SUZANNE BROCKMANN

sidewalk outside was crowded with those reporters and photographers.

Hank didn't give them as much as a glance. 'Tell me you don't love me, and I'll sign these papers right now,' he said. 'Otherwise I'm ripping them up.'

He didn't have to rip them, I did it for him.

'I'm afraid you'll have to come to me so I can kiss you,' he said. 'But you better do it quick, because I'm about to knock this table over to get to you.'

'But . . .' I looked at the window. Didn't they realize how terribly rude they were being, staring in at us like that?

Hank started to move the table, and I quickly stood up.

As soon as I came close, he pulled me down, right onto his lap and kissed me. Oh, what a kiss that was.

And oh, how those cameras flashed!

One of the more bold reporters knocked on the window. 'Who's the lady, Prince?' he shouted through the glass.

Hank wouldn't let me up. He turned his chair with me still in his lap, so that we faced the window. I laughed and blushed and he kissed me again, and again the cameras flashed.

Then Hank's voice rang out, loud enough for them to hear him in the street. 'May I present the daring double agent who helped me penetrate the Nazi war offices in Berlin during the last years of the war, Mrs Ingerose Rainer von Hopf – my wife, whom I love with all my heart.'

The cameras flashed again and again and again, and just like that the crowd of reporters dispersed. I could almost hear the newsroom phones ringing. With one sentence, Hank had irrevocably changed both of our lives.

He kissed me a few more times, and then helped me off his lap. 'How about taking me home to meet my sons?'

He knew about Alex and Karl! I was surprised for a second,

508

but then I realized – of course he would know. This was a man who had been gathering intelligence for most of his adult life.

'They'll be asleep when we get home,' I told him as I wheeled him out of the dining room. 'But of course we can wake them.' I smiled down at him, my dear, wonderful Hank. 'Or we could sneak into their room, you could take a peek, and then we could let them sleep . . .'

His smile made my heart sing.

And so I took my prince home, and together we lived happily ever after for thirty wonderful years.

Alyssa closed Rose's book as the seaplane prepared to touch down in the harbor. Jules glanced at her and opened his mouth as if to speak, but she shook her head. She didn't want to talk right now. She was afraid if she opened her mouth, she would start to cry.

A short boat trip to a shorter taxi ride, and then they were at the temporary FBI headquarters.

The elevators were out, and as they climbed the stairs, Jules finally spoke. 'Are you all right?'

'No,' Alyssa said as she pushed through the door to the fourth floor. She turned back to glare at him. 'I want to live happily ever after. Where's my goddamn happy ending, huh? That's what I want to know.'

She left Jules standing there, gaping at her as if she'd gone mad.

It was entirely possible she had.

There was blood on his runway.

There were bodies, too. Several still sprawled on the concrete, but four were neatly lined up in the shade of the Quonset hut, covered with tarps.

Jones landed on his first pass, searching for Molly among the missionaries and villagers who were moving the bodies.

She wasn't there.

At least not among the living.

He leapt from the plane, running past Otto Zdanowicz, who lay clutching his bloody chest, eyes staring sightlessly at the sky. Running for those tarps.

Please God . . .

'She's not here.' It was Angie, one of the missionaries, but Jones wasn't satisfied until he lifted those tarps and stared down at the unfamiliar faces.

'Where is she? What happened?' And then he saw it.

The metal attaché case, open and empty. Lying several feet from Zdanowicz. Oh, God.

'They came to the village,' Angie told him. 'Threatened to kill Billy. Molly said she knew where the money was.'

Angie had sent Tunggul running to get the other men, to get their guns, and she'd raced up the trail to the airfield.

She'd seen it all. By the time Tunggul and the others joined her, General Badaruddin's men had come, and the battle was over. There were far too many of the soldiers. It would have been madness for the villagers even to consider attacking.

And so Badaruddin's men had left, taking Zdanowicz's helicopter and Molly and Billy – both of whom had been wounded – as well.

According to Angie, Molly had been shot and pistol whipped. And right now she was the prisoner of General Badaruddin – a man who'd learned torture techniques from the Thai.

Sickened, Jones turned and headed toward his plane.

'What are you doing?' Angie called after him.

'I'm getting Molly out of there.' He checked his arsenal of weapons, slipped on the flak jacket he'd taken in trade for a twenty pack of toilet paper about four years ago, and climbed into the Cessna.

Angie came running toward him. 'There's nowhere to land a plane on Badaruddin's island!'

'Then I guess I'll have to improvise.' With a roar, he taxied to the end of the strip and took off into the brilliant blue of the afternoon.

Nineteen

Ken sat next to Savannah on the floor of Badaruddin's 'guest quarters' and held her hand.

'Tell me again what's going to happen,' she said.

He couldn't blame her for being nervous. He was a little nervous himself. All those assholes out there had weapons capable of killing instantaneously. All they'd need was one person to see them and to fire his weapon and . . .

'We'll leave through the hole in the back,' he told her, 'as soon as we have contact with the SEAL team. We'll split into smaller groups – it'll be easier to move covertly that way.'

'But I get to stay with you,' she said. 'Right?'

'Right. You get to stay with me.' Ken looked down at their hands. She was playing with his fingers. 'You know, I was thinking, Van, you know, kind of about that. About you staying with me and . . .'

He laughed, suddenly uncertain as to her reaction to what he was about to say. There were times when, inside his own head, it sounded completely crazy, but there were other times when he was absolutely convinced it was the only thing to do. He decided to start with a slightly less crazy variation on the theme. 'I think you should move out to San Diego.'

Her smile was slightly hesitant but completely pleased. 'You really want me to?'

'Oh, yeah.' Fuck it. He was just going to say all of it. 'I think you should marry me.'

She made a sound that was sort of like a laugh, but not quite. He couldn't tell if it was a good sound or a bad sound. So he kept talking.

'I know I'm not what your parents want for you,' he said. 'I'm no prince – I'll never pass for one. I'm legitimate – my father was married to my mother, so I guess that might win me about a half a point. Right now, as a lawyer, you probably earn four times as much as me. But that's going to change as soon as I retire from the Navy. I've got people who want to pay me a million dollars for my tracking device – except that's not going to happen for a while. A good long while.'

'You're a SEAL, you're gone a lot of the time. That's not going to be much fun.'

He looked at her.

'Just thought I'd add that to the con list,' she said, 'since you brought it up before.'

'You're making a list – pro and con – for whether or not you should marry me?'

'I'm not making the list,' she pointed out. 'You are. But as far as I'm concerned, the pro side of the list completely cancels out the cons.'

Hope warmed him from the inside out. Not that he particularly needed warming in this heat, but it still felt nice. She was going to say yes. She was going to spend her life with him, the luckiest son of a bitch on the planet.

'What's on the pro side?' he asked. 'I'm great in bed, cute as hell, got a frog tattoo on my—'

'You love me,' she said softly. 'That's all.'

'Wait a minute, you don't think I'm great in bed . . . ?'

Savannah laughed as she rolled her eyes.

'I'm sorry,' Ken said, inwardly kicking himself. 'This was one of those times when I shouldn't make a joke. I know that. I don't always say what I'm supposed to say. You should probably add that to the con list, because it's a serious offense. Things just kind of come out, and I hear myself say 'em, and I *know* what I should've said just then was that I'll love you and cherish you forever. That I have no freaking clue how to be a good husband or God, a good father, and that scares me to death, but I'll figure it out, I know I will. I'll try harder not to say too many stupid things, and I'll work my ass off to make your life with me as wonderful as you'll make *my* life, just by being in it.'

He knew he'd won when he saw the tears in her eyes. 'I'm a control freak,' she said. 'I'm going to drive you crazy.'

'Probably,' Ken agreed.

She laughed. 'You don't care?'

'You love me,' he said. 'That's all I need to know.'

'You always say the right thing,' Savannah told him, her eyes so filled with love that *he* almost wept. 'Sometimes it takes you awhile to get to it, but you always get there, and what you say is always worth waiting for. And the rest of the time you make me laugh, so . . .'

Ken kissed her. It was that or start to cry. The woman had just told him she loved him exactly the way he was. Who would've thought that would ever happen?

She kissed him back the way she always kissed him – as if she were starving and he was a five-course meal. God, she made him so hot, he had his hand up her shirt before he remembered they weren't exactly alone.

He put his mouth to her ear. 'How about you pretend you've got something in your eye, and I'll go with you into the bathroom? We can see how many times I can make you come inside of ten minutes.'

'Kenny!' Savannah pulled away from him, laughing and blushing, but he could see from her eyes that she was actually considering it. She looked at the bathroom door, looked at him.

Ho, now! She wanted to go for it. It was probably not the most professional thing in the world for him to do, but hey, he wasn't here in his official capacity. He was on leave, on vacation. And they could wait for evening to fall just as well in the bathroom, getting it on, as they could out here . . .

'Come on,' he whispered, grinning at her. She was going to say yes.

She opened her mouth to speak, but he stopped her. 'Wait.'

He heard a sound that could only be some kind of aircraft approaching. It wasn't a helo, though. It was some kind of small plane.

'Hold that thought,' he said, and pushed himself off the floor, crossing to the window.

It was getting louder.

Savannah and Molly came to stand beside him. 'What is it?' Billy asked from his place on the floor.

'Small airplane. Single prop – one propeller,' he translated. 'Whoever it is, our hosts aren't expecting him. Lookit.'

Outside the window there was a great deal of activity as soldiers ran in all directions, probably heading for battle-stations. The guard in front of the house took several steps out into the yard.

'Be ready to move,' Ken said.

515

'It's not dark,' Savannah observed.

'Sometimes a good diversion trumps cover of darkness,' he said. 'Let's get Alex up and out of bed and Billy ready to roll.'

The mood in the FBI headquarters was tense. Alyssa could feel a trickle of sweat slide down her back.

How did Max Bhagat always manage to look so cool? He was wearing a suit with a jacket, too.

Several hours ago there had been visual contact – both Savannah and WildCard Karmody had been seen in Badaruddin's compound. They were being held in the same structure where Alex was believed to be. That was good news. Now it was just a matter of the sun setting so that the SEAL team could bring them out.

Rose's son Karl and his wife, Priscilla – Savannah's parents – had finally arrived. It was obvious, about ten seconds after they entered the room, that Priscilla got on Rose's nerves. Without saying a word to each other, Jules intercepted Priscilla and Karl, and George pulled Rose into the opposite corner of the room.

Alyssa bounced back and forth between them, feeling Max's gaze upon her.

He didn't look away when she caught him staring. It was entirely possible that he was deep in thought and didn't even realize that he'd fixated on her. But he tracked her when she moved, and he was still looking five minutes later.

She took the opportunity to gaze back at him, trying to see evidence of the surgery in which he'd had his sweat glands removed.

But then he smiled, and she turned away.

The radio crackled to life and everyone sat forward in their seat. 'Unidentified aircraft approaching the island.' The voice was Jenk's – Petty Officer Mark Jenkins. 'Request air support be stepped up to full stand by. Be ready to come in fast. We've got a lot of activity in the compound.'

'What does that mean?' Priscilla asked anxiously.

'Lieutenant Starrett may decide to take advantage of all the activity,' Max explained. 'If the chaos factor is high enough, he may decide to pull the hostages out right now.'

'It's Jones,' Molly breathed as a red Cessna made a pass overhead, and Ken came back to the window.

It did look an awful lot like the plane he'd seen on the smuggler's runway. But whoever it was, they were flying at tree level and scaring the crap out of the soldiers on the ground.

Some of them – just an erratic few – opened fire.

Skinny came running down from the general's house, screaming at the top of his lungs, probably for the troops to hold their fire. He went on for quite some time, no doubt giving them a crash course in physics. If they shot and hit the pilot while the plane was heading north like that, it would crash directly into the general's house.

Ken was betting Badaruddin's homeowner's insurance didn't cover things like self-inflicted acts of aggression.

'What is he doing here?' Molly asked. 'Go away!' she shouted, although there was no way in hell the pilot of that plane could have heard her.

Jones made one more low pass over the road, getting up his nerve to give this a try.

It was going to be fucking tight, but he'd landed in

517

fucking tight places before, for far less important reasons.

Molly was down there.

He was going to get his ass down there, too, and get her out of there.

The red Cessna was landing. Ken could tell by the sound of the engine.

The crazy son of a bitch flying that thing was actually going to try landing on the road.

One false move, and one of the wings would get tangled in the trees, and he'd somersault and crash.

'Okay,' Ken said. 'Everyone in the back room. Let's get ready to move.'

But Molly, the missionary, wouldn't budge from the window.

The Cessna got lower and lower and lower. Jesus, the guy had balls of steel. It had to be like flying an X-Wing through the canyons of the Death Star – without any of the technology.

The wheels hit the dirt, and the plane jerked and lurched, but it stayed in the dead center of the road.

It was only at the very end, after it had slowed significantly, that the left wing caught a tree, and it spun out and crashed headlong into the brush on the opposite side of the road, almost directly across from the guest quarters.

It was entirely possible that Jones – if that's really who it was – had done that on purpose.

The engine cut out, and the silence was amazing. No one moved.

All weapons were aimed at the Cessna.

'I don't know whether to pray for him to be dead or alive,' Molly said. There were tears on her cheeks. 'They know who he is. They'll send him back to . . . oh, God.'

'Who is he?' Ken asked, but she just shook her head.

The Cessna door opened, and every weapon in that compound that wasn't locked and loaded got locked and loaded. It was quite an impressive sound.

'Jayakatong, old friend,' Jones's voice called out. 'Tell your troops to back off. I have the money you were looking for and I'm willing to trade it for something of mine that you've got.'

Skinny stepped forward. 'And what would that be, Jones? I don't recall taking anything of yours.'

'Some friends,' Jones called back. 'Molly Anderson and Billy Bolten. They're missionaries for chrissake. You have no business holding them here.'

'Actually, I do,' Skinny replied. 'It seemed Miss Anderson had some interesting information that I wanted her to share with the general.'

'Jones!' Molly called out. 'He knows who you are!'

That was Molly's voice. She was in earshot. Jones had guessed right in assuming she'd be held in the same little 'guest cottage' that he'd spent some time in about a year ago.

She was alive, and conscious. That was good.

What wasn't so good was that she'd let slip – either on purpose or unintentionally – the fact that he was Grady Morant, the most hunted man in all of Southeast Asia and Indonesia, thanks to the price on his head, which translated to roughly five million US dollars.

Jones had pretty much known on his way over that there was a very real possibility this was going to be a one-way trip. He'd already considered the possibility that Molly had given him up, and he didn't blame her for it at all. He'd run with the money, putting both her and Billy in mortal danger. He deserved what he got.

And right now what he got was the chance to be a dead man, rather than a barely living man kept alive only to be tormented and tortured.

No, there was no way in hell he was going back to the Thai alive.

He reached around to his arsenal of weapons and grabbed a hand grenade. He pulled the pin and took the duffle of money and climbed down out of the plane.

Molly was as white as a sheet, and Savannah came up beside her, ready to catch her if she should faint.

Out the window, she could see Jones, climbing down out of his plane.

'Tell your troops to hold their fire,' he said. 'Tell them that while the reward for bringing Grady Morant in alive is five million, it's only a hundred thousand if I'm dead.'

'What did he do?' Savannah asked softly.

'He destroyed a drug lord's business,' Molly said, 'but the bastard bounced back. God, Grady should have killed the Thai when he had the chance.'

Those were pretty harsh words for a missionary.

'Here's what we're going to do,' Jones-Grady said. 'I'm holding a grenade,' he held it up for the officer and everyone else to see. 'I've pulled the pin, but as long as I'm holding onto it, it's not going to go off.'

'Oh, Lord,' Molly whispered, pressing her hand to her mouth. 'Oh, Grady, don't do this.'

'What I'm going to do is keep holding the release,' he

continued. 'What *you're* going to do is march all of your American hostages out of your guest quarters and down the road to that helicopter you inherited from Otto Zdanowicz. You'll give them weapons and a map and a pilot, if they need one. And then you and I will stand and wave goodbye as they head back to Jakarta. After they're gone, I'll put the pin back in the grenade, and we can have a nice dinner before you call the Thai.'

'Holy shit,' Ken said. 'He's negotiating our release.'

'I'm not going,' Molly said. 'I'm not going to leave him here.'

'No one's going anywhere yet,' Ken said.

The officer paced in silence for several long moments before he responded to Jones's proposal.

'What's to keep you from blowing up both yourself and the money after they're gone?' he finally asked.

'I'm not exactly the suicidal type,' Jones said with a laugh. 'Do I look like I want to blow myself up?'

'I would hug a grenade before spending the rest of my life in Nang-Klao Chai's dungeon,' the officer said.

'I'll give you my word that I won't.'

The officer laughed. 'Your word. Wonderful. How about: If you blow yourself to bits with that grenade, I will track down your friend Molly. I'll deliver her to Chai, and tell him to keep her alive in your place.'

'He warned me that this would happen,' Molly whispered. 'He said if we became friends that they'd use me to get to him.'

'Can't we do anything?' Savannah asked Ken.

'I think Jones is doing a pretty good job all by himself,' Ken told her. 'He's going to get us out of here. And then they'll probably toss him in here. And tonight Sam and the

521

rest of the team will have to rescue only one person instead of five.'

Molly turned toward them, hope in her eyes. 'Your friends can get him out of here? But will they have to arrest him? He's wanted in the US as well.'

'I didn't hear what his real name was,' Ken said. He turned to Savannah. 'Did you?'

The walk to the helicopter was excruciating.

Grady was holding a duffle filled with money and that grenade and looking at Molly as if he was never going to see her again.

'I'm sorry I got you and Billy shot,' he said. He was walking on one side of the road with the slender officer he'd addressed as Jayakatong, the hostages were on the other. Soldiers with huge guns were in front of them and behind them. 'I was planning to tell you that I took the money for safekeeping, but we both know that would be a lie.'

'But you came back,' she said.

'Too little, too late.'

'It's never too late.'

'Yes, actually,' he said, 'sometimes it is.'

As Savannah helped her uncle and the two missionaries get comfortable, Ken wrestled the helo off the ground. They lurched and swooped and flopped around for quite a bit before things evened out.

She came forward. 'Do you really know what you're doing?'

'I do now,' he shouted. 'Took me a sec to figure out the controls.'

She sat down, uncertain whether to laugh or cry. 'You haven't really ever flown a helicopter before have you?'

He glanced at her, glanced at her again.

'It's okay,' she said. 'You seem to have the hang of it now – you can tell me the truth, I won't freak.'

'I've had some training, but this is a first for me,' he admitted. 'And I have this wicked, awesome simulator game for my PlayStation2. It's really not that different.'

'Will you just do me a favor and check to make sure we aren't going to run out of gas?'

'Fuel gauge,' he said, pointing to the intricate control board. 'Here and here. Computer says . . .' He made an adjustment to another device. 'We've got enough to fly for . . . three hours at this speed.'

He reached up and flipped several more switches, pushed other buttons. 'Navigation computer says . . . Port Parwati, ETA fifty-eight minutes.' He smiled at her. 'Plenty of fuel. We'll land there and transfer to a Navy helo – get us back to Jakarta that much quicker. Besides, we don't want anyone mistaking us for Otto Zdanowicz and blowing us out of the sky.'

God, she hadn't even thought of that. Still . . . Fifty-eight minutes until Ken didn't need to be the pilot, until she could ride the rest of the way to Jakarta in his arms. 'I can't believe this is almost over.'

He looked at Savannah and grinned. 'Honey, it's just beginning.'

On General Badaruddin's island, as the helo carrying Molly and her friends faded from a speck to nothing, Jones put the pin into the grenade and handed both it and the duffle to Jayakatong.

Who turned to a squad of his soldiers and ordered, 'Beat him. Make sure that he won't be able to run away tonight, but be careful not to kill him.'

They circled him cautiously, and he knew what they were thinking. Grady Morant. Any man who had angered the Thai enough to place a five-million-dollar price on his head must be just one degree of separation from the devil himself.

Except, no, wait. The Thai was the one who was one degree of separation from the devil. Thanks to Molly, Jones was just two degrees of separation from the other guy, the one who lived upstairs.

Imagine that.

Her mother and father were waiting, along with Rose, as they disembarked from the Navy Seahawk.

Savannah had been extremely aware of Molly for the entire trip – aware that she'd left her lover back in Badaruddin's camp. She'd tried to be discreet about holding tightly to Ken, who made it much more difficult by whispering all the ways he was going to blow her mind that night – as soon as they found a hotel room where they could be alone.

But after they landed and helped Molly, Billy, and Alex off the Seahawk and into the waiting ambulance, Savannah was ready to never let Ken go.

They came off the helicopter arm in arm, and she could see her mother's horror in the way she took a quick step back.

Savannah looked at Ken, trying to see him with her mother's eyes and . . . oh dear. He looked like Robinson Crusoe's younger, grunge-loving brother. But what a smile, and what incredible eyes . . .

'Savannah! Darling! Thank God you're safe!' Her mother practically yanked her out of Ken's arms and enveloped her in a cloud of perfume.

Ken held out a dirt-streaked hand to her father. 'Mr von Hopf. I'm Ken Karmody. How do you do, sir?'

Her father shook his hand. 'I understand you're responsible for saving our daughter's life, young man. I'd like to offer you a reward.'

'Well,' Ken said. 'Thank you, sir. I'll accept. As a matter of fact, I've already picked out something pretty special and . . . Mrs von Hopf! You're *exactly* as I pictured you.'

Savannah bit the inside of her cheeks as Ken brushed past her mother's gingerly offered hand and gave her a bear hug.

Rose, who'd returned from a quick visit with the still heavily sedated Alex in the ambulance, was also trying not to laugh.

On impulse, Savannah hugged her grandmother. And got a very big hug back. 'Thank you for bringing Alex home.'

'I had more than a little help,' Savannah replied. 'There's a man still in Badaruddin's camp who sacrificed himself for us. Kenny says they'll get him out tonight. I hope so . . .'

'They will.' Ken jumped into the conversation. He squeezed her arm. 'Trust me, they'll bring him out.' When she nodded, he turned to Rose. 'Mrs von Hopf, it's a pleasure to meet you, ma'am. I'd love to have the chance to sit down and talk to all of you, but I need to do a debriefing with my CO and Max Bhagat – he's the FBI team leader,' he told Savannah. 'And then I've got a date with a shower and a scrub brush. I'll meet you back at the hotel, okay? Don't go anywhere without an FBI escort.'

'I won't,' Savannah said.

He pulled her into his arms and kissed her goodbye. Right in front of her parents and Rose. It was not an 'I'm kissing you in front of your parents' peck. It was an 'as soon as we can find some privacy I'm taking off your clothes' kind of kiss.

'Later, babe,' he said, and was gone.

'My . . . goodness gracious,' Savannah's mother murmured.

'I like him,' Rose announced.

Savannah laughed. 'I do, too.'

'What's this reward he's already picked out?' her father asked suspiciously.

'Me, Daddy,' she said. 'He wants *me*.'

The floor was cool.

Jones floated in a place where there was only the cool floor, the darkness, and the pain.

He'd been here before, and he'd sworn he'd die before he came back.

Why had he come back?

Molly.

She'd been standing right there, right in front of him, and yet he hadn't said it. He'd had the chance, but he'd choked. Still, maybe she knew. 'I love you,' he whispered. He had no problem saying it now, even though his lips were battered and split. 'I love you, Molly.'

'I'm afraid I'm not Molly,' a voice said quietly from the darkness. 'I'm Lieutenant Sam Starrett, US Navy SEALs, and I'm here with my friend and hospital corpsman, Petty Officer Jay Lopez, to get you out and bring you home.'

His first thought was that they came for him. After all these years, they finally came for him.

But then he realized with a sickening certainty that he couldn't go.

'If you take me, they'll go after Molly.'

'We're a step ahead of you, sir,' said the voice with its trace of a Texas drawl. 'She and all of the other missionaries have already been taken to safety. You can put her out of your mind right now, Mr Jones, and concentrate on helping us get you out of this shithole.'

'Your right leg's broken, sir,' said another voice. 'I'm going to put on a temporary splint. I'm working with night vision glass, so even though it might seem dark in here to you, I can see what I'm doing quite clearly. I'm going to give you some morphine—'

'No!'

'All right, but I need you to stay still and not cry out. Do you understand me, sir?'

'Yes.'

There was a sharp flare of white-hot pain that then slowly subsided, leaving just the dull roar from the rest of his bruised and battered body.

'Let's get you out of here,' Starrett said.

Twenty

Alyssa left the press conference and went out into the hotel lobby for some air.

What a pain in the ass it must be to be a von Hopf and have to hold a press conference every time some bad personal shit reared its ugly head. A son kidnapped. A daughter missing. Okay, maybe those were news stories, but still. There were reporters in there asking Priscilla von Hopf about an alleged fender bender she had in the Lord and Taylor's parking lot during a recent business trip to Natick, Massachusetts. That wasn't anyone's business.

The lobby wasn't that much more of a fun place to be right now, Alyssa realized. The SEALs – with the exception of WildCard Karmody – were checking out and going wheels up this afternoon.

They'd brought the man known only by his obvious alias of Jones back late last night, and spent the morning in debriefings.

Jones, yeah right. That was really his name.

But Max had given her a direct order not to dig into records of missing military personnel, so she'd spent the night reading. She was supposed to be Savannah von Hopf's FBI escort, but Savannah didn't leave her hotel room. Not once. She went in at five in the afternoon, and

528

didn't emerge until ten-thirty this morning. With WildCard Karmody, who was actually a good-looking guy when he bothered to smile.

He was smiling a lot this morning. Thank God Alyssa had their room checked for hidden cameras. A video like the one she was imagining would have played on the Internet until the end of time.

Alyssa started to hide behind a potted fern as Sam Starrett came out of the elevators and crossed the lobby.

But there was no need. He didn't even look at her. He just walked his long legs out the door, toward a group of his teammates who were waiting on the sidewalk.

He didn't look back, didn't even glance at her through the window. He just got into the hotel's airport shuttle and drove away.

'Hi.'

Alyssa turned to see Max standing behind her. 'Hi.'

'Ready to go home?'

'Oh, yeah.'

'Are we on the same flight?'

'I don't think so,' Alyssa said. 'I'm not going back until tomorrow morning. Alex won't be released from the hospital until then, so . . .'

'Ten thirty-five flight to Hong Kong?' Max asked.

'Yeah, that's right.'

'We *are* on the same flight.'

There was a ripple of laughter from the press conference, and Alyssa glanced toward the slightly open door. 'I better get back inside.'

'Why rush? They're not going anywhere,' Max said. 'Besides, Jules is in there, right? Any bad guys come in, he'll kick ass.'

Alyssa narrowed her eyes at him. 'You're not making fun of my partner, are you?'

'No, I'm serious. He's great.'

'You're not just saying that so I'll have dinner with you?'

'No, I'm . . . No. Of course not. I haven't asked you to have dinner with me, have I?'

'No.'

Max shrugged. 'See?'

'How come you haven't asked me?' God, had those words really come out of her mouth. What was she doing?

Max got very still. 'Are you asking me to ask you to have dinner?'

'If I wanted to have dinner with you, don't you think I'd ask you myself?'

Max looked at her hard. 'You want me to be honest?'

'Do I have a choice?'

'I don't think you know what you want.'

Alyssa laughed. 'You are so wrong about that.'

'Besides Starrett,' he said. 'You can't have him, Alyssa. So now what are you going to do? Be miserable for the rest of your life?'

She turned toward the conference room. 'I have to go.'

'Have dinner with me tonight.'

Alyssa stopped. Didn't turn back around. 'What time?'

Max drew in a deep breath and then let it out in a rush. 'Six. Meet me out front. We'll leave the hotel, maybe see a little something of Jakarta while we're at it.'

She looked at him. 'I'd like that.'

He smiled at her, and she smiled back, aware that for the first time in a long time, she actually felt like smiling.

*

Jones left the hospital on crutches.

He'd spent the night and most of the morning pretending to swallow but then spitting out his pain meds because he knew if he didn't get out of here soon, someone would find him.

Five million dollars was a very big motivator. And it didn't matter that this was supposed to be some safe house type hospital facility. He would be found.

Jayakatong would be searching for him particularly vigilantly. He was going to be triple pissed when he found out that the bounty on Grady Morant's head was five million dead *or* alive.

Jones had slept very little last night. Ironically the only time he'd actually fallen asleep was when Molly came to see him. He couldn't face her – what he'd done was unforgivable. So he pretended to be asleep, and while she was holding his hand, he'd actually drifted off.

But he'd awakened as she was leaving, as she'd whispered to the nurse that she'd be back again in the afternoon.

So early this morning he'd gotten on his clothes and he'd walked out.

For a place that was supposed to be so secure, it had been laughably easy to leave.

He took a bus to the harbor, and stood in line to buy passage on a boat heading for Malaysia. It was then, while he was digging in his pockets for his roll of cash, that he found it.

A letter. From Molly.

It started out all business. She gave him her mother's address and phone number in Iowa, as well as that of her daughter.

'You can always find me by calling my mother or my

daughter,' she wrote. And then she got down to it, direct and to the point as only Molly could be.

'I want to tell you to turn around and come back,' she wrote. 'Come back to me, because I already miss you desperately. Yes, Dave, you are missed.' Her words made his chest ache more than the hellishly persistent throbbing in his leg. 'But I know that if you left it's because you know you're not safe here, and I want you to be safe more than I want you by my side.

'I know you think you're probably saving me by leaving. I know you probably left because you were afraid that when Chai came for you, the innocent people here would be hurt or killed – that *I* would be hurt or killed.

'You probably think we'll both be better off by your leaving. The man who took the money and put the woman and her friends in mortal danger. The woman who betrayed him. Two human beings who made very human mistakes.

'You did take the money. And I did betray you. I won't pretend otherwise. They pointed a gun at Billy and I told them who you were. I didn't trust what I knew deep in my heart – that you were going to bring that money back.

'I've already forgiven you. I hope you'll find it in your heart to forgive me. I know you're capable of it, because when you returned the money it proved that I was right about you all along. Oh, honey, I know you're no angel, not by any means, but you're a good man with a good heart.

'I know that I once promised all I wanted from you was friendship, but see, you're not the only one who knows how to lie. I love you. I love all of you – even your scars and your mistakes – and I hope someday you'll forgive both me and yourself enough to find me again.

'And even if you don't,' Molly wrote in her loopy

handwriting, 'even if we never meet again, take extra care of yourself. Because you are loved.'

'Where are you going?' the ticket clerk asked as Jones moved to the counter.

'I don't know,' he said. And for the first time in a long time, he honestly didn't know. For the first time in a long time, he didn't want to drift, to tell the man to put him on the next boat out of the harbor, regardless of its destination.

The clerk took it upon himself to describe all the various shitholes that his company sailed to, making them sound like heaven.

Jones ignored the man as he memorized the phone numbers Molly had given him. He folded the letter carefully, putting it into his deepest pocket. He knew where heaven was. Heaven was Molly – who loved him – and she sure as hell wasn't going to Malaysia or Thailand.

He cut the clerk off midsentence. 'You got anything heading for Africa?'

'Of course.'

Jones put his money on the counter. 'That's where I want to go.'

Ken slipped into the back of the room. This press conference thing was a completely new experience for him, and he wasn't sure he liked it.

Savannah didn't look all too comfortable sitting up there with her parents and grandmother, in front of a roomful of reporters. She was wearing a dress that was a little too tailored and high-necked for his taste, but she'd managed to do her hair in a style that was a compromise between scary and wild. It was cute, he decided. Although five minutes alone with him, and he'd mess it up, guaranteed.

He caught her eye, and she smiled.

Oh ho, he knew what that smile meant. She was thinking about the same thing he was. He sent a similar smile right back to her.

'Savannah,' one of the reporters asked, and she looked away from him. 'Is there any truth to the rumors about your engagement with Count Vladamir Modovsky of Romania?'

She leaned forward to speak into the microphone, the perfect little princess. 'Absolutely not.'

'Can you tell us a little bit about your ordeal on Parwati Island?'

'It wasn't entirely an ordeal,' she said, avoiding the question like a pro.

'Who exactly were you with when you were abducted?' a reporter asked. 'The airline has stated that you weren't traveling alone.'

'That's right,' Savannah said, the queen of cool. 'I was with a friend.' She called on the next reporter.

'A male friend, isn't that right?'

'Yes, that's correct.'

'Can you tell us who he is, what he does for a living—'

'No, I'm sorry.'

'Is he an intimate friend?'

Savannah looked at him across the room, a very clear message in her eyes. *Are you sure you want to be a part of this for the rest of your life?*

'Yes,' Ken said, answering both Savannah and the reporter's question as he headed toward the front of the room. 'Yes, he's a very intimate friend. In fact, he's her fiancé.'

Rose was grinning at him. Priscilla looked as if she were

going to have a cow for about two seconds and then she quickly hid her reaction behind a carefully pasted-on smile. Karl was talking to his broker on his cell phone, and Savannah . . . she was just shaking her head.

'You are so in for it now,' she said as he came up onto the little stage.

'Watch me work,' he said. 'I'm a chief in the US Navy. I can handle anything.'

The questions were flying so fast he couldn't hear above the din. 'One at a time,' he shouted.

'What's your name?'

'Ken Karmody.'

'How did you and Savannah meet?'

'Technically, we met back while Savannah was going to Yale. And then we met again when she had a flat tire in front of my house. But we really didn't *meet* meet until we were stranded in the jungle on Parwati. Needless to say, as we got to know each other, neither of us voted the other off the island.'

The crowd laughed.

'What do you do for a living, Mr Karmody?'

'That's Chief Karmody. I'm employed by my Uncle Sam's Navy.'

'Why would Savannah von Hopf want to marry you, an enlisted sailor?'

That was one hell of a question. 'Well, she told me she either wanted to marry a prince, or a guy with a frog tattooed on his butt. I'll let you guess which one I am.'

There was more laughter, but Ken leaned in to the microphone. 'Seriously,' he said. 'She's marrying me because she knows that on a scale from one to ten, I love her an eleven. Now, if you'll excuse us, I have a few more days of liberty and we have plane tickets. You'll understand if I don't tell you where we're heading.'

Rose stood up. 'I must leave as well. I'm due to visit Alex in the hospital. He's doing much better and will be released in the morning. I'm hoping to convince him and his longtime companion and personal assistant to pay me an extended visit in New York.' *There Alex, I've outed you. It's about time.*

Savannah paused at the door to look back at her and give her a thumbs up.

Yes, my dear, I'll be hoping to spend a lot more time with you in the near future, too.

Savannah smiled as if she could read Rose's mind.

Rose followed her granddaughter and her fiancé out into the lobby. Alyssa Locke joined her, ready to accompany her to the hospital.

Just as she'd suspected, the two lovers didn't make it very far before Ken pulled Savannah into an alcove and kissed her.

Such passion, especially for two o'clock in the afternoon. But what else could be expected from a man whose love was an eleven on a scale from one to ten?

Rose watched Savannah and Ken slip into an elevator. They were in each other's arms again before the doors had fully closed.

Her granddaughter was infinitely lucky. Rose knew this first-hand. She'd had a husband who had loved her an eleven, too.